THE SHARECROPPER'S SON SHOULD HAVE BEEN BENEATH HER

Desiree had been trained to look down on a man like Christopher Fairfield. Strong and striking as he might be, he still was poor white trash, lower even than the black field hands. Even worse, he was a convicted killer, pursued by the law.

But now, naked in his arms, her body still shocked by his fierce and fevered penetration, Desiree felt all she had been taught melting away.

"I'll let you go," she heard him saying. "What do I want with a thin-blooded Miss like you anyway?"

Even as he spoke, Desiree felt the pain subsiding, and in its place an exquisite trembling frenzy, a madly racing heart, a blazing response to the throbbing of his flesh within her. When she felt him try to withdraw, she moved with him, desperately held him to her.

"I want you, Christopher Fairfield. I want you so much."

Always Desiree had been mistress of her feelings. Now for the first time she was learning what it was to be their slave. . . .

Flame of the South

Have You Read These SIGNET Titles?

- ☐ **ROGUE'S MISTRESS by Constance Gluyas.** (#E8339—$2.25)
- ☐ **SAVAGE EDEN by Constance Gluyas.** (#E8338—$2.25)
- ☐ **WOMAN OF FURY by Constance Gluyas.** (#E8075—$2.25)*
- ☐ **HARVEST OF DESIRE by Rochelle Larkin.** (#E8771—$2.25)
- ☐ **TORCHES OF DESIRE by Rochelle Larkin.** (#E8511—$2.25)*
- ☐ **MISTRESS OF DESIRE by Rochelle Larkin.** (#E7964—$2.25)*
- ☐ **THIS PASSIONATE LAND by Harriet Janeway.** (#E8462—$2.25)
- ☐ **LORD OF RAVENSLEY by Constance Heaven.** (#E8460—$2.25)†
- ☐ **THE FIRES OF GLENLOCHY by Constance Heaven.** (#E7452—$1.75)†
- ☐ **THE PLACE OF STONES by Constance Heaven.** (#W7046—$1.50)†
- ☐ **THE QUEEN & THE GYPSY by Constance Heaven.** (#J7965—$1.95)†
- ☐ **GLYNDA by Susannah Leigh.** (#E8548—$2.50)*
- ☐ **WINTER FIRE by Susannah Leigh.** (#E8011—$2.25)*
- ☐ **VALENTINA by Evelyn Anthony.** (#E8598—$2.25)†
- ☐ **THE CORMAC LEGEND by Dorothy Daniels.** (#J8655—$1.95)*

* Price slightly higher in Canada
† Not available in Canada

To order these titles, please use coupon on the last page of this book.

Flame of the South

By

Constance Gluyas

NAL BOOKS ARE ALSO AVAILABLE AT DISCOUNTS IN BULK QUANTITY FOR INDUSTRIAL OR SALES-PROMOTIONAL USE. FOR DETAILS, WRITE TO PREMIUM MARKETING DIVISION, NEW AMERICAN LIBRARY, INC., 1301 AVENUE OF THE AMERICAS, NEW YORK, NEW YORK 10019.

SIGNET TRADEMARK REG. U.S. PAT. OFF. AND FOREIGN COUNTRIES
REGISTERED TRADEMARK—MARCA REGISTRADA
HECHO EN CHICAGO, U.S.A.

SIGNET, SIGNET CLASSICS, MENTOR, PLUME AND MERIDIAN BOOKS *are published by The New American Library, Inc., 1301 Avenue of the Americas, New York, New York 10019*

FIRST PRINTING, MAY, 1979

1 2 3 4 5 6 7 8 9

PRINTED IN THE UNITED STATES OF AMERICA

For my husband, Don,
always with love, and
for Jay Garon, outstanding agent,
and my editor, my very good friends

1

Disturbed by a crashing in the undergrowth, the flock of roosting birds rose high in the air. For a moment they hovered motionless, looking like black pencil streaks against the vivid blue of the sky; then, with shrill indignant outcries and a heavy beating of wings, they flew away to disappear into the vast distance.

The man who came bursting out of the dark green gloom of the forest into the sudden and startling blaze of sunshine which bathed the forest clearing did not hear the rustling sounds of wildlife or the clamor of the birds. He heard nothing but the drumming of blood in his ears. The breath laboring in his tortured lungs, his black skin greasy with sweat, he stood there swaying, his tall, muscular form quivering with reaction, his blurred eyes trying to adjust to the piercing light. He shook his head in an effort to clear it, his broad nostrils flaring as though endeavoring to pick up a scent, his ears straining for the sounds of pursuit. For the first time in three days he could detect no menacing sounds in the distance, and yet still he could not bring himself to trust the silence and tranquillity about him. His pursuers were out there somewhere; perhaps even now they were watching him. They would never give up, and eventually he would be hunted down.

Alarmed by his thoughts, he took a quick step forward. Then, weighted down by the weariness of his body, he stopped again. He must rest for a while, or else be felled by his lurching heart. He rubbed at his burning eyes, running the trembling fingers of his other hand through his damp, tightly kinked hair. His flight, born of desperation and a woman's pleading, might well be useless. His only hope lay in finding the man he sought. If he failed, he was in trouble.

His full mouth trembled and he tightened his lips against the betraying weakness. The man he sought! The words rang in his brain, echoing with a sound of hopelessness. His people had named the man "the Flame" Flame of Freedom, the champion of the oppressed, who had helped so many to cast off the shackles of slavery and escape to the North. He shook his head again. He did not know whether the man was black or white, whether he was real or existed only in the imagination of his people. He only knew, if he did exist, that he had to find him. But how, when his only lead was a whisper among the slaves of Twin Oaks, the great plantation that was owned by Master Elton Grayson, and of someone there who might possibly aid him and ultimately bring him to the protection of the Flame. "Elton Grayson." His words were only a whisper, but to his inflamed imagination the sound of his own voice seemed to boom through the silence. Shocked by the thought that had sprung full-fledged into his mind, he looked furtively about him. He must be mad! Elton Grayson, one of the most respected planters in Georgia, could not possibly be the man known as the Flame.

The thought, so heavy and frightening in its significance, was too much for him, and he cast it from him as he would a loathsome object. To even think of the master of Twin Oaks in that connection could be dangerous. Suppose he were to grow careless, suppose he were to speak the wonderings in his mind aloud. That way lay agonizing death. His mind clouded, and all coherent thoughts fled, yielding instead to an overwhelming consciousness of thirst and hunger, of the pain of his scratched and thorn-lacerated flesh, the throbbing of the gash in his forehead, still exuding a sluggish trickle of blood. Groaning, his knees giving way, he slumped down on the mired narrow track that snaked between close-growing trees, and which led, he perceived with a rising of despair, into yet another part of the dense forest. Lying on his stomach, he thought of the three days of running, of hiding, of listening to the distant shouting of the white men who hunted him. Above the sound of their voices, like a strain of doom, he had detected the deep-throated baying of the dogs.

He turned his face downward, heedless of the mud left by a week of continuous rain. He well knew, if the white men found him, what his fate would be. Certainly they would not kill him, once they had flushed him from cover, they would not even allow their dogs to savage him, but it was only a temporary respite from the terror to come. He knew how runaway slaves were handled, he had seen them brought in before. The slaves, called by the clamor of the big house bell, would assemble, so that they might witness the runaway beaten to death. "An object lesson," their mistress called it. If caught, the same thing would happen to him. Like those other poor wretches, he would first be tightly bound and his mouth gagged so that he could make no outcry, and then, flung like a sack of meal across a horse, he would be taken back to Murray Hill Plantation, and to Miss Youtha Murray.

A shudder shook his broad shoulders as he reflected upon his mistress. Miss Youtha, grim-faced, elderly, her gray hair scraped back from her bony face and further hidden by a battered black bonnet, had been an only child. When her father died, she had inherited the plantation. Her sex had not proved a stumbling block, for she ran the huge place with all the skill and efficiency of her father before her. Her neighbors, seeing her as a helpless woman who had courageously assumed a great burden, an impression which she encouraged, helped her in many ways. So, with the full backing of these sympathetic neighbors, who could be counted upon to help her suppress the first signs of insurrection, the use of the whip as well as her viperish tongue, she had managed to subdue black and white men alike.

The black man turned his face sideways, blowing the mud from his nostrils. Miss Youtha's father, Simon Murray, had been a big, hearty man, thoughtful of the needs of his slaves. His daughter, generally thought to be frustrated and embittered by her single state, was quite another matter. She had none of her father's humanity, and upon his death all that was merciless and cruel in her nature had been given free rein. She ferociously punished both minor and major infractions, and aside from the constant floggings, her cruelty took other and more subtle forms. The fraternizing between male and female slaves, overlooked in her father's time, was instantly abolished. Simon Murray had allowed and even encouraged his slaves to go through a form of marriage known as "jumping the broom," but this too the daughter had done away with. "Animals do not marry," Josh had once heard his mistress say, "and what else are Negroes but slightly superior animals?"

With a savage flash of anger the big black man dug his fingers deeply into the oozing earth. How he hated that scrawny white woman. How he hated his own black skin that robbed him of the right to human dignity! And yet, strangely, there was one thing he had to thank Miss Youtha for. His mistress's harsh decree did not extend to mating for the purpose of procreation, and it was through this forced mating that he had come to meet Martie. Sweet Martie, with her low, husky voice, her soft and gentle eyes, her overwhelming love for him, expressed in so many small and tender ways. It was Martie who had urged him to run. As clearly as though she lay beside him, he could hear her voice. "You run, Josh. Ain't no future for us 'less you make the break. You fin' that man, the Flame. He's a good man, he'll help you git up North. He'll help me too when the time comes."

"No, Martie, I cain't never leave you."

Her hands had touched him, stroking, cajoling. "Hush, honey, mah big man. I'll find you, never fear. No matter where you are, I'll find you."

Martie the maternal, Martie his love. Agonized, he had held her close against him. "Don't you ask me to run off an' leave you, woman," he mumbled against her soft neck.

"You can, Josh, you must! It's the only way I know for us to have the chance of a life together. You want that, don't you, honey?"

He wanted it. Just how much, he had not known until that moment, but still he protested. "You talkin' foolishness, woman. How you knowin' this Flame man real? Maybe it's all a makeup, you ever think of that?"

"Ain't no makeup, Josh." With a sudden violent movement that took him by surprise, she thrust him away. Amazed at the anger that glimmered in her expressive eyes, he could only stare. "He's real," she panted. She put a hand over her heart. "I know in here that he's real. Don't you never agin say to me that he ain't."

He knew then what troubled her. She could not bear to abandon the hope that this romantic figure gave to her. Tenderly he drew her back into the shelter of his arms. "I understand, sweet baby, cain't none of us live without hope. If this Flame man yours, then I ain't blamin' you none."

"Josh, Josh!" He felt the trembling of her slight body, the almost feverish burn of her face against his own, and he knew that he would give in to her pleas. Besides, he could not deny that he more than half-believed in the existence of the Flame himself. "I'll go," he told Martie.

Engulfed in memories, heedless now of possible danger, Josh turned over on his back, his eyes narrowing against the fierce glare of the sun. It had been raining on the day he had first met Martie. Rain falling heavily from a sky of sullen gray, blown in slanting lines by a boisterous wind, dashing against his half-naked body, making him shiver, and increasing his anger against the white overseer who was leading him to the breeding hut.

"Don't you show me that face, boy," the overseer had rapped out, startling him. "Not 'less you a-wanting me to report you to Miss Youtha. That your desire, boy?"

He had wanted to turn around and smash his fist into the overseer's face, but to strike a white man came under the heading of the ultimate sin, and would result in him being beaten to death. He swallowed hard against his seething resentment. Sometime, somehow, he told himself, he would have vengeance, but for now it was best to seem to comply. Hating himself for the humble note he was compelled to force into his voice, he had replied, "No, suh, Master Tring, that ain't my desire."

"That's real good, boy, smart too. Reckon you know that if I was to tell Miss Youtha that you ain't willing and happy to be the bull to the cow she done picked out for you, she wouldn't like it none at all." Tring chuckled. "Why, she'd have you strung up in a trice, she would, and tickled up something powerful with the whip. You just take my word for it."

Josh's hands clenched at his sides. "Yes, suh, I'll take your word."

"Fine. Thought maybe you would." The overseer's red-knuckled hand had pushed the door of the hut wide; the butt of his coiled whip had thrust against Josh's back, pushing him inside. "You have yourself a good time, boy." Chuckling again, he scratched at his stubbled chin. "Hot damn! I don't know but what I don't envy you at that. Nice little piece of female flesh is Martie." His pale blue eyes squinting, Tring licked his full lips. "Give it all you got, boy, ram it right up inside her." He shook a stubby finger in Josh's face. "But don't you go crippling her up now. Might be wanting to give it to her myself. Yes sirree, just might." With a wink and a final push, Tring had departed with seeming reluctance.

With the door of the windowless hut firmly shut, Josh had found himself enclosed in a musty darkness that was only feebly enlivened by the light of one flickering candle. He listened to Tring's retreating footsteps, but he made no move to go forward. Shaking, his body slick with sweat, a prey to mingled hatred and confusion, he simply stood there. For a long time now, excited by tales of his friends' prowess, he had yearned to stud a wench. He even prayed that Miss Youtha might select him as the next, but now that the moment was upon him, he had a terrible fear that he might prove unequal to the task. He thought back to the time when, with great daring, he approached Miss Youtha. Keeping his eyes downcast in the approved way, he first greeted her. Then, shuffling his toes in the dust of the yard, he mumbled, "I'm ready to stud for you, Miss Youtha, ma'am. I'll stud any wench you tell me, 'cause I'm truly ready."

Miss Youtha had stared at him with her hard eyes; then she cut him across the shoulders with the small whip she always carried. "That's just to remind you that I say when, Josh. Approach me again on the matter, and I'll have you strung up and flogged. Now, get back to the pen."

A sighing breath came from the semidarkness, followed by the rustling of a mattress. His heart leaping, despising the fear that beset him, Josh took a backward step. He had the bitter thought that Miss Youtha had done her work of repression well. No doubt he could stud for her, but could he ever feel a natural desire? This was to be no joyous coming together of a man and a woman; it was simply a service for the white woman he hated. The ultimate degradation for him.

Josh took another backward step, his quivering fingers

groping for the latch of the door. Even as he touched the cold metal, he knew that he lacked the courage to raise it. Tring had departed, but there would be others watching, for Miss Youtha left nothing to chance, and these watchers would be happy to report his insubordination to her. Bitterness welled up in his throat as he thought of the pens his mistress had erected. The two pens, well separated, held a number of small wooden huts, and these huts were jokingly referred to as "pure houses." In one pen dwelled the virgin males, and in the other, the females. Both boys and girls were placed in the pens at the start of their teens, and until Miss Youtha decreed otherwise, the state of virginity between both sexes was strictly preserved. In the case of the wenches, usually when they reached the age of fourteen, Miss Youtha would give orders that they be groomed for their coming encounter with the opposite sex. The frightened girls, their imagination supplying them with fearful and lurid details, would be given richer food to eat. If they so desired, they could ignore the work detail and rest all day. Their supple young bodies were massaged and oiled daily by a squad of carefully picked men, who were, in turn, supervised by Miss Youtha. The stroking hands of the men were deliberately sensuous, guaranteed to bring about a reaction. If the reaction did not come, the unfortunate masseur was ejected from the hut and led away for a flogging. As if nature would not deliver the message to them in good time, the girls were even taught the correct position in which to receive a man, legs invitingly wide apart, their nervous fingers plucking at their nipples to make them rigid. At a certain peak in their training, Miss Youtha herself would take over. Her hands oiled, lest their touch be harsh, she would fondle their bodies, her hands moving slowly, caressing these frightened black women while she murmured to them of the delights to come. "You black wenches were born to pleasure men," she would tell them almost tenderly. "And you shall, you shall. Your mistress cares for you. She is good to you." It was her set speech, and it had been repeated to Josh many times. "I will fill you up with men," Miss Youtha would go on, "men that are potent, and men that will put their seed into you. You will enjoy yourself, I promise you. Your belly will quicken and swell, and in the course of time you will bear me many little black animals. Ah, yes, your bodies will enrich me and my lands. Do you understand what I am telling you?"

The girls understood only too well. They were to be brood mares. Hating her, they tried to resist her knowing hands, but eventually they came to a point where they could only writhe and moan. Shortly after, Miss Youtha would declare them to be ready for the grand experience. Like the unknown wench who now awaited Josh, they would be put into breeding huts. Only when they could report to Miss Youtha that they were pregnant would they be allowed a measure of freedom from the unceasing demands upon their bodies.

Refusing to allow his eyes an attempt to pierce the darkness, Josh put a balled fist to his mouth. The lot of the virgin boys was not so very different from the girls'. They too were oiled and massaged and exercised. They too suffered Miss Youtha's fondling, the thoughtful weighing of their genitals in her scrawny hand. And because there was no actual passion in the woman, it made it all the more horrifying. Josh and his comrades had been angry and excited by turns, and they could talk of nothing else but the sexual experience awaiting them.

Coming back to the present, Josh rubbed his cold hands together in an effort to warm them. He had wanted to be a stud, and here he was in the breeding hut, at the start of his career. Josh bit his lip. Foolishness! He had been lying to himself all along. He did not want to stud for Miss Youtha. His needs were simple; he wanted to love a woman, and to be loved by her. But that particular emotion, the tenderness that went with it, was not for black people. Miss Youtha had said so. Yes, that skinny old bitch had said it repeatedly.

Trying to control his anger, Josh took in a deep breath and began to grope his way forward. He heard a gasp from the girl lying huddled on the plank bed, but he did not look at her. Better not to do so, he told himself, or he might weaken. It was simply a job he had to do, and he must force himself to think of it that way; the sooner it was over, he thought, the better for both of them. "You there," he said harshly. "You ready, woman?"

"No!" The cry that came from the huddled form made him jump. "Go 'way, ain't wantin' you to touch me."

The futility of her words made him shrug. "Cain't be helped, woman, an' you knows it. Don't like it no more'n you. Ain't takin' me no pleasure in ramming an unwillin' woman, but it got to be done."

She sat up on the bed, but still he kept his eyes averted. "You stay for a while"—her tremulous voice was eager, pleading—"jus' long 'nough for them to think you done it, an' then when you go out, you say you done it." Her hand touched his arm. "Please."

He jerked away from her touch as though it had burned him. Pitying her, he said roughly, "Ain't easy like you make it sound. Miss Youtha, she have you examined afterward, always does. She findin' you ain't been bedded, it's a floggin' for both of us. Better we get it over with."

With a cry of hopelessness she fell back on the bed. "I'd like to be dead right now."

"Well, you livin', so hush your foolish mouth." He turned her over on her back and pulled up the single coarse garment she was wearing. With scarcely a pause, he forced her thighs open and thrust the already-hardened length of himself inside her.

She screamed at the penetration, and struggled desperately against him. Her hands pushed at him, her fingers pinched his flesh. Ruthlessly he restrained her. He had no words of comfort to offer as he rode her, for there was only a blankness inside him. And then, suddenly, as though giving in to the inevitable, her sobs ceased and she was moving with him.

After it was over, she lay very still, her eyes avoiding his. For the first time since he had entered the hut, Josh was drawn by a need to see, to have some contact, however fragile, with the person with whom he had shared such an intimate experience, and so he allowed himself to look at her. Her long black hair, coarse and rainwater-straight, giving more than a hint of Indian blood, was scattered over the thin pillow. Her Indian blood was further borne out by her fine-featured face and the light tawny shading of her skin. His heart jumped as he gazed. She was so beautiful that he wanted to touch her again, to assure himself that she was real, but he could not summon the courage. Touch, stroke—this was the language of tenderness, and he was a stranger to that emotion. Her deep sighing breath, the rustle of her garment being smoothed over her hips as she tried to cover herself, broke in on his thoughts. "What you doin', woman?" he said sharply. It was something to say, and he had no other words.

She did not answer at once. When she did speak, her husky voice caused him to start. "Thinkin' maybe this your firs' time at breedin'," she said.

He nodded. "It's my first time, but I know all about it. I know Miss Youtha have you examined after it done, 'cause I heard the other men talkin' 'bout it." Then, his masculine pride stung, he added, "How do you know it's my first time?"

She hesitated. "Just do, that's all. Women know these things."

Woman! She was a child, sixteen at most, while he himself had a full nineteen years. Her stillness, her air of waiting, invited him to answer. When he did not, she turned her tear-streaked face toward him, her huge doelike eyes studying him closely. "I want you to know that I ain't blamin' you none," she said. "I know you had to do it."

For some reason this simple statement caused his eyes to sting with tears. He waited, hoping she would go on. "After Miss Youtha release you from the pure houses, you worked a time or two in the fields, I seen you," she resumed. Her hand stole out and touched his shoulder timidly. "I liked what I seen. You are big and strong and fine. If I had to be studded, then I ain't sorry it was you who done it."

He felt stifled, so shallow and painful had his breathing become. On Miss Youtha's orders he had raped her—there was no other word for it—and yet her words and her tone sought to console him for this crime against herself. Her fingers, gently stroking his shoulder now, aroused a dangerous emotion that he did not fully understand. He only knew that he wanted to bury his head against her breast and beg her forgiveness. He wanted to release all the burning rebellion that had festered inside him for so long. Rebellion that he had not been aware of until this moment. Instead, he said abruptly, "What your name?"

"Martie. But you knows that, I hear Tring tell you."

"I forgot. My name's Josh." With a movement as abrupt as his tone had been, he grasped her hand and held it tightly. "Ain't seen you before. Where you work, Martie?"

"After Miss Youtha release me, she set me to work up at the big house." Now Martie's fears seemed to be forgotten, for her nose crinkled impudently and her sorrowful eyes were lit with laughter. "You hear that, man? I a house slave, an' that make me too good for a messy ol' field hand."

He could not take her gentle teasing. "Ain't messy," he jerked out. "You ain't to be sayin' that." He stared at her with somber eyes—sullen eyes, Miss Youtha called them—and then quite suddenly he was laughing with her. The sound emerged rusty and uncertain, so little laughter had there been in his life. Those lighthearted shared moments had been the start of their love. How strange, then, that loving and being loved in return, he had been unable to get her with child.

Josh closed his eyes against the burn of tears. He should never have left her. By running, he had lost her as surely as if he had killed her with his own two hands. Someone else would be sent to service his Martie. Maybe it would be Plute, or Thomas. Both had a reputation for planting their seed at the first try. And if they did not succeed, Miss Youtha would send another and yet another, until Marie's slender body was worn out.

His lips puckering, Josh put an arm across his eyes. What of the Flame, the mysterious man he sought? The answer came to him quickly, springing into the recesses of his despairing mind. There was no such person. The Flame existed only in the minds of his people, the hero of a tale told by them to bolster flagging courage and to revive waning hope, and he had actually thought to find him! There could be only one end to his flight from Murray Hill Plantation, a slow and agonizing death, for he was bound to be recaptured. What made him think that he, of all his brethren who had fled Murray Hill, would succeed? And Martie—she would be assembled with the other slaves to watch him die. For her it would be not only the death of love, but of hope and joy and dreams.

His mind went blank for a moment, shutting out terror and hopelessness; and then, lighting the blankness, came a memory of the words he had heard Miss Youtha utter to Master John Sutridge, her neighbor at nearby Magnolia Plantation. "I have heard much of this man," she had said, her voice high-pitched and querulous. "From what I can gather, he is an uncouth and uncivilized lout whose declared aim is to abolish slavery, and yet you stand there and tell me he has been elected." Miss Youtha's voice dropped, throbbing now with horror. "No, John Sutridge, you are lying to me. It's just not possible, the things you are saying."

"I'm not lying, Youtha. Why in the hell would I do that?" John Sutridge's voice crackled with impatience, and his usually smiling and gallant manner was noticeably absent. He looked, Josh had thought, risking a quick glance at him, like a man with a burden on his mind. "Abe Lincoln was elected on May 18, almost four weeks ago. Surely you must have heard?"

Miss Youtha had stared at him, her mouth hard and set. "I did not. I have no time to be forever listening to idle gossip."

"Idle gossip!" John Sutridge looked as if he were about to explode. "Your words tell me that you did hear, but you just don't choose to believe. A lot of Southerners are like that, but I am not one of them, let me tell you. I—"

"How dare you!" Miss Youtha had interrupted. "Mind your manners."

Disregarding the interruption, John Sutridge rushed on, "Be blind, if it suits you, but I was in Chicago on the day Lincoln was elected. Everybody went wild when the news was announced. Bonfires were lit on almost every corner, and I thought my eardrums would split with the noise of the cheering and the thunder of the guns."

Miss Youtha looked quite unlike herself, with her trembling mouth and the fear peering from her eyes. "Cheering?" Her voice was hesitant and uncertain. "But I don't understand. Why would they cheer a man like that?"

"Everybody does not think as we do, Youtha. Even those who were staunchly for Seward, and believed that he was bound to be elected, have turned now to Lincoln. And I'll tell you something else. The South Carolina Legislature has already called for a convention to meet in December of this year. They are going to consider secession."

"Secession!" In an uncharacteristically feminine gesture, Miss Youtha had put her hands to her head. "Seward, Lincoln, secession! John Sutridge, you are bewildering me."

Sutridge sighed. "Sorry, Youtha. But with Lincoln elected, 1860 is going to be a dark and sorrowful year for the South. If the abolitionists continue to make trouble, and Lincoln, in his turn, persists in the stand he has taken against slavery, it could very well mean war."

"War! How ridiculous you men are. Lincoln, I feel sure, is

no great threat to the South." Miss Youtha laughed on a shrill, almost hysterical note. "Abolish slavery indeed! Let Lincoln but try, and we will very soon send him scuttling off with his tail between his legs. The South would simply never stand for that . . . that Republican's interference, and what's more, John Sutridge, you know I'm right."

"Of course you are, Youtha, and that's why it could mean war."

"Bah! There are other ways of dealing with the likes of Lincoln."

"Are there? I wish I knew what they might be." The picture of gloom, John Sutridge turned to his horse. Remembering his manners just in time, he turned back to Miss Youtha, bowed, and then mounted. Riding away, he had glanced casually at Josh, his expression unchanging, and the black man knew that he had not really seen him.

Abe Lincoln. Who was he, Josh wondered, and what did it mean to abolish slavery? Later, still wondering, he had gone to Delby, the ancient black man who was known among his fellows for his learning, and he had asked him what "abolish slavery" meant.

Delby had looked frightened, and his eyes, with their yellowed and bloodshot whites, had shifted uneasily. "To abolish slavery means to free all us slaves," he told Josh, "what them Yankee abolitionists always rantin' 'bout."

Bewildered, Josh had pressed for more details, but the old man stubbornly refused to answer. All he would say in conclusion was, "This freedom won't never happen, Josh, so don't you be frettin' your head none 'tall. An' I ain't never hear tell of this Master Lincoln, an' ain't sure I wants to."

Josh, disregarded the old man's advice. From carefully listening whenever the white folk gathered together, he found out that on February 11, 1861, Abraham Lincoln had made his inaugural speech and was now officially President of the country. Once again he had sought out Delby, and the old man patiently explained what it meant to be a President. But Delby had no answer when, after overhearing another conversation, Josh had asked him to explain the word "secession."

"Don't know nothin' 'bout no 'cession," Delby answered him gruffly "an' I purely gittin' tired of your fool questions."

Genuinely puzzled, unable to believe that this wise man

was letting him down, Josh persisted, "But, Delby, how come you ain't knowin'?"

"Cain't be knowin' ever'thin'."

"It's a pity you don't, Delby. Could maybe be important. Them white folks sayin' that South Carolina seceded on December 20 of last year. An' this year, Georgia, Louisiana, Florida, Mississippi, Alabama, and someplace called Texas done seceded also."

"Cain't help that." Delby shook his bald head impatiently. "Tol' you, Josh, don't know nothin' 'bout it."

"Delby, what 'Confederate States of America' mean?"

"Don't know." Delby withdrew to a corner of the cabin. Wrapping his old coat tightly about his skinny frame, he had glared angrily at Josh. "What for you keep botherin' me, boy? Why you want to know these things?"

"Just do. Them white folk say 'nother thing."

"What that?"

"Sayin' they draws up a constitution." Josh pronounced the word with difficulty. "Sayin' that Jefferson Davis be President."

Delby sat up straight. "Now I know you talkin' foolishness, boy. Ain't you been tellin' me that Master Lincoln the President?"

"That's what I hear. How come there's two presidents?"

Delby shrugged. "White folk done take notion, I reckon." Lying down on his plank bed, the old man cautioned him, "It's dangerous to think on white folk's notions, so don't you do it, boy."

This time, taking Delby's advice to heart, Josh had dismissed the Confederate States of America, along with Jefferson Davis, as being an unsolvable mystery. But for a time the glorious dream of freedom had persisted, nudging his mind with dazzling pictures. Excited, he and Martie had discussed Abraham Lincoln in careful whispers. He had even wondered if Lincoln might not be a black man, until Martie said crossly, "You nothin' but a big ol' stupid. How come you think the white folk let a black man be President?"

Staring at Martie's suddenly closed face, Josh had felt the dream dying. More and more, Martie's conversation had centered on the Flame, and he had understood from this that the first natural flaring of her excitement was gone. For Martie, the Flame had more reality than Abraham Lincoln. It was shortly after this, at the beginning of April 1861, that he had run from Murray Hill.

A rustling in the undergrowth jerked Josh from his thoughts. Stiffening, he let his arm fall slowly to his side. They were here. His pursuers had found him. His heart pounding, his limbs paralyzed with dread, he waited, his dilated eyes fixed on the mass of greenery just ahead of him. The rustling came again, and a small, twitching, furred face peered out at him. "A squirrel." The thankful words were forced from Josh's dry throat. "My lord, it ain't nothin' but a li'l ol' squirrel!"

Quivering at the sound of a human voice, the small creature vanished in a blurring movement. With its disappearance Josh felt his courage come pouring back, healing, revitalizing. Twin Oaks must be near, he told himself in a rush of confidence, and he would surely find it soon. If, as Delby said, freedom would never happen, then he must pray that he would find somebody at Twin Oaks who would aid him on his way North. Anxious to be on his way, Josh bounded to his feet and followed the track into a new part of the forest.

2

The long white plantation house gleamed in the April sunshine. Smooth white columns reared up to support the roof of a large veranda, above which were velvet-and-net-draped windows. Wild roses twined along the veranda rail, adding their sweet scent to the drowsy air. A jay, perched on the rail, made a flashing blue flight to a nearby tree, and was immediately lost to sight among foaming peach blossom. Stretching out, some distance from the house, were the turned and prepared cotton fields, and edging the fields, the ubiquitous forest. The house, set amid slightly sloping velvety lawns, its white bricks splashed with the pastel colors of the close-growing flowers, was aloof from the normal activity of the plantation, and on this mild spring afternoon there was about Twin Oaks an air of dreaming peace.

The little black girl stopped before the house and eyed the large white building with a mingling of awe and suppressed excitement. The jay called its harsh cry from the peach tree, and the child started and looked furtively about her. Seeing nothing to alarm, she mounted the veranda steps. Skirting a table and two chairs, she looked longingly at the covered pitcher of lemonade on the table's surface, then crossed the smoothly planed wooden floor and disappeared through a half-open door. Inside the house itself, she stopped to admire the dark oak paneling embellished with a fascinating array of copper plates, warming pans, and various other ornaments. In front of her the staircase curved gracefully to the top of the house, its balusters carved in a pattern of fruit and leaves, its wide treads carpeted in a deep red. She looked at it wistfully, wishing she could mount and explore the upper regions. Finally, sighing, she moved toward a door on the left. Mammy had told her that she would find Miss Dessi in the front parlor, where she generally was at this hour of the day. She hoped very much that her mammy was right, for if Miss Dessi should be out, and old Wilmers, the butler, found her in the house, he would likely kick her down the front steps. A sound from the rear of the house made her heart leap, and she tapped quickly on the door and turned the big knob.

Desiree Grayson rose from the couch with a rustle of starched petticoats and silken lace-trimmed gown. Her red hair, caught back from her face with a wide white band, shone fierily in the sunlight streaming through a round window; the inquiring eyes she turned on the black child standing timidly in the doorway were an almost exact match to the deep violet hue of her gown. "Mandy Lou," she exclaimed in surprise, "what in tarnation are you doing in the house?" She advanced toward the girl, her ringed hands controlling her swaying hoop skirt with some difficulty, a faint rose fragrance wafting from her person.

Mandy Lou looked frightened, though it was apparent that the fear was for the tall slender girl rather than for herself. "You knowin' you ain't supposed to say 'tarnation,' Miss Dessi," she burst out. "I heard master tellin' you so more'n once, on account of he sayin' it ain't l-l—"

"Ladylike," Desiree supplied. She smiled, her teeth showing white and even against her faintly bronzed face, a deep dimple creasing each side of her full, generous mouth.

"Your daddy likely to whup you he hearin' you 'gain," the child went on. "Ain't wantin' master to whup you, Miss Dessi."

"Land sakes, Mandy Lou, my daddy won't do that."

Relieved, Mandy Lou grinned. "Another thing," she rushed on breathlessly, "master sayin' you ain't to go out without your hat. Sayin' you git all burned up and then you lookin' just like a nigger gal."

Desiree laughed, amused by the earnest little face. "So you heard all that, did you?"

"Did. Cain't help hearin'. Master, he always bellowin' so."

"You hear too much for your own good, you little scamp." Desiree put her hand on the child's head, her fingers gently stroking the tightly plaited wiry hair. "Lucky for you my daddy's away. He'd skin you if he found you romping through the house."

Mandy Lou's round eyes widened in indignation. "Ain't rompin'. Mah mammy tol' me to tell you that she needin' you."

Desiree's smile disappeared. "Why didn't she come to the house herself?"

"Cain't, Miss Dessi. She got a misery in her back, an' she sayin' you understan' why she wantin' you."

Desiree moved away from the child. "Was anyone with your mammy?" she asked.

"Yes, ma'am, big black buck." Mandy Lou giggled. "Mammy didn't think I saw her hide him away in that old abandoned root cellar, but I did. He all sweaty and cut up, real wore out an' shaky. I heard him sayin' that he ain't thought to git to Twin Oaks alive. What for my mammy hide that buck, Miss Dessi?"

"I have no idea." Desiree swung around quickly, her skirts flaring out to show a glimpse of rainbow-hued petticoats and long, frilly, ribbon-threaded underdrawers. Her beautiful face had hardened into tense lines, and she looked older than her twenty years. "You must not speak of this to anyone else, Mandy Lou. You saw nothing. Do you understand?"

Mandy Lou nodded. She did not understand, but if her mistress did not want her to speak of what she had seen, then she would not. Seeing that look on Miss Dessi's face, she was reminded of the dark and stormy night when, unable to sleep, she had stolen from the cabin. Knowing that her mother would be back soon, and fearing to be seen, she had carefully concealed herself behind the broad trunk of a tree. It was then she had seen that other Miss Dessi. In Mandy Lou's mind she had two mistresses. One was the scented and curled lady with the lovely rustling gowns, the shady flower-laden hats, the soft, low voice, and the dimpled smile. That one was

Miss Desiree Grayson, of Twin Oaks Plantation, the daughter of Elton Grayson. The other was the one she had first glimpsed on that stormy night. That Miss Dessi had been dressed in breeches and shirt and a wide-brimmed felt hat. At first she had taken her for a man, but then she had seen the red hair escaping from beneath the hat, and she had known her at once. "Fire hair," her mammy called Miss Dessi's hair.

The strangely dressed and almost unrecognizable Miss Dessi had led her horse past the slave cabins, whose windows showed a faint candle glow behind drawn sacking curtains. She had gone down the incline just behind the cabins, and Mandy Lou knew that she was headed for the forest that edged the plantation. Frightened by her own daring, but determined, she had followed. What harm could come to her, she reasoned, when her beloved mistress was near?

Miss Dessi did not look around. She led the horse a good way into the forest, and Mandy Lou heard the soft exasperated sounds she made when a branch whipped out at her, causing the horse to shy and whinny. The darkness was spooky, there were rustling sounds all about, and she had some difficulty in keeping her mistress in sight. Once, hearing the bloodcurdling scream of a disturbed wildcat, Mandy Lou had had to bite her lip to keep from crying out. Her short, plump legs were tired and her heart beating very fast when Miss Dessi finally stopped in a clearing.

Torchlight had flared, startling Mandy Lou, and, blinking her eyes against the sudden light, she had scrambled silently for cover. She had seen a small wooden hut set well back amid concealing, draping trees. Grouped before the hut were several black men and women, some of whom she recognized and others she had never seen before. The men and women had stared at her mistress in silence, but even though they knew secret gatherings were forbidden by Master Grayson, they did not seem to be particularly frightened at being discovered.

Miss Dessi spoke to them, and her voice was so different from her usual soft tones that Mandy Lou had found the change somehow frightening. "Sorry I'm late," she said. "My father was entertaining Frazer Phillips, and I had difficulty in getting away. After he left, I had to wait until I could be sure my father was safely in his bed."

"It seem like your daddy purely set on you marryin' up

with Master Phillips, Miss Dessi. A pity he ain't knowin' that man like his slaves does, reckon then he change his mind in a hurry." Mandy Lou recognized the voice as belonging to Clover, one of the house slaves, and she trembled at the girl's boldness.

Miss Dessi did not rage at Clover's impudence. She did not threaten her with a whipping, as Master Grayson surely would have done, she just said quietly, "Few know Master Phillips as well as his unfortunate slaves. But don't worry about me, Clover, I'll handle him when the time comes."

"Surely hopes you does, Miss Dessi, but Master Phillips, he's a slippery one."

"So am I, Clover, real slippery, as you all have reason to know."

When the laughter following this remark had died down, a man's deep voice put in on a note of seriousness, "It real bad at Woodgrove Plantation, Miss Dessi, an' it gitting worse all the time. Heard that Master Phillips taken to whuppin' his slaves even when they ain't done nothin'. Been hopin' things be diff'rent now that Master Lincoln done got 'lected an' made his Pres'dent speech, 'specially since you tol' me that he's so clear set on abolishin' slavery." His heavy sigh carried clearly to Mandy Lou. "Never been so 'joyed as when Master Dunhill rode in an' tol' you the news, but seem like nothin' ain't changed."

"It's no use expecting miracles, Tom. Change doesn't happen overnight. For myself, I happen to believe strongly in Mr. Lincoln and his ideals. When he puts those ideals into practice, you may be sure we will see change."

"Might, if he ain't all jus' talk," Tom answered, apparently unconvinced. "But them other white folk 'bout here ain't like you, Miss Dessi. They ain't wantin' change nohow. I hear that Master Phillips went on like he gone mad when he hearin' 'bout Master Lincoln. Done whupped him some niggers that day, surely did."

"There is nothing you can tell me about Frazer Phillips and the situation at Woodgrove. You can be sure that Amos has his sources, and he keeps me well-informed."

Mandy Lou shivered. There was something about Miss Dessi's voice that, for some reason she could not understand, made her think of the sharp cutting edge of the knife her brother, Sam, used to chop down the weeds. Miss Dessi had always disliked Master Phillips, and she did not trouble to hide it, not even from her daddy, who wanted her to marry the master of Woodgrove Plantation. Master Phillips was handsome, he was tall and blonde and blue-eyed, with a smile that made you think he was kind, only he wasn't kind at all. Mandy Lou had listened to her elders when they were discussing the shameful treatment of the slaves at Woodgrove Plantation. Some of the stories had so terrified her that she had prayed, if she had to be sold, that it would never be to Master Phillips, whose bright smile hid such terrible cruelty.

Mandy Lou started to attention when Miss Dessi spoke again, straining her ears so that she might hear every word. "Tom, all of you, we did not gather here to have a long discussion. Martha, did you bring food and water?"

"Yes, Miss Dessi."

"Tom, you were responsible for clothing."

"Brung ever'thin'."

"Good. Amos, where are you?"

"Here." A big burly man stepped from the shadows into the circle of torchlight. Mandy Lou saw his big white teeth flash into a smile. She wondered who he might be, for he did not belong to Twin Oaks. "Knows what you goin' to ask, Miss Dessi," the burly man said, "you always so careful 'bout details. Ever'thin' prepared. Mark even forge 'nother set of freedom papers, jus' in case the one you give us gits lost. He say it always handy to have 'nother." He tapped his shirt pocket. "Got that paper right here."

"In that case, Amos, you must make sure that nobody stops you and discovers the paper. Two sets might be hard to explain."

"Ain't likely to be stopped, Miss Dessi. I know them ol' tracks like the back of my hand and I'm too careful to be stopped, and I know all the places to hide."

"I know that, Amos. Go on, please."

"Soon's we hit North, I'll take the old man to John, who'll fit him out with city duds."

"And then?"

Amos, impatient with the cross-examination, shuffled his feet. "After he fitted out, John'll take the old man to his daughter. But we gone over this a hun'red times before, Miss Dessi. Seem like it happen ever' time we gits a new one."

"And it will happen many times more." Mandy Lou heard

the sharp note in Miss Dessi's voice. "In an operation like this, there is no room for slipups. It doesn't do to grow careless and forgetful."

"Ain't never let you down yet, Miss Dessi." The burly man sounded hurt.

"And I know you never will, Amos. I trust you completely. The questions are more to reassure myself."

Mandy Lou saw the burly man's grin flash again in immediate response. Mumbling something, he nodded and stepped back, the shadows swallowing him again.

"All right, question time over." Miss Dessi nodded toward the hut, and, raising her voice, she said, "Bring him out here, please."

The door of the hut opened slowly. Mandy Lou caught her breath in a startled gasp as her mother and her brother, Sam, emerged from the dark interior, leading between them a frail old man. In the torchlight, the old man's incredibly wrinkled face was even blacker than Sam's.

"You sure ever'thin' go all right?" Mandy Lou heard her mother say anxiously. She nodded toward her tall son. "Sam here's been tellin' me that since Master Lincoln got hisself made Pres'dent, they watchin' the roads extra careful for run'ways."

"Not the roads Amos takes, which are not really roads at all." Miss Dessi gave a short laugh. "Don't worry, Tildy, I know what I'm doing, and so do all the others in this organization. Everything will be fine."

"If you say so," Tildy replied. "You ain't never led us wrong yet. It on'y that I ain't wantin' nothin' to happen to you. Cain't help wishin' you give up soon, 'fore you gits discovered."

Mandy Lou's eyes widened as Miss Dessi approached the old man. "You must not worry," she said gently, placing her hands on the stooped shoulders. "You will pass through many hands before you reach the North, but all who work for me are to be trusted. Eventually you will be with your daughter and her husband, you will see your grandchildren, and then you will know you are truly free." She smiled. "I guarantee this, Caleb . . . we have never yet had a failure."

The old man stared at her for a long moment. "Why you do this, mistress?" his cracked voice asked. "You a Southern lady, you used to havin' slaves 'bout you to do your bidding. So how come you bother your head 'bout us black folk?"

"Because I don't believe in slavery, Caleb. From the time I could think and reason, I have been against it. Is that answer enough?"

"Reckon the Lord's answer be the same as yours, mistress, so it's enough for me."

Without answering, Miss Dessi patted his shoulder. Mandy Lou, seeing the tears coursing down his seamed cheeks, felt embarrassed for him. "Bless you, mistress," he continued in a difficult voice. Reaching out a trembling hand, he touched a lock of red hair that spilled from beneath the hat. "Flame of Freedom," he said, winding the lock about his finger. "Your hair matches your name."

Gently disengaging her hair, Miss Dessi stepped back. "The arrangements have all been made, Caleb, so my part in this is over. It only remains for me to wish you Godspeed."

"I thank you, mistress." The old man hesitated. "But Tildy here, she right to worry 'bout you. White folk real riled up 'bout the Flame."

"Do you know my name, Caleb? My real name, I mean?"

"No, and it's bes' I don't. Only know you by the name my people call you."

"Well, then, do you know where I live, or anything at all about me?"

Caleb's face fell into slack lines and his eyes were bewildered. "Cain't say I do."

Mandy Lou saw a smile light Miss Dessi's face. "No one knows the true identity of the Flame, Caleb, except these people about you, and I would trust them with my life. So you see, there is no need to worry about me."

"I hear you, mistress, but I cain't help it. I hear they posted a reward for the capture of the Flame. Master Elton Grayson of Twin Oaks, he's the one sugges' it to my ol' master. If they catch you, they hang you for sure."

Mandy Lou saw Miss Dessi's violent start, she heard the tremble in her voice as she said, "Nonsense, Caleb."

"Ain't nonsense," the old man said stubbornly. "It don't make them folks no never-min' who you is. Jus' 'fore I make my plans to 'scape, I heard my old master talkin' to Master Grayson. Master Grayson say that come time they catch the

Flame, they hang that goddamn renegade from the highest tree. That's what he say, mistress, and he mean it."

Mandy Lou saw the sick look on Miss Dessi's face, and a great panic afflicted her. She did not understand the old man's ramblings about a flame, but she did know that some kind of danger threatened Miss Dessi, and that the danger would come from Master Grayson, Miss Dessi's own daddy. Deaf now to the voices, her mind in a turmoil, and her heart hammering, Mandy Lou had fled as though pursued by devils. With her fear of the dark forest and the prowling night creatures quite forgotten, she did not stop running until she reached the safety of the cabin.

Dawn was tinting the small window with a delicate pink mist before the door finally creaked open to admit her mother and Sam. They made no attempt to go to bed, for it would soon be time to start the day's work. Instead, they sat at the rickety old table, heads close together, talking. Lying stiffly on her corn-shuck pallet, her eyes tightly closed in a pretense at sleep, Mandy Lou had listened intently to the low murmur of their voices, but, to her chagrin, she had been unable to distinguish one word.

For a while, the panic still with her, Mandy Lou had watched Master Grayson from a safe distance, waiting with dread for disaster to befall Miss Dessi. Master Grayson, however, seemed much as usual. He spoke harshly to the slaves, if they displeased him, and sometimes threatened them with a flogging, but Mandy Lou knew, from her short experience with life, that he was mostly bluster and very little bite. With Miss Dessi, too, he was the same, loving and kind, strolling about with his arm lightly clasping his daughter's slender waist, making his small jokes, and laughing a great deal at his own wit. When day followed day and nothing terrible happened, Mandy Lou gradually ceased her anxious vigil, and when Elton Grayson went away on one of his periodic trips, she relaxed altogether. She could not forget the scene she had witnessed in the forest clearing, and the ominous words the old man had uttered often troubled her dreams at night, but some innate wisdom kept her usually talkative mouth tightly sealed.

"Mandy Lou"—Desiree's voice recalled the child to her surroundings—"why are you staring in that peculiar way?"

Blinking, Mandy Lou looked about the parlor, and immediately the worry lifted from her mind. The big room with its white walls, soft rose-pink carpet, the curving couch, and the deep armchairs upholstered in a lime green that matched the drapes at the long double windows, dazzled her with its splendor. She looked at Miss Dessi, slender and beautiful in her rustling violet gown with the lace trim at the low neckline and scallops of lace decorating the huge bell skirt, and saw that she was smiling at her. It was all so reassuring, so normal. A bee droned ineffectually against the windowpane, smothered laughter sounded from somewhere in the house, and through the slightly opened round window came the everyday sounds, the rustle of a bird in sudden quick flight, the monotonous chirping of the cicadas, and the sighing of a gentle breeze through the magnolia tree that grew close to the house. It had all been a dream, Mandy Lou decided. She had not really seen that other Miss Dessi in her strange clothing, she had not heard that old man saying that Master Grayson would hang her mistress. White folk, she knew, sometimes hung bad black men, and sometimes black women, but she had never heard of them hanging one of their own kind, so it must have been a dream.

"Well, I do declare, Mandy Lou"—Desiree's voice penetrated again—"if you don't stop staring at me, I'll shake you until your teeth rattle in your head. What in the blue blazes is the matter with you, anyway?"

Mandy Lou knew quite well that the threat to shake her was an empty one, and she was pleased to be diverted. Screwing her small face into a stern expression, she said accusingly, "Ain't nothin' the matter with me that I know of, Miss Dessi, but you is cussin' agin. Leastwise, I think you is. Is 'blue blazes' as bad as 'tarnation'?"

Desiree lowered her long lashes to hide the amusement in her violet eyes. "Well, now, Mandy Lou," she said in a serious voice, "I reckon it's every bit as bad. Worse, maybe. Why, my daddy would likely lock me in my room if he heard me."

Or he might do worse. Mandy Lou's conviction that it was all a dream vanished, and into her mind flashed a frightening picture. She could see Master Grayson throwing a rope over a branch of the magnolia tree, see him placing a loop about Miss Dessi's neck and hoisting her up until her feet left the ground. "Then you ain't to cuss," she burst out on a note of real terror. "If you do, your daddy goin' to punish you real bad. Don't say them things no more, Miss Dessi, don't!"

"Why, Mandy Lou, honey!" Desiree's skirts billowed as she knelt and pulled the trembling figure into her arms. "What's wrong?"

"Don't wan' for you to say it, Miss Dessi," she sobbed. She flung her arms about Desiree and buried her face against the soft scented flesh of her neck. "Ain't wantin' your daddy to git mad at you."

Desiree cradled the child close and murmured soothingly, "There, now, honey, my daddy wouldn't harm me. But if it makes you happy, I won't say it again. I promise."

Mandy Lou drew back, her tear-flooded eyes searching Desiree's face. "You really promise?"

Desiree smiled. "I surely do." Wetting her forefinger, she drew a line across her throat. "I swear I hope to die if I ever utter another cussword. That suit you?"

Mandy Lou felt a renewal of fear at this unfortunate choice of words, but since she had never known Miss Dessi to break her word, relief was predominant. Nodding, she smiled a watery smile. "That's good, Miss Dessi, now your daddy don't git mad."

Desiree's arching bronze eyebrows drew together in a puzzled frown, but she said nothing. Rising to her feet, she propelled the child over to the door. "Scoot, Mandy Lou. Tell your mammy I'll be with her soon."

3

When Desiree Grayson played innocently in the nursery, her doting father had nicknamed her "Puss," and over the years the name had clung, though, had he but known it, he would have been nearer to the truth had he named her "Wildcat." Elton Grayson saw his daughter as the epitome of beauty, charm, grace, and becoming modesty. Desiree had been just sixteen when her mother died, and the way she had taken over the reins of the household had evoked his sincere admiration. That she had also been a bulwark of quiet strength in the face of disaster, he did not acknowledge. Men were strong, but females were to be petted and taken care of and shielded from the harsh realities of life. In this way of thinking, Elton Grayson was no different from most of his contemporaries. It was true that his fond picture of Desiree was sometimes marred by the occasional fiery arguments she directed against the evils of slavery, but he tolerantly put this down to the growing pains of youth. Unthinkable, he reasoned, that his daughter could seriously rebel against the charming and leisurely way of life made possible by the institution of slavery.

When Desiree reached the age of eighteen, the arguments

ceased. Elton Grayson was well content. It was not in his nature to look too deeply, and so he did not see the new purpose in his daughter's eyes. At the age of twenty, Desiree had rejected numerous suitors, and seemed to have no desire for the stability of marriage.

Twenty was almost spinsterhood, and Grayson began to worry about his daughter's future. When he was afflicted by severe chest pains, and was told by his doctor that he had a heart condition, he cast about for a suitable husband for Desiree. His choice fell on the handsome and wealthy Frazer Phillips, their nearest neighbor. The match would be eminently suitable, Frazer was deeply in love with Desiree, and the Grayson fortune, joined to his, would make a powerful and formidable combination. Unfortunately, Desiree seemed to despise Frazer, making dark hints about his cruel and inhumane treatment of his slaves. Grayson did not believe her. Frazer Phillips was popular with the white community; there had been no ugly rumors about him. "If it were so," Grayson told Desiree, "I would have heard. If Frazer is sometimes overstern with his slaves, I don't doubt that he has good reason. A sullen and intractable slave must be disciplined."

Desiree gave him a look of scorn. "I wonder how sullen and intractable you would be, if you were enslaved?"

"Don't talk nonsense," he answered her coldly. "That is quite a different matter."

"Different, how?" Suddenly he was confronted with a Desiree he had never thought to see, eyes blazing, vivid spots of color in her cheeks. "How different?" she cried. "Because you are white, is that what you would tell me?"

"Yes," he had shouted, his temper rising. "And curb your tongue, miss. Damned if you don't sound just like those cursed abolitionists."

Desiree looked at him steadily, the fire still in her eyes. "I believe in freedom, so I guess you have been cursed with a cuckoo in your nice comfortable little nest." Turning, she had swept from the room.

Elton Grayson had paid little attention to his daughter. Female vapors! If she wished to indulge herself in such absurdities, then let her do so. Her notions would soon pass. Unfortunately, though, her words had sent his mind in an unwelcome direction. There was trouble in the air, what with the abolitionists kicking up a dust, to say nothing of the election of Abraham Lincoln, with his pronounced antislavery sentiments. And if that were not enough, there was the audacity of that scoundrel known to the Negroes as the Flame. The damned fellow was still at it. There was not a planter for miles around, himself included, who had not lost slaves. In place of the valuable slaves, a note would be found, stuck in a prominent place—"Freedom for all," it said in large block capitals, and it was always signed "The Flame."

He had heard the name again from Wilmers, his butler. Wilmers, serving his coffee, had said unexpectedly, "There's big talk 'bout the Flame, master. They say he promise to double the number of niggers he sent to freedom."

"Who says that, Wilmers? Give me names."

"Ever'body talkin', master. Flame leave a note on the tree near Folly Stream. It addressed to white masters. Ol' Hugh, the smithy, his last master taught him to read a few words, an' he tell what that note say."

"I see." His eyes hard on the butler's square-jawed face, he said slowly, "And what of yourself, Wilmers? Do you, too, want to follow this Flame? Do you yearn for the freedom the Flame promises? If you succeed in running, boy, it will be the biggest mistake of your life. You'll likely end up starving in some Northern gutter. Speak up. Tell me if that is what you want?"

Wilmers felt sick. Why had he, slyly nursing his delicious secret, mentioned the Flame? Why had he not left well enough alone? If Elton Grayson should ever find out that his own daughter was the Flame, and that the black people had banded together to keep her identity a secret, his rage would be terrible. Just now, his voice had been mildly inquiring, pleasant even, and yet Wilmers had not been deaf to the dangerous undercurrent. He swallowed hard against a sudden constriction in his throat. He had been born at Twin Oaks, some sixty years ago, and he was too old for running now. In his youth, when his blood had been hot in his veins, his mother and his brother had been sold away from Twin Oaks, and at that time, filled with hatred and resentment, his heart breaking, he would have run, had he seen the opportunity. As for Elton Grayson, he had a certain fondness for him. They were much of an age, and they had played together as boys. As masters went, Elton Grayson might be said to be a good one. He never punished without cause, as he had heard that

Master Phillips did, but all the same, it was not wise to cross him.

"Boy, I spoke to you." Now Grayson's voice cracked like a whiplash. "You wanting to run?"

"No, suh." Wilmers' hands trembled in a spasm of nerves. "Ain't wantin' nothin' like that." His eyes slid away from the blue ones regarding him so closely, too closely, he thought. "You mus' be knowin' I ain't. I's content. All the slaves at Twin Oaks content."

"Are they? Now, you listen to me, boy, I've lost five valuable properties in the last three weeks to this Flame. Maybe you know something, maybe you don't. But if you do, I advise you to speak up, boy."

Wilmers winced at the continued use of the word "boy," and a muscle beside his mouth began a spasmodic twitching. "Tol' you, don't know nothin' 'bout no Flame. I swears it."

"I wonder. Tell me, Wilmers"—he shot the question abruptly, hoping to catch the man off guard—"what is the real name of the Flame?"

Wilmers wanted to shout: Your daughter, she the Flame, an' how you like that? Suppressing the words, he picked up the empty tray from the table, his long fingers squeezing at the fluted edge. "Ain't knowin' the name," he gasped. "Don't know nothin' 'bout him. That's the truth, master."

"For your sake, boy, it had better be."

Wilmers' taut sweating fingers made smears on the silver tray. "Why you say that to me? I ain't never lied to you."

Despite his mild harrying of the man, Grayson found himself believing in his innocence. He had known Wilmers a long time, and he flattered himself that they understood each other well. Wilmers was loyal. If he had been guilty of complicity, he would hardly have been stupid enough to mention the Flame in the first place. No, he could rule Wilmers out. Later that afternoon, his anger still simmering, he had sent for Hugh. His abrupt questioning, his pointed remarks concerning the strict law that forbade slaves the privilege of reading or writing, had caused the grizzled-haired blacksmith to shake with fear, but it had produced nothing of importance. Two days later, Hugh had disappeared, and, as added fuel to Grayson's rage, the usual note from the Flame was discovered.

It was fortunate for Elton Grayson's peace of mind that his

doting love blinded him to the true nature of his daughter; otherwise he would have been a most unhappy man. Desiree was not only beautiful, she was courageous and strong-minded, a firebrand who found it expedient to hide behind a demure manner and a sweet smile. Composed of intense emotions, burning ideals, and an indomitable will, there were reserves of passion in Desiree that had never yet been tapped, certainly not by Frazer Phillips, or by any of the beaux who clustered eagerly about her at balls, parties, and picnics. To the young men who sometimes gathered hopefully on the wide veranda of Twin Oaks, she was as beautiful as a dream, but an enigma. Had they known the real Desiree, they would, like her father, have been shocked, even faintly repelled by the very qualities that made her unique. But with no idea of the things that seethed inside her, the young men sipped at their tall, minted drinks, conversing easily, but always alert for a word or a sign from her. She smiled on them alluringly, spoke to them in the low seductive voice that seemed to promise so much, and yet, to their dismay, they found her to be cold and untouchable. The alluring smile, seen close to, appeared to them to be mocking and even faintly cruel. It was as though she toyed with them, deriving a secret amusement from their various reactions. Discouraged, they slipped away one by one, yielding their positions to Frazer Phillips, who seemed to thrive on opposition to his will.

Desiree's views on slavery, unusual for a girl of her age and position, had always been directly opposed to those held by most Southerners, but apart from an occasional heated argument with her father, which, most times, feeling that her strange ideas were of little importance, Elton Grayson blandly ignored, she kept her views to herself. Nevertheless Desiree yearned to right the injustices she saw all about her, and yet she did not know how to go about it; everything she thought of seemed both childish and impractical. It was not until shortly after her eighteenth birthday that an incident occurred that was to point her in the right direction. She told herself then that if she could not stop slavery, she could at least take direct action against the slave owners. As for her father, her deep love for him must not be allowed to cloud the issue, for he too was a slave owner.

On the particular day that was to prove so fateful, her hatred of slavery burst into active flame. She had decided to visit with Tildy, who had once been her nurse. Tildy was not in her cabin, but Mandy Lou, Tildy's seven-year-old daughter, was playing in a patch of dirt before the cabin. When Desiree inquired for her mother, the child, eager to be helpful, pointed toward the root cellar. "Mammy in there, Miss Dessi," she said. "She say for me to stay here, an' it seem like she mighty upset 'bout somethin'."

"Upset. Why, what's happened, Mandy Lou?"

"Cain't say, Miss Dessi." Mandy Lou grinned engagingly. "Mammy never tell me 'bout anythin'. She say my ears too big, an' my mouth bigger still."

Reaching the root cellar, Desiree found the door slightly ajar. She was about to call to Tildy, when an anguished voice from within came to her ears. "I hurts, Tildy, I hurts so bad!"

"Hush, gal," Tildy's soothing voice answered. "Knows you hurts, but ain't no use to cry. Seem like you be knowin' that by now."

"Cain't help cryin'. I give him two sons, and this what he do to me. That worse'n the pain, knowin' I ain't nothin' to him. Cain't bear it, jus' cain't!"

"Got to, Blossom. You foolish lovin' that white man. He jus' use you. Us black folk knowin' from the time we birthed that we's dirt to the whites." Tildy paused, and her voice, which had been heavy with bitter knowledge, softened slightly. " 'Course, it ain't fair to say they all de same, there's some good white folk."

"He sell my chil'ren, Tildy, he a-sayin' that when he whup me. Ever' stroke he put on my back, he a-sayin', 'I sell the black bastards, I sell 'em!' " A storm of weeping followed this; then the voice, broken with tears, went on. "What I do, Tildy, ain't never goin' to see my chil'ren agin!"

"Don't know, Blossom. Here, I brung this salve for you. It's real good for them cuts. Stan' still while I spread it."

The answering voice rose on a note of wild hysteria. "What for you botherin' your head 'bout them cuts? Cain't you understan' what I been sayin' to you? Ain't needin' salve, ain't needin' nothin' 'cept a place to hide. When he say he sell my chil'ren, I know he means it, so I run from Woodgrove. I'm sorry now, 'cause I could have seen the chil'ren one more time 'fore they was sold away from Woodgrove."

"Quiet your voice, Blossom. What if someone hears you?"

"Master Phillips know by now that I run. Cain't go back, not lessen I's wantin' him to carve the meat from my back worse'n he done this time. Tildy, Tildy, if he catch me, an' if he's a mind to, he likely whup me to death!"

Frazer Phillips! Despite the warmth of the sun, Desiree felt herself turning cold. The man her father wanted her to marry! Phillips was responsible for the pain and terror in that voice. She had always disliked him, but now dislike hardened into hatred.

Tildy's voice came again. "I understand how you feel, Blossom, 'deed I do. That Master Phillips, he purely scum, but he hide it from the white folk, and they ain't knowin' him the way we do. All the same, cain't nothin' be done for you till you get them cuts tended. Let me spread this salve, then maybe I think of somethin'."

"If Master Phillips finds me, I'll kill myself 'fore he kin do it!"

Desiree pushed at the door with a trembling hand, the creaking sound it made shivering along her nerves. "Tildy!"

Tildy's head jerked up at the sound of her young mistress's voice, but beyond a slight widening of her eyes, she showed no fear. The other woman stood there frozen, her eyes staring with horror at the slender figure descending the short flight of stone steps. The white silk flounces of her swaying skirts brushed the steps, making a whispering sound, the sun behind her made a fiery halo of her hair, but her face was in shadow, and it was that shadowed face that stirred a primitive terror in Blossom. "No!" She flung out her hands as though to ward off an approaching evil. "No, no!"

Tildy's huge bulk moved quickly. "You jus' hush," she hissed, clamping a large hand over Blossom's mouth. "That Miss Dessi, an' she ain't goin' to hurt you none." Her fingers exerted pressure. "If I take my hand away, you promise to hush?"

Tears spilled from Blossom's terrified eyes and splashed on Tildy's hand; then her stiff posture relaxed and she nodded. "Tha's jus' fine, Blossom, gal," Tildy soothed, cautiously withdrawing her hand.

Tildy was still for a moment, her thick shoulders slumping; then she straightened and turned slowly toward Desiree. "Miss Dessi, I know how this looks to you, but Blossom here been whup bad, and I think she cain't take no more."

Desiree's lips felt dry and tight. "Why was she punished?" she whispered.

"She punish for nothin', that's what I think." Tildy's white-turbaned head rose, and her eyes flashed with anger and defiance. "Blossom belongin' to Master Phillips of Woodgrove, an' he mad with her 'cause she late bringing' his meal to the table." She took a step forward. "Miss Dessi, maybe Blossom ain't needin' to run, not if you was to tell Master Phillips you ain't wantin' her to be whupped agin, an' ain't wantin' her chil'ren sol' away. He wantin' to marry up with you, an' I know he listens to you."

"Perhaps, Tildy. But I have no intention of marrying him."

"Don't matter, Miss Dessi," Tildy pursued, "Master Phillips believe whatever you say, an' you don't need to tell him Blossom try to run, do you?"

"Don't matter, Tildy," Blossom whimpered. "I'm done for anyway. Your Miss Dessi ain't goin' to help me, an' don't you think it. She white, and that's all I'm needin' to know."

"Shut your fool mouth," Tildy said angrily. "Miss Dessi ain't like the others, she's different."

With a moan, Blossom sank to the floor. Pulling up her knees, she wrapped her arms about them, rocking herself to and fro. "White folk all the same. I'm tellin' you, it's the end of me!"

Desiree's sickened eyes looked at the crisscrossing of suppurating lash marks on the black woman's thin shoulders and back, and she felt a terrible anger. With the anger, resolve was born, welling so strongly inside her that she trembled with the force of it. "This is not the end for you, Blossom." She spoke in a hard clear voice. "It is the beginning of a new life. You shall be free, and I intend to help you attain that freedom."

Blossom was suddenly very still. Then, as Desiree came to kneel beside her, her head lifted slowly. "Ain't knowin' what you mean, ma'am." Her eyes flinched away from the face so close to her own.

"You are afraid of me, Blossom, I know, but there is no need to be. I have said I will help you, and I will. Just how, I am not quite sure, but I will find a way."

The soft honeyed tones Tildy was used to had been replaced by a hard, determined note that bewildered and frightened her. "Miss Dessi . . ." She made small ineffectual movements with her hands. "That floor's filthy, an' you is spoilin' your pretty gown."

"To hell with my gown!" Desiree looked up, and Tildy was startled afresh by the glitter in her eyes. "Listen to me carefully, Tildy, Blossom will stay here until dark. Make up some kind of a bed for her." She looked from one face to the other. "It is important to me that you trust me. Somehow or other I'll get Blossom away."

Shaking her head, Tildy said hoarsely, "Cain't think you know what you're sayin', Miss Dessi."

"Yes, Tildy, I do. Instead of moping about the place and brooding on the evils of slavery, I'm going to do something about it at last."

Tildy's heart accelerated, the hard beating drumming in her ears. She had always felt that Miss Dessi was against slavery, but still she had never been quite sure. Looking into the almost feverish violet eyes, she was still shaken with doubt. There were things she could say, but could she trust the girl? The struggle was mirrored in her face, for Desiree said gently, "It is asking a lot of you both, I know, but once again I ask you to trust me."

Tildy's face softened. "Then I will," she burst out impetuously. "If I'm wrong 'bout you, Miss Dessi, I'm takin' a mighty big chance on my life, but I . . ." She stopped, overcome by the enormity of what she was about to say.

"You're not wrong, Tildy," Desiree said quietly. "Go on, please."

"I . . . I know someone who might help," Tildy stammered. "He's a free black man, an' he hate slavery. He been wantin' to help slaves git North, but he's afraid to make the first move. If he know you with him, maybe he be strong."

"We'll be strong together." Desiree's face glowed. "His name, Tildy, tell me his name."

His name. . . . Lord have mercy! Sweat sprang out strongly on Tildy's face, beading there in large drops and then running down her face to her neck. If she were wrong, she had just sentenced herself to death. It was true that she had known and loved Miss Dessi from the moment of her birth, and yet she also knew that white people sometimes took strange notions. She gripped her hands tightly together. Should she let her life depend on the whim of a girl? In a sudden revulsion of feeling, she tried to retrieve herself. "I'm jus' joshin', Miss Dessi," she mumbled. "Don't know any man."

The coldness of Desiree's disappointment vanished quickly before the look in Tildy's eyes. "You're lying to me," she said sharply. "Tell me this man's name and where I may contact him."

"Ain't lyin'. Please, Miss Dessi, I told you that I'm joshin'." Tildy flicked a look at Blossom, hoping to draw strength from her, but the woman's head was resting against the wall, her eyes staring at nothing.

"Poppycock!" Desiree rose to her feet and approached the trembling Tildy. "Land sakes, don't be a fool! You must know you have nothing to fear from me. You do know that, don't you, Tildy?"

"Ain't had a whole heap of reason to trust the white folk, Miss Dessi."

"I know. But I beg you to trust me."

Tildy's nerves steadied as her eyes met the clear violet gaze. If there was malice or cruelty in the girl, she had never known of it, or seen it demonstrated. With a wrenching sigh, she capitulated. "His name Amos Wilson, Miss Dessi, and like I told you, he a free black man. I know how to get hold of him, if you wants."

"I want." Desiree laughed, her face glowing and triumphant. "I have such plans stirring in my brain, Tildy, such magnificent and daring ideas."

Blossom's pitiful condition, a few reluctant and frightened words from Tildy—that was how it had all started. It had sprung rapidly from a one-man-and-woman operation to a complicated network of many people, with Desiree as its heart and brains. Through Amos Wilson she met others of a similar mind with the same rage against the enslavement of a human being, black men and women, Northern whites. And through Tildy, the black men and women of Twin Oaks, many of whom had known her all her life. Once they were reassured, their suspicion dropped from them and they eagerly offered their help. There were some who, given the same opportunity to go North, refused it, preferring to work behind the scenes with their beloved mistress. They seemed to thrive on the danger, on the thrill and the excitement of the gigantic gamble they took in the name of freedom.

Desiree had no idea how the name "the Flame" got

started, but it appealed strongly to the dramatic streak in her nature, causing her to leave behind the mocking notes that so enraged those planters who had lost valuable slaves. Two years from the time the organization came into being, the Flame, thought by most planters to be a renegade white man, was the most coveted prize of bounty hunters, not only for the immense bounty promised, but for the glory that would be theirs if they brought him in.

Desiree was thinking of Blossom as she crossed the hard-packed earth that led toward the slave cabins. Blossom had been living in the North a full year before Desiree, with the aid of Jonathan Barker, her contact in Virginia, had managed to locate Blossom's two children. They, too, had been abducted and smuggled North to join their mother. The last report Desiree had had on Blossom, brought to her by Amos, was that she had married, and all four, including her new husband, were gloriously happy.

Desiree started out of her thoughts as Tildy, calling her name, came waddling rapidly toward her. "I thought you'd never come," the woman exclaimed breathlessly, halting before her. "I was thinkin' that scallywag Mandy Lou skip off without givin' you my message."

"Mandy Lou gave me the message. I came as soon as I could." Without appearing to do so, Desiree studied Tildy closely, noting the carelessly wrapped headcloth and the trembling mouth. "What is it, Tildy?" she said quietly.

"I know I shouldn't be runnin' at you like I done," Tildy said in a strained voice, "and I'm sorry I forgit myself." She looked furtively about her. "But we got trouble, Miss Dessi. Got me a big buck run'way in the cellar, an' he mighty sick. Ain't been whupped, but seem like he been travelin' a long time. His name Josh, an' he come from Murray Hill Plantation. Told me just 'fore he collapse." Tildy's brow wrinkled with anxiety. "You know that place, Miss Dessi, it's the big property owned by Mistress Murray."

"Naturally I know it," Desiree said, suddenly irritated. "I am also, unfortunately, well acquainted with Miss Youtha."

"So am I," Tildy said gloomily. "I hear what she's sayin' that las' time she visit at Twin Oaks. She's sayin' that the Flame's somebody from one of the plantations."

"What if she did?" Desiree's small foot in the low-heeled violet silk slipper tapped the ground impatiently.

"What if she did!" Tildy repeated incredulously. "But, Miss Dessi, ain't you hearin' the rest of what Miss Youtha say? She sayin', if she missin' a slave, she search every place till she fin' her property."

"I heard her, Tildy." Desiree's head lifted haughtily. "But what Miss Youtha states, and what she is allowed to do, are two different matters. My daddy, for one, would never permit her to search Twin Oaks. Other planters will feel the same way, believe me. Why, a search of their property is as good as saying that they are implicated with the Flame, don't you see that?"

"I'm seeing what you mean." Tildy wiped her sweating palms on her white apron. "But the point is, Miss Dessi, she ain't needin' to search. Dat big buck, he out of his head with fever. He hollerin' 'bout the Flame, and 'bout Master Lincoln, and somebody call Martie. Miss Youtha hear him a mile 'way."

"Will she? I don't hear him."

Tildy sighed. "He's quiet for the moment, but he likely to start up agin."

"Then somebody must stay with him night and day," Desiree said briskly. "Should Miss Youtha visit, the news will be relayed. If he is still noisy, he must be gagged until she leaves. The same applies if others should visit Twin Oaks."

Tildy looked shocked. In the past two years, her young mistress had been called upon to make many harsh decisions, and she had made them without faltering, but Tildy had never been able to reconcile the utterly feminine Miss Dessi with the breeched-and-shirted authoritative woman who so coolly directed operations and took such tremendous risks. "Don't seem right to gag him, Miss Dessi," Tildy mumbled. "That buck awful sick."

"Nevertheless, it must be done. If we are to go on with our work, we must protect ourselves."

"I'll do what you say," Tildy answered. "By the way, Miss Dessi, last time I see Amos, he tell me there's goin' to be a war between the North and the South. That the truth?"

"I don't know, Tildy." Desiree frowned. "But it seems likely to me."

"Praise the Lord!" Tildy grinned widely. "If war comes, Amos say that Master Lincoln swear to free all the slaves.

Won't be no more need for the Flame then, Miss Dessi, and you'll be safe."

"No one is safe during a war, Tildy, especially such a one as this could be." Desiree shuddered. "Civil war, it could turn brother against brother, father against son. Think of my case. I am on one side, my father on the other."

"Miss Dessi!" Tildy's eyes were wide and frightened. "Why you say that? I ain't likin' that kind of talk."

"Because it's true!" Desiree said passionately. The fire died from her eyes as she saw Tildy's troubled face. "Never mind. What makes you so sure that the North will win?"

" 'Cause Amos say the North got right on their side, and they sure to win. What you think, Miss Dessi?"

"I think that right doesn't always make for victory, and I also think that Amos is very far from knowing everything." With fingers that suddenly trembled, Desiree pushed back a lock of hair from her face. "If war does come, my father will fight, and so will all the boys from around here. Tildy, do you realize that they could all be killed?"

Tildy's soft heart twinged at the girl's stricken expression. "No one will get killed, Miss Dessi," she said bracingly. "Pish, fiddlin' little old war like that, it all be over 'fore you can turn 'round, you'll see."

Desiree did not seem to hear her. "You remember me telling you about that troop of men Frazer Phillips got together," she went on, "and how they were all set to lick the Yankees, well, two weeks ago, when I was in Dudleyville with my father, I saw them drilling and marching. I . . . I don't know why, but it frightened me a little."

"You, Miss Dessi? You ain't frightened of nothin'." Tildy stroked the girl's arm. "You prove that to us over and over."

"You're wrong, Tildy. I'm frightened of many things."

"Ain't showin' it, then." Anxious to change the subject, Tildy said quickly, "Amos tell me somethin' that's a lot more exciting than that old war."

Desiree drew in a deep, calming breath. What she had seen in Dudleyville had seriously alarmed her. Aside from the drilling and marching, the men, all handpicked by Frazer Phillips, had indulged in ferocious mock attacks on the Yankee enemy, represented by a well-filled bag of straw, yelling at the top of their voices as they charged. "The rebel yell," her father had called it.

"Miss Dessi, don't you want to hear what Amos told me?"

"Of course." She smiled at Tildy. "Well, what exciting news did Amos bring you?"

Pleased that she had recaptured Desiree's attention, Tildy said quickly, "Amos say we best look out, 'less we're wantin' to be murdered in our beds."

Desiree stared at her. Tildy's flights of imagination were sometimes comical, but more often than not exasperating. With thoughts of the fugitive in the cellar troubling her, she said with a trace of impatience, "Tildy, what on earth are you talking about?"

Offended, Tildy drew in her lips in the obstinate manner that Desiree knew so well; then, relenting, she went on, "I'm talkin' 'bout that killer, Christopher Fairfield. Seem like he 'scape from prison where he was sent. Might be he on his way to see his sister, Christine, on account of they bein' so close. You hear of him, Miss Dessi? He's the one done that robbery over at Dudleyville, and he killed that gal who raised the alarm."

Desiree nodded. "Yes, I've heard of him."

"But ain't likely you met up with him, Miss Dessi." Tildy sniffed. "I hear them Fairfields ain't nothin' but poor white trash. Amos say their daddy die soon after his son go to prison."

"That's true, John Fairfield died, some say of a broken heart. As for Christopher Fairfield, no, I never did meet him, though I've seen him once or twice. A dark, surly-looking boy, as I recall."

"Ain't no boy now, Miss Dessi, he's a good five year older'n you, which make him 'bout twenty-five."

"I suppose. I've spoken to Christine, his sister, occasionally. She's a nice girl."

Tildy's fat cheeks quivered with outrage. "That Chrissie ain't no one for you to be knowin', Miss Dessi. What would your daddy say if he knew you speak to that trash?"

Desiree felt a rush of annoyance. "I speak to whom I please," she answered coldly. "And the Fairfields are certainly not trash. Chrissie's father, as you know, was a sharecropper, and a damned hardworking one at that."

"Ain't no need to swear, Miss Dessi," Tildy said in a censorious voice. "You brung up better'n that."

Ignoring the rebuke, Desiree went on, "As for Chrissie herself, since her father's death she has made a fair living with her sewing. I once took her some work, and she keeps a very clean and tidy home."

This last, uttered for Tildy's benefit, did not impress her; all she said was, "I'm ashamed of you, Miss Dessi."

"I don't care what you think, Tildy, at least not when it comes to Christine Fairfield. Another thing, Chrissie believes in her brother's innocence. She says that one day, if she lives long enough, she will prove that he is innocent."

"Oh. And how she gonna do that?"

Feeling as though she were in the nursery again, Desiree flushed beneath Tildy's critical eyes. "I don't know. But if it can be done, Chrissie will do it."

"She's a fool, Miss Dessi. Everybody know that Christopher Fairfield's a killer. As for the daddy bein' hardworkin', could be, but I know that he drank most of the time."

"And what if he did drink? I daresay it was only to dull the pain of his son's arrest and imprisonment."

"Ain't seein' how that excuse him nohow. Anyway, why you takin' up for dem Fairfields, Miss Dessi?"

"Never mind." With a desire to gain the upper hand over this woman who had ruled her childhood with a rod of iron, and who, despite all evidence to the contrary, apparently still saw her as a child, Desiree added in a frosty voice, "I'll come with you to the cellar. Perhaps there is something I can do to make . . ." She paused inquiringly. "What did you say the man's name is, Tildy?"

Relenting, Tildy smiled. "It Josh, Miss Dessi."

Desiree nodded. "I must see if there is anything I can do to make Josh comfortable. Amos is due to report to me tomorrow morning. If Josh's fever has broken by then, we can make the arrangements to get him away."

Tildy's smile became a proud beam. "Josh is safe in your hands, Miss Dessi. I'll back you anytime 'gainst whole army of slave catchers."

Following behind Tildy's rapidly waddling form, Desiree returned her thoughts to the Fairfields. Christopher Fairfield, as dark as his sister Christine was fair, had been a wild boy, and eventually, as people later said they had always predicted, this unfortunate streak in him had led to tragedy, for he had murdered a young girl.

The story went that Christopher Fairfield had actually been

discovered standing over the murdered girl, his hands stained with the blood that still seeped from her slashed throat and dyed the front of her white cotton gown. The victim, Charlotte Elliot, had been just fourteen years old.

Feelings ran high, for Charlotte had been popular with the people of Dudleyville, and though the knife with which the deed had been done had never been found, Christopher's fate was already decided. Protesting his innocence, Christopher declared that he had found the girl huddled in the alley behind the general store. He had no idea that she was dead until he turned her over on her back and saw her throat. "Why would I kill Charlotte, you fools, she was my friend. She never gave me a hard word or a look, which is more than I can say for most of you!"

Asked about the blood on his hands, Christopher spoke with barely concealed violence. "Naturally I touched her. God damn, what would you have done?"

Christopher Fairfield's plea of innocence was treated with contempt. There was too much against him. He ran with a crowd as wild as himself, and in every way he had showed a disregard for law and order. Shackled hand and foot, he had been taken away to serve life imprisonment. Even then, knowing that there was no hope, he had still insisted that he was innocent. Staring out of the train window at the stony faces turned his way, he had sworn revenge on those who had sentenced him. "No prison can hold me!" he had shouted. "Watch yourselves, for one day I'll be back. I'll be even with the lot of you!"

Elton Grayson, telling the story to his daughter, had said, "Let me tell you something, Puss, young Fairfield only narrowly escaped a lynching. The people were so worked up that they were drawing lots as to who should be the one to place the rope about his neck. And that's another thing, he was lucky not to hang in the legal way. For that he can thank that damn fool judge who pronounced sentence. Judge, bah! A fool, I tell you, and likely a cursed abolitionist into the bargain. Fairfield is a brutal swine, and I say he deserved to swing!"

Her father's face was so flushed with anger that Desiree could not help wondering what his reaction would be if he knew that she was wholeheartedly in sympathy with the despised abolitionists. Brushing the uncomfortable moment aside, she had ventured. "Are you so sure, then, that Christopher Fairfield is guilty?"

"Of course I am. All murderers plead innocence, Puss, but Fairfield couldn't fool me. Why, his guilt was written all over him."

"You are hard on him," Desiree murmured. "Would you be so hard, I wonder, if he were in a similar position of life to your own?"

"Desiree!" Her father only called her by her given name when he was angry. "Are you trying to be impudent?"

Her own rage kindling, she had sprung to her feet and raced over to the door. "Everyone condemns him," she shouted. "Isn't it just possible that he is innocent, as he claims? Perhaps he is a little wild," she had rushed on, refusing to be intimidated by her father's outraged glare, "but what of it? Have you always been so dull and respectable yourself? Weren't you ever wild and high-spirited, weren't any of your friends? It seems to me that Christopher Fairfield has never been given a chance."

"A chance? What the devil are you gabbling about? I think you must be mad. If you think it through, you will realize that there is a world of difference between high spirits and the kind of brutality that prompts murder."

"But you don't know that he is brutal. You told me yourself that the murder weapon was never found. Don't you understand, Christopher Fairfield might be innocent, he might have been speaking the truth."

"I've had enough of this. Go to your room and stay there until I send for you."

As Desiree had told Tildy, she had never met Christopher Fairfield, not, at least, in the conventional way, but even before the tragedy of Charlotte Elliot, she was already very aware of him. Sometimes she went out of her way to catch a glimpse of him at work in the field that adjoined his father's cabin. Tall, broad-shouldered, lithe, his body burned by the sun, his hands caked with the red earth—that was how she remembered Christopher Fairfield. She had wondered then, just as she wondered now, how that strikingly handsome face of his would look if his sullen expression ever melted into a smile. He never had smiled at her. But sometimes, if he were near enough to her, he would doff his battered straw hat in an exaggerated gesture of courtesy. Once, when she had passed by, he had been standing on the edge of the footpath. He was hatless, the sun gleaming on his thick mop of curling blue-black hair. He had given her a long look, his dark eyes somber in his sun-browned face, but all he said was, "Howdy, Firetop."

Firetop! How dare he make remarks about her hair? Suppressing her anger, she had said coldly, "Good afternoon, Fairfield. You should not be idling here, should you? I am quite sure your father has need of your help."

"Oh, my, such venom! Don't you fret, pretty girl, he'll be getting it."

His tone, the mockery in his eyes, had caused Desiree's face to flame, and she had felt small-spirited, mean. Now she hated herself for the snobbery that had prompted her words, and she had sped away from him, her wide skirts swaying and rustling with her agitated walk. Just before she turned the corner, she had paused. He would be thinking of her, he would be staring after her. Slowly, expectantly, she had turned her head, only to find that he was already on his way back to the fields. Furious, bitterly disappointed, she had walked on.

Forgetting Tildy and the present-day problems that beset her, Desiree continued to reach back into the past. Try though she might, she had not been able to get Christopher Fairfield out of her mind. Waking or sleeping, he continued to invade her thoughts. At nights, tossing and turning in her bed, she would imagine him making love to her, and her skin would burn and tingle as though with a fever. In her favorite fantasy, he would accost her as she strolled by. She would turn and face him, his arms would sweep her close, and his dark eyes would look deeply into hers. There would be no need for words between them; the urgent message of their bodies said it all and could no longer be denied.

Snuggled beneath the bedclothes, Desiree would embroider the fantasy, and quite suddenly it would become reality. She was actually there, standing at the edge of the field with the sun blazing down on her uncovered head. She could even feel the prickle of heat between her breasts, the hard, excited thrusting of her nipples against the thin fabric of her bodice. "Christopher . . ." She said his name softly.

Christopher turned and came toward her, but there was no surprise in his expression. It was as if he had known all along that she would come to him, that the joining together of their two vibrant, passionate young bodies was meant to be. Smiling, his dark eyes strangely gentle, he held out his hand to her. She put her own into his, her heart jerking at the clasp of his strong fingers. Wordlessly, she let him lead her to the hut at the far end of the field.

The hut, where she had so often played as a child, was exactly as she remembered it. To her, it was not just a building, it seemed to have always been there, a part of the earth that she loved. It still leaned crazily to one side; the slats on the roof had warped from the relentless bombardment of the sun, letting in stray fingers of sunlight. Inside the hut, the cobwebs of disuse hung from the rafters, low and gray and dusty, fluttering in the slight breeze occasioned by the opening of the door, and decorated with the dwindled specks of long-dead victims. She stood still, sniffing the well-remembered pungent odor of sun-blistered rotting wood, and then all coherent thought was driven away as Christopher's arms drew her close against him. His hands caressed, his mouth crushed hers in a long, hungry kiss that set her brain reeling and her body trembling with a storm of desire. "Desiree"—his voice was deep, shaken, urgently pleading—"I want you so much!" His warm, faintly tobacco-scented breath fanned her face as he began kissing her closed eyes, her cheeks, and once again her tremulous mouth. "Let me love you, my darling. Let me!"

Astonished that he should even feel the need to ask, Desiree opened her eyes and looked at him intently. The tenderness with which he had looked at her had vanished. His face had frozen into that proud and forbidding mask that she had come to know so well. Feeling bereaved, she gave a little cry. He must not return to his former aloofness, he must love her. Couldn't he feel the response of her body, didn't he sense her driving need to be possessed by him? He took a step away from her, and she flung her arms about him, straining herself against him. "Christopher, please!" she said huskily. "Don't you know how much I need you?"

"Need?" His lips curled into a sardonic smile. "Is that all you have to say to me?"

For a moment he hesitated, and she had the panic-stricken feeling that he meant to leave her. Then, the words issuing forth harshly, he said, "There are other things besides need between a man and a woman, and perhaps, in time, you will understand that." The sardonic smile touched his mouth again. "So you need me, Miss Desiree. Are you quite sure of that?"

"I know what I want." Desiree's fingers fluttered over his face, lightly, caressingly, stopping at his grim mouth and trying to coax it into a smile. "And never let me hear you call me Miss Desiree again. Things are different now."

"Are they, I wonder."

"Yes, oh, yes." She was eager to reassure him. "For a long time I have known that we were meant to belong to each other. You have known it too. You cannot tell me that you have not."

"You were determined that I should know it," he answered her savagely. "You and your pretty swaying gowns, your wafting perfume, the flame of your hair, and that look in your eyes that enticed me on, that made me dream of something that could never be mine. You should have left me alone. Why didn't you?"

"I tried." Desiree's answering voice trembled. "I really did. I even tried to think of you as the grubby, rough, older boy who was always fighting with me, mocking me, snatching my hair ribbons, and tripping me up, but it was no use. When you came back from that school where your parents sent you, you had become the type of man that I had always dreamed of. I saw you, Christopher, and I was lost." Tears filled her eyes and ran down her cheeks. "Oh, please say you want me. Please!"

Christopher stared into her tear-suffused violet eyes. She was so beautiful, her slim, perfumed body was so willing to belong to him. Why shouldn't he take what was freely offered? "Christ, yes, I want you," he answered her roughly. He gripped her shoulders tightly, wringing a muffled cry from her. "I will always want you. Always! But tell me, Desiree, do you really know what you want?"

Her brain whirled with speculation. Always, he had said. Was he trying to tell her that he was in love with her? Love? Oh, no, there could be no question of that between them, and he must know it. Firmly she closed her mind against troubling questions. Nothing mattered now but her driving need for him. "I know that I want you," she assured him. "Please believe me."

"I warn you, Desiree, this is not a passing thing for me. If you're playing with me, you'll be sorry."

She felt a moment of fear at his possessiveness, at the leashed-in violence that she sensed, and then the fear was swept away. "I'm not playing with you," she murmured, "so I'll never be sorry."

"You are sure?"

"I'm sure."

He gripped her even tighter. "Once you belong to me, I'll never give you up, and you had better know that now. Despite all of your father's objections, and there will be plenty, I'll hold you."

Desiree frowned faintly. Why must he be so intense? Why couldn't he live for the moment, as she was doing? She opened her mouth, intending to say something light and frivolous, something that was designed to disabuse him of the dream he so obviously nurtured, but the words she would have uttered died in the surge of passion that swept her. Of course her father would disapprove, but she would not think of him now. Her father's objections, the objections of the whole world, could not sway her from her desire. Only Christopher mattered. Just to look into his gypsy-dark eyes, just to see him move with his lithe, slightly arrogant gait, was enough to send the throbbing madness coursing through her.

"Desiree . . ." Christopher's voice was brusque. "Did you hear what I said? Did you understand?"

He was so handsome, so breathlessly exciting. He was the meaning of romance, of passion, he was everything to her. "I only care about you," she answered. She touched his face again, her finger tracing his strong, deeply clefted chin, the line of his nose, the slightly prominent cheekbones. She undid the buttons of his blue shirt and let her hands rest against his broad, lightly downed chest. "Tell me you want me."

"How many times must I say it? Shall I show you how much I want you?"

"Yes," she breathed. "Please show me."

Clumsily Christopher loosened the pale green ribbons that tied her bodice. Through the fine lace-trimmed chemise beneath, he saw her breasts as tantalizingly vague outlines. Thrusting down the confining material, he drew in his breath sharply as her breasts sprang free, firm, pointed, the nipples a thrusting dark red, the delicate surrounding skin almost startlingly white in contrast to her lightly bronzed face and shoulders. He put out a hand, but Desiree, as if suddenly shy, shook her hair forward in an attempt to cover herself. Fire against snow, Christopher thought, pushing back the fiery strands. He let his fingers play over her breasts, gently teasing the aroused nipples, and then, without looking at her, he bent his head and kissed them lingeringly.

Desiree stiffened. The touch of his hands seemed to sear, and his gently suckling lips released all that was primitive in her nature. Heat flushed her body, and her breathing quickened, a hoarse, labored sound that was loud in the tiny room. Trembling violently, she stroked his thick blue-black hair. "Christopher, Christopher!" Her wild utterance of his name was a cry of desire.

Christopher raised his head and looked at her, and Desiree saw an echo of her raging hunger mirrored in his eyes. Without speaking, she stepped back a pace, her fingers fumbling for the tiny hooks at the waist of her gown. It fell about her feet in a soft froth of green silk and amber-tinted lace; the chemise followed, her petticoats, and finally, her long lace-flounced and ribbon-threaded underdrawers. Naked, she felt no shame, she simply stood before him, waiting, her eyes slumberous with passion and her mouth slightly unsteady.

His hands clenching, Christopher's eyes traveled over her slender form, lingering on the full, pointed breasts, the tiny waist, the long, beautiful limbs. She was like an exquisite statue, he thought, a statue that had stepped out from her casing of cold marble to reveal herself as a living, breathing, passionate female. He thought of the dreams he had so foolishly cherished, and despite the turmoil of desire that possessed him, bitterness intruded. Miss Desiree Grayson of Twin Oaks, and himself, the sharecropper's son. That he had even allowed himself to dwell on the idea was sheer lunacy, as improbable as the idea he had had of a statue coming to life. Despite the words he had flung at her, he knew that he could never hold her, that he would not waste his time by making the attempt. Inner laughter rose, scalding in its bitterness. Desiree, as his wife, Desiree living in a cottage, trying to make do with the pittance he would earn, putting aside her silks and satins and expensive cottons for homespun! It would be like trying to turn a gorgeous bird of paradise into a drab mud hen. The girl was strongly attracted to him, perhaps at this moment she even loved him, but for her it was no more than a passing amusement, something with which to while away the sun-drugged hours. She was very beautiful, very young, and in a year or two, maybe less, she would do what was expected of her by her father and the society in which she moved; she would become engaged to someone of her own social class. Someone, of course, who was equally as wealthy as her father, or perhaps even more so, and then, after the prescribed interval, she would be married. Christopher's lips tightened. This thing that she felt for him now—fascination, passion, summer madness, call it by any name, but never call it love—would become a disgraceful episode in her life, and if she could avoid it, she would never think of it again. Curious, he thought, how very much it hurt to think of himself relegated to a dusty and forgotten corner of her mind.

Desiree moved, her eyes widening with uncertainty, and he knew that she was wondering if she had been rash, if she had perhaps mistaken his feelings for her. His gaze traveled over her again, lingering on the delicate shading that shielded her womanhood, and he felt the prickle of perspiration. God, how he wanted her! Put aside your dreams, you fool! he told himself. She is here, warm and willing and waiting, entirely yours, and you must live only for this moment. His eyes fixed on her, he kicked her garments to one side and swept her up in his arms. As he carried her over to the narrow, blanket-covered bed beneath the grimy window, his nostrils were teased by the subtle fragrance that rose from her body and her cloud of fiery hair.

Desiree trembled as he laid her down. Aware of the fast, almost suffocating beating of her heart, she concentrated a desperate attention on the dust motes rising from the ancient, moth-eaten blanket. She heard the rustling sound of his disrobing, and she wondered what it would be like with him. Would it be wonderful, as the highly romantic novels she managed to smuggle into the house intimated, or would it be the dreary boredom, the distasteful duty, of which she had heard so many of her married girlfriends complain? After a hesitant moment she turned her head his way, and found that he was standing very still, his dark eyes watching her intently. If a man could be called beautiful, she thought, her heart leaping, then Christopher Fairfield would surely deserve to be called so. Naked, he lost none of his dignity, he was as tall and commanding in appearance as ever, his body smooth-skinned and as sun-browned as his arresting face. Her eyes lingered on his broad shoulders, his powerful chest and arms, the lean waist and the narrow hips, went lower still to the rigid proof of his manhood. Flushing crimson, caught up in the spell of his dark fascination, she closed her eyes. Thinking of the question she had asked herself, she wanted to laugh aloud. Dreary boredom, distasteful duty? With Christopher, no, never!

Studying her, Christopher noticed the change in her face. His conscience stirred. Foolish and headstrong she might be, but she was, after all, little more than a child. If she was regretting her wayward and impulsive action, then while he still had the strength to do so, he would let her go. He said abruptly, "There's no need to be afraid. You can leave, if you wish."

Feeling a curious disappointment, Desiree opened her eyes and looked at him. From all the reports she had heard on the wild Christopher Fairfield, there was nothing tame in any of his actions, nothing even remotely decent. Why must he choose this moment to be noble? "Why do you say that to me?" she cried indignantly. "I am most certainly not afraid."

"No?" Christopher smiled mirthlessly. "All right, I'll concede that. But suppose you tell me if you'd like to leave."

"And if I did wish it," she cried challengingly, "are you telling me that you would make no effort to stop me?"

Christopher shrugged. "Stay here or get out, it's all one to me." The words cost him an effort.

Desiree pouted. How cool he was, how uncaring. Or was he perhaps trying to mask his true feelings? The last thought was soothing to her vanity, and conquering her petulance, she smiled brilliantly. "You don't really want me to go, I know that," she said seductively. "You must know that I want to be with you, that I want you to love me."

"Your actions would seem to indicate that." Christopher answered dryly, his eyes going over her unclothed body.

"Well, then?" Her smile lingering, Desiree closed her eyes again. "If you want me to say it again, I will. I want you to love me, Christopher Fairfield." The words made her feel deliciously wanton, and her smile deepened.

Christopher stared hard at that smile. Child? Woman?

Which was she? "Then I'll love you," he said harshly, "and to hell with conscience!"

Why was he talking so strangely? Desiree thought, her brows drawing together in bewilderment. The handsome and wickedly fascinating Christopher Fairfield was the devil's spawn—everybody was agreed upon that—so it followed that he could have no conscience. All coherent thought fled, and she tensed with excitement as she heard the protesting creak of the plank bed. She felt his weight upon her, the hard throbbing of his desire. This was the moment she had yearned for. Her pulses began a rapid fluttering, and for the first time a flicker of fear mingled with her excitement. Despising herself, she stammered. "You . . . you will be gentle? It is the f-first time for me."

Christopher did not answer. His hands caressed her, trailing fiery paths. He kissed her face, her ardently parted mouth, her throat. His lips found her breasts, lingered there, then moved downward, searching out every vulnerable place, making her writhe and pant. God damn her, Christopher thought, she had asked for this, and he would take what he could get.

Desiree clutched him closer, her fear quite forgotten. She could not seem to control her thrusting limbs, and there were sensations in her body such as she had never dreamed possible. She was on fire, burning up with the force of her desire. Now she no longer wanted him to be gentle, she wanted him to take her with all the savage force that lay just below his civilized exterior. Her hands moved, giving him back caress for caress, trailed lower until she found what she sought. She heard him gasp, and she opened her legs wide, eagerly inviting him. When he did not come into her immediately, she arched upward, pressing herself urgently against him. "Please," she whispered, "please!"

The taste of her in his mouth, Christopher raised his head and looked into her perspiration-glazed face. Her eyes were closed, the long lashes fluttering, the ripe, tremulous mouth parted as she drew in panting breaths. She was all fire, all passion, he thought. She was a wild and lovely thing, and she had been born to belong to him. Yet, in a few years' time the passionate girl would be transformed into sober matron, indistinguishable, except for her haunting beauty, from the rest of her breed. Words whirled through his head: I hate you,

Desiree Grayson, but most of all, God help me, I love you! Suddenly, at the thought that she would never be his, he wanted to hurt her as he was hurting. He raised himself, and poising himself above her, thrust her legs farther apart and drove inside her with a force that was governed by his rage and despair. He heard the gasping scream she gave, but he continued to move inside her. She had been seeking a new thrill, so let her take the consequences!

The pain of penetration quickly vanished, succumbing before the mounting fire of passion. Moaning, Desiree inched her legs upward to circle his waist, went higher still to lock themselves about his neck. His slow strokes became faster and faster, and her battered body jerked with his in a frantic, matching rhythm. Her heart was hurting her with its pounding, and her head felt light. The ecstasy was too much, she could bear no more without screaming aloud! Even as the thought sprang into her mind, the heat of his release spilled inside her, and her own gushed forth to meet and mingle.

For a time, Desiree clung to him tightly, loath to surrender the sensation of him inside her. "I want you again," she whispered. She stroked his hair. "For a while I thought I could bear no more, but I don't want it ever to be over."

The anger had drained from him, and he felt suddenly weary. Gently he unclasped her legs and lowered her down on the hard bed. "Everything must come to an end," he said tonelessly.

With the feel of the gritty blanket beneath her, Desiree reluctantly returned to the world of reality. "We won't ever come to an end," she told him fervently, her violet eyes looking into his. "I won't let that happen!"

His eyes sad, Christopher smiled at her. "I'm afraid you'll have no choice." He twirled a lock of her hair about his finger, and then he bent his head and gave her a quick, hard kiss. "There will be other interests in your life, dearest Miss Desiree, and you'll forget me soon enough."

She had wanted to protest the mockery implicit in his tone, but she choked back the angry words that sprang to her lips. He was a devil, and just by a look, a word, a gesture, he could make her furious, but she would not fight with him now. Instead, she smiled at him and returned his kiss. "I'll never forget you, Christopher. We must never be parted. I'll be back, you'll see."

"Perhaps."

"I mean what I say. I'll be back. Will you be waiting?"

Christopher rose from the bed and began to put on his clothes. "For a while," he answered her curtly. "But I won't embrace a lost cause." Completing his dressing, he walked out of the hut, slamming the door behind him.

Desiree sighed. She had gone back to the hut, but only in her fantasies. The passionate interlude between herself and Christopher Fairfield had never happened. The scene had been set by her vivid imagination, the action, the thoughts, the words, all supplied by her. In that fantasy, Christopher had intimated that he loved her, and his innermost thoughts had confirmed this. But she had never said that she loved him. The words that had come from her mouth had always been "I need." "I want." Desiree grimaced. How vain and selfish and shallow she had been in those days, how conscious of her beauty, her superiority. Even if the fantasy had become reality, Christopher Fairfield would never have been able to stand her. She was still sometimes selfish, still pleased with her reflection in the mirror, but the shallow girl who had believed herself so superior had been left behind.

Desiree frowned. It was all nonsense, of course, and she must stop daydreaming. But all the same, she admitted ruefully, she had never quite managed to forget Christopher Fairfield. He was the kind of man a woman could never forget. And now he had escaped from prison. Would he come back here to carry out the threat he had made?

Desiree's heart skipped a beat. Her father had been one of the men who had brought in a guilty verdict against Christopher Fairfield. Frazer Phillips had been another. Phillips could take care of himself, and if he died at Fairfield's hands, she would not weep. Her father, however, was another matter. They might be on opposing sides concerning the question of slavery, but she loved him dearly. Just lately he appeared to her to have grown very frail; even his deep-rooted convictions seemed to have paled. The one thing he wanted, her marriage to Frazer Phillips, she would not, could not grant him. How could she marry a man she hated and despised, even to please her father? Christopher Fairfield's face rose strongly in her mind. Imagining those dark eyes blazing with the light of vengeance, she stumbled. Surely he would not wish to harm her father.

Tildy turned quickly at the clumsy sound. "You wrenched your ankle, Miss Dessi?" she inquired anxiously. "You sure lookin' mighty pale."

"It's nothing, Tildy. I'm fine." Putting the disturbing thoughts of Christopher Fairfield firmly from her, she followed Tildy the remaining few paces to the root cellar.

4

Josh heard the sound of the opening door, the protesting squeal it made as it was closed again. His heart leaped with suffocating terror. Where was he, what door had opened and closed? Frantically he tried to move, but his weighted limbs refused to obey. He moved his head from side to side like a goaded animal as light began to steal back into his brain, bringing with it the memory of the fear that had driven him on for so long, and that he now no longer had the strength to combat. He listened to the footsteps coming closer and closer, thudding like hammer strokes in his wincing ears. So he was finished. They had tracked him down at last. He heard the rustle of feminine garments, and he knew Miss Youtha was there. He might have known that she would be in on the kill. Jesus, help me! The words sounded deep inside him. Sweet Jesus, have pity!

Shuddering, Josh heard the rustle of garments again, and the momentary protection afforded by the prayer flew away from him. Miss Youtha was the devil, and at this moment the devil was the stronger. He knew exactly how she would look, now that she had him cornered. Her narrow bleached face, with the thick spattering of freckles over an incongruously tip-tilted nose, would be wearing the tight and merciless expression that the slaves of Murray Hill Plantation had good cause to fear; her small eyes, devoid of all compassion, would have the glisten of wet stones. Soon now her voice would issue the command that meant death to him. Rough hands would seize him and bind him with ropes to the flogging post that stood in the center of the baling yard. The post was stained with the blood of other victims, and now his own would be added. The house bell would begin tolling its message, bringing the slaves and the overseers from all parts of the plantation. Some would look on stolidly, hardened by repetition of the same nightmare scene. Others would half-close their eyes, trying not to look as the great whip with its heavily weighted tip tore the flesh from his bones. His blood would spatter the dusty ground, and children would shriek hysterically, while still others would begin to sob in frantic terror. His sweet Martie, little more than a child herself—she would cry for him.

Josh heard the soft sound of breathing near to him, and his fingers twitched in feeble protest. Not yet, he thought. Dear Lord, delay the moment. Now he tried to will Martie's face to come to him, wanting desperately for her countenance to be the last image he beheld before he died. Sweat stood out on his face and rolled down his neck in great drops as he struggled to conjure her up.

"Praise be, Miss Dessi," a voice said. "Will you jus' look at that boy, he's got fever.

Josh heard, but the words were a confused jumble that made no sense to him. He only knew that the voice had driven Martie from him, she was gone, vanished forever. In her place, horrifying pictures, sounds, and smells flashed into his mind. Stunted trees, their trunks gray and lifeless-looking, growing close to the forest floor. Snakelike vines that spread a trap for the unwary, the overpowering odor of dank vegetation combined with the smell of animal droppings, the slinking of heavy bodies through the undergrowth, the drone of countless insects competing with the sometimes raucous, sometimes sweet tones of the many varieties of birds, and, dominating, the giant trees that reared interlocking leafy branches toward the sky, shutting out the daylight.

"Wipe his face, Tildy, and raise his head a little."

Josh was deaf to the voices now, he was back in his nightmare. He swerved away as something touched him, and then he was running through that endless forest. Brambles whipped across his face, tearing great gashes near his eyes, half-blinding him with the flow of warm, sticky blood. Thorns drove deeply into his flesh, leaving behind patches of festering poison.

Again he heard whispering voices, and something again touched him. His stomach was cramped with hunger. Thirst had dried his tongue to an unwieldy lump that cleaved to the roof of his mouth, and he thought longingly of the clear, sparkling streams that were occasionally to be found rippling over a deeper depression in the forest floor.

He had no idea how long he ran. When he finally found a natural cave almost hidden by an overhanging fountain of greenery, it seemed to him to be a haven. Silence greeted him and he crawled thankfully inside, curling himself into a tight ball. He no longer cared; if death came, it came; he could not run anymore, he had reached the limit of his endurance. His uneasy dreams were haunted by the dogs and the men who had pursued him for so long.

After the dawn had broken to full splendor, Josh crawled from the cave. A rabbit, startled by the sight of the man, stood upon its hind legs, front paws flopping and its nose twitching with agitation. As he rose to his feet and took a lurching step forward, the small creature loped away with a flit of its tail.

All around him the forest was stirring to life. As his brain cleared somewhat, he thought once more of the dogs. The men would drive the dogs until they at last succeeded in sniffing him out. Perhaps, after all, since he had led the slave catchers such a long chase, they would not return him to Miss Youtha, but would instead take their revenge by letting their animals tear him to pieces. "Don't care," Josh mumbled defiantly through his cracked and bleeding lips, "just don't care. Whupped to death or tore to pieces, it's all one to me."

"What's he sayin', Miss Dessi?"

"I don't know, Tildy. His lips are badly swollen, it's difficult to make out his words."

He began to laugh, a harsh racking sound that brought

fresh torture to his body. Twin Oaks, and Master Elton Grayson. They would make him safe. Laughter turned into tears. There was no safety anywhere for his kind. His head shook from side to side as his delirious shouts turned into more laughter.

Tildy drew in a shocked breath. "He's ravin', Miss Dessi." Her anxious eyes sought Desiree's; then, looking down at the tossing black man, she caught one of his flailing hands and held it firmly in hers. "He's sweatin' so hard, the fever must be breakin' now."

The words cut through Josh's confusion, blowing the last lingering mists of fever away. He lay very still, remembering how he had come stumbling out of that forest. He had felt more dead than alive, and at first he had been conscious only of the blessed sun and the clean fresh air on his face. Then, with the fading of his first rush of joy, he had seen the white-painted outbuildings, the fields stretching wide beneath the April sunshine, the rows of stooping black people in the fields, and he knew, or hoped, that he had reached Twin Oaks. Everything had begun to swirl crazily about him, and then he was falling. The next thing he remembered was an enormous black woman bending over him. Her breasts were pendulous beneath a severe black cloth gown enlivened by a crisply starched white apron. Her round face, topped by a tightly bound white headcloth, was dewed with sweat and wrinkled with concern. Her upper arms were the size of hams, but her hands, in comparison, were ridiculously small. The little dimpled hands had touched him gently, and he had felt the calluses on the palms. "You a runner, boy?" Her voice had struck pleasantly on his ears; it was as rich and as warm as the good red earth.

Struck dumb by her directness, he had nodded. There was no fear in this woman; he sensed it. She would not turn him over to white authority to save herself, as some of his people had been known to do.

"I thought so," the fat woman said. "Ain't likely you run here with a message, not the condition you're in." She laughed a little at her own joke, her sides shaking. "What's your name?"

He swallowed hard, and after one or two attempts he managed to bring it out, "Josh," he said.

"You lookin' to find the Flame?"

Frightened, his eyes had flared wide. "I know he's made up."

Tildy chuckled, and her face broke into a smile that puzzled him. "Well, now, you're a right clever buck, ain't you?" she went on, her deep-set eyes dancing with mischievous lights. "In fact, you so sharp that you cut yourself if you don't watch out." She had stood up, looming over him, her hands planted on her hips. "The Flame ain't no makeup, and I'll prove it to you 'fore long."

Josh lay still after Tildy had bustled away, his mind grappling with her words and making no sense of them. Finally, feeling the darkness trying to catch at him again, he surrendered to it gratefully.

The cool touch came again, and Josh's rapidly awakening senses became aware of the soft touch of fingers on his arm. Opening his eyes slowly, he stared into the face bent above him. A white woman. Momentarily he stiffened; then, as she smiled at him, he relaxed. Whatever might come of this, at least she was not Miss Youtha.

"You are feeling better now, Josh?" Her voice was beautiful, low-pitched, friendly, and the sound of it made Josh want to smile at her. Unable to speak, he nodded. Her face was as beautiful as her voice, and her eyes were unlike any he had seen before. Bordered by thick black lashes, they were the color of the violets that grew wild and free in the patch of earth behind Martie's cabin. Sunlight shafting through a crack in the roof touched her hair and turned it to flame, reminding him of Martie's ridiculous notion. His clearing mind slipped slightly. To his chagrin, he heard himself mumble, "Flame."

"You have found the Flame," the violet-eyed girl said clearly, commanding his wandering attention.

Josh was filled with resentment at her words. Why must she make fun of him? "No I ain't," he answered roughly. "Cain't find him, 'cause there ain't no such person."

Desiree looked at Josh again. Seeing the angry bewilderment in his eyes, she said softly, "I am telling you the truth. I am known as the Flame."

Josh stared at her, wondering if the fever was hitting him again. Her extraordinary eyes were upon him, waiting for his reaction. "But you cain't be," he burst out, "you only a gal. If the Flame's real, he's a man."

"Mah land!" Tildy exploded again. Does you hear him?" Seems like these menfolk got the notion we women cain't do nothin'."

"Tildy, be quiet."

Ignoring the excited and wrathful Tildy, Desiree began to speak. From the first moment she captured and held Josh's full attention. Motionless, his fascinated eyes never leaving her face, he heard how her organization had first started, how it had steadily grown until its members had penetrated every slave-holding state in the South. She told him that some of the most active and valuable members were actually slaves themselves, and that in most cases these people, offered their freedom, had declined. They knew, once they reached the North, that they would be faced with the need to earn a living. Work did not frighten them, for they had known little else in their lives, but the responsibility of being a wage earner did. Even more important, it was generally thought that this new way of life would absorb so much of their time, attention, and energy that it would, of necessity, preclude them from taking their full part in the cause that meant so much to them. Having thought over all the risks, they embraced the danger gladly, for they felt that freedom for one must, in the end, mean freedom for all.

His eyes speaking his wonder and awe, Josh sensed the great dignity of manner this slender white girl had. A calm strength which unquestionably stamped her a leader, and which told him more clearly than any words could have done that he did indeed behold the Flame.

"There is something else troubling you, Josh. Would you like to tell me about it?"

Josh blinked his tears away and looked at her again. "I'm thinkin' of my woman, ma'am," he said huskily. "Knows if I takes my freedom that I ain't never goin' to see her 'gain."

"If you take your freedom, Josh?"

Josh heard the question in her voice, he saw the change in her face, the doubt clouding her eyes. Eager to make her understand, he touched her arm with hesitant fingers. "Cain't go on without my woman, ma'am. I'm thinkin', if I go to Miss Youtha and tell her I'm sorry for runnin, then maybe she let me live."

Desiree shook her head. "You know she won't, Josh. We both know how Miss Youtha thinks. Even if she wanted to let you live, she would feel that she had to make an example of you."

It was true, Josh knew it, but, remembering Martie, the feel of her in his arms, he refused to allow his hope to be crushed. "Maybe Miss Youtha be different this time." His words tumbled over each other. "Miss Dessi, ma'am, ain't never goin' to tell Miss Youtha 'bout the Flame. She could whup me to death, and wouldn't never breathe a single word."

Desiree heard Tildy's snort of indignation, but she did not look at her. "It is not a question of trust, Josh, but of what is best for you. Tell me, would your woman want you to go back to Murray Hill?"

Josh started to assure her that Martie would want him to return, but the lies he had been about to utter stuck in his throat. Somehow, with those candid violet eyes upon him, he found that nothing less than the truth was possible. "No, ma'am"—his words came out in a reluctant mumble—"she wouldn't want me to go back to Murray Hill. It was her that begged me to go."

"She begged you?"

Pride in his woman put warmth in Josh's haggard eyes. "Yes, ma'am, she say someday she be free too, an' then she'd find me. But won't never happen."

"So she put you before herself," Desiree said warmly. "I like that. What is her name, Josh?"

"Her name Martie, ma'am." Even the mere saying of the little name sent the pain twisting deeper inside him.

"Martie," Desiree repeated. Her smile flashed. "Your Martie sounds like a fine brave person to me, Josh. I don't think we can possibly leave her behind."

"Ma'am?" Josh's heart was behaving strangely, leaping wildly, pounding in his ears, seeming to flutter in his throat. Martie, who was dearer to him than his own life, Martie was to go with him. To make sure he had not misunderstood, he said in a faint voice, "Wh-what you meanin', ma'am?"

"I mean, Josh, that Martie will make the journey North with you."

She had said it again, he had not misunderstood. Stifling a sob, Josh looked at the white girl through a mist of tears.

Even for Martie, how could he let her take such a terrible chance? Her seeming fragility was, he knew, a delusion, for there was steel beneath that delicate feminine appearance, but all the same, she was not infallible. What if something should go wrong with her plan to get Martie away from Murray Hill? And if it did, how could he live with his conscience? She was the Flame of Freedom, the precious hope of so many people, and he must not allow his own selfish desires to quench that flame. He had to say something, he had to stop her; somehow he was quite sure that Martie would expect that of him. "No, ma'am"—he forced the difficult words out—"cain't let you do it. Reckon you ain't knowin' Miss Youtha as well as you think you do. She's a devil, and she'll be on the rampage now."

"Nevertheless, Josh," Desiree answered him calmly, "it will be arranged."

"I tellin' you that woman's a devil. If she catches you, ma'am, she'll—"

Tildy, who seemed to take Josh's words as a personal affront to her mistress, glared at him angrily. "You jus' tell her what she needin' to know 'bout that Martie."

"But—" Josh's voice broke into a startled gasp as the door at the head of the crumbling flight of steps opened, letting in a stream of bright light. He felt the white girl's fingers touch his wrist and tighten, trying to impart courage, but he had been through too much, and he could not stay his trembling.

"It Clover, Miss Dessi," Tildy said in an indignant voice. "She knows she ain't to come to the cellar without you sayin' so."

Shutting the door carefully, Clover turned and came down the steps in a rush. Her eyes flickered over Josh, but she made no comment. "I been lookin' for you, Miss Dessi," she said in a breathless voice. "Couldn't find you nowhere, and the cellar the only place I didn't look."

"What was it you wanted, Clover?"

"Your daddy's home, and he got that Master Phillips with him. They're all excited and talkin' a blue streak 'bout some place call Fort Sumter. Master Phillips, he laughin' like a loon and sayin' he glad the war got started. What war he meanin', Miss Dessi?"

"There's no time to explain, Clover." Her face very pale,

Desiree rose swiftly to her feet and headed for the steps. "Tildy, look after Josh. Sick or well, you must ready him for a journey, for there is no time to be lost. Do you understand?"

Tildy wrung her hands together. "Yes, Miss Dessi," she said in a subdued voice.

Desiree nodded. "Clover, send Tobias to Amos, he'll know where to find him. Tobias is to tell him to go to the usual place. I will meet with Amos as soon as possible."

"I'll do that, Miss Dessi." Clover's voice shook on the last word. "Miss Dessi, suddenly I'm scared."

"So am I, Clover. The world is about to crumble around our ears."

Desiree turned quickly to Josh. "If Clover heard aright, it would seem that the South has decided to fight to preserve its way of life. The North, which is solidly against slavery, will fight back."

"War, then, ma'am?"

"War, Josh, civil war."

Josh's gasp was drowned by Clover's startled cry. "Ma'am," he said, when Clover had subsided, "hope you know I ain't meanin' no disrespec' to you, but sure ain't got no call to love the South. I like to be in on that war, an' thinkin' maybe them North folk could use me."

Desiree's hands clenched. "I . . . I understand, Josh. I have no doubt the Yankees could use you."

Josh was touched by the flash of pain he had glimpsed in her face, and understanding came to him. She hated slavery, and yet she loved the South, and perhaps there were many of those who would fight who were dear to her. If the Clover girl had heard correctly, and war had indeed broken out, she would be torn both ways. He said in a diffident voice, "Understand what you goin' through, ma'am, but will this make a diff'rence to your plans?"

Desiree smiled brightly. "Difference, Josh? No, not as far as you are concerned. I had intended to wait until you were fit to travel, but instead, you will be smuggled away tonight."

No matter what her pain was, his own and that of his brothers was the greater; forcing back the weakness that bade him be silent, he questioned, "An' . . . an' Martie, ma'am?"

"She will be with you. I give you my word."

Josh sank back and closed his eyes. He heard the silken

rustle of her gown as she sped away, and the distressed breathing of the two women left behind. Delby had been wrong. Freedom would happen, it must! Surely the North would win this fight.

5

Her feet noiseless in their soft silk slippers, Desiree crossed the veranda and let herself into the house. She stopped short at the unprecedented sight of a group of servants standing near the swinging doors that led to the kitchen quarters, all of them openly listening to the conversation that came through the open parlor door. Wilmers, clutching his inevitable tray, was motionless in the shadow of the stairwell. The old butler, usually the sternest of custodians where the lower servants were concerned, would normally have sent them about their business, but today he had no rebuking words, he appeared as frightened and as uncertain as the others.

"Wilmers," Desiree said in a low voice, "what is going on?"

Wilmers started. "I'm sorry, Miss Dessi," he said apologetically. "Knows we shouldn't be standin' here like this. It just that the gentlemen made such a clatter when they came in, and they were talkin' about war . . ." He hesitated. "They're still talkin' about it."

Desiree smiled at him. "There's nothing I can tell you now, Wilmers. In the meantime, it might be best if you resume your duties."

Wilmers returned the smile. "I'll do that, Miss Dessi." Assuming a fierce scowl, he flapped his hand at the other servants. "We all know Miss Dessi will come to us when she got news, so scat now, you lazy no-goods."

Desiree waited until they had disappeared; then, straightening her rumpled skirts, she moved over to the parlor door. The two men in the room, oblivious of her presence, continued their loud conversation. Elton Grayson, a glass of peach brandy in his hand, was seated on the couch. Despite his excitement at present, Desiree thought her father looked far from well. His lips were pale, and there were deep shadows beneath his gray eyes. Frazer Phillips, lolling in the deep easy chair opposite her father, was in complete contrast. He was unusually flushed, his blond hair was rumpled, and his bright blue eyes were flashing. He exuded health and vigor as he lifted his glass and shouted, "Here's damnation to the Yankees, El. We'll lick those bastards in no time at all."

"Surely will." Elton Grayson, looking slightly drunk, leaned forward and clinked his glass against Frazer's. "Hands off the South, I say. No interference, we'll not stand for it." His mouth twisted with scorn. "As for this Lincoln, the jumped-up uncultured oaf is not even to be regarded. How can he be expected to understand the affairs of gentlemen?"

"You're right there. Just who does he think he is, anyway?"

"The next thing to God, perhaps. Who knows?" Grayson laughed harshly. "But whatever Lincoln thinks he is, we'll soon cut him down to size."

Frazer stared at him, the blue blaze of his eyes darkening with a shadow of uncertainty. "El"—he set down his glass on the side table—"what if the Yankees won't fight?"

"After the way General Beauregard blasted them out of Fort Sumter, what the hell choice do you think they've got?"

Frazer shrugged. "Could be they'll find a way to ignore Beauregard's gallant action. It's a well-known fact that the Yankees are cowards."

"Well-known to whom?" Desiree said, stepping into the room. "Whatever else the Yankees might be, I doubt you'll find them to be cowards." She looked steadily at Frazer, all her scorn of him evident in her eyes. "But of course, I had forgotten. You are an authority on cowardice, aren't you?"

As always, when he first saw her, mixed emotions battled

in Frazer, intense hatred and burning desire. Now, under the sting of her words, he flushed a dull red. Rage flickered, and for one barely controlled moment of violence he wanted to leap from his chair and smash his fist into that lovely mocking face. God damn the nigger-loving bitch, he thought, what right had she to judge him? Whatever she knew, or thought she knew about him, she could prove nothing. He ran his plantation as he saw fit, and it might be that some of his niggers had gone whimpering to her with tales of his brutality. For some time now he had suspected that there was a leak in the affairs of Woodgrove, and if ever he should find out that any of his black bastards were responsible for that leak, he would string them up by their heels and flog them to within an inch of their miserable lives.

Unaware of Elton Grayson's puzzled eyes upon him, Frazer moved restlessly in his chair, his fair brows drawing together as he continued to brood. To his neighbors and friends he had the reputation of being a strict but just master, but Desiree saw him in quite another light, and because she saw through all his pretensions so clearly, he could not forgive her. But be damned if he would pamper his stinking black animals just to earn her regard. One way or another he would have Desiree Grayson in the end, and then he'd teach her a lesson she would never forget. His mind leaped to a familiar grievance, the increasing number of runaways from Woodgrove. He would not be surprised to find that Desiree had had a hand in some of his niggers running off. Perhaps she was even in league with that cunning and tricky bastard who called himself the Flame. For a moment he toyed with this intriguing idea, and then regretfully rejected it. He had the certain notion that there were hidden depths in the girl and that she was capable of almost anything except, perhaps, that. No, there was no perhaps about it. She was a Southern lady, and a lady would not sink so low as to throw in with a renegade white man. All the same, it was a pity he had to reject the idea; he would like to have something on the bitch.

"Frazer seems to be sunk in thought, Puss, but he'll tell you it's true." Elton Grayson's excited voice broke in on Frazer's thoughts. "General Beauregard made a surprise attack on Fort Sumter. Yes, yes, it's so. He's shelled the Yankees every which way to hell. The Yankee commanding the fort, a Major Robert Anderson, was forced to surrender.

I'm told that he was defiant to the last, and that he and his men vacated the fort with flag flying and drums beating."

"Defiant?" Desiree clasped her hands together, her face glowing at the picture he had invoked. "I would not call it defiant, I would call it splendid."

Annoyed by his daughter's enthusiastic tone, Grayson regarded her from beneath lowering brows. "Splendid perhaps," he said, making a grudging concession to fairness. "But what of Beauregard? What do you say, Frazer?"

Feeling that something was expected of him, Frazer nodded absently, but he was not really listening. His senses were caught and held by the fragrance that wafted from Desiree's person and by the seductive rustle of her gown. However much he might hate her for her arrogance and her too-obvious dislike of himself, he could not deny that the merest glimpse of her was sufficient to make him ache with raw desire. There was something about her that set his blood on fire, a cool and elusive something that would challenge any red-blooded man to grasp and hold her against all comers. That was why, knowing he had Elton Grayson's full approval and support, he had determined to marry her. He glanced at her quickly, and his imagination ran riot. His fingers itched to tear the silken gown from her body. He wanted to feast his eyes on her slim perfection, and to fondle those ripe young breasts until the nipples stood out like tiny dark pink spears. His lips would suckle those nipples and his mouth would be filled with the taste of her scented honey-smooth flesh. He imagined himself grasping her thighs and parting them to expose the shadowed triangle of love, felt himself thrusting inside her. Sheathed in her moist heat, he would ride her so deeply and so long that she would scream aloud her desire for him, just as Christine Fairfield and others before her had done. He thought of Phoebe, his current mistress, and somehow her musky black body became one with Desiree's. His hands gripped the arms of the chair, and a trembling afflicted him.

"Frazer?" Elton Grayson raised his voice. "You're shaking. Are you sick?"

Frazer started, looked at Grayson vaguely. "What was that you said?"

"I asked if you were sick."

"No, I'm fine, El." He managed a smile.

Grayson shrugged. "Perhaps I was mistaken." He grinned. "A while ago you were full of Beauregard and the happenings at Fort Sumter, but now you seem to have forgotten about it."

"Forgotten? Not I. And speaking of that, there is something I would like to ask you."

Aware of Desiree's hostile eyes upon him, Frazer hesitated. Then, reminding himself again that he had Elton Grayson's support, he made up his mind to speak. "Sir," he said, reverting to the formal, "do you remember the matter we discussed in regard to your daughter?"

Grayson looked at him sharply. "I remember," he said quietly.

Frazer smiled. "Well, since we are both agreed that war is coming, there will be no time for a lengthy courtship of Miss Desiree, so I would like your permission to address her now."

"You must give me a moment to think, Frazer." Elton Grayson glanced at Desiree. She was standing stiff and straight, the violence of her shock reflected in her pale face and her accusing violet eyes. He waited for her to speak, even hoped that she would vent her anger, so that he might justify himself. When she said nothing, he looked quickly away.

Frazer's malicious eyes were on Desiree, enjoying her anger and embarrassment. She might hate him, but he was the best catch in Hawleigh County, and she knew it. Many girls of his acquaintance had married for expediency rather than love, and he did not think that this one, unique though she had proved herself to be in many ways, was so very different from the rest of her sisterhood. When her father died, Desiree would be wealthy in her own right, but could one ever have enough money and power? Frazer, who did not believe in love, smiled complacently. "Miss Desiree," he said smoothly, "won't you sit down?"

"No, thank you," Desiree answered in a cold voice. "I prefer to stand while I await the interesting results of my father's thinking." Her lip curled slightly. "But don't you bother to get up, Mr. Phillips."

By God, but she was insolent! Were he in Grayson's shoes, he would whip her for that smart mouth alone. The old man was too easy with her. Glowering and defiant, Frazer settled back in his chair.

Elton Grayson winced at the sarcasm. He loved his daughter dearly, but too much free thinking was bad for a female. He had given her too much license, and now he was reaping the reward. If only she were more like her mother, who had been so gentle and submissive. Desiree had tried to emulate her mother, but he was no fool, and he was well aware that it was a mask she donned for his benefit. Desiree, he imagined, was a throwback to his grandmother, who, from all accounts, had been just as fiery and independent in her thinking. Grandmother Eloise had been quite a lady, but she must have given her husband some uncomfortable moments.

"Have you reached a decision yet?" Frazer's voice prodded.

"Not yet." Grayson's tone was suddenly as cold as his daughter's. He believed Frazer Phillips to be an excellent young man, well-suited to Desiree, but all the same he did not care to be hurried. Sighing inwardly, he went back to his thoughts. Desiree, he told himself, had never known what was good for her, and that being the case, it was up to him to think for her. As far as Frazer was concerned, she was stubborn and unrelenting, and all because she had got hold of some garbled and completely untrue story about Frazer Phillips' brutality toward his slaves. Useless to tell her the story was untrue; she had made up her mind, and that was the end of it. Over and over he had enumerated Frazer's good points, dwelling on his strength, his steadiness, his desirability as a husband, and all he had got for his pains was a derisive smile or, even worse, a stony silence.

The burning log in the hearth collapsed, scattered a shower of sparks and flaky ash, and brought Grayson's attention back to Desiree. She was maintaining that stony silence now, but her eyes had switched to Frazer. He believed that she would come to love Frazer in time, and that, in favoring this marriage, he was surely doing the best thing for his child. Surreptitiously he lifted his hand and massaged the pain about his heart. His heart condition was worsening, and Dr. Baker, usually the most cheerful and optimistic of men, had grown increasingly pessimistic about his chances of living beyond this present year. That was why he wanted to see Desiree settled into matrimony. Once this was an accomplished fact, he had made up his mind to join the fighting. Better by far, he thought, to fall on the battlefield than to linger on, a nuisance to all, until death decided to claim him. He was greatly obliged to Beauregard for his action at Fort Sumter; it had opened the way to him. With Desiree secure as Frazer's wife, he could leave the running of Twin Oaks to Wilson, his head overseer, and depart with an easy conscience.

Desiree regarded her father's down-bent head with a mixture of anger and tenderness. He had grown very gray lately, and there were times when he looked quite ill. He had been attending Dr. Baker, that much she knew, but the doctor, apart from recommending that he take a tonic, had given him a clean bill of health. Desiree's arching bronze eyebrows drew together in a frown. Her father had always made it a rule never to lie to her, and she hoped he had not broken that rule when he had quoted the doctor's report.

Her gaze skimming with distaste over Frazer's lounging figure, Desiree stopped and picked up the poker. As she absently stirred the fire, her thoughts reverted to the present situation. Her father must know that nothing in this world would persuade her to marry Frazer Phillips; she would as soon marry a rattlesnake. All this deep and thoughtful silence on his part was not only silly but a great waste of time. Why didn't he just consult with her? She would give him a definite no, and the distasteful matter would be closed once and for all. Returning the poker to its stand, she straightened up. Frazer Phillips indeed! As though it had been waiting there to erase Frazer's fair image, another face flashed into her mind. Dark intense eyes in a strong, sun-bronzed face, blue-black hair that fell curling over a broad, intelligent forehead, a deeply cleft chin, and a sensitive mouth that had assumed a cynical and bitter twist. Christopher Fairfield. Now, why in the world had she thought of him? She shivered. Christopher Fairfield, the wild one, the exciting one—she had the strangest feeling that he was very near.

Grayson heard the rustle of Desiree's gown as she moved abruptly. He gripped his hands tightly together. The one thing he would not do was use his illness to coerce her. She knew, of course, that his health had declined somewhat of late, but she had no idea of the seriousness of the situation, and he did not intend her to know. In the past, Desiree, for all her headstrong ways, had always endeavored to please him. Perhaps it would be that way again, he thought hopefully. Yes, it was quite possible she would get over this foolish animosity she now felt toward Frazer, and consent to marry him. He did not ask himself what he would do if she issued an outright refusal, for he had not allowed himself to think beyond the point of his own earnest wish.

Annoyed by the long silence, and made increasingly uncomfortable by Desiree's unspoken hostility, Frazer contemplated Grayson through narrowed angry eyes. What was the matter with the fool, why did he appear so quivering and uncertain? The old man had been eager enough before to see him wed his daughter, and Desiree, whose one weak spot seemed to be her father, would surely not go against him . . . or would she? Biting his lip in the anger inspired by her possible refusal, Frazer's thoughts drifted to Melody Hampton. Everybody in Hawleigh County had known that Melody did not wish to marry Graham Carter, and that she was breaking her heart for Wayne Frobisher, a penniless adventurer recently come to Hawleigh. A word of command from James Hampton, Melody's father, had quickly banished Melody's foolish romantic dream and had set the wedding bells ringing for herself and Graham Carter. Grayson should command Desiree, as Hampton had done with Melody.

Frazer glared at the slender girl standing by the fire. Bitch, he thought with a spurt of viciousness; that was the word that best described Desiree Grayson. So why did he want to marry her? The answer came to him immediately. It was because he could not have her any other way, because, even while he hated her, she maddened and excited him. Beautiful Desiree, with her flame-red hair and her huge violet eyes, the fragrance that always clung to her person—she was like an exotic butterfly, and he must possess her. But, by God, if they should be married, he would crush her like the butterfly to which he had likened her. Yes, he'd break her proud spirit. If she did not come instantly to heel, he'd flog her as he would a disobedient nigger girl. She would pay for every contemptuous glance, for every insult she had uttered.

Grayson stirred, and Frazer leaned toward him at once. "Well, sir," he said, still maintaining the pretense at formality, "have you changed your mind? Our past conversations have led me to believe that you would not be unwilling to see a match between your daughter and myself."

"And I am not unwilling." Grayson saw Desiree's furious movement, the blaze of her eyes, and he hurried on. "But in the long run it will be up to Desiree. Much as I desire the marriage, we are not living in the dark ages, and I cannot force her."

Frazer's dark blond eyebrows rose. "I suppose you could say that James Hampton forced his daughter into marriage, but as it turns out, he did the right thing. I met Graham the other day, and he tells me that Melody is not only gloriously happy, but she is blessing her father for insisting on the marriage."

Liar! Desiree glared at Frazer. Melody was far from happy. She had taken to her bed the day after the wedding, and she refused to leave it. Lying there in a darkened room, the door bolted against her husband—that was Melody's happy marriage. But if Frazer imagined her to be a meek little mouse like Melody, he would very soon find out his mistake. Her head held high, she turned on her heel and swept from the room.

"I take it she has given me my answer," Frazer said bitterly.

"She'll come round, I feel sure," Grayson said soothingly. "I'll speak to her again. I trust you, Frazer, and I know you'll make my daughter a good husband. It's true that the war is upon us, but you're young and strong and you'll know how to survive." His worried eyes went to the open door, as though expecting Desiree to walk through it. "Don't give up hope, my boy."

Old fool! His lips turning into an automatic smile, Frazer rose from the chair. "I'll go on hoping, and certainly I'll know how to survive. In any case, I don't think the war will last very long. Now, if you don't mind, I'll go find Miss Desiree and put the question to her again."

6

Frazer caught up with Desiree just as she entered the forest that edged the plantation. Walking along behind her stiffly held figure, he said mockingly, "I have come for my answer, dearest Dessi. Will you marry me?"

"I will not." She lengthened her stride so that he had to hurry to keep pace with her. "I'd rather be dead than married to you."

"So dramatic, Dessi, but you know your father wishes this marriage. He is your weakness, and I know you won't disappoint him."

She flung around to face him, her eyes blazing. "And so you imagine that I will marry someone like you? You are very much mistaken. Now, go away and leave me alone."

Stung by her contemptuous expression, Frazer let his simmering rage boil over. His eyes dangerous, he grabbed her and slammed her hard against the trunk of a tree. "Nigger-loving bitch!" He ground out the words savagely. "You have a reputation for coldness where white men are concerned, don't you? But I know there's a fire inside you, I've seen it looking from your eyes. Who is it for, your niggers? Do you lie with them?" He twined his fingers in her hair and yanked viciously. "Answer me, slut!"

Tears of pain bright in her eyes, Desiree managed to pull one arm free from his crowding body. Lifting her hand, she raked his cheek with her long, pointed nails. "How dare you say such a thing to me, you swine?" She stared at the blood beading along the shallow furrows her nails had made, and she laughed on a note of hysteria.

That laughter was her undoing. His face contorting, Frazer hit her open-handed, the sound of the blow like a pistol shot in the green dimness. "Nigger's whore," he snarled. Flinging her to the ground, he threw himself on top of her, laughing as the breath rushed from her lungs. "I'll teach you a lesson you won't forget in a damned hurry."

Her senses swimming from the blow and the hard contact her head had made with the ground, Desiree went limp beneath him. Dimly she heard the sharp report of a breaking branch, a flurry of wings accompanied by an agitated twittering as a flock of roosting birds rose in sudden alarm, and then Frazer's raised voice. "Where the hell did you come from?" His angry tone seemed to Desiree to hold an undercurrent of fear. "Who are you?"

Footsteps approached, and Desiree felt Frazer stiffen. She tried to open her eyes, wanting to see the cause of his fear, but the pain in her head was too intense. With a gasping sigh she surrendered to the darkness that was fast closing in.

Frazer looked down at Desiree's unconscious face; then he rose slowly to his feet, his wary eyes on the apparition who had emerged so suddenly from the crowding undergrowth. The man standing before him was very tall, and thin to the point of emaciation. Above an untidy growth of rough dark beard, deep hollows scored his cheeks. Dark eyes glowed with a fierce light from beneath a mop of tangled black hair. His stained clothes were little more than rags, and the exposed flesh was coated with mud and green slime. He looked, Frazer thought, as though he had made a difficult passage through boggy Colter's Way. He saw the red, scabbed, worn places on the man's wrists that must surely come from the wearing of manacles, and his heart leaped in renewed fear. Convict! The word flashed into his mind, and with the thought came the dismaying realization that he had forgotten to wear his gun.

The man laughed at the groping movement he made toward his empty holster, the sound harsh and curiously menacing. "No gun," he said in a deep voice. "A pity, that—you could have shot me down like a mangy dog, and no questions asked."

Frazer did not answer. He took a backward step, then another, his eyes never leaving the gaunt bearded face. He had a feeling that their shock was mutual; the man obviously had not expected to come upon anybody, and it would not do to antagonize him. He had heard that there had been an escape from Buxton Prison, but he had not paid it much attention. This man had to be the one who had successfully broken out of the almost impregnable prison, and even now the authorities must be hunting him. "Who are you?" he asked again.

The question echoed in Christopher Fairfield's brain, and rage filled him at the irony of it. Had he changed so much in the four years of hell he had spent in Buxton Prison, he wondered, that this elegant gentleman, in his casual well-cut clothing, failed to recognize him? Well, he had not forgotten him. He felt a rush of hatred. Frazer Phillips' name was burned in his brain, together with Elton Grayson's and those others who had condemned him. Guilty, had been the verdict they had brought in against him, and for a crime he had never committed. The murdered girl's face rose in his mind, and he felt a stab of familiar pain. Sweet little Charlotte Elliot, with her wondering blue eyes and her little kitten face, had been as much a sister to him as Christine, and he would have died before hurting her. On the day of the murder, when he had found her in that alley with her throat slashed from ear to ear, he had been taking her a wooden animal he had carved for her fourteenth birthday. Even now his heart jolted from the remembered shock of that gruesome and pathetic sight, and it was as if he could still feel her blood on his hands, warm, sticky, horrifying. Blood—there had been so much of it. It had spattered his shirt, it had marked an innocent man as Charlotte's murderer.

Frazer flinched before the gaze of those dark tortured eyes. What was the man thinking about, why didn't he answer his question? Like an animal scenting danger, he moved uneasily, for he knew instinctively that this man was dangerous to him, that he threatened him in some way. Recognition struggled to surface. He was almost certain he had seen him before—but where, when, and under what circumstances?

Christopher's bitter mouth tightened. Frazer Phillips and his kind, masters of their great plantations, so wealthy, so sure of themselves, and so intolerant of those in lesser positions—they had helped to send him to the mind-destroying stench and filth of the infamous Buxton Prison, to weekly floggings, to the torture and degradation of the chain gang. They had taken four years from his life. His scarred hands clenched. Why should he not kill Phillips now? He took a step forward, and then checked. No, it would be over too quickly. Phillips, he was confident, would eventually remember him, or at least put two and two together and come up with the right answer. When he did, the shock would be that much greater, so let him sweat for a while, let him wonder when Christopher Fairfield would kill him, as he promised to do on that day before the train carried him off to Buxton.

His thoughts drifting to his sister, Christopher cast an unseeing look at the crumpled figure of the girl on the ground. Chrissie would have a shock when she saw him. She must know by now that he had escaped from Buxton, for the news was at least ten days old, but perhaps she would not be expecting him to head this way. His face softened. He could rely on her to find him a place to hide, to bring him food and clothing. Chrissie believed wholeheartedly in his innocence, and she had said so at the trial, shouting her belief into the hard, unmoved faces of those who had already condemned him. His father had been present too, but Christopher had had no way of knowing if he believed in him. Looking into John Fairfield's set face, he had been unable to detect the slightest trace of emotion. He had disappointed his father many times, of course, wild and unruly and rebellious as he had been, but he was no murderer, and he hoped his father had known that before he died.

Frazer glanced quickly at Desiree. Her eyes were still closed, but she was stirring feebly. He would have to carry her, he decided reluctantly, for certainly he could not leave her here, at the mercy of this man with the fiery and dangerous eyes. He had better make a move now, before something happened. He took a step forward, and then froze as the tall man's voice halted him. "Get away from her. The girl stays."

Frazer swung around to face him, his expression almost

ludicrous in its dismay. "What the hell do you mean by that?"

"Exactly what I say." Christopher smiled a cold, mirthless smile. "She stays. And by the way, if you're thinking of leading a party to her rescue, you'd best think again. Before you could reach her, I'd kill her."

So Desiree was to stay, and he was to go. Ashamed of the surge of relief he felt, Frazer tried not to show it. "You can't hurt her," he said in an unsteady voice. "You wouldn't really do that?"

"I can and I would, if driven to it. I've nothing to lose by killing her."

"Why should you want to kill her? What harm has she done to you?" Frazer cried desperately.

Christopher ignored the last question. "I said I would kill her if you came after her. Her life is in your hands, wouldn't you say?"

Frazer took a deep breath and tried again. "It doesn't matter, she's going with me."

Christopher's mirthless smile turned into a sneer. "That's reckless talk from a coward. I know all about you, I'd say the whole of Hawleigh County knows. You're a big man with the ladies, aren't you, and an even bigger one when it comes to beating the hell out of your slaves."

Frazer stared at him, and again he felt recognition trying to stir. "Who the devil are you," he shouted, "what do you want from us?"

"You'll know the answer to those questions soon enough." Christopher waved a hand toward Desiree. "Well, there she is. Take her, if you think you can."

Frazer felt a chill as he met those dark, implacable eyes. He was suddenly quite sure that he was facing not only an escaped convict, but a lunatic as well. It might not be wise to try to take him, although he would not have hesitated had he had the backing of his gun. The instincts of self-preservation rising strongly, he decided that although the fellow might look emaciated and worn-down, there was obviously a great deal of power left in that lean body, the sinewy arms, and the scarred fists. With as much dignity as he could muster, he said in a threatening voice, "Now, you listen to me. If any harm comes to that girl, I'll see to it that you pay dearly."

"I'm tired of listening to you." Christopher moved toward

him. "As to the rest, I'm sure you will. That is the specialty of you and your friends, isn't it, making people pay, especially when they are innocent of wrongdoing. Now, get out of my sight."

Frazer looked frantically about him. It was ridiculous to stand here arguing with a madman, and he certainly wasn't going to indulge in an unseemly scuffle in which, possibly, he might be injured, which would leave both of them at the mercy of the man. Much better to go for help. He felt a sense of unreality as he hastily backed away, as though he had dreamed the whole thing. It was best to leave Desiree, he argued with himself. In the short time he would be away, he doubted if she would come to any harm. And when he returned with help, he'd make damned sure his party moved as silently as possible. He made his way over the branch-littered ground, falling once, the hot blood of humiliation scorching his face as the gaunt stranger's mocking laughter followed after him.

With returning consciousness, Desiree had become aware of voices, although not of the words being said. Turning her aching head to one side, she forced herself to listen intently. Only silence greeted her concentrated effort; then, startling her, she heard a scrambling rush, as though somebody had just fled; this was followed by laughter that had an oddly chilling sound. Frowning, she opened her eyes a slit and tried to raise herself on her elbows. Pain immediately lanced through her head; with a stifled groan she closed her eyes and fell back. Footsteps, slow and deliberate, came toward her; her lids darkened. Stubbornly, filled with an unreasoning panic, she kept her eyes tightly closed. Who was standing over her? Was it Frazer, or was it the owner of the deep, rich voice?

Christopher Fairfield looked down at the girl. She was pale and disheveled, but far more beautiful than he had remembered her. Her breasts had budded to an enticing fullness, and through the disarranged laces at the low-cut bodice he had a misty glimpse of taut, rosy nipples. Her waist, always trim, had narrowed still more; her face, exquisite with its delicate planes, the saucy, slightly tip-tilted nose, the full, sensuous mouth, and the shadowed hollows beneath high cheekbones, had lost that too-rounded look of extreme youth. What age would she be now, he wondered, nineteen, perhaps twenty? Lying there, her hair bright even in the uncertain light that filtered through the trees, her violet silk skirts ballooning about her, she reminded him of a fallen flower.

Christopher half-turned away, his hands clenching in anger at his poetic flight of fancy. He was a fool to allow himself to be caught off guard by her glowing beauty. No fallen flower, this one, he reminded himself savagely. She was Miss Desiree Grayson of Twin Oaks, the daughter of his enemy, and a snobbish bitch, as he had cause to know. With a fresh surge of bitterness he remembered how she used to come strolling past the field where he was working, her graceful bell skirts swaying and rustling and looking like the brilliant petals of a giant inverted flower, her head bare, her bright hair a flame in the sunlight, or sometimes enticingly shaded by a tiny lace parasol.

Christopher blinked his tired eyes. The incident, if one could call it that, between himself and Desiree Grayson had not been such a tragedy, but he had been four years younger then, and sensitive. The road where Desiree had chosen to stroll led past the field, but it was little more than a rutted cart track, abandoned a year since in favor of a broader, smoother road. There had been no need for her to use that difficult way, and so it would seem that she had deliberately flaunted herself to invite his attention. Only he had not thought so then.

Christopher put his hand against a leaning oak tree, his fingers playing with the delicate ghostly beards of Spanish moss that hung from the branches. No, he had not thought so then. He had believed, romantic fool that he was, that she was genuinely attracted to him. Dazzled by her, his strong pride and the wary suspicion with which he viewed most things temporarily subdued, he had made up his mind to speak to her. One afternoon, his heart beating rapidly, he had stood on the edge of the track, waiting, hoping she would come by. As though his longing thoughts had conjured her up, he heard the rustle of her silken skirts before she came into sight, and as she appeared and drew level with him, he had smelled the delicate fragrance emanating from her person. He had felt stupid and awkward when her beautiful violet eyes had looked into his, and he could not bring himself to smile, even though there was a smile lurking inside him. Somehow he had managed to force out words, and to this day he had no idea what they were. She had drawn back from him with a look of anger, switching her voluminous skirts to one side, as though he were diseased and loathsome to her. Recovering herself, she had given him a haughty appraisal which seemed to see right through the bold front he had assumed, and then her cold voice had recommended him to be about his work and not to idle. Looking after her departing figure for a brief moment, his cheeks burning with an overwhelming humiliation, he had vowed that never again would he lay himself open to a snub, not from her, not from anyone. His dream of a romance between the fine lady of Twin Oaks Plantation and the sharecropper's son was definitely over.

His fingers tightened on a strand of Spanish moss. After that episode, his behavior had become wilder and even more defiant. He knew it, but he could not seem to stop himself, did not even want to. He was Christopher Fairfield, he told himself, and as good as any man. He had done many things of which he was ashamed, and some things he was vaguely proud of, but he had never robbed, never deliberately set out to hurt anyone, and certainly he had never committed murder. Christopher's hand fell away from the tree, clenching at his side. "That wild Fairfield boy," he had been called, and in the end his reputation had trapped him. He had always believed that those who had condemned him had known he was innocent, and he could not shake the conviction. Somehow, before he killed his enemies, he would choke an admission from them.

Desiree moved restlessly, bringing Christopher's attention back to her. Strange, he thought, but no matter how hard he had tried, he had never been able to forget Desiree Grayson. In his grim nights at the prison and during his even grimmer days, he had thought of her constantly, not with sentiment and tenderness, but with anger and the biting memory of humiliation. He had cursed her then for the sway she held over his mind, and he cursed her now. Damn the bitch, she was well-fitted to be Elton Grayson's daughter.

As though his angry thoughts had reached her, Desiree's arching bronze brows drew together in an uneasy frown and her slim hands opened and closed spasmodically. Christopher watched her broodingly. She appeared to him to be conscious and aware, so why didn't she open her eyes? Had she perhaps seen him standing there with Phillips, and was she hoping, if she remained still, that he would go away? His mouth tightened as another and even more disagreeable solution occurred to him. It might be that she believed he was Phillips, and that she was waiting for the interrupted seduction to be resumed. With this thought, an idea was born. He would take Phillips' place. He had not had a woman in a long time, and this was fitting; one might even call it a rough justice. Through this girl he could strike at both Grayson and Phillips and even part of the score.

Stooping over her, he saw a tremor pass across her face, and he hesitated, fighting the fundamental decency that not even prison had quite been able to erase, and then the moment of indecision passed. Stooping lower, he gathered her into his arms. Her breathing accelerated and he felt the tensing of her muscles. Giving way to an impulse, he brushed his lips against her hair, smelling again that light, delicate fragrance that seemed to be so much a part of her. "Don't struggle, Firetop," he said in a low voice. "It will only exhaust you, and it won't do you a mite of good."

Firetop? The word danced through Desiree's brain. Only one man had ever called her by that name, and that man was Christopher Fairfield. She stiffened in the arms that held her so tightly. It could not be. He must know that the prison authorities would search Hawleigh County first. Her eyes flew open, widening as they gazed with shock and horror at the face bent over hers. "It *is* you," she gasped. "My God, what are you doing here?"

So she had thought he was Phillips. Christopher felt the anger all through him. "It would seem that you, at least, remember me," he said roughly.

Despite her alarm, she wanted to laugh at the absurdity of his words. Her trouble was that she had found him impossible to forget. He looked very different now, bearded, haggard, mud-daubed, and yet it was not so much his appearance that alarmed her as his air of menace. She stared up into his eyes, and found them unaltered in his gaunt face, deep, dark, disturbingly intense, carrying her back to that day when he had first spoken to her. The eyes of Christopher Fairfield—how often they had haunted her dreams. To cover her confused emotions, she said sharply. "Naturally I remember you. Why would I not?"

Christopher's shoulders rose in an eloquent shrug. "Then your memory is better than Phillips'."

She felt a spasm of alarm. She had forgotten about Frazer. "Where is he?" She blurted out the question. "What have you done with him?"

"Why, I've murdered him, what else?" He laughed at the expression on her face. "No, I'm reserving that pleasure. I'm afraid your lover just scuttled off and left you."

He was reserving that pleasure? Desiree flinched inwardly. Christopher Fairfield had promised to take revenge, and he had come back to fulfill that promise. Frazer need not concern her; he could take care of himself. But what of her father, who had grown so frail? Biting back the words that rushed to her lips, she said coldly, "Frazer Phillips is not my lover."

His dark eyes mocked her. "You appeared to be enjoying yourself when I came upon you."

Color swept into her face. "Don't be a fool," she snapped. "If you think that, then you could not have observed very closely."

"You are ready with your tongue, Miss Desiree." Christopher's voice was soft and drawling. "Perhaps a little too ready. But tell me, you are not angry because Phillips ran off and left you, you are not afraid to be alone with me?"

He was deliberately goading her. Of course she was afraid, and he must know it. "I would expect nothing else from Frazer," she said in a carefully controlled voice. "You know as well as I do that he has always been a coward. And as for you, I am certainly not afraid."

She was lying—he had seen the flash of fear in her violet eyes—but obviously she did not intend to give him the satisfaction of knowing it. "And now if I have answered all your fool questions"—Desiree's voice was overloud—"please put me down."

Christopher's response was to crush her closer. He heard her gasp, quickly stifled, and he smiled to himself. She had courage, he thought with a stir of admiration. He had heard that she was spirited and fearless, and possessed of a flaming temper to match her hair. She would not beg him to let her go; somehow he knew that. She would fight him until there was no fight left in her, and he found the prospect curiously exciting.

"Fairfield"—Desiree jerked in his arms—"perhaps you did not hear me. I said put me down."

"I heard you." Christopher's temple flared at her imperious tone. "But you are not talking to one of your unfortunate slaves, you arrogant bitch."

"No," Desiree shouted, losing her head completely, "I am talking to a murderous scum!" In a sudden frenzy combined as much of anger as fear, she doubled her fists and battered at him furiously. "Turn me loose, you swine!"

Startled by the unexpected rain of stinging blows, Christopher automatically loosened his arms and sent his burden sliding heavily to the ground. For a second Desiree lay there stunned; then, recovering herself, she bounded to her feet. She heard his enraged shout and the heavy sounds of his pursuit. Impelled by blind panic, she ran faster, and she did not see the branch that tripped her and sent her sprawling into a thorn bush. Her hands and face stinging, half-sobbing with pain and frustration, she tried desperately to tear her skirts free.

Panting, Christopher caught up with her. Her struggles, he noted, had only succeeded in entangling her still further. Her face, her hands, and her arms were crisscrossed with bright red scratches; her eyes poured angry tears; and her hair, loosened from the carefully arranged curls, streamed over her shoulders in shining confusion. "Are you in difficulty, Miss Desiree?" he said mockingly. "Can I be of some assistance?"

She turned her furious eyes on him. "Go to hell, I'll get myself free."

Christopher laughed softly. "Caught like an animal in a trap," he taunted. "Not a very pleasant feeling, is it, as I should know. How do you like it?"

"Shut up!" Desiree almost choked on her fury. "Don't you dare say another word."

Christopher regarded her with an amusement that did not match his eyes. "I would not say your speech is very ladylike," he said, shaking his head reproachfully. "But then, what else can one expect from a member of the illustrious Grayson family?"

Desiree flushed before the mockery, hating him, hating herself for feeling so strongly. "Damn you," she blazed, "enjoy yourself while you can, convict. You won't be laughing when you are caught and sent back to Buxton Prison."

Christopher's face was suddenly expressionless, but Desiree had the uncomfortable feeling that it was only a mask to hide the seething emotion within. This was borne out when he spoke again. "I won't go back again," he said, thrusting his face close to hers, "never. Do you hear? I'd kill myself first. A man would be better off dead."

The savage tone, the awakening of those somber eyes to fiery suffering life, erased Desiree's anger and sent a pang of sympathy through her. That he was dangerous, she knew, and it was better to say no more; yet, remembering that she had always believed him to be innocent, she could not stop the words from coming. "They will catch you, you know," she said uncertainly. "I would not like—"

"And you'd help them catch me, if you could," Christopher interrupted harshly. "And why not? Treachery is a pattern in your family."

Desiree's newborn sympathy vanished abruptly. "You have no right to speak of treachery. I know what you're trying to say, but you're wrong. My father would not have given a guilty verdict against you, had he not genuinely believed it to be the case."

"Genuinely believed," Christopher repeated, his lip curling into a sneer. "I wonder."

Desiree stared at him in outrage. "Do you suppose he had some other and personal reason?"

Christopher shrugged. "I must have asked myself that question a million times. Perhaps he just wanted to rid Hawleigh County of my presence. I remember, even before the murder, that he was always loud in his condemnation of my behavior."

"And so were many others. Have you forgotten that?"

"Forgotten? Why, no, Miss Desiree."

The sarcastic inflection he laid on the last two words brought her anger rushing back in full force. "I have heard many things of you," she said in an icy voice, "and chiefly, I believe, you were noted for your arrogance, so this mock attempt at servility ill-becomes you."

Christopher's brows rose in sardonic amusement. "You do not care to be addressed as Miss Desiree?"

"Not when it comes from your lips."

"Forgive me. I had thought you expected such an address from a member of the lower order."

The cool audacity of him! Except for his tattered clothing and his haggard appearance, no one would ever believe him to be a fugitive. Resentful of the amusement that tried to conquer anger, Desiree answered him in a hard voice. "Be quiet. When have you ever considered yourself to be a member of the lower order?"

"Many have tried to make me feel that way," Christopher answered with a faint smile, "but they never succeeded. No, Miss Desiree, I have never thought of myself as inferior, so at least we are agreed on that."

Desiree could not resist the thrust. "I am well aware that you do not consider yourself inferior, Fairfield. But I do not remember giving my opinion."

"Very true." The flash in his eyes belied the dry voice. "But since your opinion is of little importance to me, it hardly matters." He leaned forward, carefully keeping out of reach of the thorns. "Hold still," he said, grasping her firmly about the waist. "I'll get you out of there."

"Take your hands away." Desiree's voice rose on a note of panic. "I don't need your help."

"Don't be so stupid," his curt voice admonished her. "And for God's sake stop that struggling, you're only making it harder on yourself." His fingers dug into her waist, wringing a cry from her. "Keep still, damn you!"

Her mouth obstinately set, she continued to resist him, with the result that her gown ripped down the front. Thorns stuck her in a dozen fresh places before he at last succeeded in pulling her free. "Fool girl, you've no more brains than a flea." He set her on her feet with a thump that jarred her body. "You're badly scratched up now, and you've no one but yourself to blame."

Blinking back tears of pain and conquering a wild desire to strike him, Desiree rubbed her stinging arms. "So I'm scratched up," she answered him through gritted teeth. "And what of it? I can bear it."

"Brave girl," he applauded. "Anyway, what's a few scratches? It's better than a flogging, wouldn't you say?"

Desiree's eyes flashed as his meaning penetrated, and indignation rose in a hot tide. "I don't happen to believe in flogging," she snapped.

"Ah, I hope that comforts your slaves when they're under the lash. Li'l mistress, she purely an angel," he mocked.

"Ain't b'lievin' in floggin' nohow. She jus' likin' to grin' us under her li'l ol' dainty heel."

He was goading her again. "You swine!" she burst out, unable to contain her words. "How dare you speak to me like that. Don't you know who I am, don't you know that I am . . . am . . ." She broke off, her face flushing crimson.

Christopher's eyes narrowed as he considered her. "I have been in prison, remember? Is there something I ought to know about you?"

Cursing herself for allowing her foolish pride to dictate incautious words, and horrified to realize she had almost given away her carefully preserved secret identity, and to this embittered man of all people, Desiree shook her head vehemently. "No, there is nothing."

"But you were going to say something," Christopher pressed, made curious by something he glimpsed in her eyes. "You said, 'Don't you know who I am?' So apart from being Miss Desiree Grayson, who are you?"

Her heart leaped at his persistence. "I don't know what you mean," she said, schooling herself to calmness. "I am exactly what you see, no more, no less."

His small flare of interest dying, Christopher shrugged his shoulders. "If you say so." His eyes went to her face. "The thorns have certainly spoiled your pretty looks. You are quite sure you can bear the pain?"

Curse him and his mock solicitude! "I can bear anything I have to bear. Sorry if I have disappointed you."

Christopher laughed, the sound flat and without mirth. "Dear Miss Desiree, I am not in the least disappointed, especially since I have plans for you. If it had not been for that, I'd have left you to wallow in the bush."

"Yes, I'm sure you would." Again Desiree fought a losing battle with self-control. "And I wish you had left me. Anything would be better than having to endure your hands upon me."

"The hands of a murderer, I presume you mean."

"You presume correctly."

"I am repulsive to you?"

"Yes, yes!" Fuming, hating herself for the many foolish and romantic thoughts she had expended on him, Desiree pointedly turned her back. As she stared at the pieces of material impaled on the long, sharp thorns, her mood was not improved to realize that he had been right. Instead of fighting him so furiously, like a child in a tantrum, she should have been sensible and accepted his help. Had she done so, she would not have been reduced to her present deplorable condition, flesh irritated and burning, her ripped bodice exposing most of her breasts, and her overskirt and petticoats hanging in tatters. Very conscious now of her half-naked state, she glanced over her shoulder. Involuntarily, meeting his intent gaze, her hands came up to cover her breasts.

"I have already had ample chance to admire them," Christopher said lightly, "and I think it's a pity to cover them. You have full breasts for such a slight girl, but they are really quite beautiful."

Glaring her defiance, Desiree tightened her fingers, digging hurtingly into the tender flesh. "I can do well without your comments," she said in a cold voice, turning her head away. "I would like you to go away, please."

"And leave you all alone? Oh, no, my lovely, not yet." Reaching over, Christopher touched her hands lightly, laughing softly as she flinched. "Be careful. It would be a pity to bruise such delightful breasts."

"You are indecent, sir." Her heart beating wildly, Desiree took a pace away, stopping abruptly as he put a restraining hand on her shoulder. "How dare you touch me!" she exclaimed, shrugging his hand away. "If you have any sense, which I am beginning to doubt, you will go. You must know that Frazer is bound to come back for me, and he will bring men with him."

"I am chilled at the very thought."

"Oh, to the devil with you and your infernal sarcasm!"

"Temper! Have I misjudged you, then, Miss Desiree? Can it be that you are actually thinking of my welfare?"

"Yes, I am," Desiree answered him firmly, "though I don't expect you to believe me." She paused, suddenly startled to realize that she meant it. Her fear forgotten, she turned to face him. Staring into his eyes, she acknowledged a truth. He still held a dangerous attraction for her. Dirty and haggard though he was, the dim ghost of the vital and attractive man he had been, the fascination, was still there. Whatever he had been, whatever he had become, she did not want him to be captured and taken back to Buxton, where, conceivably, they might hang him this time. "Despite what you may choose to think," she went on in a different voice, "I don't wish you to be caught."

"Do you know, I find that very touching." He lifted his hand, his finger tracing a line down her cheek. "Touching, but a little hard to believe. You said you were not afraid of me, beautiful lady, but I think you are, just a little."

"Should I be?" Desiree held his gaze unflinchingly. "Are you really a murderer, Christopher Fairfield?"

Dark color flushed his face, and his eyes gleamed dangerously. "Your father was one of those who was pleased to judge me guilty. Does that answer your question?"

"No, it does not. I want to hear it from you."

The light caressing touch of his fingers turned harsh, but still Desiree did not move. "You'll get no more from me," he answered at last. "I made my plea of innocence a long time ago, and I'll not amuse you by repeating it now."

"No, you don't understand. I really want to know."

Christopher's fingers slid from her cheek to her throat, lingering there. Beneath his touch, he could feel the contraction of the muscles. "Perhaps you're right," he said slowly. "For the last four years, I have understood very little." The gleam in his eyes intensified. "But surely you should not be urging me to escape. As a righteous citizen of Hawleigh County, is it not your duty to try to prevent me?"

Goaded once more, she said hotly, "I think you must be the most infuriating man I have ever met. What should I do, hit you over the head with a stone, stab you with a knife? Even if I wanted to, I couldn't stop you from walking away."

"No, you couldn't. I will allow no one to stop me now." His hand dropped away from her throat. "But I have the feeling that you would like to stop me. Come, Miss Desiree, the truth."

How she hated his sarcastic use of her name. How she hated him, and yet was at the same time drawn to him. "Of course I don't wish to stop you." Her voice reflected her confusion and anger. "How can you be such a fool?"

"I wonder. I can't help but remember the endearing names you called me. 'Convict' was one, 'murderous scum' another."

"I was angry. Besides, that was then and this is now. If you want the truth, I have never really believed you to be guilty of that girl's death."

Christopher glanced away, and he appeared to be weighing

her words, but when he looked at her again, she saw rejection in his eyes. "I believe you, of course, Miss Desiree."

Desiree colored beneath the soft mockery, and suddenly she felt very weary. "No you don't." She put a hand to her burning face. "You've grown so bitter that I doubt you'd believe God himself. Anyway, what does it matter? Believe what you please, as long as you go away and leave me alone."

"In time, ma'am, you will be free of my distasteful presence, I guarantee it, but for now, I can't oblige you."

"But why not now," Desiree said desperately, "why should you risk your safety to stay here? I am nothing to you."

"No, nothing!" He said the words savagely, wanting to believe them, wanting to erase the memory of this girl who had haunted him for so long. He gripped her shoulder, shaking her slightly. "You are less than nothing to me."

Desiree drew back, her heart beating wildly, relieved when his hand fell away from her shoulder. "Well, then"—it cost her an effort to speak calmly—"why don't you go?"

"When I'm ready, not before." Christopher stared at her, his bitter eyes taking in the beautiful, flushed, scratched face, the bold defiance in the wide violet eyes, the tangle of vivid hair, and the naked, heaving breasts. She was right, of course, he was a fool to stay here and risk capture, but on the other hand, he'd not go until he had struck a blow at Elton Grayson. He saw the thin aristocratic face in his mind's eye, and for the first time a tremor of doubt struck him. Was it right to make the girl pay for her father's sins?

Desiree moved, her lips opening as though she was about to say something, closing again as she scanned the dark, frowning face. Christopher's doubts fled, snapped by her movement. Of course she was innocent, but so was he. He had not laid one finger on little Charlotte, but his protestations of innocence had fallen on deaf ears. He had been found over the body, therefore he must be the murderer, or so those worthy men had decreed. Four years in hell, four years taken out of his life. And it would have been the rest of his years, had he not found the means to escape. He looked down at his scabbed wrists, remembering the prolonged effort, the pain of the sharpened stone grinding away at his manacles. Well, he had freed himself from those iron cuffs, and he had survived the pain. He had conquered starvation, eating of the forest's bounty, stealing food where he could. He had drunk from the forest's many streams, and he had bathed constantly. This last had been important to his pride, it had served to remind him that he was a man, not the stinking animal the prison guards had tried to make of him. He was unkempt in appearance, it was true, but except for his torn and soiled shirt and trousers, mute evidence of his hazardous passage through the bog at Colter's Way, he was clean, and reasonably healthy.

"Sir?"

Christopher's lips curled. The Grayson bitch was treading carefully now. "Sir," she called him; no longer "Fairfield," but "sir."

Summoning her courage, she touched his arm pleadingly. She felt his muscles flinch and shudder, and before the look in his dark eyes, she hastily withdrew her hand. "For your own sake, please go."

"Shut up!" Christopher said the words with a snarl. In memory, he was back in Buxton. The prison guards, rifles at the ready, were parading the upper walls, eager for a chance to shoot at the collection of miserable humanity below them. In his ears was the clink of chains, the scraping of tools, and the stifled groans of his fellow prisoners. He remembered how old Ezra Jones, bound to him, had collapsed and died. The guards, two of them, big burly men with florid, well-fed faces, had been suspicious of a trick. Taking no chances, they had flogged both him and the dead body of Ezra. The savage, crippling punishment had gone on and on, leaving him torn and bleeding and in excruciating agony before it was at last decided that Ezra was truly dead. Contemptuously the guards had unlocked the dead man's manacles and hauled him away, dragging his terribly maimed and wasted body over the dusty, stony ground with no more care than they would have given to a side of beef.

Christopher's eyes blurred, his lips tightening against the pain of memory. That same night, as though he had been responsible for Ezra's death, he had been manacled hand and foot, and after a bucket of salt water had been thrown over his wounds, he had been left alone in the prison yard. Hungry for the bowl of thin, wormy gruel that served as the evening meal, his lips swollen and cracked, he had lain there in torment, unmoving. After a while he had no longer been conscious of hunger and thirst, and even his pain had been subdued by his implacable hatred of the men who had put him into Buxton Prison. It was then, in those moments of desperation and weakness, that he had made his vow to escape. He would kill the men who had sent him to Buxton; one by one he would hunt them down. How this was to be accomplished, he did not know, but somehow he would find the strength and the means.

Desiree stirred, a small, restless movement that brought Christopher's attention back to her. His mouth moved into a sneer of self-contempt as he thought of how often he had allowed this girl to intrude on his waking and sleeping dreams. Miss Desiree, perfumed, curled, arrogant, useless, had certainly been a strange companion in hell. She was one of the autocrats, taking her good fortune as a God-given right. Slaves ran to do her every bidding, lest she strain a muscle or soil the flounces of her dainty gowns. Husky blacks and, in many cases, poor whites labored to keep her and her kind in the comfort to which they were accustomed. They tilled the red earth, producing the bountiful crops of corn, cotton, and tobacco, and all without hope of reward. Contempt was usually the lot of the poor whites, as he had good reason to know. For the black men and women, it was the threat of punishment, being parted from loved ones, or even death. And this girl standing before him epitomized all of those white autocrats, she was everything he despised and hated. But he would humble her, bring her low. Before he had done with her, she would be no better than the painted-up whores to be found in Madam Pinkney's house on the edge of Hawleigh County. He looked away from her almost reluctantly, concentrating instead on the thing that had exercised his mind for the past four years, the day of the murder. It struck him with fresh force that it was important he remember every detail of that fateful day.

"Why won't you listen to me?" Desiree's voice, prodding, persistent, sounded again. "It must be obvious to you that you should get far away from here. If you will let me, I will help you."

Like hell she would, the treacherous bitch! Christopher surveyed her with a narrowed gaze, seeking for the lie in her eyes. "Sure you will, Miss Desiree," he drawled, "you'll help me right back to prison."

"No, you fool, no. I could arrange for you to go North. I don't suppose it would matter to you which side you fought on, would it?"

Her words touched his mind briefly, bringing with them a vague memory of the rumors of war he had heard in the prison, about which even the guards had displayed a strange, almost feverish excitement. On himself it had made no impression, and so he had shrugged it aside. War and rumors of war, they were always there, and hardly worth dignifying with deep thought. It had seemed to him that no matter how unjust the Southern system might be, it was impossible to think of brother fighting against brother. The civil war the guards spoke of so openly could not come, it would be a catastrophe, and even worse, an offense in the eyes of God. So obviously Miss Desiree Grayson, having heard the war talk, was trying to confuse him. Which side would he fight on indeed. On no side but his own. Looking at her, he knew a moment of mingled amusement and admiration for her spirit, her deviousness, and for the angry and unsubdued flash of her violet eyes. She would be a wildcat worth conquering, by God she would! His voice betraying nothing of his inner excitement, he said quietly, "And why should you help me?"

Her anger increased at his tone, and yet, beneath the intent regard of his eyes, she was moved to an urgent trembling that had nothing to do with anger. "I've . . . I've told you," she stammered. "I believe you to . . . to be innocent." Her eyes fluttered away from his face and concentrated on his hands. What would it be like, she wondered, if those hands should touch her in tenderness and love? Appalled by the direction of her thoughts, she jerked her head up arrogantly.

Christopher, noting her change of expression, and misconstruing it, found his amusement vanishing. "Don't try feeding me any of your lies," he said furiously. "There have been enough lies already, enough for a lifetime."

"Damn your ornery hide, I am not lying! Can't you get it into your thick head that I want to help you?"

Placing a restraining hand on her arm, Christopher put the other to his forehead, his fingers digging hurtingly into the flesh in an effort to force memory to the surface. There was Frazer Phillips, for instance. He had met him a scant five minutes before he had gone on to discover Charlotte's body in the alley. Phillips had been quite unlike his usual immaculate self. His clothing was rumpled and dusty, his bright blue eyes dazed, and there was a streak of blood on his frilled shirtfront, at which his nervous fingers constantly dabbed. "Horse threw me," he had explained, answering the question in Christopher's eyes. Then, his voice gathering irritation, he said loudly, "Well, Fairfield, why are you staring at me, and what the devil are you doing here?"

For once Christopher had not resented the tone. "I wasn't aware that I was staring," he answered mildly. "As to being here, why not? It's a public road."

Frowning, biting at his lower lip, Phillips nodded. "Yes, of course, Fairfield. Sorry if I spoke sharply."

"Not at all, sir." Christopher's tone was tinged with the irony this man could always arouse. "Think nothing of it." Looking more closely at Phillips, he felt a twinge of sympathy. He must have taken quite a toss, for his eyes looked very strange. Odd to think they had played together as boys, yet they had, and there had been no class distinction then to mar their relationship. Softened by the fleeting memory, he had shown him the small animal he had so laboriously whittled from a block of oak. "For Charlotte," he said simply. "It's her birthday. She's fourteen years old today."

"What?" Phillips had swayed, his face going so pale that the freckles across the bridge of his nose stood out in stark relief. "I . . . I . . ."

Thinking he was about to fall, Christopher took a step toward him. "Here, let me help you."

Phillips drew back hastily. "I'm all right now. The fall rattled me a bit, that's all." He inspected the wooden animal on Christopher's palm. "A fair piece of work," he said condescendingly, nodding his head. "You're really quite clever with your hands, Fairfield."

"Why, thank you, sir. You are much too kind."

Phillips flushed angrily. "Now, then, Fairfield, there's no need to take that tone. You must learn to accept a compliment graciously. The toy is for Charlotte, I think you said. That conveys nothing to me. Who is she?"

The grand manner he had assumed, his suddenly haughty expression, amused Christopher. Charlotte, the daughter of a shopkeeper, was not in Phillips' social circle, therefore it behooved him to disclaim knowledge of her. He had known the man a long time, and he knew exactly how his mind worked.

It might even be that he was suffering some embarrassment at being seen in conversation with the son of a lowly sharecropper. "Charlotte Elliot," Christopher said dryly. "Surely you remember little Charlotte. I have often seen you stop and speak with her."

"I'm afraid I can't place her." Shrugging, Phillips made another ineffectual dab at the streak of blood on his shirtfront. "Cut myself when I fell," he mumbled. "Damned nuisance, too, the shirt is probably ruined."

Half-smiling, Christopher nodded. "I've always heard that bloodstains are hard to remove."

As though he suspected sarcasm, Phillips looked up sharply. "Never mind the conversation, Fairfield. Haven't you anything better to do than to stand there gaping at me?"

The rare moment of comradeship Christopher was experiencing fled, and all his arrogance surfaced. He remembered his anger, the derisive laugh that cloaked it, the biting mockery with which he had answered. "I surely sorry, suh, 'deed I am. Ain't nohow meanin' to offen' you."

Phillips' hands clenched. "You'll go too far one of these days, you surly beggar. Get along with you, and keep that smart mouth of yours closed. God damn, but I've a mind to take my crop to your back!"

Christopher's eyes looked deeply into his, their glitter conveying a warning. "Why don't you try it, massa suh?" he drawled. "You jus' do that li'l thing, an' I surely breaks you in half, massa suh."

The warning in the dark eyes was not lost on Phillips. Coloring, he turned away. "To hell with you. Take your toy to the child, and less of your insolence. The next time, you may not get off so easily."

Mastering an overpowering urge to lash out with his fist, Christopher had gone on his way. Seeking Charlotte, he had found her with her throat cut. So little, so young and innocent. Who could have done such a thing?

Christopher's fingers tightened on his forehead as a sudden monstrous suspicion struck him. Phillips! His dazed eyes so strangely at variance with his agitated manner, blood on the crisp frills of a white shirt. Had it been Charlotte's blood? Had he really taken a fall from his horse, or had he killed the little girl? One thing was certain: Phillips, in common with his peers, had been quick to condemn him, and yet he had known he was innocent of the crime. How could it be otherwise, when, according to the time the investigators had fixed for the murder, he had been engaged in conversation with him? And Elton Grayson—had he known from Phillips of his innocence? Christopher had always believed so. His mouth turned hard and bitter at this last thought.

Frightened by the expression on the dark, brooding face, Desiree tried to tug her arm free of his tight grip. "What is it?" she said in a light voice that sought to mask her alarm. "Why do you look like that?"

Christopher did not answer. His hands dropped heavily to his sides, his fingers opening in mental relinquishment of the little toy that had played such an important part in the tragedy. He had taken Charlotte a toy, and he had been branded her murderer. A choked sound escaped him. It was hopeless. He could suspect, he could accuse, but to whom could he carry his accusation? The fact remained that Charlotte was four years dead, and the real murderer as yet undiscovered. As for himself, he thought bitterly, he would no doubt go to his grave under the undeserved stigma of murder.

Desiree made a restless movement. It was obvious to her that he was reliving the terrible events that had sent him to Buxton. Without stopping to think, she said hesitantly, "Would . . . would you like to tell me about it?"

"You want me to confide in you?" The dark eyes turned on her, examining her as though she were some curious specimen. "You'd like to hear all about the murder, would you, ma'am?"

She flushed. "I thought perhaps if you spoke of it, you would not feel so—"

"So bad?" he interrupted fiercely. "Is that what you were going to say?" He looked at her contemptuously. "Shall I tell you of the way Charlotte screamed before she died, would you like to hear of how she crawled at her murderer's feet and begged him for mercy? The gory details would amuse you, I'm sure."

"Stop it! Don't you dare say such hideous things to me."

Revenge, Christopher thought, it was all that remained to him. Revenge, of which this girl was a part. He looked at her breasts. In contrast to her faintly bronzed skin, they were startlingly white; the nipples were aroused as though they anticipated a lover's touch. By God, but she was beautiful! The eyes looking into him were so huge, so vivid, the thick lashes made little shadows on her face, and her tumbled hair was like a flame. Though he died for touching her sacred person, he would have her. The blood drumming in his ears, he moved closer. His hand touched a lock of her hair, then dropped to settle on her shoulder. "Come here to me," he said hoarsely.

"I'll do nothing of the sort." The agitated beating of her heart seemed to shake her body as she shrugged his hand away. "I think you must have gone mad, Fairfield."

"Fairfield," again; she had dropped the polite, placating "sir"; the grand lady was back. He laughed harshly. "No, not mad," he said, reaching for her again, "just determined to pay back a little of what has been done to me."

"What has been done to you," Desiree replied, "has not been done by me." She went on firmly, "You cannot hold me responsible for your troubles."

"You might call them troubles, but that is surely a polite little word for the ruination of a man's life, wouldn't you say?"

"You ruined it yourself," Desiree flashed. She looked desperately about her, wanting to run, and yet knowing he would be on her before she had gone more than a few steps. "Yes, you did," she continued in an uncertain voice. "You were heedless, wild, determined to go your own way."

His dark eyebrows rose sardonically and his teeth flashed white in that curious, mirthless smile. "My land, Miss Desiree, but what a catalog of sins you quote. I was young, I was resentful, I considered myself to be as good as any man, and I refused to knuckle under to my so-called superiors. I hated to see my father working himself into an early grave, and to know that he expected me to do the same. I wanted something better for myself and my family. It may be that I went about it in the wrong way, but that is the sum total of my sins. Yet for all my reputation, sometimes undeserved, I am no murderer, lady." With a swift movement he pulled her into his arms and crushed her close against him. "I am no murderer, do you hear?"

Desiree strained against the barrier of his arms. "Let me go at once, or it will be the worse for you."

Christopher rubbed his bearded face against her cheek, laughing softly as she winced. "I'll take that chance," he murmured. "Elton Grayson owes me something, and I aim to collect the first payment from his daughter."

Desiree did not hear his last words. She felt the rapid beating of his heart, the slight trembling of the arms that held her, and she was suddenly devastated by a thrill of intense excitement. In shame and confusion she acknowledged what the hard contact of his body was doing to her. She knew well that she must fight him; her pride demanded it, and yet she had this insane wish to surrender, to pull down that shaggy dark head and fasten her lips to his. Now she could put a name to her earlier feeling—desire. It was true, she had always desired this dark, handsome man, Christopher Fairfield, the rebel. Desire had been the reason for the tingling in her flesh whenever she saw him, the reason why she had never been able to forget him. Now he was back, harder, older, dangerous in his bitterness, and still, despite his gaunt and unkempt appearance, her mind and her body were drawn to him. So nothing had changed, except that she had now been forced to face the truth. She looked up at him. "Please," she whispered, "you must let me go."

He looked at her for a long moment, and she felt as if she were drowning in the depths of those dark eyes. "No, lady," he said slowly, "I have no intention of letting you go."

It was clear to her now. He would use her, degrade her, and all because he wanted to get back at her father. Pride and anger rose, drowning desire. "You must stop this," she shouted, "you don't know what you're doing."

"Oh, but I do. I am going to do this,"—Christopher kissed her hair, her face, her throat—"and this." His mouth covered hers for what seemed to her to be an eternity. "And then, dear Miss Desiree," he said, raising his head to look at her, "I'm going to make that lovely body mine."

The breath catching in her throat, she stared at him in horror. "You can't," she said, pushing at him frantically. "It would be rape!"

"You are bright today. So it would, my lovely, and will be."

Her eyes blazed with the vehemence with which she sought to convince. "You fool, aren't you in enough trouble? If you do this thing, my father will hunt you down. He won't rest until he catches you, and when he does, he'll see to it that you hang."

"I'm sure he will. That has been his aim all along. He must have been very disappointed when the judge gave me life."

"You don't know what you're talking about. My father is good, kind."

"Enough talk." With a lightning movement Christopher thrust her from him. Then, almost lazily, he ripped the tattered remnants of clothing from her body. "That's much better." His eyes traveled over her, taking in the tempestuously heaving breasts, the graceful curving of her waist and the delicate flaring of her hips. "Ah, Miss Desiree, unclothed, you are just like any other female. More exquisitely formed, perhaps, but very like. How astonished your slaves would be if they could see you now. The poor bastards must treat you with such reverence, such awe, that they must surely think you are made of pure gold." He gripped her arm, his fingers sinking into the flesh. "But you are going to show me that you are just like any other woman, aren't you, Miss Desiree?"

As though unconscious of her nakedness, Desiree stood there unmoving, her head raised proudly. "I will show you nothing," she said in a quiet voice. "You will have to kill me first."

Her dignified stance brought an unwelcome touch of admiration. "Kill you?" Christopher made his tone rough, deliberately menacing. "Well, now, I might just do that." He saw the expression of horror, quickly concealed, that flickered across her face, and he smiled grimly. "The thought of Charlotte Elliot has no doubt crossed your mind," he went on, "but it doesn't matter, does it, since you believe me to be innocent? You do believe that, don't you?"

Beneath his taunting, a sob broke from her when her wildly aimed foot failed to find its target. "Oh, damn you, damn you, don't dare to touch me!"

Christopher tightened his grip on her arm. "But I am already touching you." Snatching her to him, he bent over her naked body and eased her to the ground, enjoying the feel of her against him. Subduing her with an effort, he managed to divest himself of his ragged garments. "Your father will see me hang, you said; therefore it only makes sense to take what I want first."

Desiree was suddenly very still as she stared at his naked, muscular form. Raised white ridges circled his neck and crisscrossed his broad chest, standing out in bold relief against the brown of his skin. The marks of the lash! He turned slightly, scanning the distance, and she saw that the ridges extended far down his back. The scars had healed, but he must have been flogged brutally, many times, to be so disfigured.

Christopher turned back to her and saw the expression in her eyes. "Buxton," he said briefly. "Courtesy of my gentle guards."

Desiree swallowed. "I'm . . . I'm sorry."

"No need to be, since you are about to console me." He laughed at her changing expression. "That makes quite a difference, doesn't it, Miss Desiree, so what price your tender pity now?" He lowered himself upon her. "Believe me, I would far rather throttle your father, but since he is not here and you are, need I say more?"

Seething with anger, humiliation, and despair, Desiree writhed madly beneath him. "Let me up!" she cried. Her hands clutched at his thick hair and pulled savagely. "I'm glad they flogged you, I hope they do it again. May God curse you, you pig!"

Christopher jerked his head away sharply. "He has, many times, so I don't doubt you'll get your wish." His eyes went to her heaving breasts. "But whatever happens, it will be worth it."

Desiree's head darted forward with the speed of a striking snake and her teeth sank into his hand fondling her breast.

Christopher stared at the tiny beads of blood on his hand. "Damn you for a savage bitch," he growled, wiping the blood against her skin. "Do that again, and I'll wind your goddamned hair about your throat and choke you."

Desiree looked down at the rusty smears; then she lifted her head and spat into his face. "Why not slit my throat," she shouted, "as you did with Charlotte Elliot? Well, go on, what are you waiting for?"

"Be silent."

For answer, she clawed at his shoulders. "Murderer, murderer!" Her voice rose on a note of pure hysteria.

Fury mastering him, Christopher slapped her face hard. "Put that label on me again, and you'll regret it in more ways than one. Whatever you may think, I am innocent, but damned if you don't make the idea of murder very tempting."

Gasping, her ears ringing from the force of the blow, Desiree stared with stunned, wide-open eyes at the leaf-laden branches above her head. As through a mist, she saw a thin, sharp beak part the dark green glossy leaves, and then the owner of the beak, a small red-and-brown bird, hopped onto a branch and surveyed her with bright eyes. A sweet trilling sound came from the feathered throat, and then, with a whisk of tailfeathers, the bird was gone. Now the giant trees seemed to be moving, their foliage blending, whirling, dipping low, making a great green weight that would surely crush her. She closed her eyes, opened them again quickly, and was relieved to see that all was as before, the leafy branches swaying innocently and casting shifting patterns of light and shade over her burning face. She tensed as a voice spoke her name softly, urgently. "Desiree!"

Desiree's dulled senses awakened to her own faint cry, and to sensation so sharp, so piercingly sweet that the cry was wrung from her lips again. Christopher Fairfield's lips were against her breasts, their touch strangely gentle as he kissed first one breast and then the other. His dark head moved lower, his lips seeking, tracing a fiery path down to her thighs that overwhelmed her with a rush of desire. Involuntarily, as though obeying some inner command, her legs relaxed, parting to accommodate him. "Desiree . . ." his voice came to her again. "Oh, my beautiful girl!"

The spell that bound her was shattered, and now she could feel only loathing for her own weakness. She struck out at him again, her doubled fists pummeling at his head and shoulders. "Stop it!"

"Oh, no, ma'am, not now." Christopher caught at her wrists and forced her arms down. "It will be better for you if you accept it. Much better."

Panic-stricken by the memory of the sensuous melting weakness that had attacked her before, Desiree spat the words at him defiantly. "You . . . you filthy convict scum!"

She winced inwardly as his hand lifted as though about to strike her again, and tensed herself for the blow. "No," Christopher said, correctly reading her expression, "I'm not going to hit you and justify your words." His hand dropped heavily to his side. "Though I'm sure you'd like that."

"You already have justified my words."

"You think so?" Christopher smiled slowly, tauntingly. "Compared to my recent playfellows, I am gentle. They were hard and tough, and not much given to regarding a woman's fragility as a drawback to violence."

"Then I can only say that you emulate them very successfully."

Christopher regarded her grimly. "Fortunately for you, lady, I do not, or you would long since have ceased caring. Do you know, with that smart mouth, that you should count yourself very lucky that I don't knock your teeth down your throat. Much more from you, and perhaps I might be tempted."

Desiree's face flamed with outrage. In all her life no one had ever spoken to her in such a fashion. With difficulty she forced out words. "Do as you please, but I'm not afraid of you, and don't you think it."

"Afraid?" Christopher's fingertips traced lightly over her breasts as he pretended to consider the question. He heard the quick gasping breath she drew, felt the leap of her flesh, and for a fleeting moment he had the strange idea that she was not as indifferent to him as she pretended to be. Frowning, he contemplated this novel idea, then dismissed it as absurd. "I don't think you're afraid of me," he went on slowly, "or if you are, you're determined not to show it. On the contrary, I think you have courage and a fighting spirit, which will make the conquest of such a grand and superior lady that much more interesting." He smiled at her. "No, my sweet, whatever else you are, you are not afraid."

He was wrong, Desiree thought, turning her head away. She was more than afraid, she was terrified, not of him, but of herself and the feelings he aroused in her. Her heart was beating like a drum, her flesh so hot that it seemed to her distorted fancy to be melting into his. "Go to . . . to hell!" she managed.

Shrugging, Christopher pushed his hand down roughly between their bodies and touched the slight mound of her belly, feeling the contraction of her muscles as he caressed her gently, lingeringly. He started as her body thrust suddenly upward, trapping his hand and pressing it even harder into her flesh. Was it a convulsive movement that had no meaning, he asked himself, or was it what it appeared to be, an invitation, and if so, had she made it consciously or unconsciously? Fool, he berated himself, looking into her set, expressionless face, you are starting to imagine things again. Abruptly, determined to make her say something, he put his hands on her breasts, his fingers playing with the taut, swollen nipples. He saw the glazing of her eyes, which, in any other woman, he would have construed as desire. But no, he told himself, he would not make that mistake again. Deliberately he bent his head and fastened his lips about a thrusting red spear of flesh. He heard the gasping breath again, and felt the writhing of her limbs. "I told you that you have beautiful breasts," he said softly. "I think I envy the child you will suckle."

Desiree tried to gather her rage, and failed. How could she think clearly when her emotions were in such a tumult? "Such things are not spoken of casually," she said weakly, "especially under such circumstances. It is indecent, you are indecent."

Christopher nodded. "So you said before. But then, what else can you expect from a scum of a convict?"

Desiree saw him as from a distance. The fire inside her was roaring out of control, fed by those insidious lips, the stroking hands. He was kissing her breasts again, and she was having trouble breathing. She had known many men, some of whom had professed to be in love with her, but never one who affected her like this man with his dark, piratical face. In an effort to hang on, to somehow hold out against him, she forced herself to think of those other men. Sometimes, in her wish to experience all facets of emotion, she had permitted kisses and caresses, the pressure of a body against her own, and even, in rare cases, the touch of a masculine hand against her breast, but she herself had remained unmoved.

Christopher's lips moved; his tongue found the little hollow in her throat. "Look at me, lovely girl," he breathed.

Desiree closed her eyes tightly, forcing her thoughts on. She could not claim a virginal innocence to account for her former indifference to men, for although a virgin, she was well aware of what went on between a man and a woman. As a child, she had witnessed the sexual acts in the breeding huts.

Dismissing those long-ago memories, Desiree came back to the present and Christopher Fairfield. Now was the only reality, this man and herself, the woman beneath him, and the shocking discovery that she was as ready and as eager as he was. Unable to bear her thoughts, she stammered. "L-let me go, please."

Christopher's eyes smiled into hers. "What, give up my conquest? Not likely."

"You m-may force yourself upon me, but you can hardly call it a conquest."

"Not in the sense you mean, perhaps." Christopher touched her quivering mouth lightly. "But just the same, it will be a conquest."

She turned her head away from his teasing finger. "I ask you again to let me go."

"I might, if I did not think that you want me as much as I want you."

"You're wrong," she cried out wildly, "I loathe you and despise you!"

"Do you?" Christopher murmured. Desiree saw his small, disbelieving smile, and she felt faint with shame. "Shall we find out, Miss Desiree?"

She had no words as his rough hands swept away the strands of bright hair that had fallen over her shoulders. He began to kiss her, wild abandoned kisses that rapidly lifted her to a frightening peak of ecstasy. She, who had always believed she knew herself intimately, had needed only his touch to bring forth a stranger, a woman with fire in her veins, shameless, incredibly wanton!

Christopher's eyes dropped to Desiree's moist red mouth, and the stirring in his loins increased. Words began to hammer in his brain, inciting him on. Grayson's daughter. This girl who lay beneath him now, her limbs quivering, her rigid nipples prodding his chest, was the child of his enemy. The proud and arrogant bitch who had plagued his thoughts for so long. Raising himself, he stared at her heaving breasts. His hands shook as he caressed them, and his breath came harshly from between his lips.

Desiree flinched from him, but the eyes that she opened looked drugged.

Seizing her legs, Christopher pushed them apart. He knew her terror, even her desire, both seemed to touch him like palpable things, trying to give him pause. For a moment longer he hesitated, fighting conscience, and then with a sound curiously like a sob, he thrust inside her.

Desiree gasped at the white-hot flash of pain that came as she felt his hard sex coming into her. Her resisting hands were feeble against his shoulders.

Looking into her pain-clouded eyes, Christopher felt a pang of remorse. Elton Grayson should be the target of his revenge, not this girl. "Ah, to hell with it," he said in a rough, angry voice, trying to hide his guilt, "you're probably not woman enough for me anyway. I'll let you go. What do I want with you, anyway?"

Desiree did not hear him. The pain was subsiding. It was no longer important. In its place was an exquisite trembling frenzy, a madly racing heart, and a blazing response to the throbbing of his flesh inside her. Instinctively, as she felt his effort to withdraw, she moved with him and held him to her. A rush of heat stung her body, and with it the last of her inhibitions fled. Words that she had never thought to speak came huskily from her lips. "I want you, Christopher Fairfield"—she pressed herself hard against him—"I want you so much."

Although he had guessed at her desire, Christopher was stunned to hear it put into words. He gripped her shoulders tightly. "Do you know what you're saying?"

Desiree could no longer think clearly, she could only feel, and he was spoiling the moment. She moved her head restlessly, nodding her assent, longing to feel him moving inside her.

Christopher saw the frantic fluttering of the pulse in her throat, the desire-drugged eyes, the sultry mouth that awaited his kisses, and he was lost in a fascination that had begun some years ago, a fascination he had tried his best to destroy. "Desiree,"—he put his face close to hers—"you are so beautiful." He kissed her parted mouth, and felt her tongue twine about his own like a small searing flame.

Hearing the note of tenderness in his voice, Desiree frowned uneasily. How strange to think of tenderness in connection with this bitter and dangerous man. She started as his hands lifted her hips higher, and once more all coherent thought vanished as he plunged deeper inside her. "Desiree . . ." He said her name as though it was sweet on his tongue, as though he could not get enough of saying it.

A wild wailing cry, pagan in its sound, broke from Desiree's lips as his slow strokes quickened, became battering, savagely demanding. There was no room in her mind now to take account of her actions, there was nothing but this moment, this man, whom she wanted so desperately. Motivated by a purely primeval need, she inched her quivering legs upward to circle his neck, clinging tightly with her own demanding response. Her body, oddly knowing, thrust fiercely with his as they rushed toward a violent climax. She felt his shuddering convulsion all through her, and it seemed to her that she exploded into flaming fragments as his release mingled with her own. As suddenly as the shattering moment had built, it was over, the ecstasy, the primitive passion, the feeling that they alone existed in a world that had been made expressly for them.

She accepted the fact that she would never be the same again; Christopher Fairfield had branded her, he had seared himself and his memory into her mind, her heart, her flesh, but for all that, he could never be more to her than a memory. A sigh welled up inside her as the hard practical streak that had ruled her nature thus far took over, telling her that there was no percentage in continuing to want a doomed man, for that was what he was. She would forget him, she decided firmly. She would stop the wanting at its source; it was the only way. For all her sensible decision, her heart quivered at the thought, and she did not know that it was the beginning of the pain of loving where love was forbidden.

Christopher heard her sigh. Bewildered by the tenderness, the rushing of his emotions that the small mournful sound evoked, he tightened his hold on her slender body. There was no thought in him of possible danger, no memory of being a fugitive; there was only this precious interlude in time in which everything was forgotten but her. Resting his chin against her bright hair, smelling the delicate fragrance which still persistently clung to her, he was like one in a dream. He felt lightheaded, strange, as though he had been born again into a world where injustice and cruelty had no place. Surely a miracle had happened, and this vibrant and lovely girl had brought it about, for against all logic, he knew that he had fallen in love with Desiree Grayson. Perhaps he had always loved her, only he had not recognized the emotion for what it was. A cold whisper of sanity intruded. There is no miracle, the whisper went on, there is no future for you. Even were you a free man, she would never love you in return. Face it, it is impossible. Unaccustomed tears stung Christopher's eyes as he closed his mind and fought to keep his dream a little longer. "No," he whispered soundlessly, shaking his head in vehement denial of sanity.

As though his emotions had communicated themselves to her, Desiree was swept by a terrible desolation. What was the matter with her? she asked herself desperately. Why did she have the feeling that her world would come to an end if she were parted from Christopher Fairfield? Her nails dug into her palms as she rejected the idea of love. No, no, she did not love him. She must not, for that way lay tragedy. It was lust she felt, nothing more than that, only lust. Finding herself unconvinced, she reminded herself again that it was over. It was best for both of them that the disgraceful episode be buried and forgotten. Drawing in a deep quivering breath, she made an effort to assert herself. "Fairfield," she said in a tight, cold voice, "take your arms away at once."

The harsh tones in her voice were like hammer blows, smashing his miracle. The truth was that Desiree Grayson had given herself to him in a gust of unbridled passion, and for her that was the end of it, he must face it. Cursing himself for those unguarded moments when he had allowed himself to dream, he drew on the fierce pride that had always sustained him. "Of course, ma'am," he answered her with soft mockery, "anything you say." His arms dropped away from her. "I apologize for . . . er . . . for forcing myself upon an unwilling woman."

Scalding color rushed into Desiree's face. For a moment she could not speak; then she managed in a choked voice, "I don't appreciate your sarcasm, Fairfield, even though I deserve it."

"Yes, ma'am, you do deserve it." Christopher sat up straight, his bitter eyes sweeping over her naked figure. "You surely do."

Desiree put her hands to her hot cheeks. "All right," she snapped, "that has been established." She glanced at him quickly. "But a gentleman would not labor the point."

"Of course not." Christopher smiled tauntingly. "But then, Miss Desiree, in case you have forgotten, I am not considered to be a gentleman."

"No," she flashed, "no one could ever accuse you of that."

"True," Christopher agreed. Driven by hurt, he stabbed at her again. "But then no one could call your own conduct that of a well-brought-up young lady, could they? I think that makes us even."

Hating him, struggling with another emotion that was trying to make itself felt, she nodded her head in agreement. "Yes," she said stiffly, "I suppose you're right."

Looking at her, he knew that the new and painful love was waiting to trap him into weakness, and he mentally armed himself against her. "There is no suppose about it," he said harshly, "but tell me, what happens now, do you run home to Daddy and cry rape?"

Desiree met his eyes with some difficulty. "I became a willing partner, as you were at pains to remind me."

Christopher shrugged. "As far as I'm concerned, you can say what you please, it will make little difference to me." His eyes swept over her again. "You will have to give a reason for your appearance, so you might as well put the blame on my shoulders, since the intention to rape you was there."

"I shall do no such thing," Desiree snapped. "At least give me credit for some decency."

"Whatever you wish," Christopher said with assumed indifference. "And what of your appearance?"

"That can be explained by my encounter with the thorn bush."

"Admirable," Christopher answered sarcastically. "I almost get the impression that you wish to protect me."

His words jolted Desiree, giving her the uncomfortable impression that his penetrating dark eyes could see into her mind, that he knew of her confusion, her doubts, and of that other feeling, warm and sweet, that she was trying so hard to suppress. Protect him, no. Christopher Fairfield needed no protection from a woman. But she did want him to get away, to some place where he would be able to make a new start. Unable to think of anything else to say, she said haughtily, "And if I do, is that so surprising?"

Christopher studied her flushed face. "Why, yes, under the circumstances, I find it extremely so. In any case, by now Phillips will have connected me with Christopher Fairfield, and I think you will be called upon to say something."

"That's right, you mentioned that Frazer did not recognize

you." Unthinkingly, Desiree caught at his arm and held it with tense fingers. "And that means you have a chance."

"Does it?"

"Of course. You must go now. You must get away as far as you possibly can. When I am asked, I shall say that I was unconscious, that I did not see you. It is not altogether a lie—I was unconscious part of the time."

With a nonchalance that belied the stirring in his blood, Christopher brushed her hand away. "So you'll say that, will you? And I should trust you, I suppose?"

"Yes," she said impatiently, "you can." She looked at him with defiant eyes. "And I don't care whether you believe it or not."

Christopher rose slowly to his feet. "You will forgive me if I don't," he said, looking down at her. His eyes took in her beauty in an unconscious effort to seal it into his mind, the huge thickly fringed violet eyes, the full, sensuous mouth, the bright hair falling over her shoulders and veiling her lovely breasts. Abruptly he turned away. There was a limit to self-deception, and he had reached it.

Desiree watched through half-closed eyes as he began to dress himself in his ragged garments. Checkered patterns of light and shade filtered through the gently swaying trees, playing over his lean brown body and highlighting the terrible ridged scars, and the sight of his mutilation added to her already heavy weight of misery. Questions whirled in her mind. Where would he go now, would she ever see him again? "Christopher . . ." She said his name gently. "I'm sorry for my attitude, sorry for everything."

"There is no need for sorrow, and I don't need your pity." Christopher turned slowly to face her. "Another thing, why assume a comradeship you do not feel? I am 'Fairfield' to you, remember?"

"Don't, please!" Desiree clasped her hands together, working them nervously. "What will you do now, where will you go?"

Christopher's eyes narrowed. "You expect me to tell you that, you must take me for a complete fool."

He hated her, he was suspicious of her. She could not bear it. "I don't take you for a fool," she blurted with an edge of desperation in her voice. "I wish you well, truly, Christopher, I do."

She looked so forlorn. Conquering an impulse to speak to her softly, Christopher said curtly, "Stop your playacting, I have no time for it." Dropping to his knees, he pulled her roughly into his arms. "Time to say good-bye," he muttered, "but before I go I'll take a little token with me." His lips crushed hers in a fierce, lingering kiss. He felt the quiver run through her body, the leaping of his own pulses as her lips parted and clung. Before he could weaken, he thrust her away. "Try not to forget me altogether." Dismayed by his own foolish words, he looked at her for a moment longer; then he rose to his feet and walked away without a backward glance.

Try not to forget me altogether. His parting words ran through Desiree's head with a melancholy sound. In the past she had tried to forget him, but he had always been there in the back of her mind. His kiss still stinging her mouth, she fought the mad temptation to call him back. Instead, she listened dully to the dry snap of fallen branches as he walked out of her life. Where would he go, what would happen to him now? Let him get away, she prayed silently, don't let him be caught. She put her clenched fists over her wet eyes as she faced the truth. It was more than passion she felt for Christopher Fairfield, it was love. "I love you, Christopher," she whispered. "God help me, but I do." Her hands dropped away, and she looked with bleak eyes as he walked through the dense foliage that hid him from her view.

7

Her full lower lip outthrust, her eyes brooding, Tildy trudged wearily along the almost invisible branch-littered forest trail. Her feet hurt, her throat was hoarse from calling, and she felt ill-used and extremely sorry for herself. "Where you at, Miss Dessi?" she mumbled. "I know you must be here somewhere, so why don't you answer when I call?"

Weighed down by the worry on her mind, Tildy surrendered to her need to rest. Sitting down on a fallen tree trunk, she placed the heavy cloak she had been carrying across her knees, looking round as though expecting an answer to her question, but hearing nothing but the creaking of branches and the rustle and slither of the secret forest life all about her. Her frown deepened. Drat the girl! she thought, her fat black fingers fidgeting with the smooth gray fabric of the cloak. Miss Dessi was always going off these days. She had been quiet and unlike herself ever since the day when she had returned to the plantation all scratched up and her gown hanging in rags. She had tumbled into a thorn bush—that had been her explanation for her alarming appearance. Master Grayson had seemed to believe her story, Tildy mused, but as for herself, she felt sure that Miss Dessi was hiding something.

Tildy absently brushed a leaf from the cloak. Master Phillips was mixed up in it too, of that she was certain. Because he would shortly be going off to the war, he was visiting Twin Oaks more frequently now, and whenever he was there, Miss Dessi looked at him with more than her usual scorn. Only yesterday, passing the two, Tildy had heard her mistress say sharply, "I'm tired of your excuses, Frazer, I don't want to hear them anymore. All I know is that you left me alone with that man, not knowing what would happen to me, and that you made no effort to come back." She laughed on a hard note. "You are a coward, Frazer, why trouble to deny it?"

Intrigued, Tildy had lingered just out of sight. "I took a tumble," she heard Frazer Phillips say frantically. "I have told you that over and over again. When I came to myself, it was too late to do anything about it. You were already back at the house when I arrived, remember?"

"'I also remember that you very carefully refrained from saying anything until you got me alone. Were you afraid that my father would also accuse you of cowardice?"

"I was hurt, I tell you. My mind was jumbled. And why upset your father, when you were quite obviously safe? You did say your scratches came from a thorn bush, didn't you?"

Tildy had heard the sneer in his question, but Miss Dessi had chosen to ignore it. "You were not hurt, Frazer," she said in a cold voice. "The plain truth is that you were drunk. I have no doubt that you had been drinking steadily ever since you left me there with him."

"It's not true." Peering out, Tildy saw Phillips attempting to catch the girl's hands in his. When he was rebuffed, he said in an angry voice, "Did he touch you, Dessi?"

Miss Dessi had looked more scornful than ever. "You are scarcely in a position to ask me that. You do remember what happened between us?"

Even from where she was standing, Tildy could see the flush staining Frazer Phillips' face. "I apologize for laying hands on you, Dessi," he said in a gruff voice. "Surely a man is allowed one mistake."

"A man, yes."

"God damn you and your insults, does it mean nothing to you that I am going away?"

"But of course, Frazer. It means that I shall have a welcome respite from your unwanted attentions."

Strangely, and much to Tildy's surprise, Master Phillips had not been angry. He had smiled rather sadly, and then said in an almost gentle voice, "You might at least tell me if that convict touched you."

Convict. Tildy had been seriously frightened then, and she had remembered that Christopher Fairfield was still being hunted. Straining her ears, she had heard her young mistress's hard laughter again, and then her icy voice. "He did not, Frazer. Does that satisfy you? All I had was a glimpse of his back as he made off." As though she had tired of the conversation, Miss Dessi had turned and walked away, and Master Phillips had followed after her.

Tildy frowned down at the ground. What had happened on that day to make Miss Dessi forget so completely that Amos was awaiting her orders in regard to Josh? Had she met up with Christopher Fairfield, or had it been some other fugitive? She had longed to ask, but dared not. Her thoughts reverted to Amos. Amos had waited patiently at first, but when there was no sign of Miss Dessi, he had ignored her entreaties to wait just a little longer. "Cain't wait, Tildy," he had said firmly, "Miss Dessi wantin' to get Josh to safety, and that's what I'm goin' to do. Besides, she knows she can trust me to do the job."

"But I ain't trustin' you," Tildy had argued, dismayed by his mulish look. "I know you ain't got a smidgen of sense in that woolly head. You got to wait, you hear?"

"'Ain't waitin'," Amos had retorted coldly. "An' what's more," he said, pointing to Josh, "This big fella told me Miss Dessi promise to get his woman, Martie, away from Miss Youtha, so I'm goin' to keep that promise for her."

A cold chill had run through Tildy. "I ain't listenin' to no more of this foolishness," she said sternly. Then, seeing his adamant expression, she had resorted to pleading. "You cain't, Amos. What will you do if Miss Youtha catches you?"

"She ain't goin' to catch me, not that ol' gal." Amos' head lifted proudly. "Miss Dessi taught me some tricks, I taught her some, so I know what I'm doin'." He had turned his back, his manner indicating that the discussion was closed.

Remembering her fear, Tildy sighed heavily. She had prayed that the three would be safe, for it had seemed to her that without Miss Dessi's guidance things were sure to go wrong. Whether from luck, or from more skill than she had given him credit for, Amos had managed to get both Josh and Martie away. The two of them were in the hands of the Northern members of the organization. There would be no more slavery for them. If Josh chose to enter the war on the Yankee side, as was apparently his wish, the decision, for the first time in his adult life, would be his alone to make. When Amos had returned, Miss Dessi had met with him in the usual meeting place, and she had been alone with him in the small wooden hut for at least half an hour. Tildy, hovering outside, yearned to know what was being said. Was Miss Dessi angry because Amos had taken things into his own hands? This fear was dispelled when Amos finally emerged, for his round black face had worn a look of beaming satisfaction. Passing Tildy, he had said, "Ain't I tol' you Miss Dessi trust me, Tildy? Perhaps now you have more faith in me."

Tildy rose from the tree trunk, hoisting the cloak over her arm. Dusk was falling and there was a chill in the air. No doubt Miss Dessi, once she caught up to her, would be glad of the warmth of the cloak. Walking on, she pondered the subject that seemed to occupy all minds—the war. Did she wish to be set free? she asked herself. The answer came to her swiftly. No, not at her time of life. She was too old now to make her own way in the world, and she wanted nothing to do with bloody violence. Freedom was for the younger ones, they deserved their chance. She hoped with all her heart that the conclusion of this war would bring it to them. Like a ghostly echo, the memory of what Miss Dessi had said came back to her—"Civil war, brother against brother, father against son. It could be that way, Tildy, and it frightens me."

It frightened her too, Tildy thought. The young ones, burning to set aside the shackles of slavery, would call her a coward. They did not fear the changing of the old order, as she did; they welcomed it. They were right, of course, and she was wrong, but she had grown old in slavery; she had never known outright brutality, and she could not easily set aside the habits and thinking of a lifetime.

Tildy shuddered with that chill that seemed to be constantly with her now. Already, in a short space of time, the war had caught up with Hawleigh County, and the young men were disappearing. When she had gone marketing with Biddy, the undercook, she had seen scores of them at the railroad station, surrounded by weeping women and red-faced, proud-looking older men, waiting to board the train that would carry them away from home and their loved ones. Some of the young men, the sons of planters, wore new gray uniforms, with shining sidearms, their horses loaded into boxcars and their black servants hovering near, alert for a command. There were others in everyday dress, and still others in buckskins, bowie knife and large pistol thrust conspicuously into belts. She had recognized the buckskin-clad men as backwoodsmen. All of them appeared to have one thing in common, a shared embarrassment at the emotional atmosphere that surrounded them. Trying their best to cheer the weeping relatives, they laughed aloud, made jokes, and sung patriotic songs.

Jostled by the crowd, Tildy, with Biddy beside her, drew nearer. She saw the sparkling fervor in the eyes of the departing men, and realized that it had not occurred to them that they might not return. Death and injuries were far from their minds. Their one thought was to come to grips with the Yankee enemy who had dared to challenge their way of life. "The Glorious Southern Cause"—that was what they called it—and no "ol' blue-belly" was going to be allowed to set one foot in their fair land. As for Abe Lincoln, that cursed upstart, he'd be showing the whites of his eyes before too long, damned if he wouldn't!

Listening to their proud boasting, Tildy had succumbed to rare tears. The colors of the women's gowns, the grays, the blacks, the butternut colors of the men, blended together in a haze, and her heart was desolate. Biddy, looking at her curiously, had asked, "What for you blubberin', you ol' fool?" Tildy could not tell her; she did not know herself.

The war had finally stretched its long finger to touch the master of Twin Oaks Plantation. This afternoon, Clover, trembling with excitement, had told her that some men in uniform had called upon Master Grayson. They had been closeted with him for a long time. After they left, riding off with a jingle of spurs and sabers, the sun shining on new gray cloth, Master Grayson had immediately shouted for Willie and John. They were excused from their other duties, he told them. He would be going away to the fighting, and they were to help him pack his trunks.

Coming down from the master's bedroom later, John, the older of the two black men, swaggered with self-importance when he informed Clover that he had been chosen to travel with his master. "Must be goin' to be a long war," John had said to her. "Master takin' two great big trunks, and thinkin' he maybe needin' more'n that." When Clover asked why, John, obviously influenced by his master's thinking, answered her indignantly, "why you think, dull-head? Master a gentleman, and ain't wantin' just clothes. He wantin' china an' silver, so's he'll be comfortable. He's takin' linen as well, 'cause he says there ain't no need to be livin' like a savage. Says he ain't likin' it without his table set proper, and clean beddin' to sleep in."

Tildy smiled sadly. She had not thought that Master Grayson would go off and leave Miss Dessi alone, but it seemed that he had made up his mind to take part in the "Glorious Cause." This direct action on his part, combined with John's ceaseless boasting, had, not unnaturally, thrown the house slaves into a state of almost hysterical confusion, and as the news reached the ears of other workers, the same emotion reigned. The master was going away. What was going to happen to them, what were they supposed to do now? They had not really believed a war would come, certainly not a war whose purpose seemed solely to free them from bondage, but since it had come, were they to consider themselves free now? At this last thought, faces changed, and self-confidence took the place of apprehension. Very well, then, perhaps they should gather together their few belongings and just leave. The slave catchers would not dare to stop them now. If they tried, Master Lincoln would punish those white men. He was white himself, but he was the big boss, and he loved his black people. Hadn't he proved that by taking action against those who wished to hold them enslaved? They had nothing to fear now.

Listening to all this hopeful talk, Tildy had wisely kept her silence. Even if she had spoken her thoughts aloud, told them that nothing had, as yet, changed for them, and that Master Lincoln, though she had heard that he was a good and gentle man, would not be on the spot to guide them, as they seemed to believe, or to instantly punish offenses against them, they would not have listened to her. With deep foreboding she watched the excited black men form a group. Without asking permission from their overseers, they had determined to go up to the house and see Master Grayson. "Master will listen to us now, cain't very well refuse."

When Tildy heard the results of that interview, she had known that her sense of foreboding was amply justified. The men had wanted to discuss the war with Elton Grayson, and, out of habit, to politely request his permission to leave Twin Oaks. After all, they were of importance now. A war was being fought by the North to ensure their rights to exist as free and dignified human beings. The master, being a reasonable man, would, they felt sure, recognize the justice in this, and he would talk to them as man to man. If there was anything they did not understand, he would make it clear to them. Elton Grayson, however, had not seen it their way, and he had quickly disabused their minds of this dangerous and seditious idea. Outraged, his customary reserve lost in anger, his face mottled, he had shouted, "So it's starting already, is it? Niggers entering my house without permission, getting big ideas, and thinking that they're as good as white men. Well, you're not, and never will be." Almost choking on his anger, he paused to draw in a gulping breath, and then he continued his tirade. "Freedom, is that what you want, freedom to leave my plantation and wander where you will? Freedom to molest our white women, is more like."

Jeremiah, the spokesman, had been shocked by this lack of control. He had never seen Elton Grayson in such a mood before. "No, sir," he had answered respectfully, "ain't wantin' to touch no white women."

"Get out!"

"Please, sir," Jeremiah had persisted, "we only want to be free."

"You'll be free if I sign papers stating so, not before," Elton Grayson continued to shout. "Now, get the hell out of here. If I see one of you within a minute from now, I'll lay leather across your goddamned stupid backs." In his rage, Jeremiah later told Tildy, the master reminded him of Demon, the prize bull in the west field. His eyes had been red and glittering, and, just like Demon, he had looked ready to gore and trample.

Once again, out of the ingrained habit of instant obedience

to the master's will, the men scattered hurriedly, but they had been far from humbled. In time they would be free. They had something to live for now. The only cloud on their horizon was the troubling thought that the North might be defeated. As a result of their going off without permission, and their new and almost arrogant attitude, several floggings had occurred within the space of two hours.

Tildy, herded together with the rest of the women, looked on at one such flogging. There was a trembling inside her at the viciousness of the strokes, and she had been badly frightened by the virulent hatred in the faces of the white overseers. It was almost as if they were punishing the men for something other than their offense, as though they delighted in this opportunity to slice black flesh. Did Master Grayson know what was happening? she asked herself wildly. If he did, and there was little that went on that he was not aware of, then why didn't he come out and put a stop to it? He was a firm master, but he had always been just, and he had never believed in cruelty for its own sake. Miss Dessi—where was she? Why wasn't she here to raise her voice against this display of senseless violence? Looking from face to face, it seemed to Tildy that all those about her, both black and white, had suddenly become strangers to her. A man called Beauregard had shelled a fort, so she had heard from Amos, and this action, marking the beginning of war, had, within a short space of time, produced this alien atmosphere, this bitter enmity. Even Master Jacobs, normally friendly to the black men who worked under him, had changed. His eyes slitted, his teeth showing in a snarling smile, he shouted, "Lay it harder on the uppity black bastard!"

Sickened and bewildered, trying hard not to give way to the tears that threatened, Tildy turned blindly away. There was one idea in her head as she made her way to the main house. She must see the master. She must tell him what was happening, and beg him to stop the punishment before somebody was killed. If he would not do it for humanity's sake, then perhaps she could remind him that his valuable property was being ruined. How would it look if, in the future, he should display to prospective buyers scarred and crippled flesh? It was not often that Elton Grayson sold his slaves away, but when he did it was an event. Twin Oaks coffles, though rare, were famous for bright, handsome, and healthy stock, and Elton Grayson could be justly proud. Surely, Tildy thought desperately, he would not want that reputation ruined.

Almost at the door of the house, Tildy met Clover. "Ain't a bit of use askin' to see the master, Tildy," she said firmly. "Except for Miss Dessi, he ain't wantin' to see no one." Clover smiled, displaying large, very white, even teeth. "He surely rarin' to go off to that war, but I guess he's feelin' badly about leavin' Miss Dessi. He doesn't know that that gal as good as any man about managin' and lookin' out for herself."

"Yes, yes," Tildy said impatiently, "listen to me, Clover, I'm sure the master'll see me. You go ask him."

Clover shook her head. "I got my orders. 'Nother thing, Jeremiah and them others comin' to the house upset him."

"It's about that I've come. The overseers got together, and they're likely to kill those men."

Clover's expression lengthened into gravity, but she remained obdurate. "Cain't risk it, the master's in a mean mood, he'd kill me for sure if I disturbed him." She paused, then added in a lighter voice, "Reckon master ain't wantin' Miss Dessi to marry up with Master Phillips now, not the way he is. That man always ridin' over from Woodgrove these days, it seems like he's hauntin' Twin Oaks. When he comes he's so drunk he cain't hardly sit on his horse. I hear the master say he's disgusted and disappointed with him."

Tildy, who would normally have welcomed this news, gripped the girl's thin arm with tense fingers. "I'm asking you one more time to call the master for me."

Clover frowned impatiently. "If you're so all fired up about stoppin' them floggin's, whyn't you talk to Miss Dessi?"

Tildy sighed; she should have known she was wasting her time with Clover. Clover had worked willingly enough for the organization, but only if it did not mean that she was risking her own precious skin. Ideals, however grand and glorious they might be, meant little to her in the face of danger. Miss Dessi knew of this weakness in her, and she used her unwillingly, and only when no one else was available. "All right, Clover," Tildy said heavily, "I'll talk to Miss Dessi. Where is she?"

Clover giggled. "Ain't no tellin', when she tumble in that thorn bush, she maybe get a thorn in her head."

"Hush your fool mouth," Tildy rebuked her, frowning. "You ain't to be talkin' of Miss Dessi that way."

"Why not?" Clover shrugged. "Miss Dessi ain't God. Besides, if the North win this war, we all be free. Ain't no more need for the Flame then."

Tildy gasped; what did she think she was doing, talking in that loud voice about the Flame. Had she lost what little sense she possessed? "Be quiet," she said in a low, warning voice. She looked upward, her eyes widening in apprehension. "The master's window is open. What if he heard you?"

Clover tossed her head nonchalantly, but she looked scared. "That window was shut when I turned down his bed."

"Ain't shut now, fool!"

"Don't mean nothin'." Clover's fingers twisted nervously at the hem of her white apron. "He didn't hear me. He's tired to death. He said he wanted to sleep for a while."

Tildy looked at her grimly. "You don't know for sure he's sleepin'."

"Anyway"—Clover's whispering voice was anxious to change the subject—"last thing he said to me was go find Miss Dessi. I was about to do that when you came."

"Too late for you to go whisperin' now," Tildy said. Relenting, she said in a softer voice, "I'll go after Miss Dessi. She's likely to be wanderin' about the forest, and ain't got no notion of the time." She glanced up at the sky. "Sun keep hidin' himself, and there's quite a nip in the air. You go get me one of her cloaks."

Clover hesitated, inclined to resent the authoritative command from this fat woman whom she envied, and had never really liked. Then, seeing Tildy's set expression, she said reluctantly, "Master said for me to go, but maybe it's all right if you go instead. I'll get the cloak."

Returning, Clover thrust the garment at Tildy with shaking hands. "The master's callin' me," she gasped. "You think he heard what I said?"

Tildy folded the cloak carefully over her arm, not looking at her. "Don't know," she mumbled. "You best pray he didn't." She turned away with an air of indifference that masked anxiety. If Master Grayson had heard Clover's reference to the Flame, he was sure to question the girl. It would be like her to break down and tell him everything if she thought it might save her from a licking. Tildy's heartbeat quickened at the chilling thought. Elton Grayson was a loving and indulgent father, but what would his reaction be if he learned that Miss Dessi was the notorious Flame? As most of the planters, he hated all that the Flame stood for, and his one aim was to capture this destroyer of his peace. "Hanging's too good for the bastard," he had been heard to say, "but it's the quickest way to be rid of him. I'd like the job of stringing him up myself, and maybe we can rough him up a bit first. You know, pay him back some for what he's done to us."

This disturbing thought and others going through her mind, Tildy stopped short on the trail and looked about her. Since taking leave of Clover, she had been searching and calling for over an hour. If she didn't find her mistress soon, it would be full dark. She had never liked walking in the forest; there was something eerie about it, but in the dark, and without company to support her, she would be terrified. "Miss Dessi?" She raised her voice to a bellow. "Answer me, child, where are you?"

Desiree raised her head. She had been aware of Tildy's voice calling for some time now, but, occupied with her thoughts of Christopher Fairfield, she had not troubled to answer. Tildy called again. This time, responding to the note of urgency in the black woman's voice, Desiree scrubbed at her tear-streaked face with her handkerchief and then jumped lightly to her feet. "Over here," she answered, hastily straightening the rumpled skirts of her primrose-yellow gown. What an idiot she was, she thought angrily, to sit here blubbering over Christopher Fairfield like some lovesick schoolgirl. It had been some days now since her encounter with him, and she had successfully resisted the temptation to visit Chrissie Fairfield, who might have known where her brother was headed, and perhaps have been persuaded to tell her. Desiree shook her head at her own naiveté. Even if Chrissie had known, which was probably unlikely, she would have told her nothing. Desiree's chin firmed. Christopher was far away from here by now, and she must get over him. She could do it if she tried. Indeed, she would do it! Taking a deep breath, she raised her voice. "This way, Tildy."

There was a silence; then heavy footsteps came nearer. The

greenery that had screened her from sight quivered as it was swept aside by an impatient hand. "So there you are, you bad gal," Tildy shouted, waddling into the clearing. "I ought to take my broom to your back." She broke off in the middle of her tirade to detach the hem of her skirt from a bramble. "Ever'thin' upset," she went on, pulling her skirt free. "Master's leavin' for the war, and he fit to be tied 'cause you ain't there." Her eyes widened as she caught sight of Desiree's face. "You been cryin'?" she asked.

"I have not been crying," Desiree said coldly, "and what's this about my father?"

Tildy, looking at the girl's tearstained face, was about to pursue the subject, then she decided against it. She had learned to read her young mistress's expressions, and this one quite clearly conveyed a warning. "Well, now, Miss Dessi," she said slowly, "you know how your daddy been itchin' to go off. When those men came to see him today, it probably helped him to make up his mind."

"What men?" Desiree asked the question without interest. For the moment, even the news that her father was going away could not shake her.

Putting the cloak about Desiree's shoulders, Tildy shrugged. "Some men in uniform, that's all I know. Miss Dessi," she said, stepping back, "there's somethin' on my min'. It's about that Clover." Tildy hesitated. Now was not the time to tell Miss Dessi about the floggings; that could come later. Her recent worry was of more importance. "Clover's been shootin' off her mouth about the Flame, and I think maybe your father heard her."

Desiree's curious detachment held. Already, in her mind, she had removed herself from that part of her life which had been so important. Unless the North lost the war, there would be no more need for the Flame. "It doesn't matter if my father heard, Tildy," she said in a low voice, "it's over. The coming of the war has altered circumstances."

Tildy stared at her in disbelief. "Maybe it's over," she burst out, "but how come you say it don't matter? You know how your daddy feels about the Flame. If he heard Clover, and makes her tell all she knows, he's like to kill you." She paused, gulping. "For that matter, he's likely to kill all of us."

Desiree smiled. "You know Clover as well as I do, Tildy. She won't tell on the others for fear of involving herself. She will make up some reason to explain the fact that she has discovered that I am the Flame."

Struck by this, Tildy nodded. "You're right, Miss Dessi, Clover won't dare tell about us, 'cause she know's we'll get back at her. But you . . ." Tears started to brim over Tildy's fear-widened eyes. "Clover never liked you, and she'd tell on you for sure. It makes me shiver to think what your daddy will do to you."

"Don't worry." Desiree took Tildy's quivering hand and pulled her gently along. "If Clover has told my father about me, he will be shocked and terribly angry, but he loves me, and he would never harm me."

Did Miss Dessi truly believe it would be so simple? Unconvinced, Tildy allowed herself to be led along. "I'm afraid for you, Miss Dessi," she mumbled. "I think that he would hurt you bad, maybe even hand you over to the law."

"No, Tildy, you're wrong. I should know my own father, I think."

8

There was rain in the air. A full moon showed briefly, a few stars winked a faint silvery gleam before being hidden by the heavy cloud cover. In the distance, lightning streaked, looking like fiery javelins thrown toward the rearing mountains. The thunder that rumbled in its wake sounded oddly like the deep-toned menacing laughter of demons.

Pushing his horse at high speed along the rutted road, Frazer Phillips cursed the darkness and the rain that had already begun to fall. He was very drunk, and filled with a vicious anger as he thought of Desiree Grayson. "Bitch!" he shouted into the turbulent night. "By Christ, I'd like to kill you!"

Breathless, his voice blown away by the buffeting of the steadily rising wind, Frazer sawed on the reins and pulled to a skidding halt beneath the dark shadow of a tree. The rain was coming down so fast now that it was almost a deluge. Beneath him, his horse whinnied nervously, rearing slightly. "God damn you!" Frazer tightened the reins, bringing the animal under control. Motionless, his eyes blinking in the rain, Frazer was unaware of the chill discomfort. His mind was filled with his obsession, Desiree Grayson, who still persisted in rejecting him. "Cursed nigger's whore," he growled. His vicious thoughts conjuring her up, he suddenly saw her plainly, and it was as if she lay before him in actuality, her naked body superimposed on the dark ground and shining with an unearthly radiance. The giant Negro who crouched above her was, in contrast, a great black hulk without lines to define him. The Negro touched her; his hands upon her body were ebony against ivory.

Frazer reeled drunkenly in the saddle, the fumes of brandy whirling sickeningly in his head. Afraid of the vision his confused mind had evoked, he closed his eyes tightly. Opening them again, he half-expected to see Desiree Grayson and her nigger lover in physical contact, but he saw only the rain, a gray curtain that caused the dimly seen landscape to waver in a mist. The horse snorted uneasily as the rain bounced off the earth and splashed his hocks with mud.

Frazer put a hand to his throbbing head. So he was seeing ghosts now. The Grayson bitch was surely driving him insane. Filled with panic, heedless of the condition of the road, he urged the horse forward at full gallop. Rain stung his eyes, causing him to drop the reins. Shouting, he clutched at the animal's soggy mane, only just saving himself from a fall. Recapturing the reins with some difficulty, he slowed the pace to a walk. Hunched over, rain streaming from the wide brim of his hat, Frazer thought of the other women who had played a part in his life. There was Phoebe, his latest black mistress. Phoebe had a beautifully shaped and exciting body; she also had a fertile brain that could invent numerous ways to make the sexual act highly novel. There had been many others before Phoebe, but, like her, they had all been slaves. Black flesh. He had been content enough until the child Charlotte Elliot had come to his notice. Fourteen-year-old Charlotte, so blond and dainty, so finely made, had stirred him to a raging passion that was akin to that which he now felt for Desiree Grayson. God, how mute, how terrified Charlotte had been when he had violated her. Afterward, fighting back tears, wincing at his threats, she promised him that she would keep silent. But when he followed her into the alley in back of her father's store, he saw her eyes, wide and accusing, and he knew that she would talk. What choice had he then but to silence her, for he could not face the scandal that would result. It had been so easy, the knife had slid through the tender flesh of her throat as easily as if it had been butter. Memories of Charlotte brought Christopher Fairfield into his mind, and he moved uneasily. Fairfield, so haughty, so goddamned arrogant, one would think he was a master instead of white trash. He had always hated him. Even when they were young boys together he had felt small and insignificant beside Fairfield's commanding presence. He had been glad when he had been blamed for Charlotte's murder.

Frazer's lips tightened as the horse stumbled in a pothole on the muddy road, scattering thought and almost unseating him again. "Damned useless old bag of bones." He jerked on the reins, straining the chestnut head upward at a cruel angle and causing the animal to whinny with pain. "Lousy hay chomper, I ought to shoot you." The throbbing in Frazer's head increased in intensity; even his voice sounded strange in his ears, as though his words had been caught up and tossed by the wind before being bounced back to him with a hollow echo. Hastily he returned his thoughts to Phoebe and those other women who had shared his bed. Women? No, he used the wrong term. Certainly they had breasts, and they had that hot, throbbing center of love, but they were not really women. They were his black slaves, his playthings, creatures not wholly human, but capable of satisfying his lust. Some came to his bed eagerly, others with reluctance and hatred written plain in dark, sullen eyes, but all of them feared a flogging if they did not please.

Diverted from his uneasy thoughts of Charlotte and Fairfield, Frazer chuckled low in his throat. Actually there was no question of his creatures not pleasing, for they were born with the knowledge of how to pleasure a man, but he flogged them anyway. Although they performed well, his belief was that their performance would be even better once they had been stripped down and hung up by their heels to await the caress of the lash. This had been his father's belief too.

Frazer frowned. Montgomery Phillips, his father, had been bearable, but Ellen Phillips, his mother, so thin and pallid and listless, he had hated. Her eyes were always so accusing as she looked on at the excesses of husband and son. She had been a nothing, always in a state of bad health, incapable of being either wife or mother. Frazer, when he was not ignoring the pitiful wreck of a woman, had taken a cruel delight in flaunting his black mistresses before her pained and shadowed blue eyes.

Frazer's hands clenched on the reins. Both his parents were dead, had been for some years, but he could not truthfully say that he had mourned either of them. Sometimes, though, more often than he liked, his mother's plaintive voice would sound in his ears. He stiffened as words she had spoken came back to him now: "If you should ever marry, son, and I pray you will join your life with a good religious woman, don't treat your wife as your father has treated me." She had held up wasted arms in an appeal for his understanding, his compassion. "Look at me, at what he has made of me. White women are not meant to be handled and abused like black wenches."

He put his face close to hers, enjoying her instinctive shrinking. "What makes white women so different?" He asked the question jeeringly. "Have they not the same thing up their skirts to pleasure a man?"

Staring in horror and shock, Ellen Phillips lifted feeble arms and thrust him away. "My God," she exclaimed, "have you no shame, no proper feeling?" Without waiting for an answer, she closed her eyes. Making for the door, Frazer had seen the tears escaping from beneath her pale, scanty lashes. She had never attempted to speak to him again. His crudity had silenced her effectively.

Laughing, Frazer thrust the memory aside. Throwing back his head, he enjoyed the sting of the rain against his face. White women. He had had one other after Charlotte Elliot. Chrissie Fairfield. Chrissie had not come to him willingly. He had been one of the men who had brought in a guilty verdict against her brother, and she thought of him as the enemy. It had amused him to woo her, to break down the barriers she had erected against him. Gradually, as she had come to believe that his verdict had not been one of malice but rather of a genuine belief in the guilt of Christopher Fairfield, her enmity had faded and she had come into his arms willingly. "If your brother is not guilty, Chrissie," he had encouraged her, "be sure that I will do all in my power to find the real murderer of Charlotte Elliot."

Chrissie's arms hugged him close, her mouth pressed eagerly against his. "I know you will, my darling. I trust you, I believe in you."

Laughter caught Frazer again. She trusted him, she believed that he was going to try to prove Fairfield innocent. What a grand joke that was. Chrissie was good for his ego, she flattered him with her attentions and hung on his every word, she made him feel like a god. But then there were those times when she lay in his arms, her slender body hot and eager for his caresses, when he would find himself indescribably bored by the little tender names she called him, by the bright glow in her soft brown eyes. He would be tempted to jolt her then by telling the truth. "I killed Charlotte Elliot," he imagined himself saying. "I slit her throat and left her in the alley to bleed to death. As you have said all along, your precious brother is innocent. Yes, Chrissie, as innocent as a newborn babe. But no one else save you and I will ever know the truth, will they?"

How would she react? Frazer wondered. Did she love him enough, despite everything, to cling to him still, or would her brother come first with her? Frazer smiled complacently. He rather thought that he would win, for not only did Chrissie love him to distraction, but she also believed that he intended to marry her and give his name to the baby she was carrying. Marry Chrissie Fairfield! His smile turned into a sneer. She had to be weak in the head if she truly believed that. It was Desiree he would marry, her or no one. But still, it might be amusing to test Chrissie's love.

The horse sidled beneath him, causing a queasy sensation in his stomach. God, Frazer thought, half in amusement and half in dismay, he really was bloody drunk. Gasping, his head reeling, he belched loudly, regurgitating brandy. Retching, he leaned over and spat out the vile taste. For a few moments he hung precariously over the horse's neck, vomiting helplessly; then, recovering himself, he straightened up and wiped his mouth on his sodden sleeve. Almost immediately, with the easing of his discomfort, his thoughts returned to Chrissie. Why not test her love? Which one would she choose, Fairfield or himself? His mouth tightened. If she chose Fairfield, she would regret it. Eager to find out, he dug his heels into the horse's side, urging him on to a faster pace. He had not intended to visit Chrissie tonight, but now was as good a time as any.

9

Chrissie Fairfield's heart pounded rapidly as she made her way through the rain-blustered darkness toward the tree-shaded washhouse at the end of the long vegetable garden. She shivered beneath her rain-soaked shawl, and the covered dish she was carrying trembled in her hand as she cautiously descended the four crumbling stone steps. Outside the door of the washhouse, she rested her fingers lightly on the latch, listening to the clattering of the rain upon the corrugated tin roof. She wondered how much longer she could hide Christopher. How long would it be before the prison authorities discovered him?

Chrissie's fingers tightened on the latch. For seven days and nights, stricken with the fever that had come upon him so suddenly, Christopher had lain hidden in the cellar beneath the washhouse. "Jail fever," Christopher had called his illness. He had suffered with it many times before, he told her, he knew the course it would take, and it would be several days before he was free of it. Chrissie bit her trembling lip. The men from Buxton Prison, evidently not satisfied with their first searching of the premises, had turned up again the day after Christopher's arrival. Scowling, eyes flinty with suspicion, they had searched the house, the grounds, the sheds, and finally the washhouse.

Remembering her terror, Chrissie drew in a deep, shuddering breath. Standing there in the washhouse, surrounded by rough-spoken, hard-featured men, she had been so frightened that they would discover the trapdoor that was hidden beneath the heavy rush matting. Her hands gripped tautly together, she had prayed silently that Christopher would not begin his delirious ramblings. God must have heard her prayers, for there was silence from the hidden cellar, and no move was made to remove the matting; indeed, the men did not even glance at it. They had gone away finally, but not before they had issued a stern warning. "If your brother should contact you, Miss Fairfield," one of the men said, "you are to get in touch with us at once. If you try to hide him from justice, you will find yourself in very serious trouble. Remember this, Buxton Prison has a section for women too."

The threat was clear, but she had said nothing. Seething with hatred, she had stood there, her head lowered. Did they really think she would give up her brother to them? She would die first!

Dissatisfied with her silence, the tall spokesman said. "Did you hear me, Miss Fairfield?"

She had looked up then. "Yes, sir, I heard you. But I know my brother is innocent of murder."

The tall man smiled unpleasantly. "Just remember the penalty for hiding a fugitive."

The door gave a protesting squeal as Chrissie opened it slowly. Inside, she shut the door and leaned against it, breathing heavily. Those dreadful men, how could she be sure they would not return a third time, perhaps when she least expected them? And there was another thing troubling her, this eerie sensation she had of being watched. The last might be her imagination, of course. She had looked carefully about her whenever she had occasion to leave the house, but she had seen no strange faces, only familiar ones. The men, these days, wore bright smiles, their eyes gleaming with anticipation of fighting the Yankees. The women, on the other hand, went about grim-faced, shadowed eyes mirroring a fear that they might not see their men alive again. Everything was changing, Chrissie thought with a surge of despair. She had a great fear that life would never be the same again.

Chrissie's hand shook as she lit the stub of candle in the iron holder. Pulling aside the matting that concealed the trapdoor, she thought of Frazer Phillips. He, too, would be going off to fight the war. It seemed that he could talk of nothing else. It was almost as though he had forgotten their love, the child she was carrying. She shook her head in negation of this last idea. Frazer loved her, she would always be in his heart, just as he would always be in hers. Dear Frazer, how sorely his conscience troubled him about Christopher, for by now, having listened to her spirited defense of her brother, he had come to believe that he had condemned an innocent man. Once, he had even cried in her arms, imploring her to forgive him for his part in the tragedy. Crying herself, she had begged him to be easy in his mind. Holding him close, she whispered lovingly, "You must not torture yourself, darling. You believed at that time that Chris was guilty."

"I will help you, Chrissie, I swear it. I will seek until I find the real murderer. You believe that, don't you?"

His pain had touched her almost unbearably. "Oh, my darling, of course I believe you."

Frazer had looked toward the bed set beneath the window, and his tear-drenched blue eyes had glowed with a familiar and exciting light. "Then prove it to me, my angel," he had whispered huskily. "Let me love you."

As if she could ever resist him. She stood very still while he undressed her, her body quivering under the assault of his stroking, knowing hands, but the question that troubled her increasingly of late crept once more into her mind. If he loved her so much, why didn't he marry her? Why did he only come to her when it was full dark, making sure that nobody saw him enter the house? Sometimes, though she tried hard to suppress the notion, she felt that he was ashamed of her. For the first time, as he settled her on the bed, she spoke aloud the thought that had been haunting her. "Frazer, why do you always come to me at night? Are you ashamed of me?"

His hands stilled on her body. "How absurd you are, Chrissie. I love you. You must know that."

Her arms twined about his neck, her fingers stroked his crisp blond hair. "Then marry me, Frazer. I don't like this skulking and hiding."

"What an odd way to put it. As usual, you are letting your imagination run away with you. As for marrying you, I will do so in my own good time." Frazer had spoken the words curtly, and he had been so angry that she had feared he would rise and leave her. Then, as her hands slipped lower, coaxing and fondling, the rigidity of anger left him. Murmuring her name brokenly, he had begun to kiss her almost frenziedly. "Open your legs, Chrissie. Hurry. I can't wait." Impatient of her slow movement, he pinched viciously at her soft flesh. "Chrissie, for God's sake, move." He plunged inside her, and, with a few hard strokes, spilled his hot seed. Although she had not been given time to feel her own ecstasy, it was on that night, Chrissie felt sure, that their baby had been conceived.

A faint movement coming from below caught Chrissie's ears, and she started guiltily. Christopher. How could she stand here thinking of Frazer, when her brother needed her? He was the only one who should now be occupying her thoughts. Her eyes misted. "Chris," she whispered, "you must get away safely. I'll die if they take you back to that awful place. Oh, Chris, I know how much you despise Frazer, but I can't help loving him. If only I could find the words to tell you how troubled in his mind he is, how guilty and ashamed of his own blindness. He is going to help prove your innocence, if he can, he has promised me. But I know you're not going to believe that."

In sudden panic Chrissie pressed a hand to her stomach. If her brother knew about the baby, he would kill Frazer. She caught her breath in a startled gasp. She must not think that way, not about Christopher. No matter what people chose to say about him, he was innocent of murder. He was good all through, and he had always been kind and loving to her. Only she knew of the deep sensitivity that he hid behind an unfortunate manner, one that had set him at odds with his father, and had started the neighbors talking against him. "That Christopher Fairfield," they whispered, "he's no better than us, but goddamned if he doesn't carry himself like he's a lord at least."

Hearing the whispers, Chrissie had defended her brother angrily. She loved him dearly, and no one was going to talk against him in her presence. But defend him though she could and did, her heart would sink as her brother, defiantly going from one scrape to another, continued to build for himself a scandalous reputation. Thus, when he had been accused of the murder of Charlotte Elliot, people were only too ready to believe it. When Christopher had been taken away to Buxton, their father broke under the strain. For all his harsh and forbidding manner, he had loved his son, and now he seemed to have no wish to live. Within two weeks of the date of commitment, he died. It was soon after her bereavement that Frazer Phillips had entered her life. How she hated him at first, and fought against the attraction he had for her. But she must not start thinking of Frazer again. Chrissie put her hand on the iron ring of the trapdoor. Exerting all her strength, she pulled upward.

Christopher looked up as the slight figure of his sister began to descend the steep ladder. She was very wet, her shawl was dripping, and her dark hair was matted and spangled with rain. He made a rueful face. Buried here in the deep cellar, he had not even been aware that it was raining. In fact, he had been aware of very little. How long had he lain here in the grip of the fever? How had Chrissie managed to keep him hidden? The prison guards must have come to the house, questioned her, searched the premises. Poor Chrissie, she had enough to bear, and he had not meant to add to it. He had wanted only to take a last farewell of her before he traveled on his way. Instead, he had been felled by the fever that attacked him intermittently. It was typical of him, he thought bitterly. He could never do anything right. He could only bring harm to those who loved him.

Chrissie reached the last rung of the ladder, and Christopher rose slowly to his feet. "Hello, little sister," he said softly.

Almost dropping the candleholder in her excitement, Chrissie swung around to face him. She found herself looking into dark eyes that were clear and alert. "You're better," she breathed.

Smiling, Christopher took the candleholder from her and placed it on the floor. "Much better," he answered. "The fever has not completely gone, but it's on its way out." By the increased circle of wavering light, he studied her intently. Her pixie pretty face seemed to him to have sharpened, and her big brown eyes were sunk in shadows. With her wet hair clinging to her small head and wisping in little tendrils about her face, she seemed older somehow, and terribly fragile. "What the devil have you been doing to yourself?" he said in a rough voice that disguised fear. "You look terrible."

Chrissie laughed shakily. "How like you, Chris. Will you never learn how to pay a compliment?"

"To a sister, I should say not."

"Oh, Chris!" Her eyes filling with tears, Chrissie cast herself into his arms. "I've been so worried about you. The guards came here and searched the house. I felt sure they would discover the trapdoor."

"Poor little kid," Christopher said tenderly, "you have been through it."

Chrissie shook her head. "Never mind about me, I just want you to be safe."

Christopher tightened his arms about her shaking figure. "You still believe in me, Chrissie?"

"More than ever! How can you even think of asking me a question like that?"

Christopher laughed at her vehemence. "All right, don't bite me."

"You suspected me, I know you did." She looked up at him with such an expression of hurt in her brown eyes that his heart twinged.

Remembering the lurking suspicion that had haunted him through his fevered dreams, Christopher was half-minded to dispel the hurt by denying her charge. Then, ashamed, he knew that only the truth would serve here; Chrissie knew him too well to be put off by an evasion. "I'm truly sorry, my dear," he said in a low voice, "my only excuse is that prison does things to a man. He is forced to live like an animal, and, like an animal, he quickly learns the habit of suspicion."

Her hurt expression changed to one of compassion, but still she could not forbear to say the words that crowded her throat. "But I'm your sister. I love you. I would never do anything to hurt you."

Christopher squeezed her tightly, eliciting a gasp. "Don't I know that, funny face." He tried for a laugh. "Come on, it was only for a moment. Hey, you've always known you have a fool for a brother."

"I don't know any such thing," Chrissie responded in a trembling voice. "I have the best brother in the world."

"No sentiment," Christopher said, laughing. "I would prefer that you gave me a tongue-lashing. I deserve it."

Chrissie shook her head. "What happens now, Chris?"

"You know the answer to that." He stroked her damp hair. "I'll be leaving tonight."

Chrissie gave a muffled cry of protest. "You can't go now. You are still weak."

"I must go, for your sake, as well as my own."

"Stay until tomorrow night," Chrissie pleaded. "I want to get some food into you, and you must get a good night's sleep." Her hand touched his matted beard. "Besides, I want you to shave off those b-beastly whiskers."

"Chrissie, listen to me. I'll do anything you say. I'll eat, I'll shave, but I must go tonight."

"Not tonight," Chrissie said firmly. She drew away from him. "It's no use glowering at me, for I won't listen to any argument. I brought you a dish of soup. It's upstairs." She hesitated, then looked at him with shining eyes. "Chris, I have an idea. Come to the house. I know you would rest better in your own bed."

"You're crazy, girl! Against my better judgment, I'll stay for one more night, but I won't come into the house."

Disappointed, Chrissie set her mouth stubbornly. "But why not? I'm not expecting visitors, and I think it will be perfectly safe."

Christopher shook his head. "I've tangled up your life enough, Chrissie. I stay here."

Seeing that he was not to be moved, Chrissie sighed. "All right. I'll bring your shaving tackle, and anything else you need. But how long will it be before I see you again? Will it be another four years?" Tears started to her eyes. "I don't think I could bear that."

"Chrissie, don't! I'll . . . I'll see you when I see you. It's the best I can say."

"Chris, why did you never allow me to visit you at the prison?"

Christopher turned away, unable to bear the sight of her forlorn face. "It was six months before I was allowed visitors, and by that time I was too ashamed to let anyone see me."

"Ashamed, Chris, or too bitter?"

He rounded on her almost savagely. "Yes, I was bitter, can

you blame me? There's another thing too. How do you think it's been for me, knowing that I killed Pa?"

"You didn't kill Pa."

"As good as." Christopher's dark eyes blazed in his thin face. "I might just as well have taken his throat between my hands and squeezed."

"Stop it!"

"Why? It was the shame of it that killed him, you know that."

"No, Chris, you're wrong. Pa could always hold up his head with the best."

"Can you tell me he believed in my innocence?" Christopher took a step toward her. "Can you?"

Chrissie saw the hunger for reassurance in his eyes, and her generous, loving heart reached out to him. "Not at first, Chris," she said softly, "but in the end he believed. He told me so before he died. He said, 'My son is wild, but there is no way he could have killed that girl. It's not in him.' "

"He s-said that?" Christopher's hands clenched. "Is that the truth, Chrissie, did Pa really say that? Don't lie to me, please."

"It's the truth, dear. I wouldn't lie to you about that."

Christopher looked at her for a long moment; then, as he read the truth in her eyes, his stiff posture relaxed. "Ah, Chrissie, thank God, thank God!"

Chrissie put her hands on his shoulders. "It was Pa's love for you, knowing that he could do nothing to help you, that's what killed him, Chris. And I think, too, that he could not bear to remember how harsh he had been with you in the past."

"I deserved his harshness," Christopher said gruffly. "I was a blind, heedless fool. I was always striving to prove myself, to be something that I was not." A picture of Desiree Grayson, warm and yielding in his arms, flashed into his mind, and he turned his head away. "Always wanting what I could not have."

Chrissie had seen the tears in his eyes, and she knew he was on the edge of a breakdown. Tactfully, she turned away and headed for the ladder. Christopher would never forgive her if she saw him indulge in the weakness of tears. "I'll bring the food," she murmured, "and put it at the top of the ladder. I'm going back to the house to fetch you some clothes, and your razor."

"Thanks." Christopher brought out the word jerkily.

With her foot on the first rung of the ladder, a sudden thought struck Chrissie. Did Christopher know about the war? Amazing as it seemed, he might not. Without turning, she said, "Chris, there's a war on. Did you know that?"

"War? What are you talking about?"

"The South is at war with the Yankees. General Beauregard fired on Fort Sumter on April 12."

"So it's come at last. I heard rumors, but I paid them no attention. The North and the South have been rumbling for some time, but I didn't think anything would come of it."

"Well, it has, we are at war." Still Chrissie did not turn. "Perhaps it is a way out for you, Chris. The South needs soldiers. You could change your name. Ma's maiden name would do, Christopher Wakely."

Hope warmed Christopher. Christopher Wakely. Another chance. With a war on, surely they would not continue so assiduously to hunt him down. With the South aflame, as it assuredly would be, what was one escaped convict. After the war, provided he lived through it, he could get away and start a new life. When things had settled down, he might even be able to send for Chrissie. With his eyes on his sister's slim back, he said briefly, "We'll see. Off you go, Chrissie. I'm starving."

"Chris, you seem so unmoved. Does it mean nothing to you that we are at war?"

"I've learned to hide my emotions"—Christopher answered her harshly—"but the fools have been itching to fight for some time now, so let them go to it. I'll tell you something, Chrissie, whichever side wins, it will be defeat for all."

Chrissie turned slowly and looked at the gaunt, handsome man who was her brother. "I don't understand."

"You will, dear, unfortunately. Think of it, a nation divided, fighting within its own borders. The bitterness will be a long time dying, if indeed it ever does."

"You are frightening me."

Christopher shrugged. "We should all be frightened. Civil war is a terrible thing. Chrissie, this news changes things. I don't know now where I will land up. But whatever happens, promise me that you will take care of yourself."

"I will," Chrissie said, nodding, "and you must do the same."

"If prison can be said to have taught me anything at all, it is how to fend for myself." Christopher hesitated; then he strode swiftly toward her. "Chrissie"—he put his arms about her—"I'm not one for soft words, so I've never told you this before, but I care deeply about what happens to you. You mean a lot to me, funny face."

Moved, Chrissie disengaged herself gently. "And you to me." Her eyes shone into his. "Remember that, please." In an effort to cut through the emotion-charged moment, she added lightly, "I can just picture you in your gray uniform. You'll distinguish yourself and come marching home in triumph. You'll be a hero, and everything will be forgiven and forgotten."

"A hero?" Christopher's dark brows rose sardonically.

"But of course." Laughing, Chrissie clasped her hands together. "All the men will be heroes, for you must know that we're going to lick those Yankees."

"Don't count on it."

"You don't think the South will win?"

"It's hard to say, but I should think it very unlikely."

"Oh, no, Chris, you're wrong. The South will win. Frazer says that we can't be beaten. He says the Yankees will . . ." Before the look in her brother's eyes, she broke off in dismay. "Chris . . ." She faltered. "I meant to tell you about—"

He cut her short. "Frazer Phillips? You've been seeing that man?"

"Chris, you don't understand."

"What is Frazer Phillips to you?"

Unconsciously Chrissie's hand sought her stomach, lingering there. He is everything to me, she wanted to say. I love him, and I am going to bear his child. Instead, frightened by the blaze in Christopher's eyes, she lied desperately. "N-nothing, he is nothing to me, Chris. He stops by now and again, that's all."

"Why?" Christopher's voice was hard.

Chrissie swallowed, her mind fumbling. "He's sorry about what happened to you," she brought out. "He . . . he believes now that he arrived at the wrong verdict." She clutched his sleeve with tense fingers. "Chris, I have made him see that he was wrong. He wants to help prove you innocent."

"Nonsense!" A white line about his mouth, Christopher pulled his sleeve free. "If you believe that, Chrissie, you'll believe anything." He looked at her with eyes that were suddenly cruel. "I have my own thoughts on Phillips. If you want to know the truth, I'm none too sure that he isn't mixed up in the murder of Charlotte Elliot."

She swayed, the color draining from her face. "Please, Chris, don't! I know you hate him, but you mustn't say such a thing."

"It was said about me."

"I know, but Frazer wouldn't."

"But I would?"

Chrissie put her hands to her head. "You're just trying to mix me up."

She looked so stricken that an unwelcome suspicion stirred. "Chrissie," he questioned her abruptly, "is there more to this than you've told me?" He drew in a deep shaken breath. "By Christ, you're not in love with that swine, are you?"

She wanted to defend Frazer, but she was afraid. With Christopher's hatred and suspicion blinding him, he would not stop to think of the consequences. He would seek Frazer out, and such an action on his part was almost bound to lead to his capture. She looked down at his scabbed wrists, and her heart twinged painfully. She could not let it happen, she must deny her love. Christopher must have his chance. She could not bear it if anything happened to ruin it for him. Certainly no words of hers must be allowed to do so.

"Answer me, Chrissie." His voice prodded at her distracted mind. "Are you in love with him?"

"No, no, why do you keep asking me that? Haven't I told you he means nothing to me? You needn't worry about Frazer Phillips calling on me, because he's going away to the war." She looked at him with tear-blinded eyes.

"If he means nothing to you, why are you crying?"

Chrissie rubbed her hand across her wet eyes. "Leave me alone. don't keep questioning me."

"Why are you crying?" he insisted.

Goaded, she turned on him. "Because you don't trust me, that's why." Openly sobbing, she bunched her wet skirts in one hand and fled up the ladder. "The soup's here at the top," her trembling voice drifted back to him, "don't let it get cold. I'm going back to the house now. I'll b-bring everything you need."

Christopher sat down slowly. It was obvious to him that Chrissie was in love with Phillips; she could not deceive him. Her lips might say one thing, her eyes quite another. Love! Not for one moment did he believe that Phillips returned the feeling. Poor little Chrissie, she was so vulnerable to a man like that. She was a dreamer, a romantic, she would believe his smooth line of talk was genuine. Christopher's hands clenched in impotent anger. By God, if that bastard hurt Chrissie, he'd hunt him down, and no matter what the consequences were to himself, he'd kill him. A memory of Chrissie's words came back to him, and his scowl lifted. Chrissie had said that Phillips was going away to the war. He felt a rush of relief. If that were so, and he had no reason to doubt it, it would take Phillips out of his sister's life. He would no longer be a problem.

Relief making him almost lighthearted, Christopher got to his feet. Seconds later, ravenously drinking the still-hot soup, he found his mind drifting back to Desiree Grayson. Had she raised the alarm yet? She had promised not to do so, but he did not trust her. Bitch, beautiful, treacherous bitch, fighting him one minute, yielding the next. Only a fool would trust her. Christopher's lips curled. God damn her anyway, she was nothing to him. Why waste his time thinking about her?

The soup finished, Christopher lay back on the pile of old clothes that did service as a bed. Drifting off to sleep, he saw the flame of Desiree's hair again, the luster of her violet eyes, and he felt the softness of her body beneath his. As sleep drew him further and further into misty toils, it seemed to him that she lay beside him, her haunting fragrance teasing his nostrils.

10

Chrissie roamed restlessly about the tiny parlor. Her green gown, robbed of its former crisp folds by the drenching it had received, clung to her slender body, outlining every curve. Her nervous hands straightened objects that were already perfectly aligned. She twitched at the patched red velour curtains, and arranged and rearranged the lace runners that protected the backs of the shabby chairs. Why, she wondered, did she feel so uneasy? Christopher, when she had said good night to him, had not referred to Frazer again, and any suspicion that he might have had seemed to be allayed. She could not understand why she felt so on edge.

A sudden terrifying thought striking her, Chrissie glanced toward the draped window. Was someone outside, watching the house? Immediately upon the thought, she started toward the window. If someone was outside, he would at least know she was alert. Her hand was actually on the curtain, prepared to pull it back, before, chiding herself for her foolish imagination, she let it drop. Seating herself in a wing chair, she folded her hands in her lap. In an effort to force her mind away from her present and unknown anxiety, she concentrated instead on her brother. How different he had looked, once he had shaved and changed into a decent set of clothing. Her mouth grew tender. He was thinner, of course, his cheeks had hollowed, and there were lines in his face that had not been there before, but he was still the same Chris; he had not really changed that much. Looking at him had been rather like going back into time. The thick, curling blue-black hair fell over his forehead; arresting dark eyes looked at her from a clean-shaven face; the deep voice, robbed of its bitter intonation when he spoke to her, teased and chided as always. Her brother had come back to her, but only for a little while. Tomorrow night he would be gone, and she might never see him again.

Chrissie blinked her eyes, dismissing the crowding tears. Rising, she went over to the gilt-edged mirror that hung above the mantelpiece and looked into it intently. Gazing, she smiled faintly. Chris and herself, they had always been so close, and yet they did not resemble each other at all. Chris, strikingly handsome, was like their dark and beautiful mother, while she, with her piquantly pretty features, resembled her grandmother on her father's side. No, she and Chris were not alike, but they loved and understood each other. That was why she suffered so for him now.

Sighing, Chrissie returned to her chair. Darling Chris, how she prayed that he would get away safely, that he would be happy at last. It was his unhappiness, his discontent with his lot in life that had got him into trouble in the first place. Chris had never shirked hard work, but he was not meant for the grubbing life of a sharecropper, and he knew it. He wanted something more, something challenging. Perhaps, when this war was over, he would find what he was looking for. She had a sudden and horrifying flash of her brother lying broken and bleeding on some gory battlefield, the light forever flown from his vital eyes, and she shuddered convulsively. Dead before he had had a chance to live. No, please, God, don't let it happen! Her mind turned to the other men she knew, Frazer among them. How they bragged, how eager they all were to get into the fighting. They would march away from Hawleigh County, drums pounding, flags flying, but how many of them would come back?

Blindly Chrissie picked up her knitting from the side table. Such dull colors, she thought, once more forcing her mind away from her fears. Her nose wrinkled. Socks for the soldiers, and the war hardly begun. Mary Loft, who was a leader, had flung herself enthusiastically into the project, and she had called upon others to show a like enthusiasm. "Sooner or later our boys will need socks," she had said, "and we might as well be well ahead of that need."

Going carefully along the line she had started in the early afternoon, her needles clicking, Chrissie decided that she hated dull colors. Mary Loft had insisted that the socks be either gray or black, but soldiers were human, and perhaps they would prefer more cheerful colors. When this point was brought to her attention, Mary Loft's piercing blue eyes had flashed imperiously. "Nonsense, ladies," she had said in her loud, commanding voice, "you really must be sensible. How would it look if the soldiers went about flashing red or purple socks, or some other equally bright color?" Pausing, her eyes resting on the flushed faces of the ladies, she added, "It is either black or gray. There, you cannot say that you haven't been given a choice."

Chrissie started out of her thoughts as a soft rapping sounded on the door. She dropped her work, her alarmed eyes watching the ball of gray yarn roll away into a corner before she could master her voice sufficiently to call out, "Yes, who is it?"

"It's me," a well-known voice replied. "Hurry up and let me in. It's damned wet out here."

"Frazer!" Joy lit Chrissie's eyes. Jumping up, she flew over to the door. After a moment of fumbling with the bolt, she pulled the door wide, letting in a gust of rain-laden wind. "Darling, what a lovely surprise. I wasn't expecting you."

Blinking at her from beneath his dripping hat, Frazer Phillips swayed in the doorway. "Lower your cursed voice. Do you want to ruin your reputation altogether?"

He was drunk, Chrissie thought, noting the slurring of his speech, but she was too happy to care. Taking his cold hands in hers, she pulled him inside. "Fiddle to my reputation," she said gaily, "come on in and dry yourself out."

Looking at her sourly, Frazer allowed himself to be led over to a chair by the bright fire. Seating himself, he was suddenly uncertain of his purpose. Chrissie had a great love for her brother; would it be wise to put her to such a severe test? And if it came to that, why should he want to do so? "Get me a drink, girl," he growled.

Hurt by his tone, Chrissie hesitated. "Don't you think you've had enough?"

"I'll say when I've had enough. Get it!"

Lolling back in his chair, Frazer watched with narrowed eyes as she went over to a cupboard set in a corner. Opening the fretted door, she extracted the bottle of brandy she kept especially for him. It was strange, Frazer thought, watching her pour the amber liquid into a glass, that something about her should remind him of the convict he had met in the forest some days ago, for there was certainly no resemblance. A gaunt man, the convict had been, tall and dark, with eyes that blazed from beneath a mop of shaggy hair. Words the man had spoken jumped into his mind, bitter, taunting words that had seemed to him to convey a threat. And all the while he had been seized with a sense of familiarity. Frazer's eyes turned to Chrissie again, and his heart jumped as he suddenly made the association. Christopher Fairfield! My God, could it have been? Sammy, his valet, had spoken of an escape from Buxton Prison. Perhaps he had even given the name of the escapee, but Frazer had been drinking more than usual that day, and he had not paid attention. Besides, there were too many other things to think about. The excitement of the events that had led to the war. Whether his new gray uniforms would fit him as perfectly as he hoped, the thrill of battle to come, Desiree Grayson, and his fruitless frustrating courtship of her. So many things, so why then should he spend his time thinking about some scum of a convict?

Frazer leaned back in the chair, his heart beating uncomfortably fast, transported back to that sun-dazzled courtroom of four years ago. Christopher Fairfield, standing to hear sentence pronounced, his broad shoulders beneath the shabby coat held stiffly, his head high. "Guilty!" the word seemed to ring through the room, and the onlookers, leaning forward, seemed like people suspended. The look in Fairfield's eyes as he turned his head and scanned every member of the jury. His lean, handsome face had been expressionless, but murder had looked from those eyes, a threat, a promise of vengeance.

"Your drink." Chrissie's voice startled him back to the present. Taking the glass from her, he drank thirstily.

Made uncomfortable by his brooding silence, Chrissie twisted her hands nervously. "Can . . . can I get you anything else, darling?"

"You can help me take off my boots."

Kneeling down, Chrissie grasped a muddy heel. Looking up quickly, she was startled by the flash in Frazer's blue eyes. "What is it, Frazer?" she said quickly. "Has something happened?"

"I shall be going away tonight. I am to join General Johnston at a place called Manassas Junction."

His booted foot fell from Chrissie's hands. "You will . . . will be fighting?"

"What else?" Frazer's teeth showed in a mirthless grin. "Somebody has to teach those Yankee bastards a lesson, and Johnston's just the one to do it." He leaned forward. "Chrissie, I want you to answer me truthfully. Has Fairfield been here?"

"My brother?" Her misery forgotten for the moment, Chrissie shrank back. "Why do you ask me that?"

"Don't you play games with me!" Seizing her by the shoulders, Frazer shook her fiercely. "Yes, your damned brother, who else? Has he been here? Answer me!"

Chrissie's heart accelerated. She could not tell Frazer that Chris was here. She had given him her word to tell no one. "I . . . I haven't seen Chris." She could not look in Frazer's eyes as she spoke the words. "Why would he come here?"

Frazer sneered. "He escaped from Buxton. I suppose you know that much?"

Chrissie's head rose, and there was a quiet dignity about her that immediately irritated Frazer. Glaring at her, he strained forward, dreading yet knowing the words that would fall from her lips. "Yes," she answered him, "I know that much. But nevertheless, my brother has not been here."

Even though he had been expecting it, the confirmation of his suspicion hit Frazer with freezing shock. He pushed back his hat with a shaking hand. My God, and to think he had actually faced him and not known him. His face flushed, and he shifted his eyes about the tiny room, half-expecting Christopher Fairfield to suddenly appear. "You lying little bitch," he ground out, "he's been here. You can't tell me he hasn't."

Chrissie half-closed her eyes, her heart squeezing in a spasm of pain. This was a Frazer she had never seen before. That look on his face, the look of a frightened, snarling animal, the terrible savagery of his words. Where had his sympathy gone? What had happened to his belief in her brother's innocence? "Frazer," she whispered, unwilling even now to let go of her illusions, "why won't you believe me? I tell you that Chris has not been here."

"You're a bad liar, Chrissie." Contempt looked from Frazer's eyes. "Fairfield's been here, all right, although I've not the slightest doubt that he's well on his way by now." A sneer distorted his mouth. "Helped, of course, by his little sister."

"What's happened to you?" Chrissie's wide brown eyes were like those of a stricken doe. "It's almost as though you hate Christopher. You said that you believed in him, that you wanted to help him."

Frazer did not answer at once. Waiting, Chrissie thought of it as a suspension in time, with only the loud ticking of the clock and the hiss and crackle of the fire to hold her to reality. Frazer's face was a blur, his opening mouth a black hole from which issued forth coarse and cruel words. "Help him, Chrissie, I'll do that all right, I'll help the bastard to hell!" He laughed loudly as she shrank from him. "What's wrong, girl, don't you like to hear the truth?"

The truth. Was that what she was hearing now? Her hands fluttered to her breasts, pressing down hard. Surely this was no more than a dream. It had to be, for she could not bear this pain of disillusionment. Her dry lips opened, and the words she uttered were a pathetic begging for reassurance. "Don't joke with me, Frazer. You . . . you said . . . you swore to me that you b-believed in Chris's innocence." Her voice broke on a wailing cry, and tears gushed from her eyes. "Oh, Frazer, tell me it was not all a lie."

He looked into her pale, shrinking face. The stupid fool, he raged inwardly, the miserable boring bitch. Enjoying the cruelty seething inside him, he said softly, "No, Chrissie, my sweet, it wasn't all a lie. I believe wholeheartedly in your brother's innocence."

The look in her expressive eyes changed from pain to bewilderment. "But I don't understand, you . . . you seem so angry."

The fumes of brandy mounted higher in Frazer's head, driving him on. What did it matter now what he said to her? Fairfield, if indeed he had been here, was far away by now. He no longer mattered. But Chrissie was here, with her big brown eyes that even now were appealing to him to make everything cozy and right in her narrow, poverty-stricken world. She was waiting for him to take her into his arms, to speak the words of comfort and belief she craved. His eyes fixed on her face, he said in the same soft voice, "I'm not angry, little love. What makes you think so?"

A shaft of anger penetrated her misery. He was playing with her. "I think I know anger when I see and hear it."

"All right," Frazer said, shrugging, "since you are so sure of my emotions, I won't attempt to deny your charge."

Chrissie seemed to Frazer's eyes to shrink, and he saw that she was once more a prey to uncertainty. "Was I wrong, then, Frazer, is it something else that is troubling you?"

Frazer's hands gripped the arms of his chair. Fairfield or him? The words boomed in his head. Now was the time to make his test. "Chrissie," he said in a low voice, "why don't you ask me why I am so certain of your brother's innocence?" He leaned forward, putting his face close to hers. "Go on, Chrissie, ask me."

Chrissie's heart leaped, then began to pound violently. She felt cold, and she was suddenly terribly afraid. She forced her words out with a supreme effort. "Tell me why, Frazer."

Putting his arms about her, he drew her close and rested his cheek against her soft hair. She knew, he had seen her knowledge in her face, and yet she had not resisted him. Even now she was lying quietly against him, ready to accept, to range herself on his side. She would crawl to him, lick his boots, she would do anything rather than lose him. "Of course I'll tell you, darling. The reason I am so sure of Fairfield's innocence is that I killed Charlotte Elliot. It was easy, Chrissie. Poor little terrified Charlotte, you should have seen her expression. There was no beauty in her then, let me tell you. She was so frightened that she couldn't summon up the strength to fight me. She just stood there staring and staring. Her eyes were so huge, just like two blue saucers. They went wider still when she saw the knife, and I thought they would surely pop out of her head. But do you know something, even then she didn't fight. Strange, isn't it? But you, Chrissie, you would have fought, wouldn't you?"

A stifled sound came from Chrissie. Frowning, Frazer tightened his arms about her. "You shouldn't mumble, Chrissie," he rebuked, "it makes it hard to hear you." He paused, waiting for a comment. When it did not come, he went on in an almost amused voice, "How very fortunate for me that your brother was the one to find Charlotte. Had it been someone else, someone, let us say, of more standing in the community, there might have been a bigger inquiry." He kissed the top of her head. "Well, sweetheart, they say confession is good for the soul. It must be true, for I feel better already."

Her face pressed against his chest, Chrissie lay there like one dead. With a tremendous effort she opened her shocked eyes. Why couldn't she move? she asked herself desperately. Had the sheer horror of what she had just heard affected her limbs? She tried to speak, but even her vocal cords seemed to be paralyzed. Frazer was the murderer. She heard his laughter, soft, drunken, triumphant, enjoying the bitter joke against her brother. Her mind scurried in frantic circles, seeking an excuse for him. He was drunk, he didn't know what he was saying, he was mad. Dazed, frightened, she clung to this latter solution for a moment, and then rejected it. No, there had been a ring of truth in his confession that she could not possibly ignore. He was certainly drunk, but instinctively she knew that he was not mad. How was it possible that she had never sensed the evil in him? Fool that she was, she had believed him to be everything that was fine and good. The ideal man. And now this. It was beyond bearing!

"Chrissie, angel, you're so still." Frazer's light voice erupted loudly in her ears. "Say something, my pet."

Her voice was a hoarse whisper. "Why did you kill Charlotte, what had that little girl ever done to you?"

Frazer laughed. "That's easily explained. Charlotte led me on, made me think that she wanted me. Then, when I took her, she changed. She screamed at me, told me that she was going to tell her father. I couldn't allow that, could I?"

A shuddering afflicted Chrissie, a rising nausea that she fought to control. Not for one moment did she believe him. She had known Charlotte Elliot well. She had been a sweet girl, slim, pretty, quiet of manner, and almost painfully shy. Frazer said that she had led him on. She knew he was lying. Her mind went to her brother. Picturing his haggard face, his tormented eyes, and his poor scabbed wrists, she felt as though she were breaking apart inside. Chris, who had treated Charlotte as a beloved sister, had paid for Frazer's crime. Her throat worked painfully. "Chris." His name broke from her on a sob.

Frazer had expected her anguish, and he was faintly amused by it, for he knew, once the first shock was over, that she would turn to him. Chrissie loved him so much that she would be ready to forgive even this. Besides, there were other considerations too, and being a woman, she would think of them. There was the baby she was carrying, the grand wedding she hoped for. Chrissie might mourn the injustice done her brother, but she would do nothing about it. Her mind would be concentrated on the bright future she would know as the wife of Frazer Phillips. No doubt she already saw the bastard she carried in her belly as the master or mistress of Woodgrove Plantation. His mouth moved into a scornful smile. The bright future she visualized was only in her dreams, it would never become reality, but he had no need to tell her that as yet. For the moment she had had enough revelations. Annoyed by her silence, he tightened his arms again. "Chrissie?"

Chrissie tried to pull away, but she felt too weak and ill. "Take your arms away," she said in a muffled voice. "Don't touch me!"

Frazer frowned. She was carrying the game a little too far. It was surely time for her to be coming out of her shock. He could deal with a storm of recriminations, but not this stiffness, this pronounced horror in her voice. Recriminations, bah! He would still them with his kisses. Trying to gentle his voice, he said patiently, "Now, Chrissie, that's enough. You know you don't mean what you say. You love me, I love you, it's as simple as that."

"And nothing else matters, is that what you would say to me? Do you really believe that, Frazer?"

Sure of his triumph, he dropped a kiss on her hair; then playfully he extracted the pins, laughing as her dark hair tumbled about her shoulders. "You know you are going to forgive me, my sweet, so why make a big drama out of the thing? As for your brother, it's not as though he is still suffering. He's free, Chrissie. Think of that. I would imagine he's put a lot of miles between himself and Buxton Prison. I know I would, if I were he. Fairfield might have his shortcomings, but he's certainly nobody's fool."

"You dare to say that? He was your fool. You saw to that."

Frazer sighed impatiently. "That was different, and you know it." His hand stroked her loosened hair. "The war has altered things. Have you thought of that? I doubt anyone will look seriously for Fairfield. It wouldn't surprise me if he got clean away."

"Oh, I hope so, Frazer. If Chris is to have any life at all, he must be away from his enemies. All his life he has been looked down upon, but in the end I know he will prove himself the better man."

Suppressing his anger, Frazer said rallyingly, "Perhaps it will be so. But anyway, all's well that ends well, eh, Chrissie?"

The rage that flooded Chrissie released her from her strange paralysis. Raising her head, she looked with unbelieving eyes into the fair handsome face bent above her. It was like looking into the face of a stranger. His smile was as vivid, his eyes as blue, and in the leaping firelight his blond hair shone with a silvery light, but he was a stranger. She had never really known him. Perhaps she had never really loved him either, for she was drained of all emotion save a burning and implacable hatred. The words she had been about to say strangled in her throat.

Misunderstanding, Frazer smiled at her, that same smile that had once turned her weak. "Poor Chrissie," he said, "I know it was a shock to you."

Her nails dug into her palms. "For four years you have let Chris suffer. Why do you tell me this now? Are you so sure of me?"

"Why, yes, Chrissie, I'm sure of you. You love me, you are carrying my child." His smile widened as he saw her hand go to her stomach. "Have done with these histrionics. I told you the truth because I wanted to prove something, and despite your hysteria, I think I have. Everything is going to be all right now, for all of us. The prison authorities will never catch up with Fairfield now, depend upon it. If he's the same one I heard about, he's been on the loose too long. The trail is cold. Doesn't that comfort you?"

It meant nothing to him, she thought, staring at him. He had ruined Chris's life, and he dismissed it with a smile. He had no conscience, no regret for what he had done. He was unbelievable. He was horrifying.

Frazer's smiling eyes went cold and dangerous. So she had chosen to take her brother's side after all. God damn the ignorant bitch! She looked crazy with her tumbled hair, her blazing eyes, the hectic spots of color staining her normally pale cheeks. Crazy, and somehow frightening. Frazer examined the thought, and then his scornful inner laughter chased the chill impression away. He must be wandering in his own mind to even entertain such an absurdity. He touched her rigid shoulder, unable to bring himself to believe that he had lost. She would come round. For her own sake, she had to. "Try to understand, Chrissie," he said in a gentle voice that was designed to bring back the loving girl. "Do you think I liked to see your brother go to prison? Of course I didn't. But when it came right down to it, Chrissie, it was him or me."

Frazer stared hard at Chrissie. "Your brother is tough," he said roughly. "He always has been. I knew he could take a prison term better than I." He saw her wince, and in an effort to recover his good humor, he smiled at her and gave a mock shudder. "Can you visualize me in prison? Why, Chrissie, it would have killed me." He stroked her shoulder. "You wouldn't have wanted that, would you?"

Shuddering, Chrissie thrust his hand away. How monstrous was this man's ego! And she had actually believed she loved him. "It would have killed you!" she exclaimed. "What do you think it did to Chris? Do you think he thrived on brutality? When I saw the terrible difference in him, I . . . I wanted to die. And you did that to him."

Frazer's eyes narrowed to blue slits. "Then you admit that Fairfield was here?"

Chrissie's heart jerked with fear. Despite his mock sympathy and his false regrets, Frazer hated her brother. If he knew that Chris was hidden in the cellar, he would go straight to the authorities. She knew him now, he had stripped her of all illusions. "Yes, Chris was here," she answered him in a hard, defiant voice. "He wanted to see me, and to say good-bye."

"Did he say where he was heading for?"

"He did not. Even if he had, do you think I'd tell you? He's beyond your reach, you can't hurt him anymore."

Her expression of scorn, her tone, caused Frazer's undying malice to emerge. "For his own sake, he'd better be long gone," he said in a loud voice. "Next time they lay hands on that cocky bastard, it'll mean a hanging."

Chrissie's tight control broke. With a violence that was utterly foreign to her nature, she launched herself at him. "It won't be Chris that will hang, you dirty murdering swine, it will be you!" Beside herself, she raised her hand and ripped at his face with her nails, tearing a long bloody track down his right cheek. "I'm going to tell everybody!"

Shocked, he could not move for a moment. The shy, gentle, loving girl, of whom he had been so sure, was gone. In her place was this vengeful virago with her hate-twisted mouth, her eyes that held a brilliant and almost insane glitter. "Stop it!" he roared, jerking his head back. "What the hell do you think you're doing?"

"You hurt my brother," she panted. "I will never forgive you for that!" Her eyes blazed in her blanched face. "Because of you, my father died of a broken heart. Everything I valued and loved was taken from me, but you didn't lose any sleep over that, did you? Three broken lives was nothing to you. You were safe, someone else was bearing the blame, and that was all that mattered to you!" Chrissie's face twisted. With tears misting the fury and hatred in her eyes, she struck out at him blindly. "Scum! May God curse you, you unspeakable swine. I hope you die in this war. I hope your last moments are tormented!" Her nails scored dangerously near his eyes, and she laughed hysterically as he swore aloud and jerked his head back. "You're going to suffer for every moment Chris spent in that hellhole of a prison, I'll see to that." Her voice rose to a scream. "If it's the last thing I do, I'll see you exposed for what you are. I swear it!"

"And it may very well be the last thing you do, darling Chrissie," Frazer snarled. His eyes watering with the pain of her attack, he grabbed her wrists and twisted them cruelly. "You'd best forget about telling on me, for I assure you that it wouldn't be wise."

Chrissie felt a spasm of terror at the expression in his eyes, but she continued to spit out defiant words. "You can't frighten me with your threats. I meant what I said. I will be heard, if I have to scream your guilt aloud."

Frazer's eyes narrowed. "You'll never have the opportunity."

She swallowed against the sudden dryness in her throat.

"Th-there's n-nothing you can do to stop me," she stammered.

"Nothing?" Frazer's tawny eyebrows lifted in amusement. "Come, come, my precious girl, you must know better than that." He smiled as she shrank back as far as his grip on her wrists would allow. Enjoying her fear, he said mockingly, "Ah, my darling, I see that you're getting the general idea."

Murder looked from his eyes. Frantically Chrissie tried to pull her wrists free. "Let get of me. I hate your touch!"

Anger flushed Frazer's face. "You're singing a vastly different tune now, aren't you? Chrissie Fairfield," he sneered, "so demure, so meek, that is the impression you try to give, isn't it? Well, no doubt you had to do something, if only to make up for that lousy, worthless brother of yours."

"Murderer, how dare you even speak of my brother, after what you have done to him."

Frazer ignored her outburst. "You don't fool me, Chrissie. You're a hot little bitch, all right. I only have to touch you in a certain way, and just like a little performing monkey, you're gasping and panting, ready to lie down on your back and open your legs wide." His eyes narrowed. "How many others have you performed for?"

Hurt shuddered through her, but her eyes flashed up to his with a burning message of contempt. "Why add to your sins, you filthy liar!"

Frazer laughed, the sound harsh and grating. "Liar, am I? We'll see about that. Maybe I'll touch you in that certain way, sweet one." His laughter rose. "I've a mind to be gripped between those white thighs of yours, a mind to watch those red buds swelling on your cute little breasts. Shall I kiss those buds, Chrissie? Shall I suckle them as you always beg me to do? That makes you scream with ecstasy, doesn't it? It makes you heave and pant and fling your legs wider still."

Chrissie's chest rose and fell tempestuously with things that clamored to be said; instead, she remarked quietly, "I don't have to listen to your drunken ravings. I want you to leave my house at once."

Her calm infuriated him. "You'll listen to me, Chrissie. For all your pious ways, you're no better than a whore. And you actually thought I would marry you!" He watched with gloating eyes as a tide of scarlet dyed her face and her throat.

"Well, you cheap little bitch," he said roughly, "what have you to say for yourself?"

The high color drained from her face, leaving her deathly white. "There is only one thing I have to say. You make me sick to my very soul."

Releasing his grip on her wrists, Frazer flung his arms about her and strained her close. She felt hot to his touch, as though her newborn hatred was consuming her, and she was shaking like one in the grip of a fever. His anger died as the jerky movements against his body roused a flood of desire. He felt himself hardening as he visualized himself plunging deeply into her soft body, and unable to bear the constraint of cloth against his springing rod of flesh, he held her tightly with one hand while with the other he unbuttoned the front of his tightly fitting fashionable trousers. Moaning faintly, he took her trembling hand and guided it downward. "Feel me, Chrissie, feel how much I want you." He forced her fingers about his tumid flesh. "It's waiting for you, sweet."

For a moment Chrissie's fingers were frozen about his swollen member. She felt the leaping and pulsing of urgent demand, and she snatched her hand away. "Oh, God!" Tears of horror jetted from her eyes. "How can you be so vile!"

Frazer did not hear her. His heart pounding, he pawed at her bodice. "Those tits, those beautiful tits," he said in a thick, slurred voice, "I want to see them, I want to kiss them. I want to see all of you." He felt the jutting of her nipples through the thin material of her gown, and he laughed triumphantly. "I knew it, Chrissie sweet, those little red spears are ready and waiting to fill my mouth." He squeezed her breast with cruel fingers. "Get your clothes off. Get them off now!"

Desperately Chrissie tried to pull free. "You'll never touch me again. Never!"

This time her words penetrated. His lips drawing back from his teeth, Frazer lashed her savagely across the face.

Filled with panic, blind with pain, Chrissie nevertheless continued to defy him. "Frazer Phillips," she panted, "cowardly scum, killer! We are all dirt beneath your high-and-mighty feet, or so you think. My brother is dirt. I'm dirt. But it's the other way around. You could not even begin to come up to Chris's standards." A sob broke from her. "Why didn't I see what you were? Why was I so blind?"

"Shut your fool mouth!" Frazer roared. "You hear me, girl?"

"I hear you." A burst of hysterical laughter shook Chrissie's slender frame. "I hear you, master, but this time I won't obey. Before I'm done with you, everybody will know you for what you are."

Frazer's violent push sent her toppling backward, to strike her head against the sharp edge of the iron fender. "I said take your clothes off, slut."

Chrissie's involuntary scream died to a gurgle in her throat. Faces whirled in her pain-blasted mind. Christopher's, dark and gaunt. Frazer's malignant and threatening. Frazer, whose desire menaced her, and lastly her father's face, old and tired and hopeless. She felt the warm trickle of her blood, and her hands twitched in horrified protest. The faces receded, dwindling to mere dots. Now her dying senses concentrated on the man moving purposefully toward her. Frazer, naked, his eyes lusting, his jutting penis held in his hand. Her breast heaved as she tried to speak, but no sound emerged.

Frazer looked curiously at the pale, soundlessly moving lips, and then he flung himself upon her. He ripped at her clothes, stripping her bare. For a moment his greedy gaze dwelled on her slight form with its almost imperceptible curves, the softly rounded breasts. His mouth drew in a nipple, suckling it. He heard her sighing breath, and he smiled to himself as his hands began tracing the curves of her body, caressing, moving intimately. He left her breasts almost reluctantly, trailing kisses downward until he reached the place where he would shortly enter. He lingered there, his tongue prodding, licking, trying to arouse sensation in the rigid form beneath him. He thrust his hands upward, his fingers crushing her breasts. Why didn't she move, why didn't she react? He raised his head to look at her. Her eyes were staring up at the ceiling. Curse her! How dare she ignore him? In fury and frustration he thrust the swollen, throbbing length of himself inside her and began to ride her savagely. She must react, he would make her!

Chrissie's staring eyes blinked once at this invasion. The man above her was deep inside her, shaking her pain-racked body with violent movement. His sweat dripped onto her face, rolling down her cheeks like tears, the sweat of this stranger whom she had once believed she loved. Charlotte's killer. The father of her unborn child! A cry came from her lips, and panting words emerged. "God help me, save me. Save Chris!" Once more she saw her brother, only a dim outline now. He was moving away from her. He must not go. He could not leave her like this. Her heart cried out to him: "Chris, Chris, Chris!"

"Move!" Frazer's voice snarled. "Bring your legs up, put them about me."

Chrissie gasped as she felt the world drawing away from her. Darkness enveloped her, smothering and somehow unbearably lonely. She could no longer see, no longer hear. Fighting terror, she opened her eyes wider, straining to pierce the darkness.

Frazer stiffened, then a convulsive shudder shook him as his hot semen ejected into Chrissie's body. Crumpling over her, he lay there panting, his body sticky with sweat, his heart thundering. Calming after a moment, he began to stroke her rigid arm. "Chrissie," he said in a softened voice, "how long do you think you can hold out against me? You don't hate me, you love me, and I want to hear you say it. Go on, say it." Confidently he waited for a response. When none came, he frowned and rolled clear of her body. "Now, Chrissie, I've had just about enough of this foolishness. Dammit to hell, your brother is free now, and if you expect me to spend my time feeling guilty, you . . ." The words died in his throat, and he felt a shiver of icy dread. "Chrissie!" Gingerly he touched her head, his stomach lurching as his hand came away sticky with her blood. Feverishly he bent over her and placed his ear against her heart. Nothing! Oh, dear Christ, he had threatened her, but he had not really meant to kill her. "I didn't mean it, Chrissie. It was an accident, you must understand that. God, God, you can't be dead!" He grabbed her hand, his fingers fumbling for the pulse in her wrist, and again he felt nothing. Dropping her hand, he slumped down, his eyes filling with tears of self-pity. First Charlotte, and now Chrissie. But he hadn't wanted to kill Charlotte Elliot, God knew that he had not. He had been forced to stop her mouth. Her babbling tongue would have brought disgrace on the name of Phillips, a name that had been honored these many years. It would have besmirched the memory of Hugh

Phillips, who had distinguished himself in the War of Independence.

Frazer looked down at Chrissie. Firelight flickered over her staring eyes, her drained face, and her colorless mouth. A strand of her hair, dangerously near a flaming stick of wood that had fallen from the grate, had begun to burn. With an inarticulate murmur of horror, Frazer picked up the stick and threw it back into the grate. Shuddering violently, he lifted the strand of hair and crushed the singed end between his hands. As God was his witness, he had not meant to kill Chrissie. It was an accident, nothing more than that. He thought of himself making love to a body that had died, and he averted his eyes, feeling violently sick.

The parlor clock began a slow and ponderous chiming, recalling Frazer to a sense of his own danger. He could not stay here, crouched over a dead girl; he must get away. It was eleven o'clock, late by these country people's standards, and it was possible that some nosy neighbor, seeing Chrissie's light still on, might decide to investigate.

Rising quickly to his feet, Frazer wiped his bloodstained hand on his handkerchief; then throwing it to one side, he dressed quickly. "I'm sorry, Chrissie," he said in a low voice. Without glancing at the still figure, he backed for the door, his mind a whirling confusion from which only two thoughts emerged clearly. Thank God he had elected to travel by night and that he had arranged to meet with his slaves at the crossroads. There was no need to go back to Woodgrove, he had settled his affairs there, leaving the plantation in the doubtful care of Magnus Baines. Baines was in his late fifties, and sometimes slipshod in his work, but he would do until Frazer returned to take up the reins again.

Sammy and Jimpson, the two stalwart Negroes whom he had chosen to ride with him, were plainly reluctant to go anywhere near the scene of the fighting, but they would be there at the crossroads, complete with all his gear. Whatever their feelings on the matter, they would not dare to disobey.

Frazer passed a shaking hand across his damp brow, his eyes avoiding Chrissie's crumpled form. He would be well on his way before her body was discovered, so no one could possibly connect it with him. Even if they did, the war would swallow him up. He frowned in concentrated thought. Of course, what a fool he was! Nobody knew of his visits to Chrissie. He had made very sure of that.

His body feeling light with relief, his hands steady now, Frazer opened the door. Rain struck his face, and a gust of chill wind took his breath away as he strode over to his drooping horse. His hand on the wet chestnut coat, he turned to look at the little house, reflecting that it might have been wiser to blow out the lamps. He took a step forward; then, changing his mind, he mounted and rode swiftly away. He was almost at the crossroads before the thought of Christopher Fairfield jumped into his mind. Fairfield again. A spasm of silent laughter shook him. God damn, but it always came back to Fairfield. When Chrissie's body was found, the blame would undoubtedly fall on him. Smiling, Frazer straightened in the saddle.

Christopher Fairfield awoke with a start. His heart pounding, he sat up and looked about the cellar. He had been dreaming, an odd jumbled dream in which faceless figures had come and gone. Frowning, he tried to remember details of the dream, but they blew away like mist, leaving an infuriating blankness. The only thing he could remember was the voice that had called his name wildly and repeatedly—"Chris, Chris, Chris!" He was not superstitious, and certainly he did not believe in the portent of dreams, but suppose something was wrong? That voice that had called to him—had it been Chrissie's voice, was she all right?

Trying to smother his uneasiness, Christopher glanced at the single candle, which had guttered low. The candle told him that it had been quite some time since he had last seen Chrissie. He wondered what time it was and how long he had been sleeping. Cooped up in this hole, with its all pervading smell of dampness and long-decayed vegetation, it was impossible to know night from day.

Christopher rose to his feet and prowled restlessly about the small space. He must get out of here, and soon. He thought of what Chrissie had said about a war and about the South needing soldiers. It was likely, in view of events, that the guards would not be looking too seriously for him. He could borrow his mother's maiden name, as Chrissie had suggested, join up with some regiment. Perhaps he would be killed, but anything was better than rotting away in prison.

"Christopher Wakely," he murmured, "damned if it doesn't have quite a ring to it."

He turned his head and looked longingly at the steep ladder that led upward to freedom. Freedom. His lips twisted into a bitter smile. Well, so it was, of a sort. If he climbed that ladder, he could breathe fresh air, lose the feeling of being entombed. He would do it, he decided, but he would be very careful not to endanger Chrissie by revealing his presence to others. Poor girl, she had been through enough on his account. Perhaps, he thought, his spirits rising rapidly, he would take a chance and go into the house.

Moving toward the ladder, Christopher experienced a surge of nostalgia for the shabby abode that had been the scene of so much unhappiness and bitter recriminations. Did the walls still ring with his father's harsh chiding voice? Or his own voice, hard and defiant, denying the tenderness stirred in him by the sight of his father's tired face—"It's no use, Pa, I can't be what you want me to be. I've tried, you know I have."

"Then what do you want?"

"I've told you over and over. I want to get out of this place, make something of myself. Is that so hard to understand?"

"Yes, it is. You have everything you need here. Maybe we ain't rich, but we don't have to go, cap in hand, begging for a crust of bread."

"Pa, you just won't understand, will you?" His father's deep sigh had made him feel guilty. Infuriated by the feeling, driven to cruelty, he shouted, "Do you think I want to be like you, grubbing in the ground for a bare existence, toiling to make the boss richer still? Pa, don't be so blind. All of your working life you've broken your back for other people. You love the land, but not one patch of it will ever belong to you."

"Be quiet. I don't have to take this from you."

"You don't like to hear the truth, do you, Pa? Look at you. You're not an old man, but you look old. That's the pity of it, you've grown old before your time. If we'd moved away from here like Ma wanted, gone to New York and taken a chance on a better life, Ma might not have died. It was the hopelessness of it all that killed her, Pa."

The high color faded from John Fairfield's face. His veined hands, resting on the back of a chair, trembled. The look he turned on his son was almost one of hatred. "By God, you swine," he said in a hoarse, shaken voice, "how dare you say that to me? I loved your ma, and you sit there and tell me I killed her!"

Something twisted inside Christopher. With a wish to get closer to this stubborn man who was his father, he said quickly, "Come on, Pa, you know I didn't mean it that way. I know you loved Ma, and that you would never have intentionally hurt her. But she wasn't country-bred, she had needs that could never be fulfilled in this place." He flung out his hands in a gesture that pleaded for understanding. "There must be something better than this. There has to be."

"You're a bloody fool, Chris. What else is there for people like us? You just be grateful that your ma insisted that we scrape together the money to give you a reasonable education. And that's more than our Chrissie will get, let me tell you."

Christopher's anger returned. "I am grateful, Pa, but must I waste that education? Just for once, will you listen to me? I'm—"

"No, Goddamn you, Chris, I'm tired of listening to you. Your head is stuffed full of daydreams, and nothing can possibly come of them. If you'd think things over sensibly, you'd know that for yourself."

"I could be a doctor. I have the feeling for it, you know that. Uncle Timothy said he would help me get started. He wrote you about it."

"You don't need that doctoring nonsense. You belong to the land. Look, why not take up your life from this point? Stop your drinking and gambling and your racketing around with your no-good friends. Ain't likely them no-goods can help you get what you want."

"No, that's true. They can't help me."

"Now you're making sense. There's not a lick of good in the lot of 'em, so why go on seeing them?"

"My no-good friends, as you call them, are a relief from the deadly boredom of this life."

John Fairfield's face tightened as he struggled to control his anger. He loved this difficult son of his, and ever since the boy had left his awkward teens behind, he had been afraid of losing him. Christopher, he saw, was watching him warily, anticipating his anger, and his dark eyes were so like Mary's that he experienced a painful pang. Mary lived again in her son. He couldn't lose him. "Look, Chris," he said, forcing a smile, "don't let's quarrel. You and me have had more than our share of harsh words."

"I don't want to quarrel with you, Pa, believe me."

"All right, son, I know that." Always afraid of emotion, John Fairfield went on hurriedly. "Try to make the best of things. Why not marry?" The forced smile became more genuine. "Lucky for you that you inherited your ma's looks. Don't hold with turning your head, but I got to say that you're a right handsome young devil. Maybe a mite too handsome for your own good. I've seen the girls looking your way, don't think I haven't. By God, it seems to me that the silly young creatures hang on to your every word."

Christopher stared at him. His father was not a gentle man, and if he loved his children, took pride in them, he had never shown it. He had always been grim, stubborn, rock-hard, opposed to change. He did not know him in this new, almost conciliatory mood.

"Can't I pay you a compliment, Goddamn you!"

Christopher grinned. The bellowing voice was more like his father. "Sure you can, Pa. What were you going to say?"

John Fairfield glared at him for a moment; then he relapsed into the new mood. "I was talking about marriage. You listen to me, Chris, there's a rare contentment in wedded life, and who should know that better than me? Before your ma took sick, we had a wonderful life together."

"Did you?"

"We did. You trying to say different?" His thick gray brows meeting in a frowning line, John Fairfield gave his son a hard suspicious look. "Reckon I know what you're thinking, but it ain't true. Oh, your ma was another restless soul like you. She was always on to me to take the job in New York that her brother offered me. Wouldn't do it, and it upset her some, but for all that, she loved me true."

Christopher's eyes softened. "Why didn't you take the job?"

"Wouldn't have worked. I told your ma that. City life would have killed me. Got to have open space and green fields about me. Why couldn't Mary understand that?"

"Maybe she thought you'd grow used to a new way of life,

even enjoy it. I do know that she loved you and that she was ambitious for you."

"Reckon she was at that." With a quick, almost furtive gesture, John Fairfield wiped his eyes on his sleeve. "Well, your ma's gone now, she's at peace. It's over and done with, and ain't a bit of use looking back. Anyway, we're talking about you. What about that Lilian King? She's pretty and smart, and she'd marry you like a shot."

Christopher's mind drifted to another girl. A girl with flame-red hair, with violet eyes and a slender perfumed body. Desiree Grayson, the beautiful, the desirable, the unobtainable. "Well, son," his father's voice cut in, "what about Lilian? Seems to me like you were sweet on her at one time."

Shaking his head, Christopher had forced his mind away from Desiree Grayson. "Lilian's a fine girl. She'll make some man a good wife. But that man won't be me. I don't want to marry, not yet. I've got places to go and things to do." He paused, looking at his father searchingly. "Pa, why wouldn't you let me go to New York? I could have made my home with Uncle Timothy for a while. He was willing, and I know he would have done everything he could to help me."

Losing his precarious hold on his temper, John Fairfield turned a dusky red. "There just ain't no reasoning with you," he had shouted, his voice booming through the tiny room. "All right, go. Ain't no one stopping you." His eyes blazing, he took a threatening step forward. "Go to New York, wallow in luxury. I don't give a good damn what you do!"

Over his father's shoulder, Christopher had seen his sister's white, frightened face peering around the door. Poor Chrissie, she would never grow used to the violent quarrels that so often erupted between her father and her brother. Giving her a small, reassuring smile, Christopher had forced himself to answer calmly, "I'm not interested in luxury, Pa. I just want the chance to work at something worthwhile."

John Fairfield noticed Chrissie, but he made no attempt to lower his voice. "Any time you take the notion, you can git. You and your big ideas and dreams. You've never been a lick of use anyway."

Sobbing, the fifteen-year-old Chrissie had burst into the room. "Tell Chris you didn't mean what you said." She gripped his arm with both shaking hands.

Releasing himself from her grasp, John Fairfield walked

over to the door. "Ain't nothing to say, Chrissie. Let the boy go his own way. He'll likely end up riding with the devil."

"He won't!" Chrissie had flown hotly to his defense. "And he's not a boy, Pa, he's a man. Sometimes I think you forget that he's twenty years old."

John Fairfield was unimpressed. "Don't you smart-mouth me, Chrissie. A man, is he? Well, then, let him act like a man. For a start, he can give up those lousy friends of his and settle down." His threatening gaze settled on Chrissie for a moment, and then swung to his son. "You heard me. Them are my last words on the subject. The rest is up to you."

Chrissie flinched as the door banged shut behind him. Bursting into tears, she flung herself into Christopher's arms. "Why must you and Pa always be fighting?" She burrowed her head against his chest. "I can't stand it, everything's been so awful since Ma died."

He stroked her rumpled dark hair, trying to soothe her. "I know how you feel, Chrissie, I'm sorry."

She raised her tear-streaked face and looked into his eyes. "If you're really sorry, Chris, why not do like Pa says? Give up running around with those awful boys. Please, Chris, I don't want you to get into trouble."

Gently, suppressing a slight spasm of irritation, he had wiped her tears away with his fingers. "Enough, Chrissie. I promise you that I'll stay away from trouble."

"You . . . you won't see those boys anymore?"

He sighed. "Perhaps not."

"And you won't go away? It would be terrible here without you." She glanced toward the door. "Pa would . . . would be worse than ever."

"He doesn't mean anything, Chrissie. It's just his manner. He loves you."

"He loves you too, Chris." She peered at him eagerly. "He really does."

Christopher shrugged. "I doubt that."

Chrissie had made no effort to convince him. Perhaps, from past experience, she had known it was useless. The breach that had opened between him and his father was rapidly widening. Instead, she said in a small voice, "Promise me that you won't go away."

"I can promise you that." Christopher made a wry face as he renounced his dreams. "No matter what Pa thinks of me,

I couldn't just walk out. I'm old-fashioned enough to want his blessing."

Christopher's eyes misted as the voices in his head faded. Poor Chrissie. First he had been taken from her life, and then their father. How lonely she must have been. Just like their father, Chrissie had feared the bad influence of his friends, but in the end they had nothing to do with his downfall. It was when his friends had planned the robbery at Dudleyville that he made up his mind to break with them once and for all. He had joined them in their wild parties, their gambling, and their drinking, taking it all in his stride, for his presence at these affairs had been largely defiant, the outward sign of his revolt against what he considered to be his frustrating life. But when it came to outright crime, he found that he could not do it. His refusal to participate had been taken in good part by his companions, and they had agreed to go their separate ways from then on. They were aware of Christopher's disapproval of the turn their activities had taken, but they knew they could trust him not to give them away.

It might have been a misplaced loyalty, Christopher thought now, but at the time he felt he owed them that much. The robbery had taken place as planned, and Christopher, looking on from a distance, knew that it had gone without a hitch. Then came the tragedy of Charlotte Elliot.

Christopher leaned his head against the ladder, suddenly overcome with the futility of his life thus far. His hands gripped the sides of the ladder, his mouth tightening in the habit of repression so painfully acquired at Buxton Prison. A man, Chrissie had called him. Well, perhaps he had seemed so to the fifteen-year-old Chrissie, but he had been only a sullen and defiant boy, just entering manhood. He had deliberately sought trouble, but trouble had turned about and found him first, and in a form far more terrible than he could ever have conceived.

Level with the trapdoor, Christopher pushed at it with one hand. It resisted for a moment, and then clattered back with a squealing of rusty hinges. He froze. Recovering, he gave a rueful smile. He had no doubt that the fear of discovery would be with him for some time, but eventually, if his luck held, he would get over feeling like a hunted animal. His smile vanished, and his lips tightened with resolution. He had fought his way to freedom through the almost impenetrable forest, and no one was going to take away that freedom and cage him up again. Almost relaxed now, he climbed out. Carefully lowering the trapdoor, he replaced the matting. He considered lighting the candle that was always left for convenience on the long wooden table. Deciding against it, he fumbled his way to the outer door.

Outside, it was still dark, the kind of dense darkness that precedes dawn. Standing in the open doorway, shivering in the chill air, Christopher remembered the many times when, unable to sleep, he had stared into the smothering darkness through the slitlike window of his prison cell. Soon now the sky would begin to gray in preparation for the dawn. The first fragile streaks of color would appear, misty and unreal, the heralds for the glorious blazing panorama that was to follow. How often, looking at this wonder, had he wanted to die. His hands tensely gripping the prison bars, he would tell himself that if he could not see and feel and experience life in freedom, then he was better off dead.

Firmly closing his mind against grim memories, he stepped forward. Now was all that counted, and what he would become. He put out a tentative hand. The rain had stopped, but the trees overhanging the washhouse still dripped heavily, drumming on the tin roof and dimpling the puddles beneath. He hesitated, momentarily considering the wisdom of his action; then he started down the cobbled path.

The small house, previously hidden by a bend in the path, loomed suddenly out of the darkness, a bright beacon in the midst of its dark and silent neighbors. Uneasily Christopher moved toward it. Why were the lights still on? Had Chrissie fallen asleep before the fire? Mounting two creaking wooden steps, he entered the porch. "Chrissie, it's me," he called in a low voice. He tapped gently on the door. "Let me in."

He waited, listening intently, but there was no stir of movement from within. His hand raised to tap again, he let it drop and cautiously turned the handle instead. He was startled when it gave under his hand. That Chrissie, the little fool hadn't even bothered to bolt the door. What the devil was she about? "Chrissie?" Thrusting the door wide, he stepped into the room. The scene that met his eyes hit him with the force of a physical blow. Chrissie lay on her back before the almost dead fire, her wide-open sightless eyes staring up at the ceiling, her arms outflung.

His knees suddenly weak, Christopher clung to the doorjamb for support, his horrified eyes going to the crumpled, bloodstained handkerchief that lay beside his sister. Stumbling forward, he dropped down beside her. She couldn't be dead. Hardly knowing what he was doing, he picked up the handkerchief. His shocked brain registered the raised blue initials at the corner of the soiled linen—F.P.—but it meant nothing to him. Thrusting the handkerchief into his pocket, he turned tormented eyes on the pathetically sprawled body of the one being he had truly loved. Refusing to believe in the evidence of death, he examined her with shaking hands, praying for signs of life, but knowing even as he did so that his prayers were quite useless. Shuddering, he felt the death chill of her flesh, looked into the wide, unseeing eyes. His fingers touched the clotted blood at the base of her skull, and her name broke from him in a great grieving cry. In his agony, he snatched her into his arms and rocked her to and fro. Now he knew whose voice had called to him in his dream. It had been Chrissie, dying, desperate, urgently trying to communicate with him.

Even as his tears fell on Chrissie's soft hair, there was something teasing at his mind, growing, becoming a finger of fire, prodding, insistent. F.P? F.P? "Frazer Phillips!" he exclaimed on a shaken breath. Phillips had done this. There was no room in his mind for doubt; instinctively, he knew.

Christopher's arms tightened about the little figure, and then, very gently, he laid her down. Frazer Phillips, whom he was now certain had murdered Charlotte Elliot, had laid those same murderous hands upon his sister. Where was Phillips now? Would he be at Woodgrove, hiding behind the sanctity of his name, believing himself to be perfectly safe, or would he have fled, realizing that this time he had gone too far?

Bending over his sister, Christopher drew down her lids and tenderly smoothed her hair about her waxen face. A sob caught in his throat as his mind filled with pictures. Chrissie, laughing, teasing him, her face radiant with the joy of living. Chrissie, mourning for him, believing in him, when no one else would believe, comforting him, trying to erase his bitterness with gentle words, and always, despite everything, loving him. Chrissie, who would never speak to him again.

Christopher touched her cold hand with quivering fingers. "I'm going to find Phillips, Chrissie. I will, don't you worry." His dark eyes, dulled by the tears he had shed, now awoke to blazing, avenging life in his gaunt face. "It doesn't matter where he is—Woodgrove, or someplace else—he can't hide from me. I'll track him down, and I'll kill him!"

11

Desiree swept down the stairs, her wide bell skirts swaying with her movements, her multicolored petticoats frothing and rustling about her small silk-slippered feet. Despite the unusual fear afflicting her at present, for never before had she had occasion to fear her father, her head was held very high, and hectic spots of color burned in her cheeks. There would be an ugly scene with her father; it was inevitable. It had been postponed by the arrival of visitors, two young men who were to accompany her father to the military post, but now the moment had finally arrived when she must face him. Her heart shivered as she remembered the way he had stared at her. There had been such hostility in his eyes that she had turned from him in pain and rebellion. Climbing the stairs to her room, Tildy fussing behind her, she could feel his eyes boring into her back. Surely he would not judge her without hearing her out. And yet that look, it had been that of an enemy, rather than a father's.

Pausing at the bend in the stairs, Desiree looked down into the hall. The hall, usually bustling with the comings and the goings of the domestics, was deserted. Only Wilmers, grave and majestic as always, stood at his usual post. No doubt,

Desiree thought, the tactful Wilmers had found jobs for the servants that were away from this part of the house.

Wilmers turned his head and looked toward the stairs, and Desiree, not wanting to be seen at this moment, stepped quickly behind the bank of flowers at the stair bend. Uncertain, ashamed of the cowardice that had prompted her action, she stood there, her limbs faintly trembling. She, who had faced so many dangers, was like a fearful child when it came to facing her own father. An hour ago, receiving a message from the agitated Wilmers that her father wished to see her in the library as soon as convenient, she had managed to thank the old butler with every appearance of calm. "You may tell my father," she had added in a steady voice, "that I will be with him as soon as I have completed dressing."

Wilmers' eyes had traveled over the quilted dressing robe she wore, with some surprise. "But it late, Miss Dessi," he ventured, "maybe you could see your daddy like you are."

Desiree's smile belied her inner turmoil. "Nevertheless, Wilmers, I prefer to dress."

With the aid of the sleepy Juniper, her maid, she had selected her costume very carefully. It was essential, she thought, that she look quite perfect for the upcoming dreaded scene with her father. Juniper brushed her mistress's red hair until it gleamed and crackled, then piled the fiery tresses high, her skillful fingers making a mass of soft curls. The back hair had been braided into a crown from which long glossy ringlets descended to touch her faintly sun-tinted shoulders. Her silken gown, the same color as the amethysts that swung from her ears, was embroidered about the low, square neckline and the extravagantly sweeping skirt with double borders of tiny violets. She looked fragile and very feminine, and her appearance, carefully contrived in the hopes of appealing to her father's chivalry and somewhat appeasing his fury, was the only weapon she had to use at this moment.

Juniper, watching her mistress move toward the door, suddenly burst into noisy tears. Running across the room, she clutched at a fold of the amethyst gown. "Miss Dessi," she wailed, "don't you go down there. Wilmers tellin' me that the master went clean crazy when that no-good Clover told on you. Please, there just ain't no knowin' what your daddy will do to you. He ain't never goin' to get over knowing you are the Flame!"

No, Desiree thought, he would never get over it, never forget. Her activities as the Flame had struck a blow at Elton Grayson's patriotism and pride. She, his own daughter, had not only menaced his safe and comfortable and unthinking way of life, but had done likewise to the lives of his friends. She thought once again of the hostility in his eyes, the rage in his face, carefully controlled into an expressionless mask when the visitors had entered, and she wondered if he would ever be able to bring himself to forgive her. Desiree's teeth worried at her lower lip. It would be hard for him to forgive—she accepted that—but surely not impossible. At this sign of weakness within herself, Desiree's back stiffened. She wanted her father's love, but she did not require him to pardon her for doing something about the slaves, something that seemed to her to be humane and right.

Looking into Juniper's tear-streaked face, Desiree had said in a firm voice, "I am going down to my father, Juniper." She smiled slightly. "At least we have one thing to be thankful for, Clover did not inform upon you and the others."

Taking a deep breath, Desiree stepped from behind the flower bank and descended the rest of the stairs. Juniper was no doubt still weeping, but she must not let the girl's frantic fear affect her now. Calm, she told herself firmly, you must be calm.

Reaching the bottom of the stairs, Desiree glanced across at Wilmers, and the sympathy in his face recalled that moment when she had entered the house, with the nervous Tildy hovering behind her. Her ringed fingers tensed on the satin-smooth wood of the handrail. Wilmers, his rich black complexion faded to a sickly gray hue, had been hovering in the hall; behind him were clustered several weeping servants. From the open door of the library she had heard her father's roaring voice. "You filthy black slut, how dare you lie about your mistress!"

Clover's answering voice came to Desiree's wincing ears, whimpering, terrified. "You got to believe me, master, I swear I wouldn't tell you no lies about Miss Dessi."

"So my daughter is the Flame, is she?" Elton Grayson's voice, heavy with menace, dropped slightly. "You know what will happen to you if you're lying. Tell me again how you found out about my daughter." Now the menacing voice cracked like a whiplash.

"I told you, master."

"You'll tell me as many times as I demand, and after I've proved you're lying, I'll have your black hide stripped from your bones and nailed to a wall."

There was a scuffling, the sound of a chair thudding heavily to the floor, followed by Clover's piercing scream.

"Get on with it."

"I seen Miss Dessi that night." Clover's voice rose, shrill with fear. "She was dressed up like a man, and she was with some nigger I ain't never seen before. He was a big man, and he called Miss Dessi the Flame. He said she bring hope to all the black people."

"And that's your proof?"

"Miss Dessi wasn't mad when he call her that," Clover babbled, frantic to convince. "She like it, and she git to laughin' with that nigger. Then they start up talkin' about all the black people they help to get North."

There was a long pause, during which Clover's sobs reached a pitch of hysteria. Then Elton Grayson's voice cut across her wailing. "Wilmers," he shouted, "are you out there?"

Shaking visibly, the old man had stepped forward.

"Send someone to find your mistress."

Wilmers looked at Desiree, a sheen of tears in his eyes, mutely asking her what he should do. He was afraid for her, and that same fear was reflected in the faces of the others. Desiree gave him an encouraging nod and forced her dry lips into a smile. "M-Miss Dessi here, master," Wilmers quavered.

Tildy's arm went around Desiree's shoulders as Elton Grayson appeared at the library door. His face was very pale, Desiree saw, and a vein throbbed heavily in his temple. He ignored Wilmers and the frightened servants, and his eyes went straight to his daughter. "You heard Clover?" he questioned abruptly.

"I . . . Yes, I heard."

"Is it true?"

Desiree felt Tildy's arm tighten about her shoulders, and for a wild moment she thought of denying it. The impulse passed, and she answered him in a low voice, "Yes, Father, it's true. I am the one known as the Flame."

Elton Grayson stared at her, his eyes incredulous; then, his face flushing scarlet, he started forward. "Why, you . . . you . . .!" He broke off as a bustle was heard outside. "Who the devil can that be?"

"Visitors, suh." Wilmers' voice shook with relief. "It's those gentlemen you was expecting."

"Oh, Christ, what a time for them to arrive. Since they're here, you'd best show them in, Wilmers." He glared at the servants. "What are you doing here? Get back to work at once."

A flap of Wilmers' hand sent the servants scuttling away. Composing his features, the butler walked with slow, majestic stride toward the door.

"Get to your room." Elton Grayson had addressed Desiree curtly. His face a study of mingled bewilderment and rage, he turned away. "Go on, get out of my sight. I'll deal with you later."

"Miss Dessi . . ." Wilmers' deep, soft voice brought Desiree back to the present. "You're always beautiful, but tonight you're somethin' special." He chuckled as Desiree turned for his inspection. Now the smile lightened his somber eyes as he, in his turn, sought to reassure her. "Lookin' like you does, cain't hardly think your daddy stay mad with you for long."

Desiree smoothed a fold of her amethyst gown and looked at him with tender eyes. "Only time will tell us that, Wilmers. Well, I'd best go and get it over with."

Elton Grayson, seated at his desk, rose to his feet at his daughter's entry. Tall and unfamiliar in his gray uniform, his face set in severe lines, he indicated a chair.

Obediently Desiree seated herself. Conscious of the rapid beating of her heart, she tried to speak lightly. "Well, Father, here I am."

Elton Grayson regarded her grimly. So beautiful, so feminine, this daughter of his, and such an enigma. Had he ever really known her? he wondered painfully. Feminine. His mind grasped at the word again, and he felt a stir of hope. Yes, most assuredly she was feminine, too much so to have done this thing. It was just not possible. Of course, he had always known that there was both strength and an unbreakable will beneath her deceptively fragile appearance, but surely not the kind of strength required to organize a freedom movement and to sustain a double identity. But on the other hand, she was capable of playing a part. He was aware that she often did so with him, subduing her naturally fiery spirit in an effort to please him. It had amused him to see his Desiree sheathing her claws, in a parody of a meek and obedient daughter. This thing to which she had confessed must be some kind of a monstrous joke; it had to be. Desiree met his eyes with seeming calm, and once more he found himself torn by doubt. Massaging the stabbing pain in his left arm, he spoke to her abruptly. "You have put me through a great deal in the past, but this goes beyond everything. Clover lied, that's it, isn't it? You were afraid for her, and so you backed her up." With an effort he forced himself to smile. "You have always been ridiculously soft where the Negroes are concerned, and I'm quite sure they take advantage of you."

Unable to bear his fixed painful smile, the unconsciously pleading tone that was begging her to reassure him, Desiree turned her head away. With the memory of the earlier hostility in his eyes serving as a guideline, she had expected recriminations from her proud, hot-tempered father, perhaps violence, anything but the actuality. It had simply not occurred to her that he, for the sake of his own peace of mind, would refuse to believe. "Desiree"—his voice prodded at her again—"Clover did lie?"

Desiree picked up her fan, her fingers playing nervously with the lacy folds. Now, for his sake, she knew the way she must go. He wanted a denial, and she would accommodate him, but not at the price of the black girl's life. "And if I tell you that Clover lied," she answered in a measured voice, "what will happen to her?"

"Why should you care what happens to her?" A trace of tightly reined-in fury tinged Elton Grayson's voice. "She is a vicious, lying slut and she must be punished."

Desiree looked at him. "But I do care. I don't want her punished."

"Desiree, you ask too much! I can't let her go on spouting such wicked nonsense."

Desiree's soft mouth hardened slightly as she thought of Clover. She did not care for the girl, and the instinctive mistrust she had felt had been amply justified, but she could not stand by and see her punished for telling the truth. "If you will leave Clover to me," she said slowly, "she will not repeat her words, I assure you."

Elton Grayson was silent for a moment; the prominent vein in his temple throbbed as he struggled with an emotion that bade him to slash out savagely at the black girl who had shattered him; then he said reluctantly, "Very well, I must trust you to deal with Clover in your own way."

Desiree breathed a sigh of relief. Clover would be safe now. Looking at her father's drawn face, his uneasy eyes, she felt a wave of love. He had always been a man of principle, rigid in his beliefs, strong when it came to doing what he conceived to be his duty, and he must be suffering now because he had allowed his love for her to temporarily weaken him. He knew she was the Flame, and although he did not realize it, the one thing that betrayed the inner knowledge that he was so intent upon smothering was his utterance of her full name. She had always been "Puss" to him, sometimes "Dessi," but unless he was angry, uncertain, or, as obviously in this case, frightened, she was never "Desiree."

"Well"—her father's impatient voice broke in on her thoughts—"do you admit that the girl lied?"

Desiree's gown rustled as she rose to her feet, and a waft of delicate fragrance teased Elton Grayson's nostrils. "Yes, I admit it." Desiree hesitated, uncertain of what she should say now. "Clover is a foolish mixed-up girl," she resumed, "but there is no real harm in her." She smiled faintly. "Perhaps she should have been a writer of romantic fiction, like our celebrated Mrs. Dulcie Beauford." She saw her father staring fixedly at her, and she hurried on. "What I mean is, that Clover makes up romantic tales in her head, and sometimes comes to believe them." The smile touched her mouth again. "No doubt Clover singled me out to be the heroine of one of her tales."

Elton Grayson's hands clenched at this patently false explanation of what might have motivated Clover. "Romance!" he exclaimed, unable to resist the thrust. "If you ask me, the girl is crazy. And another thing, Desiree, there is nothing romantic about this so-called Flame. He is a renegade, a damned scoundrel, and he ought to be hung!" He looked at her sharply. "You agree?"

Desiree flushed. "I have never thought much about it."

Elton Grayson let out a shuddering breath. What childish

game was he playing now? She had said the words he wanted to hear, and it was best not to dwell on the touchy subject of the Flame. How strange, he thought bitterly, at this moment of his relief, that he should know beyond any doubt that it was indeed the daring and audacious Flame who confronted him now, his own daughter. How had she dared to go against all the values and traditions in which she had been brought up? What had been her thoughts when he and his friends had railed against the Flame? And what of the slaves of Twin Oaks—were they involved in his daughter's incredible daring? Hastily, becoming aware that Desiree was waiting for him to speak, he said lamely, "Thank you, Desiree. I knew you would eventually tell me the truth."

Desiree hesitated, wondering how he would receive the caress she longed to give him. He was her father, and she loved him dearly. It might well be that she would never see him again. Feeling cold and lonely and bereft, she half-turned to the door. "Where are you going?" Elton Grayson broke the silence.

Desiree turned quickly. "I . . ." She waved her hand vaguely. "To my room. It's . . . it's very late."

He could not part from her like this, his lovely girl who had so unaccountably turned against her own kind. "I shall be going away in the morning, child," he said huskily. "Won't you wish me well?"

Child. It was better than the coldly formal "Desiree." "I know." Desiree's voice broke. With a muffled cry she ran to him and threw her arms about his neck. "Of course I wish you well. I love you very much."

Just for a moment he stiffened, remembering the loss of several valuable slaves to the Flame, the mocking notes that had been left behind, adding to his frustration and anger. There was the solemn vow he and his friends had made to hang the Flame from the highest tree, the immense reward promised by them to anyone who should bring in the Flame alive or supply them with information leading to his capture. As his daughter's arms settled about his neck, other questions pelted his mind. How had it been done? Slaves had vanished, but there had never been a whisper of sound to betray an alien presence, never a clumsy movement to alert the dogs.

"Father . . ." Desiree made a small restless movement that sought his attention.

Answering her unspoken question, he put his arms about her and held her close. "I love you too, Desiree." It was true. Whatever she had done, whatever dangerous ideals she had subscribed to and put into practice, she was his daughter, and he could not stop loving her.

Desiree, who despised tears, cried openly now. "I . . . I will miss you," she gasped. "Twin Oaks will not be the same without you, and I shall be lonely."

Elton Grayson's arms tightened about her. Earlier, after the frightened and sobbing Clover had huddled in a corner, waiting for him to give her permission to leave, he had been conscious only of the blind fury occasioned by his daughter's calm confession. Forced to restrain himself and hold his fury in check by the arrival of Paul Drake and John Newton, he had willed his first violent reaction to cool. He had known then, in the light of what he had learned about her, that he could not leave Desiree alone at the plantation. And there were other things to be considered. He believed, if the war did not get him, that his failing heart would. No, he would never return to Twin Oaks alive. His daughter's future was assured, for he had not the time for or the intention of disinheriting her. After his death, Twin Oaks would be hers, as well as several smaller properties and a fortune in cash and bonds. But it was not the future that worried him at this moment, it was the now. After his two young guests left, both in a high state of intoxication, and anticipation of the war they would escort Elton Grayson to, promising to meet with him at Twin Oaks just after dawn, he had sat down to think out the problem that Desiree now presented. When the answer finally came to him, he wondered why he had not thought of it before. Summoning one of the grooms to him, he had sent him riding off with a message for his sister, Clara. From now on Desiree must be watched, she must be guided in the way she should go, and she would be allowed only those friends who passed his sister's inspection. He had every confidence in Clara's ability to handle her headstrong niece, for his sister had developed from a pious and rather boring girl into a saintly and determined woman, especially when it came to the question of doing her duty by her family. "Desiree," he said softly, "I can promise you that you won't be lonely, my dear. I've arranged things so that you will be in the constant company of girls of your own age, or thereabouts."

"Girls of my own age?" Desiree questioned, drawing away from him. "What do you mean?"

"I sent Ben off with a message to your aunt, asking if would be willing to take you in for the duration of the She replied that she would be happy to do so."

"Aunt Clara!"

Elton Grayson gave an uneasy laugh; he did not sudden blaze in Desiree's eyes. "I know you don't par care for your aunt, but there is no need to look so Anyway, it's all settled. Your aunt will be here in ing. See to it that you are packed and ready to go."

At his suddenly imperious tone, the blaze in De intensified. "Nothing is settled. I won't go!"

Elton Grayson sighed. In the end he wou way—a girl did not defy her father—but he di battle of words with her. Desiree, unlike the a ters of his friends, had always been difficult course you will," he replied. "In any case, you for long. The war will be over in a matter maybe less. In the meantime, it will relieve you are safe with Clara."

"Dead, you mean. I shall die of boredo Clara. She is a self-righteous cold-natured p

"That's enough! You will speak of your aunt

"Father"—Desiree spoke through gritted teeth— twenty years old, in case you have forgotten. I will not be treated like a child."

"I have decided what is best for you, and there is no more to be said."

Desiree trembled with the force of her anger. How dared he do this to her! She had responded to his unspoken appeal for reassurance, and he had pretended to believe her, but it seemed that he was determined to punish her. To be banished to her Aunt Clara in disgrace—it was more than she could endure! Her Aunt Clara was the mother superior of St. Luke's, a small teaching convent ten miles beyond Hawleigh County. She was a pale, stern, humorless woman with a great dislike for her niece, which she kept hidden behind her irritating air of piety. This dislike was returned by Desiree in full force, for she had always detested the woman. There was no warmth in her, no understanding, and she was unlike her father in every way. "You can't force me to go to St.

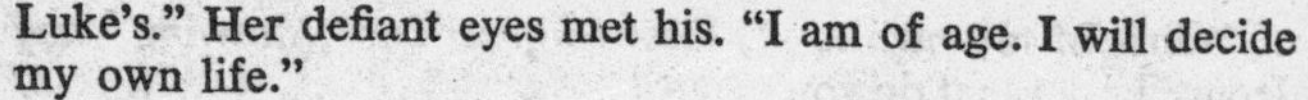

Luke's." Her defiant eyes met his. "I am of age. I will decide my own life."

"Your life!" he scoffed. "Desiree, you are being ridiculous. I am speaking of a matter of a few short months, not years."

"To me it would seem like years. As for the war being over soon, I think you are being overly optimistic. The Yankees will not be easily beaten."

Elton Grayson's face flushed a deep angry red. "You would like to see the Yankees triumphant, is that what you are trying to say?" Breathing deeply, he glared at her, the cooler part of his mind wishing he could take back his ill-considered words.

Desiree did not blaze out at him as he had more than half-expected. She did not launch into a passionate diatribe on the evils of slavery, as had been her wont in the past; she met his eyes coolly. "Neither side will win, Father," she said, unconsciously echoing Christopher Fairfield's words.

"And what do you mean by that? We'll show the Yankees a force of arms, and they'll run like rabbits."

Desiree shook her head. "They won't run, and neither will our side. Victory, for whichever side, will have a very bitter taste. That's why I say to you that neither side will win."

"Nonsense!"

"You can call it nonsense if you wish. But don't you see, reason is what is needed when it comes to the question of the South. Reason, compromise, and justice on both sides, not war."

"You know nothing about such matters, Desiree, and I refuse to continue this futile discussion."

"I thought you might. I realize it was presumptuous of me, a mere woman, to attempt to give my point of view."

Stabbed by her sarcasm, he retorted roughly, "You are quite right. Which brings us back to the question of St. Luke's."

"The question of my incarceration, you mean. I've told you, Father, I will not go."

The flush in his face deepened. The calmness of her, the brazen flouting of his authority! Despite her dainty appearance, there was a very unfeminine streak in Desiree. She should have been a boy; he had often thought so. "You will do as you're told, missy," he said in a tightly controlled voice, "in this one thing, at least, you will obey me."

"And if I refuse?"

Fighting to control his rising temper, Elton Grayson drew in a deep, steadying breath. "In that case, you will be locked in your room until such time as your aunt arrives. After that, if you continue to resist, you will be transported to St. Luke's by force."

"By whom, my Aunt Clara?"

"No, by Ben and Silas. I will detail them to stand by."

Desiree's eyes dropped. Ben and Silas. Thinking of the two husky Negroes, she was forced to hide a smile. Both Ben and Silas had worked very closely within the organization, and she numbered them among her most able men. She had nothing to fear from them, so why continue to make an issue of it with her father? He would be gone soon after sunrise, and so would she, long before her aunt arrived. She said in a faint voice, "You would really do that to me?"

"I would. Desiree, be reasonable. I only want to be certain you are in a safe place." Looking into her clear violet eyes, he felt his anger dying; in its place was that treacherous softening that only his late wife, and now his daughter, was able to inspire. "Will you do as I ask?" he said gently.

Although her pride rebelled, she responded to the gentle note in his voice, and she was conscious of a wish to please him, to give him that further peace of mind he sought. She was her own woman, she always would be, it would do no harm if she seemed to agree. Carefully, for her father could be very astute, she paused just long enough to make the hesitation convincing, and then she nodded. "I seem to have no choice in the matter." She smiled. "That being the case, I might as well give in graciously. All right, Father, I will do as you ask."

"That's my good girl. You will settle down and enjoy yourself, you'll see."

Desiree smiled inwardly. If her father's defense against what he had learned was to treat her like a little girl, it did not matter. He would be far away from Twin Oaks in a matter of hours, and who knew what hardships he might have to face? She said tenderly, "I'm not so sure that I'll enjoy myself, but I'll do my best."

He looked at her anxiously. "And your Aunt Clara, you will do your best to get along with her? I know she can be very difficult at times, but she does mean well."

"Perhaps she does. All right, Father, I can do no more than try."

He distrusted her sudden meekness—it was not like Desiree—but he was not inclined to probe further. Overcome with melancholy at the thought of the imminent parting, he put his arms about her again and drew her close.

Juniper's eyes were wide, her earrings trembling against her cheeks with the agitation that had possessed her ever since her mistress had returned from the interview with her father. She watched in silence for a moment as Desiree continued to cram a large carpetbag with items of clothing, toilet articles, and other necessities; then, unable to bear the haphazard packing, she moved forward, her hand extended. "Here, Miss Dessi, you best let me do that."

"I'll do it." Impatiently Desiree thrust the garment into the bag.

"But, Miss Dessi, these clothes goin' to get badly creased."

"It doesn't matter," Desiree answered shortly.

Juniper shrugged. "If you say so, Miss Dessi." Her eyes ran over the girl's scantily clad form. "But why are you dressed in your nightshift? Cain't very well run off in those clothes."

"I've just got through telling you, Juniper. Should my father by any chance decide to look in on me, it must appear that I am ready for bed. Now do you understand?"

Juniper thrust out her underlip, her expression faintly sulky. "You cain't just run off. A lady wouldn't behave so."

Desiree grinned. "I'm going anyway, so perhaps I'm no lady."

Agitation overcoming her again, Juniper wrung her plump hands together. "What'll become of you," she moaned, "where'll you go?"

"I'll manage," Desiree said, smiling. Although she had evaded the maid's question, her destination was firmly fixed in her mind. She was going to Blue Hollow, the pseudo-English manor house that her father, in an unusual fit of extravagance, had purchased a year ago. The house, a solitary gem set among the hills about Manassas, was fully furnished; the late owner, having set sail for England, had asked if he might leave his possessions behind until such time as he could send for them. There was also a caretaker on the premises, whose job it was to keep everything clean and in good repair. Her father was always making plans to have Blue Hollow repainted and fully staffed, but nothing had as yet been done. Perhaps, when times were less troublesome, he would decide to turn it into the holiday retreat he had originally intended. As for the caretaker, he could take a vacation, Desiree decided. It would be fun to care for the house herself.

Desiree glanced quickly at the black girl. Juniper was poised over the carpetbag, a worried frown on her face, obviously itching to dump the contents and repack. Certainly, she thought, she did not intend to reveal her destination to Juniper, or to any of the other slaves. It would be safer for them if they did not know. At the thought of leaving Twin Oaks, maybe for a long time, Desiree experienced a painful pang. And it was not only Twin Oaks she would be leaving behind, but those slaves who had aided her in the founding of her daring and ambitious venture. They were her friends, and she loved them. They had all, with the exception of Clover, been loyal to her. Working together, sharing laughter and small jokes as well as the ever-present danger of discovery, they had become like a closely knit family group. The outbreak of war had temporarily put an end to the organization, but her ties with the black people who loved and trusted her would never be broken. After the war, should the need remain for the Flame to act again, it would be a simple matter to rally her force again. The slaves of Twin Oaks, and those others, many of whom she had never met, would continue to work for a common goal, freedom, and the right to live in safety and dignity. Desiree's eyes misted. She would miss them all, but perhaps most of all she would miss Wilmers, Juniper, and Tildy.

"Miss Dessi," Juniper said in a complaining tone, "you ain't listenin' to me. I done ask you three times where you is goin'."

"I'm sorry, my mind was far away." Snapping the bag closed, Desiree thrust it under the bed. "Listen to me, Juniper"—she turned to the expectant girl—"I've told you I'm going away, and why, but I'm not going to tell you where I'm going."

Juniper bridled. "That mean you ain't trustin' me." She sniffed forlornly, and her soft eyes brimmed with hurt tears.

"You should know by now you can trus' me, Miss Dessi. It ain't as if I'm like that Clover."

Desiree sighed. "Of course you're not like Clover, Juniper, and I do trust you." She gave the heaving shoulder a pat. "Land's sake, stop that sniffling!"

"Then if you trus' me," Juniper lamented, "why don't you tell me where you're goin'?"

"Because it's better that way. It's safer for you if you don't know."

Slightly mollified by the warmth in her mistress's voice, Juniper wiped her tears away with a corner of her starched apron. "That's all very well," she continued in a mournful voice, "but you cain't just run off alone."

"I know what I'm doing, Juniper."

"Never been a time when you didn't know that."

"Remember it, then." Desiree paused, her expression growing thoughtful. "You know something, Juniper, perhaps I'll take up nursing."

Juniper's jaw dropped. "Nursing, for the soldiers?"

"Naturally for the soldiers. If this war should last longer than the predicted few months, there will be a great need for skilled nursing."

"But, Miss Dessi, you ain't skilled."

Desiree frowned at her. "Well, I know that, but I can learn."

Juniper, who was gazing at her determined young mistress with a mixture of awe and admiration, suddenly looked scandalized. "But you're a lady, Miss Dessi. These wounded soldiers'll be all dirty and sweaty and bloody."

"And you're afraid I might get blood all over my dainty gowns. Don't be silly, Juniper, nursing is a worthwhile job, and I'm not in the least squeamish."

Evidently remembering her mistress's past activities and her pronounced antislavery sentiments, Juniper said in a hushed voice, "Who you goin' to be nursing, Miss Dessi?"

"Whoever needs me, of course."

"Even . . . even Yankees?"

"If I happen to be on the spot, and if I'm needed."

Juniper chuckled. "You're a caution, Miss Dessi." Sobering, she added, "But you ain't to be nursin' Yankees. I hear they ain't nothin' but savages."

"You talk as if they're not human," Desiree answered

sharply. "They are people just like you and me, and with the same problems."

Unconvinced, Juniper dropped her voice to a whisper of apprehension. "Miss Dessi, what if the Yankee men do bad things to you!"

"Bad things?" Desiree choked back laughter and gazed sternly at the black girl. "Juniper, will you please stop this nonsense."

"Only tellin' you what I heard." Juniper paused; then, with the air of one making up her mind, she said in a strong voice, "Just ain't no other way but for me to come with you. The way I see it, you'll be needin' me to protect you."

Desiree shook her head. "It's kind of you, Juniper, and I thank you for the offer, but you will remain at Twin Oaks."

A thought struck Juniper, and her expression turned sullen with jealousy. "You say you ain't takin' me," she muttered, "but I bet you're takin' old fat Tildy with you. That woman's fat and lazy, and she cain't do for you like me. Cain't take care of clothes either, and cain't do hair worth a lick."

Desiree lost patience. "This is just plain silly," she snapped. "No one is going with me."

Her jealousy erased, Juniper heaved a sigh. "Sure as the Lord, I wasn't meanin' to rile you. You must know I'm only thinkin' of you. It seem to me—" Her words ended in a protesting shriek as Desiree's strong hands propelled her toward her room, a tiny slip just off the main bedroom.

"You're going to bed," Desiree said to her firmly. "You should have been asleep ages ago."

Thrust forcibly through the door, Juniper continued to protest.

Ignoring her, Desiree closed the door and turned the key in the lock. "Juniper," she called softly, "when you are questioned, you are to say I sent you to bed early. You knew nothing of my plans, you didn't know I had locked you in. Go to sleep, Juniper. Good night."

Ignoring the now-muted sounds of Juniper's sobbing, Desiree wandered over to the open window. Leaning out, her unbound hair falling about her, she breathed in the mingled perfumes of the night. Inevitably, as they always did in her quiet moments, her thoughts turned to Christopher Fairfield. Where was he now, would she ever see him again? Tears burned in her eyes as she thought of her father lecturing her on her boldness, her adventurous spirit, her too-independent and seeking nature. More than once he had said to her sternly, "I love you, Puss, but if you would please me, you will rid yourself of these masculine traits, for they are not seemly in a female. Especially one with your dainty appearance. It is, to say the least, incongruous."

Desiree blinked her tears away. How surprised her father would be if he could know how very feminine was her reaction to Christopher Fairfield. She was weak with longing when she remembered his caressing hands, his searing lips, the sweet and wildly passionate invasion of her body. And yet there was more to it than the appeal he made to her senses. She was in love with him. "It's true, Christopher," she said aloud, "I am in love with you. If I should ever find you again, I'll do everything within my power to make you fall in love with me. But love me or not, I'll never let you go again."

Desiree turned from the window and went over to the bed. Sitting down, she reflected bitterly on how slight were her chances of finding Christopher Fairfield. When he had walked out of her life, it had been forever. Why couldn't she accept that, why did she go on hoping that someday, somehow, she would find him again?

12

The black man moaned, his body twitching in involuntary response to the occasional deafening roar of the cannonade. He lay in a depression between two hills, shielded from the sun by their looming purple-black shadows; his torn and bloody arm, in its tattered smoke-blackened remnant of a sleeve, was flung across his eyes. From somewhere musketry crackled in a sharp fusillade. His heart pounded in alarm as he pictured the Confederate soldiers creeping up on him. "Go 'way, Johnny Reb," he muttered. "Cain't do you no harm now. Leave me to die in peace."

A fly settled on his swollen lips, and he turned his head in weak protest. He didn't want to die, not now, when he had so much to live for. With this thought, a small obstinate spark of life glowed brighter, and it was as if, in this moment of extremity, the panorama of his life was unfolding itself. Vivid pictures leaped into his mind. Growing up at Murray Hill Plantation, the harshness and cruelty of Miss Youtha Murray. Manhood, and that first sweet meeting with Martie, his woman. His flight from Murray Hill, the astounding contact with that flame-haired, violet-eyed angel of mercy, Miss Desiree Grayson. After that, events had moved swiftly, carrying him along as if borne on a relentless and roaring tide. There had been the rescue of Martie from Murray Hill—how well he remembered the feel of her trembling body in his arms—and then came the exciting moment of their arrival in the North. For the first time he was without supervision. Clad in his stiff new city clothes, he had felt big and awkward and terribly conspicuous, vulnerable. Were the bustling people summing him up, knowing him for the escaped slave he was? Were they hostile, condemning? Each time he met a pair of eyes, he had been fearful, and he had grinned obsequiously, hoping for charity and understanding, but anticipating disaster. It was Martie, clinging tightly to his hand, who had rebuked him. "Josh"—her voice had been clear and cool—"ain't no need for you to be bobbin' your head an' grinnin' like a fool at them white folk. We're free now."

Ashamed that this tiny slip of a girl was displaying more courage than he, he had answered her roughly, "Don't you be naggin' at me, woman. I'm afraid of no one."

"Prove it." Martie's voice was a goad. "Hold up your head and walk like a man."

"I'll prove it, all right. First chance I get, I'm joinin' the army." Martie's eyes had instantly been shadowed with a new fear. Seeing it, he had grown kind again. "You ain't to worry, Martie, gal. Ain't a bullet made that can get Josh Grayson."

Josh Grayson. His mind lingered over the name. White men had last names, and he needed one, but he would not take Miss Youtha's. With Amos' assurance that Miss Dessi would be proud, he had become Josh Grayson. How triumphantly he had given that name when he had been inducted into the Union Army. His life took an even more drastic turn. Hot and uncomfortable in his ill-fitting blue uniform, Josh and his newly acquired comrades received only the barest training in the use of firearms, a circumstance that left most of them more confused and uncertain than before. And then suddenly, raw recruits though they still were, they were proceeding south to a war that apparently could not wait for fully trained men. From Arlington toward Fairfax, and then the reality of war was upon them. Manassas. The awesome General McDowell. The general, his steely blue eyes looking from a florid, determined face, roared his orders, and God help those officers and recruits who did not scatter at once to take up their positions. July 21, the Battle of Bull Run. The words repeated themselves over and over in Josh's head. It was still July 21, he thought wearily, and yet it seemed to him that he had lain here for months.

Josh's arm moved, dropping heavily to his side. Shuddering with pain, he opened his eyes. Through a pall of blue smoke he saw a blur of greenery, and higher, a few fleecy clouds sailing across the serene, gradually darkening sky. Serenity. It was not in keeping with the nightmare of blood and death and destruction in which he had taken part. His brow furrowed. How had he come here, to this almost immune place between the guardian hills? The last thing he remembered was dragging himself along the ground, circling around prone, shattered bodies, his blood darkening the bright green of the grass. The screams of the badly wounded had sounded in his flinching ears, and he had screamed himself in pain and rage and grief. It could not end like this, not for him, who had barely tasted freedom. God would not be so cruel! With Martie's name on his lips, he had tumbled into darkness and known no more.

With a painful effort, Josh's fingers touched the still-warm earth, the good red earth that would shortly cover him. His fingers tensed as a frightening thought occurred to him. Would the Confederates take the trouble to bury their enemy, or would he and his fallen comrades be left to rot? Terrified, he allowed his tired mind to carry him back to the beginning of this disastrous day.

They had attacked the Confederates just before the break of dawn, but they had had no way of knowing if the attack had been successful. Then, with the coming of the light, they had seen the first of the Confederate dead. Coming across a contingent of rebs, they had tried to drive them across the Warrenton turnpike. The Confederates had turned then and stood firm. At their head was a tall figure, with dark blond faintly gray-streaked hair curling from beneath his cap, and bright blue eyes that had blazed with a fierce light as he bellowed commands. A Southern voice had cried out triumphantly, "Jackson will get us through, lads. See how he stands. He is like a stone wall." Under the leadership of this man, the Confederates had fought with an almost holy fervor, striking back with the ferocity of wounded tigers.

Josh shivered, remembering his comrades falling about him, the piercing rebel yell, the patriotic frenzy, the voices that had shouted constantly, "Hurrah for Stonewall Jackson! Kill the blue-bellies, kill, kill!"

But for all the Confederate fervor, things had gone badly for them until, at some time in the day, they had been reinforced by fresh troops. The gray hosts, unblooded as yet, had swept the tired and staggering Union troops back across Bull Run. Johnny Reb had carried the day to a resounding victory.

Josh closed his eyes. If he must die, he prayed that he would be allowed to slide peacefully and painlessly into death. It was all he had left to hope for. The occasional bursts of gunfire meant only that the rebs were conducting a mopping-up operation, herding the few stragglers and the walking wounded along. His outfit had scattered, he was entirely alone, unless one counted the bullet-blasted bodies of his dead comrades. He thought of Martie, so quick and warm and vibrant with life, and his lips moved in a soundless appeal. "Come to me, honey. Don't let me die alone!"

"I'm here, Josh. I ain't never leavin' you." Her voice was only in his head, but Josh's dry lips stretched into a smile. He could almost feel her satin-smooth body beneath his, as it had been on their first full day of freedom. In imagination he traveled back in time, and suddenly he was there, in that small room, in the tall boardinghouse, which Amos, through his contacts, had secured for him. "Josh!" Martie's voice, throaty with desire, was calling to him.

He had turned and looked at her. For the first time they were truly alone, the door locked against intrusion, and Martie, who knew how to please a man, was lying on the dingy carpet before the flickering fire, her slim arms stretched out in invitation. Her black, Indian-straight hair was spread about her, and her tawny naked body seemed to him to glow. "You come on here to me, big man. Cain't wait one second longer for you." Fingering her heavy breasts with their rigid, coppery nipples, she had parted her legs suggestively. "Of course," she said with a mock pout, "if you ain't wantin' me, then I reckons I understand."

He had stumbled toward her, already burning and heavy with the weight of his desire. Looking down into her dark, seductive eyes, he had blurted, "Won't never be a time when I ain't wantin' you."

"I can see that," Martie smiled slowly, her small hand

reaching up to pat him. "You goin' to undress yourself, big man, or do you want me to do it for you?"

Intrigued by her new behavior, he sank to his knees beside her. "You do it," he answered her gruffly.

Her eyes burned into his, her black hair fell about him in a shining waterfall as she stripped him slowly and lingeringly. Removing the last garment, she had fondled his urgently throbbing manhood gently. Then, relinquishing it, she poised herself above him, before pressing her body tightly to his. Tawny limbs tangled with ebony, the sweat stood out thickly on Josh's face, and his veins seemed to be filled with fire. Her breasts were so soft, fitting into his hands, his nostrils were filled with the rich, warm, fragrant odor of her body as he took a rigid nipple into his mouth.

Shivering, Martie tried to press even closer. "Now, Josh, I've been waiting so long for this."

There were no words for the tenderness he felt, and so he did not speak. Raising himself, he waited for her to slide beneath him. She was like a flame, urgent, demanding, uttering little whimpering cries that bade him enter her. He did not obey her at once. With her, this young girl whom he adored, the sexual act must not be a furtive grabbing and a hasty repletion as it was in the breeding hut, it must be with love, with tenderness. He began to kiss her, starting with her soft, shaking mouth, traveling downward until he had covered every inch of her body. When he came to the entry that he craved, he looked up and saw the blaze in her eyes, and he knew that it was time. Now he became strong, aggressive, pushing her legs apart, thrusting himself deeply inside her. Her legs clasped him tightly, her body jerked and thrust with his, her whimpering cry grew into a scream of ecstasy as they rushed together toward an explosive climax that left them both weak and shaken. Martie, his heart's darling, so loving, so insatiable. Her wandering fingers had aroused him again and again, and all that night they had not slept. Exhausted, but blissfully happy, Josh watched, enchanted, as the dawn's fiery light, penetrating the curtainless window, tinged Martie's body with vivid orange. It was a picture he had always carried with him. It was the picture that he would die with.

"You'll be all right, soldier." A voice spoke close to Josh's ear. "I'll take care of you."

Josh stiffened. A Southern voice, with the thick musical accent that was akin to his own. With a supreme effort he opened his tear-blurred eyes and looked into the face of the Confederate soldier bent above him. Beneath the grime of battle, he could see that it was an exceptionally handsome face, with eyes that were as dark as night, and, at this moment, filled with compassion. Mistrusting the compassion, Josh rejected it. "Leave me be, Johnny Reb. I'll die soon enough."

The dark eyes softened still more. "What are you talking about? You're not going to die, I'll see to that."

Josh's voice came out in a croak. "So you can take me prisoner."

The man shook his head. "My job is healing, and to hell with causes. After I've done with you, you'll be as good as new. Then I'll leave you someplace where your regiment or some other outfit will be sure to find you."

"Why do you do this for me, Johnny Reb?" Josh whispered.

"Maybe I like your looks, Billy Yank, or maybe I'm just for the underdog."

"Ain't no Yank." Josh felt obscurely offended.

"And I'm no Johnny Reb. I have my own reasons for joining the army, none of which are the popularly accepted ones." He broke off, grinning ruefully. "I always did talk too much. What's your name, soldier?"

I hurt, Josh thought. I'm tired, I'm afraid, and I don't understand why this man, my enemy, should want to aid me. Can I really trust him? His voice faltered as he answered the question. "Josh Grayson, doctor, sir."

"I'm not a doctor, Josh," the man interrupted, "but I do have a certain talent for healing, and I am used in a medical capacity." Misinterpreting the doubt in Josh's eyes, he added, "But you've got nothing to worry about, soldier. I know what I'm doing."

Pain clawed through Josh. He bit down hard on his quivering lower lip.

The dark eyes studied Josh thoughtfully. "Grayson, you say. Do you come from Twin Oaks Plantation?"

An alarm shrilled in Josh's brain. This man might ask questions, he might probe, and at all costs Miss Desiree's secret identity must be preserved. He answered with a surge of false strength, "I've always had that name. I'm a free nigger."

"Then perhaps your father came originally from Twin Oaks?"

His father? He had never known one. Feeling desperate, Josh invented a father. "He's free too. Both been free all our lives."

There was a bitter twist to the Confederate soldier's mouth. "You're lucky, my friend. I wish I could make that claim."

Josh stared at him, his fogged brain clearing slightly. What did he mean? Surely all white men were free? His eyes dropped to the hands that were gently peeling away his blood-soaked tunic. Through the mists of pain he saw the deeply grooved scars on the wrists, and understanding came to him. This man had been, perhaps still was, a convict. If he was on the run, he had obviously chosen the army as a convenient place to hide. Josh remembered the chain gangs he had occasionally seen, shuffling gray groups with blank faces, savage faces, hate-twisted faces. Abused men, as enslaved as he and his black brothers. It had not seemed to matter what crime they had committed; Josh only knew that God had not meant his creatures to be so brutalized and degraded. With a stirring of fellowship, Josh said with some difficulty, "What's your name?"

Christopher Fairfield smiled, his teeth showing almost startlingly white in his smoke-grimed face. "Christopher Wakely." He gave the assumed name lightly. His long, sensitive fingers examined the jagged wound just below Josh's collarbone. "Hurts like the devil, I know," he said sympathetically, "but it's not as bad as it looks or feels. You'll do just fine, Josh. You won't lose your arm. The bullet passed clean through." He grinned at Josh's relieved sigh. "By the way," he went on, "I spotted an empty house not far from here. Has a caretaker, but he's not one for staying awake on the job. I'll hide you there for tonight."

Josh's dormant suspicion awoke. After all, what did he really know about the man? On an expelled breath, his weakening voice came out harsh with doubt. "I ain't seen no houses."

Busily stanching a fresh flow of blood from the wound, Christopher did not reply. He worked for a few moments, and then threw the bloodied lint to one side. "That's better."

Digging into his big canvas pack, he produced a roll of linen and a brown bottle. "This will sting," he warned, uncorking the bottle, "but you'll just have to grit your teeth and hang on." He did not glance at Josh as he continued to tend him. "As for the house," he added, "it's to your left. The hills are hiding it from view."

Josh's fingers dug into the earth in an effort to steady himself against agony. "I should have seen it," he gasped.

"None of us were in any condition to notice. Anyway, it's there." Straightening his back, Christopher wiped a hand across his grimed forehead. "That's the best I can do for now. I've cleaned out the wound. Once the sting stops, you should feel more comfortable."

Josh averted his eyes, trying to hide a rush of panic. He was not only a black man, he was an enemy, and Christopher Wakely seemed too good to be true. Why was he being so kind to him, what were his motives? He groped for words. "How do you know the house is empty?" he blurted. "Could be folks livin' there."

Christopher closed the canvas pack. If he was aware of the other man's unease, it did not show in his manner. He looked up, a smile lighting the somber depths of his eyes. "I happen to know the house is empty. I scouted it a week ago. A pity we have to move on, it would have made a fine temporary hospital. For tonight it will be useful. I guarantee you that the caretaker won't know a thing. If I have to, I'll hide you in the cellar."

His words stirred Josh's clouded mind to remembrance of a small dramatic incident. It had happened just before he was wounded. A young woman, heedless of danger, had burst out of the undergrowth, running in a zigzag course between the enemy lines. Dirty and disheveled, her blue gown torn and covered with mud, she had ignored the furious curses hurled at her from both sides. Taking shelter behind a tree, she had demanded to see somebody in charge. When no one came forward, she had called loudly, "Listen to me. I have a home not far from this spot. Bring your wounded there."

It had been a demand rather than a request, and Josh had marveled at her audacity and daring. There were crowds of civilians massed on the hills, watching the fighting, many of them women, but this one quite obviously was not in the same class with those fluttering and overexcited females. She was more than a spectator, she wished to do something about the increasing number of wounded, and so with heedless, foolish courage she had run right into the path of the firing to voice her demand.

A bullet had thudded into the trunk of the tree that sheltered her, and a deep voice had shouted in alarm, "For God's sake, go home, ma'am! Go on, get away. This is no place for a lady."

"Lady, be damned! Remember what I have said." Crouching low, the young woman gathered up her torn skirt and prepared to run. "The house overlooks Bull Run. Look upward from there and you will see it."

"Anything you say, ma'am, just get out of here!"

Josh moved his head restlessly. He had seen a shock of mud-daubed red hair, but he had been unable to catch a glimpse of her face. He remembered thinking that there had been something very familiar about that clear, imperious voice. Josh frowned. The house she had spoken of, could it be the same one mentioned by Christopher Wakely? But he had said that he had scouted it a week ago and found it empty. Confused, troubled because it was becoming increasingly difficult to marshal his thoughts, he turned to a more pressing problem. "Will there be other folk in that house?"

"Don't worry"—Christopher patted Josh's uninjured arm—"there will be no one else. For tonight you can be comfortable. The place is fully furnished, so just by removing a few dust covers I can give you all the comforts of home."

"What about the caretaker?"

"If he's restless, we might end up in the cellar. That's a chance we'll have to take."

Josh's attention drifted. Whatever this man intended, if indeed he intended anything, there was nothing he could do about it, unless the man could be moved by an appeal. "I'd be mighty grateful if you'd let me go."

"What, in your condition, how far do you think you'd get?"

Josh's voice trembled. "You fixed me up fine. I can make it on my own now."

Christopher shook his head. "Impossible, you've lost too much blood." He sat back on his heels and studied the troubled face intently. "What is it, Josh, do you think I'm leading you into a trap?"

Never argue with a white man. Josh remembered the stern warning that had been drummed into him from earliest childhood. It was the habit of self-preservation that dictated the answer. "No, suh."

"I believe you do, and I can't say I blame you. All the same, Josh, I'd like it if you could bring yourself to trust me. I mean you no harm."

The words were so gently spoken that, against all his instincts, Josh found himself responding. Maybe he was a fool, but there was something about this Christopher Wakely that inspired trust. Something that broke through the barriers erected by the harsh years and found the soft inner trusting core that is born in most men. Josh blinked the sweat from his eyes and studied the face of the white man. The expression in repose was hard, the mouth bitter, suggesting a grimly borne inner suffering, and except when he smiled, by no stretch of the imagination could his be called a friendly face. Yet the realization came to Josh that he had been made the recipient of the warmth and the compassion that were apparently natural to the man. An old and well-worn saying of Delby's crept into his mind: "Never judge nothin' by its cover." Ashamed now of his former suspicion, Josh said in a trembling voice, "I trust you, but what will you do with me? What will happen to me afterwards?"

"First, I'll stick you in a gray uniform and take you along with me. In all this mess, no one will be counting heads. After you're able to walk, you're on your own. If you can't track down your own regiment, you can join up with some other Yankee outfit. The Yankees were licked today, but their defeat will make them all the more determined. They'll be coming back thick and fast."

Forgetting that the man bent over him was the enemy, Josh said gloomily, "More than likely the rebs'll capture me."

"Then you must see to it that you're not captured." Christopher's voice was suddenly sharp. Then, on a softened note, he added, "I'm an expert on running, and I imagine you are too. We know all the tricks of survival, eh?" He smiled as the black man's dulled eyes flashed. "It's all right, Josh, no questions. Good luck to you, I say."

Josh licked his dry lips. Was it a case of like recognizing like, or had those penetrating eyes seen through his meager disguise? A "free nigger," he had called himself, and yet this man had not been deceived for one moment. Chilled, he tried to bring out words, but found that his throat had closed against them.

Looking into that vulnerable face, Christopher cursed himself for having unwittingly brought about a return of the black man's fear. "There is no need to trouble yourself," he said hastily, "I said no more questions, and I meant it. You are a man in need of help, no more and no less than that. Do we understand each other?"

"Yes." Josh swallowed hard and felt the constriction in his throat ease.

Smiling reassuringly, Christopher rose. "I'm going to have to move you, Josh. It will be painful, but it must be done. I want to get you settled before it's full dark."

The words were casually spoken, but Josh detected the slight urgency in Christopher Wakely's voice. At this period of time the hatred that flamed throughout the South was at fever pitch, and it was not wise to give aid and comfort to the enemy. There was a great deal of danger in the undertaking, for if they were caught it would not only be he who was shot, but quite possibly Christopher Wakely too. Even though he understood this very well, he cringed at the thought of moving, and he tried to put off the moment. "Maybe . . . maybe you should go attend the others needin' you," he whispered.

"I am just one of a team, but as you have just pointed out, there are many still in need of attention, which is all the more reason to hurry. Cooperate with me, please, Josh."

Josh drew in a deep, unsteady breath. He was used to pain, for he had been flogged many times, and he had always managed to endure. Mentally girding himself, he said hoarsely, "Ready when you are."

"Up you come, then." Stooping, Christopher grasped him beneath the armpits and heaved. "Easy, now, easy!"

Josh felt an explosion of pain as his feet touched ground. This was not to be compared with the floggings. With a stifled cry he clutched at Christopher's arm, biting his lips to suppress his groans. Great drops of sweat clustered thickly upon his forehead, rolling down into his eyes, blinding him. Forgetting his resolution, he mumbled in an agonized voice, "Ain't no use. Leave me here, let me die!"

"Die, nothing. You've been badly hurt, but you're a long

way from those pearly gates. I'm going to turn my back to you. Lean forward and put your good arm about my neck."

Deprived of his support for a second, Josh wavered. Only when the instructions were repeated in a louder voice did he make the attempt. "That's good, Josh." Christopher Wakely's voice was a faint thread of sound in his ears. "Now tighten your grasp as much as you can."

Josh gasped. His arm fell away, and he lurched heavily against Christopher's dimly seen shape. "It hurts me too much."

Recovering his balance, Christopher rapped out words: "Do as you're told, soldier!"

Josh gritted his teeth. The authoritative voice of the white man. He had given a command, and he expected it to be obeyed. Out of the habit of a lifetime, Josh made a supreme effort. He thrust out his arm again, his fingers clutching desperately at cloth. As he was hoisted across Christopher Wakely's broad back, everything rushed together in a red-streaked swirling blackness, and he lost consciousness.

Desiree's steps lagged as she walked through the double iron gates and approached the house. Set on a high rise of land, the frowning hills rearing up at its back, Blue Hollow was a tall, narrow, half-timbered abode that overlooked the small stream of Bull Run. Blue Hollow, though not more than fifty years old, had a timelessness about it, Desiree thought. It fitted in as an integral part of the lushly beautiful surroundings that had, today, known such devastation by the warring factions of North and South, and yet it seemed strangely aloof from the strife.

Desiree's thoughts scattered abruptly as her tired eyes fell on the intricately carved front door. It was standing open. Someone was in the house! For a moment she felt a thrill of fear, and then, remembering that she had sent for the caretaker, her face cleared. It was small wonder, after the shattering events of today, that she had forgotten. Her heart resuming its normal beat, she ran up the two broad steps and entered the lamplit hall. "Bickford," she called, "where are you?"

The man who had been hidden by the tall back of a settle drawn up before the huge fireplace rose to his feet and faced her. "Ma'am." He inclined his head stiffly.

Desiree was annoyed to find herself flushing under his critical gaze. She felt certain that he was not missing one detail of her lamentable appearance, from her wildly disheveled hair to her torn gown, and the left shoe, which was minus a heel. "Good evening, Bickford," she said with a touch of haughtiness.

"Good evening, ma'am." Fred Bickford, the caretaker of Blue Hollow, was a lean, lugubrious-looking individual with a deeply lined face, small pale blue eyes, and an untidy mane of white hair. His sense of injury deepened as he looked at the girl before him. He was, he considered, a man with a sense of duty, and he had been outraged when Miss Grayson, arriving three days ago, had stated her wish to have Blue Hollow to herself for a time. Deprived of his comfortable berth by her insistence, he had gathered his belongings together and retired to his small cottage near the crossroads, but not before he had delivered a lecture on the impropriety of the situation. "There's trouble in the air," he had declared sourly, "and it ain't fitting for a young female to be alone in this great house. The Lord only knows what will happen to you. Why not let me stay? You needn't see much of me."

"That's not the point, Bickford," Desiree had answered. "I just want to be alone. You will be receiving your pay as usual, so I would think you would be glad of the rest."

"It ain't the pay, and I don't need no rest."

Firmly Desiree had ushered him out of the door. "You need have no fears for my safety, Bickford. I know how to take care of myself."

"That's what you say now, missy. But it's me that'll have to answer to your father if you get your head bashed in."

"I'm glad you came, Bickford." Desiree's voice interrupted his train of thought. "I wasn't sure if the boy would deliver my message."

"I got it, all right," Bickford answered gloomily, "and let me tell you, it wasn't easy getting here. As it was, the lad you sent with the message was hit by a flying bullet."

"Hit!" Desiree's voice rose shrilly. "Bickford"—she looked at him with stricken eyes—"is he . . . is he . . . ?"

"No, ma'am, he ain't dead, though that's not your fault, is it?" Looking at her drained face, Bickford felt a stab of sympathy. "Bullet grazed his upper arm," he added gruffly. "He'll be all right. I fixed him up."

"Thank God!"

"That's all very well to say, ma'am, but with all this fighting that's been going on, you ought to know that youngsters ain't got no place on the roads."

Her legs feeling weak, Desiree sank down into a chair. Thoroughly chastened, she said in a small voice, "You're right, Bickford, I just didn't think. Believe me, I would never have forgiven myself if that boy had been killed."

"That's the trouble with most folks," Bickford answered, his expression of disapproval deepening. "They're selfish, and they never take time to think."

Despite herself, Desiree felt a spasm of irritation. "You say you had trouble getting through?" she said in a harder voice.

"I did, ma'am, and it ain't to be wondered at, what with the Yankees scattering every which way. The road to and from Centerville is clogged by 'em, civilians too, all of 'em fighting among themselves in their hurry to get away. There was horses bolting down the road, dragging them ambulances and wagons behind 'em like they didn't weigh nothing at all. Some of them had a driver handling the reins, and they managed to get through, though not without knocking down the folks that stood in their way, and beating off them others that were clinging to the wagons and begging for a lift, but them horses without drivers were in a bad way. Here and there I saw soldiers shooting the animals that were too stove-up to save." Bickford looked at Desiree's appalled face and sighed heavily. "It's a mess, I don't mind telling you. One time, there, I thought for sure I'd be trampled underfoot."

For the first time, as he turned toward the light, Desiree noticed the smear of dried blood on his cheek and the bruise beneath his eye. "You've been hurt, Bickford." Impulsively she rose from her chair and went toward him. "Here, let me see that."

Bickford drew back. "Ain't nothing but a scratch, ma'am."

"All the same, you must let me bathe it for you."

"No, ma'am, I don't like females fiddling with me."

"As you please." Desiree's outstretched hand dropped.

Bickford rubbed impatiently at his cheek. "There's men lying out there, our own, who've got a hell of a lot more than a fiddling scratch, and I aim to do something about the ones still living. Seems like there ain't enough docs to go around, and we can't let our boys just lie there."

"No, there aren't enough trained doctors, that's the tragedy of it," Desiree said in a choked voice, "but we will all do what we can." Shuddering, she recalled the scene of carnage she had witnessed. Bodies everywhere, the blue and the gray mixed together in a companionship repudiated in life. Bodies lying along the ravine, waiting for burial, the dead staring eyes, the shattered limbs. There had been one soldier in particular, a Yankee, who had managed to drag himself beneath the shelter of a bush. She had been passing by, bent double in her attempt to dodge the flying lead, and she had not noticed him. It was a feeble clutch on her skirt, a voice pleading for help, that had halted her.

The Union soldier was little more than a youth. His fair curls were matted with sweat, his blue eyes dull, and it was obvious to Desiree that he was dying. Crawling beneath the bush, she had taken his hand in hers and held it firmly, all the time speaking to him in a low, soothing voice. Her presence had seemed to comfort him, and she was pleased to remember that he had died with a slight smile on his lips. She had sat there for a long time, his stiffening hand still clasped in hers, her tears falling on his white, still face. Around her the battle raged, but she could only think that a young boy, on the threshold of life, had died, and that she mourned his passing.

"Goddamned Yankees!" Bickford's loud voice startled Desiree into attention. "We whipped 'em to hell. They'll remember Manassas and the Battle of Bull Run for a long time." Bickford drew himself up, a militant gleam warming his frosty eyes. "And if we whipped 'em once, we'll whip 'em again." A shadow crossed his face. "I tried to join the army, ma'am, but I was told that I was too old. Well, maybe I can't help to whip the blue-bellies, but I sure as hell can cheer our boys on."

With the memory of the young soldier's face still in her mind, Desiree was sickened by Bickford's attitude. War, fighting, the Cause—when would it all end? "I shall be leaving in the morning," she said in a cool voice. "You may return to Blue Hollow when you please."

The gleam faded from Bickford's eyes, and an approving smile touched his lips. "That's right, you go back to Twin Oaks. In these times a young lady should stick close to home."

Desiree turned once more to face him. "I shall not be going home. When the main part of the army moves on, which will be at first light, I go with them. I have offered my aid in nursing the wounded, and I have been accepted."

"Accepted?" Bickford stared at her with incredulous eyes. "I can't believe it, ma'am."

"It's true. My first idea was to make Blue Hollow into a temporary hospital. I was not taken too seriously, I must admit, and my offer was refused. Since I was so persistent, I was then referred to a General Hunt. The general, after listening to me very carefully, decided that I would be of more use if I moved on with the army."

Bickford exclaimed in outrage, "It's not proper! That general must be out of his head."

"On the contrary, the general appeared very sane. Of course, it was I who put the idea of a traveling nurse into his head. He shared your sentiments at first. He thought that a woman going into the heart of battle was just too much of a novelty." Desiree smiled sweetly at the old man. "Nurses are badly needed, Bickford, I made him see that. I can be very persuasive when I set my mind to it." She laughed. "The general is now a little confused in his thinking. He is not quite certain whether to look upon me as a tawdry camp follower or as a lady determined to do her bit for the Glorious Cause. In any event, he has informed me that he will be keeping an eye on me."

Detecting the hint of sarcasm, Bickford flushed a bright red. "You talk like you don't believe in the Cause."

"There may be other issues at stake in this foolish and tragic war, Bickford," Desiree answered, "but the main one is a determination to preserve the plantation system and to keep slavery alive."

"And what's wrong with that?"

"Nothing, from your point of view, but I don't happen to believe in slavery."

"And loyalty, young missy, do you believe in that?"

Desiree looked at him consideringly. "I will take no side, Bickford. But if it makes you feel any better, my loyalty shall be first and foremost toward the wounded men."

At a loss, Bickford gaped at her, and then returned to his former attack. "Women have no place in the army," he said sourly. "The very idea of a gently reared female looking on at such horror makes my blood run cold."

Desiree sighed. "I'm sorry you feel that way," she answered him calmly. "But you know, Bickford, women were not meant to be merely ornaments. Neither, as you seem to believe, are they in the least delicate or helpless. You would be surprised at the strength a woman can show when called upon to do so. Before this war ends, many will volunteer their services as nurses, I guarantee it."

Bickford was not to be appeased. "I daresay, ma'am, and it's just fine if that nursing is done at home, in a respectable hospital. But a real lady don't go tramping around with a lot of rough soldiers, exposing herself to insults."

Keeping a tight rein on her temper, Desiree changed the subject. "Will you be returning here in the morning?" she asked coldly.

"I will, ma'am." Bickford looked at her fully, a dangerous gleam in his eyes. "Suppose I was to find this General Hunt and tell him just what you think of the Cause?"

"Do as you please," Desiree snapped. "However, you will find some difficulty in locating the general. He was preparing to move out when I left him."

"There are others I could talk to," he blustered, and wondered why he was making such an issue of it.

Choking back the angry words that clamored to be said, Desiree looked at him scornfully. "You must do your duty as seems fit, Bickford."

Bickford glared at her. Despite her present unkempt appearance, the girl was strikingly beautiful with her delicately formed features, her flaming hair, and her great violet eyes. Hers was the kind of heart-clutching beauty that would arouse lust in most men, but he had long since passed the age when a woman was capable of stirring him, and it left him cold. This Desiree Grayson was quite obviously a hard piece, and her lack of patriotism had been apparent in her low voice when she had spoken of the Glorious Cause. Glancing quickly at her, Bickford shifted uncomfortably. Though he was loath to admit it, her personality had, from the beginning of their short acquaintance, overawed him. There was something about her, a certain aura of command, a strength, a quiet confidence. As he reflected on this, his anger flared. It was his duty to speak out against her, for she had admitted she was against all that the Cause stood for, and speak out he would, just as soon as he had the chance.

"Is there something I can do for you, Bickford?" Desiree asked.

"No, ma'am." Bickford frowned down at the floor. Perhaps he was a fool to antagonize her. Her father was, after all, the new owner of Blue Hollow, and he had no wish to be dismissed from his comfortable job. Later, young missy, he thought vengefully, you just wait and see! He walked stiffly across the room. Pausing at the door, he attempted a conciliatory smile. "Best be careful, ma'am," he muttered. "You never know who might take it into their heads to break in." His eyes traveled over her. "You look delicate to me. If there was any trouble, I doubt you'd be able to defend yourself." Prompted by caution, he added unwillingly, "Would you like me to stay?"

Desiree shook her head. "No, thank you, though I do appreciate your concern. You mustn't worry about me, I'm really much stronger than I look. Besides, I have a pistol, and I assure you that I know how to use it."

Believing that he detected sarcasm again, Bickford flushed angrily. She had a tongue like a viper's. It was, in his opinion, quite apart from her beauty, the only feminine thing about her. "I'll see you in the morning, then," he said.

"Only if you're here by first light. Good night, Bickford."

Bickford stared at her for a long moment, the conviction growing in his head that she was a traitor to the Cause. But he'd fix her, he resolved. If she didn't land in prison, where all traitors belonged, then his name wasn't Frederick Bickford. His hand clenched on the doorknob as a new thought struck him. Suppose she was not really Miss Desiree Grayson? After all, he had only her word for it. It was true that she talked like a genuine lady, her words overlaid with the unmistakable soft honeyed accent of the South, but just suppose she was a spy for the Yankees? Mumbling to himself, pleased with the fruits of his imagination, he eased out of the door, closing it carefully behind him.

Crushing down her annoyance, Desiree smiled ruefully. As caretaker of Blue Hollow, Bickford was perhaps too much alone, and as a consequence he had developed cantankerous ways and a spiteful tongue, to say nothing of an overactive imagination. She thought of his accusing eyes, and she wondered what he thought her motives might be for traveling with the army. Surely he did not think that she intended to undermine the precious Cause by relaying information to the enemy? She shrugged. He was an old man, and it was absurd to allow his views on her patriotism, or lack of it, to disturb her.

Desiree jumped as a shutter banged heavily against an outer wall. A branch tapped against the window, a small irritating sound that further rasped her tightly strung nerves. The storm that General Hunt had earlier predicted was upon them in full force. Listening to the shrill keening of the rising wind, Desiree knew that it was not the caretaker's hostile attitude that had disturbed her, but rather the events of this terrible day. Now that she was alone, the horrifying pictures that she had been trying to block out rushed upon her like gibbering demons. Once again she saw the heavy pall of smoke that had hung over the area where the fighting was heaviest. Through that wavering screen she had seen men fall, their hands sticky with blood as they clutched at gaping wounds. The charging of the cavalry, sabers held at the ready, flashing steel fingers of death that had plunged into vulnerable flesh. She had heard the thunder of the cannon, the whine of streaking bullets, and the screaming of wounded men as their life's blood flowed out upon the uncaring earth. Frozen, she had stood among the spectators on the hill, and there was such a deep grief inside her that she had thought her heart would surely break. Her distraught mind turned to the dying Union soldier. He had been only a youth, and yet to her he had been Christopher.

Desiree put out a groping hand, her fingers tensing on the back of a chair. They had all been Christopher—the injured, the dead, the dying. It was for him, for his memory that would never leave her, that she had rushed unheedingly through a hail of bullets to demand that the wounded be brought to Blue Hollow.

Unaware of the tears streaking her cheeks, Desiree's lips silently formed his name. His gaunt, handsome face with the marks of suffering indelibly printed upon it rose up before her. She thought of the bitter mouth that she had kissed with such hungry passion, the eyes that were so dark that they were like pools of midnight, and how those somber depths had seemed to flame when they had looked upon her naked body. She had fought him desperately, but in the end she had given herself to him with an almost savage fury, and she had known ecstasy. There was no shame in her now as she recalled that mad surrender; there was only the recognition of an undying love, and a passion that separation or time could not slake. Christopher, swarthy as a gypsy, the hunted, who had walked back into her life and revealed to her the face of love, and who had departed without a second glance, leaving her world cold and empty.

The shutter banged again, a noisy intrusion upon her grief, and a draft of rain-laden air sent the heavy red drapes sailing out into the room. With dragging, exhausted steps, Desiree walked across the room. She was tired, she thought, so desperately tired. Lightning dazzled her eyes as she grappled with the stiff hinges of the window, rain gusted into her face, and her loosened hair streamed back from her shoulders before she finally succeeded in closing it. She turned abruptly away from the square of dark glass, unable to bear the thought of those men who were possibly still lying upon the cold ground, their eyes sealed in eternal sleep, the rain beating on their stiff bodies. Christopher! She put a hand to her shaking mouth. Where was he now? Was he still running, hiding from his pursuers, or had he allowed the anonymity of civil war to swallow him up? And if so, on which side would he choose to fight? For the South, where he had grown to manhood, but which held such bitter memories of humiliation and injustice, or for the alien North? It might be, in the Union Army, that his past would remain a closed book, and that after the war, he would be enabled to make a fresh start. "My love," Desiree whispered, "wherever you are, whatever you do, may God go with you."

Her heart heavy, Desiree turned to the table beside her and picked up a squat iron candleholder bearing a half-burned candle. Lighting it, she took one last look around her. The fire that Bickford had kindled earlier represented no danger; it had long since died down to gray ash. She would go to bed, hopefully to sleep.

Her hand shielding the frail flame, she wearily ascended the red-carpeted stairs. Her tears began again, and she brushed angrily at her eyes.

She paused at the top of the narrow flight, aware that another emotion had intruded, a sensation that might almost be described as fear. She looked intently down into the shadowed hall, its dark corners only faintly touched by the light from the one lamp she had left burning, and tried to pinpoint the reason for the sudden uneasiness afflicting her. She was not given to fancy, nor did she normally suffer from nerves, but the house seemed to her to be too big, too oppressive, and she too acutely conscious of her vulnerability. She leaned over the banister, her ears straining. Somewhere a board creaked, and her heart jerked in panic as she remembered that there were no bolts on the front door. There was not even a key to turn. He had lost it, Bickford had informed her. He had been meaning to have a new one made, but had forgotten about it. "Don't need no key, ma'am," he had remarked in a voice that made light of her indignation. "Prowlers do come around here from time to time, looking for a handout, or something to steal, but I soon send 'em about their business. That's only in the daytime, though. Ain't never troubled at night, because Blue Hollow's got a reputation for being haunted."

Undaunted, Desiree had said dryly, "I would imagine you sleep rather well at nights, Bickford, yes?"

"Don't matter, ma'am," Bickford had answered sharply. "Anyone strange in the house, I'd hear 'em. Look around you, there ain't a thing been stole."

"I'll take your word for it, Bickford. Unfortunately, I do not carry an inventory with me."

"Ain't no need for one, ma'am. Everything the last owner left behind is still here. I can vouch for that." Pressing his former point home, Bickford had added, "I won't deny that I sleep deep, but it's always with one ear open, if you take my meaning."

Dismissing the irritating Bickford from her mind, Desiree frowned thoughtfully. Blue Hollow's reputation for being haunted might well deter local prowlers, but times had changed drastically. What of the influx of soldiers? Biting her lip, she stood there unmoving. The ticking of the grandfather clock below was loud in her ears, and yet it seemed to her that she could detect other sounds, muffled, furtive. They seemed to be coming from the direction of the cellar. She stiffened, her hand clenching on the rail. Was someone in the cellar? It was a frightening thought. But of course there was nobody there, she assured herself at once. She was allowing her imagination to play tricks on her. It was natural for houses to creak, especially when buffeted by wind and rain. Soldiers indeed! Those who were still whole were either sleeping the sleep of complete exhaustion or painfully alert lest a stray party of Yankees, resentful of their ignominous defeat, should sneak back and open fire on those who had been left behind to temporarily hold Manassas against a possible renewed attack. The first light would see other Confederate soldiers on the move, and they would be marching fast to catch up with the vanguard. The wounded would be among them. As many as possible would be piled into the ambulances, the walking wounded would hobble along as best they could. Serious cases, failing room in the ambulances, would be carried along on litters.

Desiree winced, her heart quickening as she thought of the momentous task she had undertaken. She, together with her superiors, would be in complete charge of the wounded men. Could she do it, could she stand the sights and the sounds of suffering, of gaping wounds turned gangrenous, could she endure the agony of the men?

Her hand still tightly gripping the rail, she thought of the double life she had led. One life had been lived as the Flame, and she had faced the numerous dangers with unshaken equanimity. The other, the private life of a rich planter's daughter, had been lived in an atmosphere of idle luxury. She had never raised a finger for herself. Her every whim had been catered to, her every want lovingly attended to by the very slaves she sought to free. She had been pampered in that private life, and she had to admit that she had enjoyed it. But now was the testing time. She must and she *would* endure. If she faltered, she would think of Christopher. She would tell herself that it was he who lay beneath her ministering hands, and she would get by.

Desiree moved away from the stairs to face the darkness of the corridor. To her heightened imagination there seemed to be a menacing figure hidden in every patch of dense shadow. Her heart leaped as a shaft of lightning lit the far window with lurid light. Had something or someone moved behind the drapes? Panic-stricken, she stared hard. The lightning streaked again. No, she had been mistaken, she told herself firmly. There was nobody hidden behind the drapes. It was her foolish imagination again. Unconvinced, she tightened her hand on the iron holder, causing hot candle grease to spill over and splash onto her bodice. Why hadn't she thought to ask Bickford to light all the lamps before he left?

She started violently as the soft, unidentifiable sounds came again. Then, going limp with relief, she remembered something that Bickford had told her. Field mice, of course—that was the explanation. Bickford, waxing hotly indignant, had said, "Them goddamn pesky rodents go scampering through the danged place like they own it. Been a proper plague of 'em lately." In answer to her question, asking what he had done about the problem, he had replied moodily, "What do you think I done, ma'am? I put out traps, of course. But reckon I'll have to buy more, for I ain't got nearly enough."

Field mice! And she had been working herself into a high state of nerves. Laughing at her absurdity, she went swiftly along the corridor to the gold-and-lavender-decorated bedroom that she had chosen for her own. Once inside, she closed the door firmly behind her. Remembering that she had forgotten to ask Bickford for the key, she felt a faint flutter of apprehension. She blocked out the feeling immediately. What did she need with a key? She was perfectly safe.

Lighting the candles in the six-branched candelabrum, Desiree reflected on the caretaker. Bickford might be sullen and disagreeable, but he was certainly a hardworking man. In this room, for instance, there was not a speck of dust to be seen, and the various silver ornaments shone with a high luster. Smiling faintly, she looked about her. Lavender velvet drapes hung in gleaming folds at the long windows, matching in color the thick, luxurious carpet. The high, gold-painted walls bore a motif of flowers and cherubs along the top, and the pattern was repeated about the outer edges of the ceiling. It was a pretty room, she thought, and decidedly feminine. No doubt it had belonged to the late owner's wife, or perhaps to his daughter. The spotless hangings surrounding the wide bed were of a fine lavender muslin. The delicately carved and gilded furniture, recently rescued from beneath holland covers, was likewise in excellent condition. The rest of the furniture in the big rambling house, with the exception of the hall, was still shrouded, giving a forlorn and ghostly appearance to the place, which, she had to admit, she had not noticed until tonight.

Cheered by the warm yellow glow irradiating the room,

Desiree set about those tasks that must be done. First she packed her belongings in preparation for the morning's departure. Locking the carpetbag, she placed it on the gold-satin-covered couch between the windows. That task accomplished, she poured cold water from a flowered ewer into a matching basin. With the help of a bar of coarse soap, all Bickford had had to offer her, she vigorously endeavored to rid herself of the accumulated grime of the day. After clothing herself in a thin cotton nightgown, she brushed out her long red hair, grimacing in pain as she tried to smooth out the tangles. Her hair smelled of smoke, and it was dulled with mud and dust, but since there was nothing she could do about it, it would have to do.

Restlessly Desiree wandered over to the window and looked outside. Lightning flickered in the distance; the thunder rolling after was fainter now, an indication that the storm was wearing itself out. A watery-looking moon, appearing between the clouds, shed pale light over the wooded dales and the steep hills of Manassas, momentarily masking the devastation below. The scene, like the shrouded house, seemed to her to be ghostly and indescribably lonely. She listened to the heavy rattling of the rain against the windowpanes, and she thought of the blood that had stained the earth today. The cleansing rain would wash away those visible signs of battle, but nothing could erase the horror of it from the heart and the mind.

Shivering, she turned away from the window, trying not to think of her father, of Christopher, of countless young men who might die in the months to come. Blowing out the candles, she climbed wearily into bed. The moon disappeared, and then came out again, sending the shadows of the tossing trees racing over the wall. In an effort to make her mind a blank, she forced her heavy eyes to concentrate on the lacy patterns the shadows made. Just before sleep claimed her, a fear that was unconnected with the war touched her mind again, and she remembered that there was no grating over the cellar window.

13

For such a big man, he moved along the corridor with the stealth of a cat, his dragging, crippled left foot muted by the soft carpet. Pausing outside a door, he extracted his handkerchief and wiped his sweating palms; then, returning it to his pocket, he eased the door open cautiously and entered the room. After a while, as his racing heart calmed, he moved forward, his ears straining. The moon, unimpeded now by storm clouds, flooded the room with silvery light, throwing his huge deformed shadow across the wall. A grunt came from his lips as his ears picked up the soft, even sound of breathing. The girl was here, in this room. He had found her at last.

Slowly, lest an incautious movement betray his presence, he advanced to the bed and looked down at the sleeping girl. She lay on her back, one arm flung above her head, her thick hair tumbled over the pillow. In the moonlight her face looked soft and innocent and incredibly lovely.

His excitement mounting, he reached out a trembling hand and brushed back a lock of hair that had fallen over her face. She stirred, murmuring in her sleep, and he snatched his hand away, standing frozen until the restless movements ceased, contemplating her, his eyes glittering feverishly as he recalled his first sight of her.

He had been one of the crowd gathered on the hill to watch the fighting below. Hot and uncomfortable, he had fought his way to a clearer space, and then he had seen her. She was standing a little way from him. Fascinated by her flaming hair, he had continued to struggle through the press of people until he was standing beside her, wedged in so closely by others that he could feel the warmth of her flesh. From that moment a kind of madness seized him, and he had known then that he must have her. Disregarding the fighting, he stared hard at her, willing her to turn. He thought of her soft, naked body beneath his, her legs opening to receive him. In imagination he crushed those soft breasts with his hands as he plunged deeply inside her. She would be moaning, begging him to ease her, straining against him as she jerked to his rhythm. And then would come that ultimate moment when he would pour his hot seed inside her. After that, he would kiss every inch of her body until he had aroused her again. But he must remember to be gentle with her. His mother had warned him many times about his roughness. Brutality, she called it. His mother had been very upset when the little Jones girl had died. She had hidden him in the attic, telling him sternly that he must stay there until the hue and the cry died down. He had not liked being locked in the attic, and he had cried bitterly. The dead girl had been ten years old, and the last thing he had wanted to do was to hurt her. If she hadn't fought him and screamed so loudly, she would be alive today.

He forgot the Jones child as the red-headed girl turned her head his way. Her eyes had been bright with tears, and she had appeared to be looking straight at him. Only he knew that she had not really seen him, she was looking through him, not at him. Anger came to mingle with his wild desire. How dare she not see him! He had wanted to shout at her, to send his fist smashing into that exquisite face. All his life people had looked through him, and he knew why. They despised him for his inability to communicate with them, for his shuffling walk. They called him names: "Idiot." "Half-wit." But it was a dirty lie, for he knew that he was saner than his detractors. Sane enough to know that he wanted the girl with the hair of flame. She would not look through him, or call him names, because he would not allow it. He would do things to her body, those things which his mother had forbidden, and after he had done them, the girl would love him. He chuckled low in his throat as he pictured her huge, black-lashed violet eyes blazing with passion. No, she must not be like the others, she must not despise him. He did not want to kill her, he wanted to keep her with him always. If he begged his mother, perhaps she would allow him to keep the girl in the attic. With the door locked against his mother, he would thrust himself into the girl every night. He would lick every inch of her white flesh. She would beg him to hurry, and she would tell him that she could not wait to feel him inside her.

He had been annoyed when the people gathered on the hill had broken into his thoughts. All of a sudden they were shouting, laughing, weeping. They made a great din in his ears and distracted his attention from the beautiful girl. Glaring, he had turned his head, and he had seen that they were hugging each other, and shouting something about the Yankees being licked. Suddenly afraid of this show of affection, he had drawn back, but nobody had attempted to hug him. For a few moments of bewildered misery, he had wondered why he was so different, what there was about him that repelled. He loved his mother, but even she sometimes shrank from him when he caressed her. She was always telling him not to hold her so tightly. As though she was standing beside him, he could hear her voice in his ears. "Billy, don't! Oh, dear God, you're breaking my bones!" And sometimes, when he was sad, she would say, "Lie down on your bed and rest, or your head will begin to ache again."

His head was always aching, because there were voices in his head, and so the first time she had said it, he had been very angry. He had shouted at her that he was twenty years old and she was treating him like a little boy. He was a man, and he wanted someone to love. She had not understood him, even though he knew he was enunciating clearly, and so he had hit her very hard. He had hurt her, and he had been sorry afterward. He had told her so over and over. She had cried and held him in her arms, and told him that she loved him. So everything had been all right.

The girl had begun to thrust her way through the crowd, and he forgot about his mother. He had followed after her as quickly as his crippled foot would allow. Several times the excited people had stopped her, and he had resented them for claiming her attention, but even more had he resented the gray-uniformed officer who had taken her out of his sight for a while. Frantic, his head pounding, his body throbbing with his urgent need, he had prayed that she would reappear. When she finally came into view, his relief was so great that he could not hold back his tears.

After she left the officer, she had been smiling, as though something had pleased her very much. Once or twice as he followed, his crippled foot dragging along the dusty road, she had looked around uneasily, but he had kept his head bent, as if he had no interest in her. Every instinct told him to leap upon her and take her there in the road. But he was afraid, if he did that, that someone would interfere. His mother would cry, and the neighbors would say angry things about him, and he might even be locked away in that dreadful place where he had been taken once before. He would wait until it was dark. He liked the darkness best.

Dusk was tinging the sky when the girl stepped through the gates of Blue Hollow. He watched her walk up the drive and enter the house, and he had felt sick with alarm. Blue Hollow was haunted, everybody said so. What if something should happen to her?

He had wanted to run away then, because his fear of Blue Hollow, and the old man who guarded it, was very great. But his desire for the red-headed girl was even greater. Concealed behind the high hedges that bordered the property, he had watched the door. Some time went by before it opened, but it was not the girl that emerged, it was the old man whom he hated. Still he waited. Lightning split the sky, thunder rumbled menacingly, and a pelting rain soaked him, before he at last decided to move. As he approached the dark and silent house, his heart beat high in his throat, but he forced himself on. The door handle turned easily, and he was inside. It had taken him some time to find the room where the girl slept, because he had had to be very careful. Once, it had seemed to him that he heard low voices coming from the cellar, and someone had moaned very faintly. He had almost turned back, and then he had decided that it was the voices in his head.

Laughing silently, the man stepped back from the bed. He

had wanted her like this, soft and helpless and slack with sleep. Quickly, his movements jerky, he undressed, throwing his wet garments over a chair. He ran his hands down his chilled flesh, delighting in the hardened organ that would soon pierce the warm depths of her womanhood.

Desiree came awake abruptly. With that ingrained sense of danger that had always served her so well in the past, she knew immediately that she was not alone in the room. Her heart fluttering with panic, she sat up straight in the bed, listening intently. Her ears caught the dragging scrape of a footstep, and she was reminded of the grotesquely deformed, vacant-faced man who had followed her about all afternoon. Her mouth dry with fear, she called out sharply. "Who's there? Bickford, is that you?"

A strangled sound answered her, from which three stuttered words emerged. "W-want y-you. M-m-mine."

Desiree's eyes widened in horror as a dark, hunched form lurched toward her. Dear God, it was the deformed man! Her heart hammering, she threw herself across the bed, her fingers frantically seeking the drawer of the nightstand. "Keep back!" she shouted. "I have a gun, and I'll shoot you if I have to."

A hand chopped at hers, knocking it away from the drawer. Gasping with the sudden pain, she fell back against the pillows. "What do you want?" she gasped.

"Y-y-you. W-want you." The bed sagged as a heavy body settled beside her. The sheet was torn away from her stiff body. She felt the feverish burn of fingers against her skin as her nightdress ripped from top to bottom. Terror-stricken, nauseated by the sour odor of unwashed flesh, she began to fight in earnest. Screaming wildly, she struck out like an infuriated tigress, her nails gouging deeply.

"B-Billy h-hurts." Whimpering, her attacker caught her wrists in a tight grasp. His tears dripped onto her face as he bent his head and settled his wet mouth over hers. She gagged as he thrust his tongue into her mouth. With a superhuman effort she jerked her head free. For a moment she lay still, her mind whirling in despair; then, gathering all her strength, she began to buck beneath him in a violent effort to dislodge him. His grip on her wrists loosened, and she wrenched her hands away. Doubling her fists, she rained blows on his head and shoulders.

The man's sluggish brain registered pain. Flushing with fury, he gave a hoarse bellow, his meaty hand striking out at her haphazardly. The blow caught Desiree on the temple, but there was not sufficient force behind it to render her unconscious. Rigid with horror, she felt his tongue licking at her flesh, heard the garbled grunting sounds he made as he descended lower. Her mind flashed to the gun in the drawer. If only she could get to it. Sobbing, she struck out at him again, and then, as his rough hands attempted to force her legs apart, she began a high, mindless screaming.

The short hairs on the back of Christopher's neck prickled as the screaming struck his ears. Christ Almighty, what the hell was going on? Pulling his revolver from the holster, he leaped for the door. Behind him, Josh stirred from a light, feverish doze. "What's that noise?" he gasped in a weak voice.

Christopher turned swiftly. "I don't know," he said grimly, "but I aim to find out." Picking up the lantern from the floor, he added, "I'll have to leave you in the dark for a while."

Josh nodded, his eyes on the revolver in the white man's hand. "From the soun' of it, you'll need that."

"Maybe." Christopher wrenched open the cellar door. "Stay put, Josh. Don't even try to move."

The screaming, which had momentarily subsided, rose to a new and frantic pitch as Christopher thrust open the cellar door and stepped into the dimly lit hall. He glanced quickly about him, half-expecting to be greeted by a scene of violence. There was nothing. The hall, except that the furniture was no longer shrouded, was exactly as he had last seen it on a previous reconnoiter. A thought struck him. He knew that the caretaker had left the house; he had watched from the cellar window as the old man trudged down the path to the gate. He might very well have returned. He had a cottage by the crossroads, Christopher had found out, but he seemed to prefer to spend his nights at Blue Hollow. Perhaps he had brought a female back with him. If so, judging from the racket, he must have lost his mind, for the terrified sounds would seem to indicate that he was engaged in rape, or perhaps attempted murder. Christopher's mouth tightened to a grim line. Whatever was going on, he had to put a stop to it. The lantern swinging wildly from his other hand, he raced for the stairs, leaping up them two at a time.

Desiree's dilated eyes turned with wild hope as the door burst open and light illumined part of the room. Thank God! she thought, staring at the tall outline in the doorway. Someone passing had heard her screams and had come to the rescue. The shadowy shape moved, bringing into view a hand holding a revolver. "Whoever you are," she cried out frantically, "help me, please!" With renewed energy she twined her fingers in her attacker's hair and tugged savagely. "Hurry! Get him off me. He's crazy!"

Christopher lifted the lantern high. The man poised over the girl did not turn; he seemed to be unconscious of the increased light, or of another presence in the room. Mumbling to himself, he continued to paw roughly at his tossing, clawing victim. The rays of the lantern shone on the white, desperate face of the girl; then, as she turned her head away and continued with her savage struggle, her features were obscured by a tangle of bright hair. That hair, that face—he knew he had seen her before. With no time to analyze the vague flash of recognition, Christopher placed the lantern on the floor and ran for the bed.

The man turned quickly as a hard hand gripped his shoulder. For a moment he glared into the dimly seen face of the one who menaced him; then, his eyes taking on the flat feral glow of a wild animal, he thrust fiercely at the restraining hand. "D-don't," he stuttered. He looked at the girl who was lying motionless on the bed, her face turned away, her breast heaving with exertion. "Sh-sh-she m-mine."

To Christopher's ears the words were a low growl, garbled, meaningless. Bright moonlight, suddenly piercing through the clouds, flooded the room, mingling with the light from the lantern, enabling him to see clearly the look in the man's crazed eyes. Christopher's heart gave a hard startled throb. By Christ, he was dealing with a lunatic! Seeking for a way to handle the situation, he rigidly suppressed his first natural feeling of pity. His mind momentarily blank, he prodded the hunched form with his revolver. "Get up, you," he said with deliberate harshness. "Try anything, and I'll blow your head off."

The man did not understand. He only knew that he was threatened and that the object of his desire was about to be taken from him. He could not let that happen. He thrust out a huge hand in a gesture of violent protest, an unintelligible stream of words issuing from his lips. When the sharp command was repeated, he knew beyond any doubt that he faced an enemy. The men who had locked him away in the asylum had spoken to him in just such a way. But this time he would not be cowed, he would not let the enemy part him from the girl. He was strong, his hands could mangle flesh, could break bones, could kill! His face twisting into a mask of fury, the dangerous glow in his eyes intensifying, he lumbered to his feet, bellowing hoarsely.

Christopher's finger tightened on the trigger. "Get over to the door," he ordered. "Go on. Move!"

Swaying backward and forward on his heels, the man darted his wild eyes about the room, finally settled them on the grimly set face of the man before him. His enemy, he saw, was holding a piece of metal in his hand, and he was pointing it directly at him. His confused mind taking a tangent, he wondered what the piece of metal was called. Suddenly he remembered the soldiers on the battlefield. They too had held similar tubes of metal in their hands. Some had been long, some short, but all had spat fire. For a moment, conscious of a spurt of fear, he hesitated. Beside him, the girl moved restlessly, and he glanced at her quickly. So beautiful! She belonged to him, and he would have her. His strength was great, he need not fear the tube of metal. He would not fall before the spitting fire as the Yankee and Confederate soldiers had done. Growling, his shaggy head thrust forward menacingly, he took a step forward.

Christopher gestured with the revolver. "Don't try it," he warned. "Get over to the door." His eyes flashed to the girl. "You all right, miss?"

The girl appeared to be experiencing some difficulty in speaking, for she gave a long sigh. "I . . . I . . ." Her words trailed away.

"Answer me," Christopher said sharply. "Are you hurt?"

"Don't worry about me." Surprisingly, she answered him in a strong, clear voice. "I'm perfectly all right. I will be even better as soon as you get that . . . that creature out of here."

Christopher drew in his breath as the flash of recognition lost vagueness and sharpened into certainty. Desiree Grayson. There was no question of it, it was her! But what was she doing in this house, and how had she come to be mixed up with this pathetic man? Forgetting caution, he looked at her again, and it was in that unguarded moment that the lunatic sprang.

Christopher! For Desiree the scene of terror receded. He was actually here, in this room. He had come to her rescue. Words he had spoken began to replay themselves in her head. She could not be mistaken—surely it was he. Had she not heard that deep, drawling voice in her dreams, had it not troubled many of her waking moments? Her heart leaped, took up a frenzied beating. It was Christopher! But how, why? Lying there rigidly, her mind swirling with confusion, she became painfully aware of the struggle taking place. With awareness came fear for Christopher. He was tough, she had good reason to know that, and he was possessed of a wiry strength that would make him the master of most situations, but this was different. The creature grappling with him had the strength of madness.

Wincing, terrified, Desiree heard the clatter of the revolver as it hit the floor. "Christopher," she screamed, "For God's sake be careful!"

Only the panting breathing of the two men answered her. She heard the sickening contact of bone against flesh, and then a new sound, the grunting of the lunatic, interspersed with enraged bellowing. Desiree jerked upright as a table overturned with a crash, spilling its burden of fragile china ornaments. She saw the slighter figure slip and fall. The lunatic made a sound that might have been one of triumph as he hurled himself upon his fallen opponent. "K-kill!" The stuttered word came out in a snarl as his hands sought Christopher's throat.

"No!" Desiree jumped from the bed. The tall, white-painted, gilt-trimmed nightstand swayed as she wrenched open the drawer and grabbed up the gun. Whirling around, she shouted, "Get away from him, you madman, or I'll kill you!"

The loud voice stabbed through the lunatic's head like a knife, driving hatred and rage away, leaving behind only bewilderment and fear. His stranglehold slackening, he stared at the girl. Her hair was wildly tangled, her eyes blazing, and her torn nightdress hung in two halves, revealing her body. He could feel her hatred. Whimpering softly, he looked at the thing in her hand, the thing that would spit fire, that would hurt him. Who was she? He did not know her, he did not like her raised voice and the hatred in her eyes. He opened his mouth to speak, when the loud voice spoke again. "I said get away from him!"

His eyes vacant, he stared from her to the man beneath him. Another stranger. Where had he come from, what did he want with him? Even as he wondered, the man raised his hands and fastened steely fingers about his wrists. The grip, imbued with a surprising strength, tightened, sending fiery shooting pains up his arms.

The man beneath him spoke, but his head was turned toward the girl with the loud voice, and his words were for her. "Keep out of this," he said. "I can take care of myself."

The girl answered something, but the lunatic did not hear her. His scrambled brain was scuttling in frantic circles, trying to make some sense out of the situation in which he found himself. He watched the girl for a moment. She had lowered the gun and was hastily lighting the candles. The room bloomed with a mellow light, and he looked about him. Where was this place, what was he doing here? His eyes dropped to his pinioned wrists. He did not understand why this man should want to hurt him, but then, had he ever understood those others who had mocked and jeered at him and had bruised his flesh with stones? His mother had often said to him, "It is hard to understand the cruelty of some people, son. They seem to be mortally afraid of someone who is different. My dearest lad, I know you are hurting, and perhaps it will be so throughout your life, but try, if you can, not to mind so much." This man must be one of the cruel ones of whom she had spoken. But if he would only stop hurting him, he would try to do as his mother asked. He would even forgive, as she was always urging him to do. A sound came from his tight throat, rough-edged, and yet unmistakably a plea for mercy. His plea was answered, for, surprisingly, the grip on his wrists slackened slightly. "All right," the man beneath him said, "I think I know what you're trying to say. I'll let up if you will. Take your hands away from my throat."

He wanted to obey the hoarse, commanding voice, but he felt too weak to move, and his fingers, with a will of their own, seemed to be frozen into place. Shooting pains, like red-hot needles, were starting in his temples, burrowing deep behind his eyes. Through long familiarity, he knew that very soon the pain would spread, and that he would be half-blind and helpless before the grinding agony in his head. He thought again of his mother, she who was so calm, so sane, so soothing, and he felt a wave of longing to be with her. If only he were back in his safe, comfortable room beneath the eaves of the cottage. If he could escape from this terrifying place, he would find his way home somehow. Once there, he would go to his room and he would never leave it again.

"He's mad! Don't you understand that?" The red-headed girl's voice rose hysterically. "Why do you try to reason with him? It is a wasted effort. He doesn't understand a word you are saying."

The lunatic gaped at the man beneath him. He seemed to be annoyed by the girl's interruption, for he spoke to her in a sharp voice. His dark brows drawn together in a frowning line, he said, "Just for once in your life be silent. I think I am getting through to him. He is not so much dangerous now, as frightened. Can't you see that?"

"No, no, I can't see it. I only know, if something is not done, that he will kill you!"

"I told you to be silent. I'll handle this. He is fairly quiet now, but one wrong move from you might set him off again."

"Oh, God! How can you say that? He is choking you."

The girl began to sob, and she made a quick movement. The lunatic turned his eyes swiftly to her. These two talked and talked, but he did not know what they were saying or if it affected him in some way. The girl was pointing that metal tube at him again. Held in her trembling hand, it wavered. The pain in his head eased for a blessed moment, and he could tell that something had frightened her badly. Her red hair was tumbling over her shoulders, and her naked body with the beautiful breasts was trembling as badly as her hand. Looking at her, he felt nothing, not desire, no emotion of any kind. He wanted his mother, the haven of his home.

Christopher heaved upward, easing but not dislodging the lunatic's weak grip on his throat. "Get off me, you great ox," he panted, "or I swear I'll break your wrists!"

Threatened, frantic with fear, he instinctively tightened his fingers about Christopher's throat. The man beneath him made a gurgling sound, and the girl began to scream, a high, dreadful sound that hurt his head. Again the lunatic was bewildered. Relaxing the pressure of his fingers, he looked down at the man. The dark eyes that met his were slightly glazed, but when he eased the pressure of his hands about his throat, they began to blaze with a fierce light. All his life, he thought, the eyes of people had haunted him. There had been cold eyes, mocking eyes, contemptuous eyes, others that had shown their hatred so plainly that he had been confused and frightened. Only his mother's leaf-brown eyes were kind, and he wanted her with him now. She would tell him what he must do, she would guide and direct him, as she had always done. The pain in his temples stabbed savagely, making him lose his last tenuous hold on reality. He could not see, he was in a terrible darkness. Flinging back his head, he gave vent to a wailing, tormented cry.

Desiree drew in a sobbing breath. The deformed man was taking life away from the man she loved, and she must stop him! She shot a swift look at Christopher, and saw that his eyes were closed. Was he unconscious? Dead? Her hands icy cold, she steadied the weapon. Squinting along the barrel, fearful of missing her target and hitting Christopher instead, she took careful aim and fired. The recoil of the heavy gun threw her back onto the bed. Stunned by the blinding flash in unison with the blast from the gun, she let it drop from her numbed hand. Shuddering, she heard the spine-chilling howl that came from the wounded man's mouth. God help her, God help them both! She had meant to kill him, but she had only succeeded in wounding him. No doubt he would kill them both now. With only one thought in her mind, she raised herself from the bed. She must get to Christopher. She must be with him when the inevitable happened.

The lunatic clutched at his bloody upper arm, aware of nothing but that a new pain had been added to his torment. His dimmed eyes stared unseeingly about him, and then suddenly, like an echo of hope, he heard his mother's voice calling to him. Trying to subdue the tortured sounds that tore from his straining throat, he put his shaggy head to one side and listened intently. "Billy, don't be afraid." Clear and strong, her voice sounded in his ears. "Come to Mother, son."

"M-M-Mama!" he babbled. She was calling to him, and he must go to her. She would hide him, she would not let him be hurt. She would put her arms about him and rock him gently. He would not mind, not ever again, if she treated him like a child. Desperately holding on to the comforting thought, he lurched to his feet and stumbled over to the door.

Staring at the trail of blood spots that marked his awkward passage, Desiree felt sick. Her nails bit deeply into her palms as the howling rose to a new crescendo. Dear God! What kind of a monster was she? She had actually tried to kill that poor idiot. She heard the thudding of his body as he reeled against the wall, hitting it once, twice. In the pause that followed, her ears strained. The howling rose again, and she heard the clatter of his feet as he scuttled along the corridor and down the stairs. A chair overturned as he fell heavily; then his footsteps sounded again. With a banging of the outer door, the terrible sound was cut off. How badly had she wounded him? Should she go after him and find out? Uncertain, Desiree took a step toward the door. No, she decided, she must stay here. She could not leave Christopher. He needed her.

Trembling with reaction, she turned and looked at the still figure on the floor. For a moment she could not move; she stood there, her hands pressed to her mouth. "Christopher!" Life returning to her limbs, she rushed across the room and sank down beside him. "Oh, please," she sobbed, her fingers tracing over his closed eyes. "Oh, please, let him be all right!"

Christopher, who had been hovering on the edge of unconsciousness, felt his senses beginning to clear. Unable for the moment to orient himself, he wondered who was bending over him, breathing in such agitated gasps. Fingers were touching his face, his painful throat, a light touch, like the fluttering of butterfly wings. He breathed deeply, wincing with the pain of the effort, and his nostrils caught a drift of familiar perfume. Desiree Grayson! He turned his head away, rejecting her touch. "What happened?" His voice was husky, slightly labored, but distinct.

"I shot him. I had to, Christopher. He was trying to kill you!"

Christopher's eyes opened abruptly. "You shot him! Why? Couldn't you have left things to me?"

Desiree stiffened. He owed his life to her, and he was actually daring to criticize her action. All that was arrogant in her nature surfaced, banishing joy and relief. Men! she thought angrily, they were all the same. They were obstinate, vain, and quite unable to believe that a woman could handle a dangerous situation as well as they. "What should I have done, then?" she snapped. "Stood by and allowed him to kill you? You are a fool, Christopher Fairfield! Leave things to you indeed. If I had, you wouldn't be talking to me now." She glared at his averted face. "Well, are you ashamed to look at me?"

"Not in the least. Though I would think, in your present condition, that you would prefer me not to look at you." Christopher's head turned slowly. "Well, dear Miss Desiree, I am looking at you, and I see that you are as beautiful as ever. A little bare, perhaps, but very satisfying to the eyes." He paused, fully aware that he was being unreasonable, but unable to resist. "If you have a fault," he added, "it is that you are inclined to be too hasty."

Desiree looked at him suspiciously. "What do you mean by that?"

"I mean that I had a lock on that unfortunate man's wrists. In another moment, had you granted it to me, I would have broken his hold."

Desiree's eyes flashed. "Fiddle!" she snapped. "You were unconscious."

"Not quite." Amused by her indignation, Christopher smiled faintly. "Appearances can be deceptive."

"In this case they were not." Desiree had seen his smile, and she was forced to conquer an inclination to throw herself into his arms. He was not serious, she knew that now, but still she held on to her anger. It was, she felt, her only defense against the treacherous emotions that were threatening to overwhelm her. She could not help loving him, she told herself, but he was stiff-necked, quite impossible, and obviously incapable of showing gratitude. Why, she brooded darkly, he had not even shown surprise at seeing her. Very well, then, let him nurse his bruised masculinity. He had asked no questions of her, so she would ask none of him.

Christopher's brief moment of amusement had vanished. He had always hoped, should he ever see Desiree Grayson again, that he would long ago have come to terms with himself. Apparently the restraint he had put on his thoughts with regard to her had not worked. There was no indifference, only a painful awareness of her. Here she was, so close to him that he could feel the warmth of her flesh, and the love that he had worked so hard to subdue was stronger than ever. From the moment he had walked away, leaving her alone in the forest, it had seemed to him that he had left some vital part of himself behind. He was incomplete without her, and the mournful certainty came to him that he always would be. Wherever he went, whatever he did, the haunting memory of her was with him. He felt a spasm of bitterness. Why fight it anymore, why not admit the truth to himself? Fool that he was, he was hopelessly and endlessly in love with the high-and-mighty Miss Desiree Grayson. He did not want to throw mocking words at her, or hide his feelings behind a barrier of hard reserve. He wanted to take her into his arms, kiss her gently, and tell her of his love. But to do so, he knew, would be to invite her scornful laughter, and that he could not bear. Frowning, he sat up, brushing aside Desiree's quickly held-out hands. "Thank you," he said curtly. "I can manage."

"Curse your obstinate hide!" Desiree flared. "Why must you be so disagreeable?"

Christopher shrugged. "Possibly because I was born with a disagreeable nature." His eyes rested briefly on her flushed, tear-streaked face, slid lower to linger on her breasts. He laughed softly as her hands fluttered upward in a futile attempt to cover herself. He raised his eyes to her face again. "Well, well," he said, forcing himself to speak flippantly, "so we meet again." He touched her breast lightly. "And you, I see, are in much the same condition as I left you."

Flushing at the insult implied by his touch and his words, Desiree drew back. "Shut up!" She glared at him. "You might at least have the grace not to mention that incident." Her eyes dropped before his dark, mocking gaze. He was deliberately goading her, but she, who had dreamed so often of this meeting, should not be snarling at him like a fishwife. Forlornly she thought of all the faults in her character that her father had been at such pains to point out to her. She was not gentle, not feminine enough. Perhaps if she were, Christopher might find something in her to love.

Christopher looked at her curiously. What had brought that look to her eyes? What was she thinking about so intently? "You must know by now that I have no grace, Miss Desiree," he answered her slowly. Forcing himself on, he touched her again. "When there is time, would you care to repeat the incident?"

"How dare you!" Desiree's good intentions vanished. "Your opinion of me is not high, you have made that quite clear. But I am no trumpery whore whom you can pick up whenever the mood moves you."

Watching the hot color scorch her cheeks and spread downward to her throat, Christopher despised himself. He had been so intent on guarding his feelings, on saving himself from the hurt that must be his if she should guess how he really felt, that he had gone much too far. "I truly apologize," he said gently. "I had no right to say such a thing."

Tears sprang into Desiree's eyes. "Some of the fault is mine, I know that. That day in the forest, when you . . . when you . . ."

"When I raped you?"

"When you made love to me," Desiree substituted. "I responded to you, so why would you not think of me as a cheap person? No, let me state the truth. As a whore. For that is how you think of me. Admit it."

Christopher shook his head. "I will admit to no such thing. I have never thought that of you."

Startled by his change of manner, Desiree said uncertainly, "What do you think of me?"

Christopher frowned uneasily. What did she want from him, where was all this leading? Had she, in some uncanny feminine way, sensed the truth that he was trying so hard to hide? Hardening himself against the appeal she made to his senses, he spoke with a soft but cutting emphasis. "As a child, I saw you now and again, but for all that, I don't really know you. You were a pretty and spirited little creature, determined to have your own way, and almost unbearably spoiled. Yes, you were quite the little princess."

"And now?"

"And now," Christopher answered, shrugging, "you have grown from a pretty child into a beautiful woman. But you know that for yourself."

"That is not what I meant."

"Then what do you want from me?" Christopher said, voicing his thoughts.

"The truth."

"I've told you that I scarcely know you. But if you want my opinion, I am willing to give it. You are still spoiled, pampered, useless, and quite incapable of seeing any issue clearly. This war, for instance. I have no doubt that you find it all quite romantic."

Desiree tried to summon anger, but it would not come. "You are very scathing, Christopher," she said quietly. "Do you think you are qualified to make such a sweeping statement?"

"Perhaps not. You asked for my opinion, and I gave it." Rising to his feet, Christopher made his way to the couch between the windows. Removing the carpetbag, he sat down. "My remarks on your character are based on my observation of the rich and privileged class, of which you are one."

Desiree's lips curled slightly. "To be rich and to be privileged. There is no greater stigma in your eyes, is there?"

He ignored the sarcasm. "Let me put it another way. I have had little cause to love them."

"True. But we are not all pampered and useless. There are some who believe in justice and fair play, and who think and act much, I imagine, as you used to do." She paused. "I find you merely arrogant now, and filled with blind prejudice."

Hot blood stung Christopher's face. She had spoken without heat, but her remarks, like barbs, had gone deep. She had made him feel ashamed, a fool! With resentful eyes he watched her rise and go over to the bed. Picking up her robe, she got into it, belting it tightly about her slender waist. Unaccustomed to the feeling she had aroused in him, he said sharply, "I suppose you are trying to tell me that you are different?"

"I am." Desiree walked across the room and seated herself beside him. "At least," she went on, "I hope I'm different. And no, I don't find the war romantic, quite the contrary. But like it or not, we are at war, and I want to help the men in any way I can."

"Admirable," Christopher said tonelessly. His thoughts reverted to Josh, he moved uneasily. He must get back to him soon, and it was not only Josh who concerned him, there were others in need of help. But he was so tired. What would it hurt if he rested for a while? He thought of the lunatic and his possible fate, and then, glancing at Desiree, who was watching him expectantly, he dismissed him. "So you want to help your dashing and romantic countrymen," he said with a faint sneer. "Hurrah for slavery, eh?"

"No, down with slavery." Desiree smiled at him. "Yankee or Southerner, it's all one to me. It's just that I want to give my help to any man who is suffering."

"Oh, for Christ's sake, don't turn saint on me," Christopher snapped. "You are the least likely candidate for sainthood."

Desiree's eyes flashed. "What do you know about anything? I am not good, but I am not as bad as you make me out to be."

Christopher's lips curled in cynical amusement. "This war is a new game for the ladies, who have never had more to do than snip flowers or perhaps supervise the correct laying of a table."

"You are an ignorant boor, you are quite impossible, and there is just no talking to you!"

Once again she was right, Christopher thought. Why could he not refrain from goading her? Crushing down his shame, he answered her calmly. "I am all of those things, so why waste your time talking to me? Don't be so verbose in speaking of your noble ambition, just get on with it. Now is an ideal time to parade your patriotism. I am sure the wounded soldiers would appreciate your attention. You are not squeamish about maggots, I hope. They do sometimes develop in neglected wounds."

She glared at him. "I am wasting my time with you."

"Quite. I told you that. So why attempt to enlist my sympathy?"

The wave of desolation that swept Desiree cooled her anger. "I had hoped to get through to you in some way," she said in a small voice, "but you are determined to think the worst of me." Where was her pride? she wondered. Why must she persist? With bitterness she remembered the vow she had made to herself, that if she should ever see this man again, she would never let him go. Her soft mouth hardened with resolution. She would keep that vow. Wherever Christopher Fairfield went, she would go, and the devil take the consequences. He could curse at her, revile her, tell her to go away and leave him in peace, but it would make no difference. She thought fleetingly of her ambition to nurse the sick, to give something of herself to this unfortunate and tragic war, and having thought, she dismissed it. Christopher was right about her in one way: she was selfish, determined to have her own way, and added to that, she apparently had no conscience. She only knew that if she was to have any life at all, her place, her only place, was with him. He was a bitter and cynical man, scarred by prison life. He had no belief in others, and especially not in herself, and perhaps he had no love to give. But if he had, it might be, through her tenaciousness, her loyalty, her refusal to be turned away, that it would be given to her. It was a forlorn hope, but it was the only one she had. Studying him, for the first time she became aware of his torn and smoke-blackened gray uniform. Her eyes widened in amazement. How strange that she had not noticed it before. She felt a flare of hope. Unless he had donned the uniform as a disguise to aid him in his flight, it might be that she could nurse the wounded and yet not entirely lose sight of Christopher. "Christopher . . ." She touched his grimy sleeve, and the questions she had vowed not to utter sprang to her lips. "Tell me what you are doing here, and in that uniform?"

Christopher's mind veered to this new problem. In the emotion of seeing her again, he had forgotten his appearance. He, a convict, wearing the uniform of the Confederate Army. How must it look to her? Through various sources, he had learned that many convicts had been freed to take their places in the ranks of war, and that afterward, if a bullet did not get them first, they had been promised a full pardon, but he was not one of them. His case was different, and Desiree Grayson knew that very well. He had escaped from Buxton Prison, and as far as officialdom was concerned, he was an outcast from their self-interest and beneficence, a man on the run. If this girl should choose to betray him, it would go ill with him. No chance would be given to him to fight for the South, no promise of a pardon. He would either be returned immediately to Buxton Prison or he would be shot. He had raped Desiree Grayson, and this would be an ideal chance for her to take revenge. Of course she would expose him.

"Christopher"—her voice interrupted his racing thoughts—"please tell me what you are doing in that uniform?"

He did not hear the hope in her voice. "My duty, what else?" he said curtly. Reluctantly Christopher turned his head and looked at her, and suddenly he was not quite so certain of the action she would take. There was a difference in the violet eyes regarding him, a brightness, a softness that he had not expected to see. "I did not give myself up, if you are thinking that," he went on abruptly. "I have not been pardoned to serve as cannon fodder. I am a convict who joined the army under an assumed name. There, now you know. My fate is in your hands, and I think I know what it will be."

"You are mistaken," Desiree said gently. "Your fate is not in my hands. It is in your own, I would say."

"Are you saying that I should surrender myself to the military authorities?"

"No. You must know that I am not."

"What do you mean?" Christopher's eyes sharpened. "Are you telling me that you will say nothing about—?"

"About the fact that you were falsely convicted of murder?" Desiree interrupted. "Yes, that is what I am telling you."

He looked at her searchingly. "Is this some kind of a joke? If it is, I don't appreciate it."

Desiree's lips quivered in uncharacteristic weakness. Why must he speak so harshly? What more could she say to convince him? A wave of weariness swept over her, and against her will she found herself remembering the horrifying scene that had taken place in this room. Would she ever be able to forget her anguish when she had believed that the deformed man was about to kill Christopher, or the swift and violent action she had taken against the mindless creature? With the memory of that demented howling in her ears, she looked at the trail of blood spots leading to the door. Shuddering, trying to compose her trembling limbs, she glanced back at Christopher. He was watching her intently, and there was an expression in those dark, unguarded eyes that she had never thought to see, an expression that told her that he wanted to believe. Her heart leaping, she answered him in a shaken voice. "Of course I'm not joking. I'm convinced that you did not kill Charlotte Elliot."

Christopher's rigidly held shoulders slumped, and the sigh that came from him confirmed Desiree's belief. As further proof of that inner surrender, he took her cold hands in his and held them tightly. "Thank you for that," he said softly.

Desiree's weariness vanished as though it had never been, and the smile she gave him was radiant. "Christopher, did you hear yourself?" she exclaimed. "You are actually accepting my word."

Christopher returned her smile uncertainly. "So I am. But your amazement is not nearly as great as my own. It has been a long time since I believed in anybody." He paused;

then, with a slight return to his old manner, he went on abruptly, "I might be a stranger to myself at this moment, but I have not lost sight of the fact that I injured you. You have every right to inform against me. I would not blame you if you did."

Desiree's smile faded. "I thought I'd made it quite clear that I've no intention of doing so."

Christopher shrugged. "Perhaps you did," he conceded.

He was unused to trusting, Desiree thought, refusing to allow her hurt to develop. She must not expect too much of him, for it would take him a long time to grow out of the habits and suspicions that had no doubt been developed in prison. He had been innocent of murder; nothing now could shake her belief in him. To be caged up under those conditions, with no chance of an appeal, would surely change the mildest of men, and Christopher Fairfield, if those wild stories about him had the smallest grain of truth, had never been mild. Excitingly different, cynical, violent in some of his reactions, but never mild. "Try to remember that I wish you well, Christopher," she said gently. "It is important to me."

"Why?"

"It just is." Reluctantly she withdrew her hands from his loosened grasp. Suppressing a mad impulse to tell him of her true feelings, she said in a calm, low voice. "I know you have a particular hatred of the name of Grayson, Christopher. That being so, it is quite useless to tell you that my father did not intentionally hurt you. But I did not sit on that jury that condemned you, and even though my name is Grayson, I have the hope that we can be friends. Do you think it's possible?"

Christopher studied her, weighing her words. Her skin was golden-tinted, rose-flushed at the high cheekbones, her violet eyes were luminous, and the fiery hair framing her face and tumbling about her shoulders reminded him of curling, licking flames. She was incredibly beautiful, he had always thought so, and fool that he was, he could not help loving her. But the gulf between them was too great to be bridged, so he would never tell her of that love. Somehow this strange and unexpected meeting had reversed his opinion of her, and he knew now that she would treat a confession of love with kindness, but there would be pity there too, and he could not endure that.

Desiree stirred uneasily beneath his regard. "Why are you staring at me? I asked you a simple question. Can we be friends?"

"If that is what you want."

"I do."

"Then I don't see why not." Deliberately blocking his mind to a vision of the tempting body concealed beneath the flimsy robe, Christopher looked away. "I don't hate your father anymore, Desiree," he said almost gently.

Desiree started. "Christopher, I'm so glad! You've realized that he did not deliberately railroad you, that his verdict was based on a true belief in your guilt, and on nothing more than that?"

"I realize nothing of the sort." There was a restrained violence in Christopher's answering voice. "Like you, I am not a likely candidate for sainthood, so it is unlikely that I shall forget. But that mock trial and the outcome of it are no longer of importance to me."

"And yet there is still hatred in you. I can sense it."

"Yes, and the wish to kill," Christopher said bluntly, "but it is reserved for one man." He looked directly at her, and she suffered a shock at the sudden blaze in his eyes. "Listen to me, I did not join the army from motives of patriotism, if that's what you're thinking. I am looking for someone, and in this general upset, it seemed to me to be my best means of tracking him down."

"Don't look like that!" Desiree could not repress a shiver. "It makes me afraid for you."

"No need," Christopher said curtly. "I can look after myself."

Desiree said doubtfully, "For your sake, I hope so." And for mine, she wanted to add, for mine! "Christopher, who is this man you're after?"

"He is a very good friend of yours, I believe. His name is Frazer Phillips."

Somehow she had expected to hear that name on his lips. "He is no friend of mine, I assure you," she answered, her quiet voice carrying conviction. "But you said that the trial is no longer important to you, so what has he done?"

"I believe he has killed twice. He has to be stopped."

Desiree's eyes widened. "I don't understand. Whatever my feelings for him, I can't believe he's a murderer."

"Believe it," Christopher said in a savage voice. "He killed my sister. I believe that he also murdered Charlotte Elliot."

Stunned, Desiree felt a coldness at her heart. Whatever else she might have expected him to say, it was not this. "Chrissie!" There was horror in her rising voice. "Chrissie is dead? Christopher, do you know what you are saying?"

"I do. I am saying that Chrissie is dead. I am saying that Frazer Phillips killed her!"

Desiree put her hand to her trembling mouth. "Oh, dear God!"

Christopher laughed harshly. "Don't mention God to me! If God does indeed exist, then why didn't He protect Chrissie? She was so vulnerable, so sweet in all her ways."

Unaware of the tears on her cheeks, enduring his agony of mind as well as the burden of her own horror, Desiree began to tremble violently. "I . . . I visited Chrissie often. I came to know her quite well."

"Did you?" Christopher's fierce suffering eyes softened. "You cared for her?"

"Very much!"

"She believed the best of everybody." Christopher's voice shook. "Yes, even of me. God! Why doesn't he protect the innocents of this cursed rotten world?"

"I wish I had an answer for you." Desiree put her hand over his tightly clenched fist. "Christopher, you have kept everything inside you for too long, perhaps it would be better out. If you'd like to tell me about it, you will find that I'm a very good listener."

His dark brows rose sardonically. "Where would you like me to start, Miss Desiree?"

"Christopher, don't!" Desiree flushed hotly beneath his suddenly inimical gaze. "Suffering is better shared, you must know that." She hesitated. "Tell me about Buxton Prison, that will be a start."

"For your amusement?"

"I want to know you." Desiree persisted. "I want to help you, if I can."

"You can't help me, only I can do that, and a lousy job I've made of it so far." Christopher looked at her searchingly, and what he read in her eyes appeared to satisfy him, for he said slowly, "All right. If you want to know what it feels like to be a caged animal, I'll tell you."

Desiree's heart began to beat very fast as he hesitated, and then began to speak. Long-damned-up words came bursting from him in a torrent, creating vividly horrifying pictures in her mind. She was privy to his innermost feelings as, in imagination, she entered with him into that great bleak place that was Buxton Prison. She felt his hatred, his despair, his bitterness, the manacles that weighted down his limbs. She toiled with him in the torrid unrelenting heat, froze with him in the bitter winter, and inhaled the poisonous miasma that rose from the marshes surrounding the prison. She watched men drop in their tracks and die, broken by harsh and unremitting labor, by semimalnutrition, and by constant exposure to the merciless elements. Sunstroke, frostbite, the sting of mosquitoes, malaria, an outbreak of yellow fever. Few were the men serving a long sentence who survived the full term. They toiled, they died, and when they closed their eyes for the last time, they were buried without ceremony in the hard, stony earth. There were no headstones, not even a cross to mark the fact that they had once existed.

Staring at Christopher, Desiree wanted to beg him to stop, but she knew that she must not. Her heart beating rapidly, she saw the guards patrolling the walls, and she feared the brutal punishments that were meted out for the slightest infraction, felt the agony of the searing lash. Christopher's determination to escape became real to her. The many attempts, the failures, and then, finally, success. The hardships of that grueling journey to freedom, the longed-for sight of home. Chrissie's eyes, looking huge in her pale face at her first glimpse of him. Chrissie laughing, hugging him, full of joy that was mingled with a terrible fear that he would be discovered and sent back to Buxton. Chrissie dead, her laughter stilled, her warmth and her love vanished forever. Through Christopher's eyes, Desiree looked down at Chrissie's body, felt his grief. She saw him pick up the crumpled bloodstained handkerchief that bore the initials F.P., and she knew his burning desire for vengeance.

Christopher's voice trailed into silence. He sat very still, and then, seeing her white face, he patted her hand briefly. "I'm sorry if I have upset you, Desiree, but you did want to know."

Swallowing against the lump in her throat, Desiree found her voice. "What does it matter about me!" she cried. "Oh,

Christopher, I meant to be so wise, to advise you if I could. And now I don't know what to say to you."

"There is nothing to say. You asked me, I told you. Let us leave it at that."

Desiree shook her head. "I may not know what to say, but there is something I can do. I will inquire about Frazer Phillips. It should not be too hard to locate his regiment."

"You believe me, Desiree? About Phillips, I mean?"

"Every word," she answered him simply. "We will find him."

"We?"

"Yes. I want to help."

"Keep out of it." Christopher's voice hardened. "It is my problem, not yours."

"We are friends now, you and I, and I am making it mine."

"Don't be a fool!" Christopher said impatiently. "This is between Phillips and myself. I don't want you mixed up in this."

A new fear came to her. "When you do find him, what will you do?"

"What do you think?" He looked at her, the frightening blaze back in his eyes. "I will kill him, of course. But I will kill him slowly. I want him to suffer!"

Desiree's voice rose sharp and urgent. "You are no murderer. Frazer Phillips must be handed over to the proper authorities. They will deal with him as he deserves."

"And obviously you still believe in fairy tales." Christopher looked at her as though she had taken leave of her senses. "What possible purpose will it serve to hand him over?" he went on in a low, goaded voice. "Have you forgotten who I am? It will be Phillips' word against mine, and mine, as you know, will count for nothing."

"But you will not be alone in this," Desiree persisted desperately. "I will see to it that you are heard. You must remember that the name of Grayson carries a great deal of weight."

"I am unlikely to forget it." Christopher smiled grimly. "But Phillips also has considerable influence."

"I know. But you will be heard," Desiree repeated. "I promise you."

"Promise me nothing," Christopher retorted sharply. "I say to hell with the law. I'll go it my own way."

"You are forgetting the war. Frazer may be killed."

Christopher was very still for a moment. "Yes, he could be." His mouth twisted bitterly. "He could have a hero's death, and another Phillips would go down in the annals of glorious history." He turned to her, his expression fierce. "I can't let it happen that way. I must find him. He must die at my hands!"

Seeking for words, Desiree clasped his arm with tense fingers. What could she possibly say that would turn him from his purpose? "Please," she said at last, "let us do it the lawful way."

Again Christopher gave her that look that doubted her sanity. "I've already told you that it will be my word against his. Besides, I have no proof to offer. There is only my own deep conviction. That being so, I would not have Phillips slip through my fingers."

In her secret life Desiree was accustomed to command, and always before she had taken the initiative. But she could not command Christopher Fairfield to her will. She loved him, he was set on a headlong course to destruction, and she could not turn him from that course. She had nothing to offer him but futile words. Drawing in a steadying breath, she ventured feebly, "If one searches, proof can be found. Somehow we will find it."

Despite himself, Christopher felt his former suspicions stirring. "Why are you so concerned?" he asked in a hard voice. "What is it to you?"

Words she longed to utter sprang to Desiree's lips, but she forced them back. Now was not the time to tell him that she loved him. He would laugh at her, or even worse, he would refuse to believe. "I . . ." She hesitated, searching for words. "I believe you, and I cared about Chrissie."

Christopher's eyes narrowed in concentration, as though he sought to see into her mind. "Yes," he said at last, "I think you did." His voice, which had softened, took on hardness again. "And what of Phillips? I was under the impression that you were rather fond of him."

Color surged into Desiree's face. "And you think I am trying to protect him," she cried. "Is that it?"

"Something like that."

"You're wrong!" Desiree's temper flared, momentarily banishing her fear for him. "I told you that I have no time for Frazer Phillips, and I meant it. To hell with the goddamned swine! He is the true meaning of a slaver."

"Your father keeps slaves." Christopher's eyes were suddenly intent upon her face. "Is it for you to condemn the practice in others?"

"I condemn all slavers, my father included." Carried away, Desiree rushed on. "I have fought my father, who is reasonably decent to his Negroes, and I have fought scum like Phillips, who treats his Negroes as though they are not even human. And if the need arises, I will go on fighting, you may be sure of that."

Amazed by her vehemence, the look on her face, Christopher continued to regard her. "I have fought my father," she had said. "I have fought scum like Phillips." Desiree Grayson was the same, as fragile-looking, as feminine, as beautiful as ever, and yet she was not the same. The subtle difference was marked by her tone, her expression, the suddenly hard glitter in her lovely violet eyes. He looked at the firm set of her soft mouth, the taut aggressive line of her chin, and he found that he could not put his finger on wherein the real difference lay. Was she two different women in one, then? The languid Southern belle, full of airs and graces and fluttering helplessness, and this woman who faced him now, bold, determined, someone who, he was suddenly sure, would make a dangerous and ruthless enemy. The word "feminine" leaped into his mind again. That was it, that was what was bewildering him. At this moment she was not feminine. There was something in her stance, in her thrown-back head and her tightly clenched hands that was, for want of a better word, almost masculine. It would seem, Christopher thought ruefully, that there was more, much more to Desiree Grayson, and that he had never really known her at all. He castigated himself for an imaginative fool, but he could not help a flare of excitement as he found himself remembering the words she had spoken to him that day in the forest. "Don't you know who I am?" she had said. And then something else: "I could arrange for you to go North. I don't suppose it would matter to you which side you fought on, would it?" He had not even known there was a war on at that time, and so her words had meant nothing. But now they had taken on a peculiar significance. She could arrange for him to go North! There was her mention of fighting, her apparent hatred of slavery. Could it be possible that she was in some way connected with an abolitionist movement, that she had actually helped slaves to escape to the North?

"Why are you looking at me like that?" Desiree's voice interrupted his thoughts. "You don't believe me, is that it? What do I have to do to get through to you, you cursed stubborn mule?"

There it was again, the steely ring in her usually low and beautifully modulated voice, the voice of someone accustomed to command. His head full of conjectures and possibilities, Christopher was still far from guessing the truth. "Who are you, Desiree Grayson," he said quietly, "who are you really?"

Desiree stared at him, unable to fathom the expression in his eyes. What had she said that he should put such a question to her? Drawn by his sudden stillness, his air of waiting, she wanted to tell him who she was and exactly what she stood for, but somehow she could not find the words. Her eyes dropped. "I . . . I don't know what you mean."

The Southern belle was back. Conscious of disappointment, Christopher nonetheless persisted. "You are not what you seem, I am sure of that."

"Perhaps not. But then, very few of us are what we seem." With a cool smile Desiree brushed his observation to one side. "Christopher"—her face softened into an expression of pleading—"when you find Phillips, promise me that you will not take matters into your own hands."

The questions in Christopher's mind vanished. What a fool he was! For a few moments he had seen something in Desiree Grayson that was definitely not there. No doubt she had been playing a part, and her boldly spoken words had been uttered to impress. Though why she should attempt to impress him was beyond his comprehension.

"Christopher, please promise me." Desiree leaned nearer to him.

Christopher rose to his feet. "I can't make you that promise," he said, heading for the door.

"Wait! Where are you going?"

His hand on the doorknob, Christopher turned to face her.

"I thought this house was empty when I entered it. I have a wounded man in the cellar, and I must attend to him."

"In the cellar? Why didn't you put him into one of the bedrooms?"

"I had my reasons. The caretaker, for one."

Desiree looked at him with bewildered eyes. "But Bickford is loyal to the Cause. He would have helped you. He would have seen to it that—"

"Never mind," Christopher cut her short. "As I said, I must take care of him, and then I must get back to the other wounded. I have been gone too long as it is." He paused. "How is it that you know the name of the caretaker, and what are you doing in this house?" His eyes narrowed in thought. "I have heard of people who follow the army from place to place, who seem to find excitement in destruction and death. Is that why you are here?"

"How dare you!" Angry color scalded Desiree's face. "What right have you to sit in judgment upon me?"

"Why are you here?"

"I have every right. Blue Hollow belongs to my father. Are you satisfied?"

Christopher had a sudden wish to go to her, to kiss the anger from her mouth. Restraining himself, he said calmly. "Not quite. This hardly seems the place for you to be at this time."

"Never mind." Desiree's anger died as a thought at the back of her mind began to take shape. Rising, she went quickly toward him. "You spoke of attending the wounded," she said, an undercurrent of excitement in her voice. "Does that mean that you are attached to a medical unit?"

"It does." Christopher looked at her curiously. "I am attached to the Fifty-sixth."

"The Fifty-sixth!" Desiree's voice rose.

"That's what I said. Are you thinking that compassion is not much in my line?"

Desiree spoke without heat. Smiling, she looked at him triumphantly. "Well, well, it seems that we will be traveling together."

"What do you mean?"

Desiree's smile lingered. "It's really very simple. I went to see General Hunt of the Fifty-sixth. I offered him my services as a nurse. I was accepted."

"What!" An expression that was curiously reminiscent of Bickford's, austere, disapproving, shocked, crossed Christopher's face. "But you're a woman!"

Desiree laughed. "So I am. I'm glad that you noticed."

"But you of all people!"

"Yes, me. I see nothing wrong with a woman traveling with the army. I am strong, willing, and I am not short on compassion." Desiree darted him a quick glance. "You do not have a monopoly on compassion, you know."

"I'm not suggesting that I do," Christopher said irritably, his dark brows drawing together in an ominous frown. "But it is like you to twist my words."

"Like me! Have you ever listened to yourself?"

"We are talking of you. You are spoiled. All your life you have been sheltered and protected. You will not be able to stand the constant strain."

"You are mistaken," Desiree said firmly. "I have a great deal of strength and endurance."

"Not enough. Go home, where you belong."

"I have given my word to General Hunt." Desiree gave him an innocent look. "You would not have me go back on it?"

"Why not? It would probably not be the first time." Losing the struggle to hold his emotion in check, Christopher said violently. "You little fool! You have no idea what you will be up against. There is no place for a woman in a war."

"I think there is. When it comes to nursing, women are superior to men."

"The Fifty-sixth goes right to the war front, and the medical unit does not stay behind the lines." Christopher was unaware of the note of desperation in his voice. "We will be right in the thick of things. Did General Hunt inform you of that?"

"He did. He was most explicit."

"You could be hurt, perhaps killed."

At the look in his eyes, Desiree's heart accelerated. "Would that matter to you?" she said softly.

He wanted to tell her how very much it would matter. He wanted to fold her in his arms and tell her: I love you, I want to know that you are safe. I can't bear to think of you being hurt. . . . Instead, he said in a cool voice, "I would be sorry, of course. However, if you are determined to go, you must take your chances with the rest of us."

Desiree's heart slowed to its normal beat. Hiding her hurt and her disappointment, she said lightly, "As you say, I must take my chances. If you will open the door, we will go see to your wounded man."

"I can attend to him myself. You have had a bad shock, and it is better that you return to your bed."

"Oh, Christopher," Desiree cried impatiently, "don't be so stiff and formal. Can't you unbend? Can't you be human for once?"

"I suggested you return to your bed. I see nothing inhuman about that."

"Oh, curse you! You know very well what I mean. In any case, I would not be in bed above an hour before I would have to rise and make ready to go. I will come with you."

Christopher looked at her searchingly. Desiree Grayson had been very outspoken to him on her views against slavery, and now was the time to test her. If it had all been pretense on her part, he would see to it that Josh did not suffer. He would get the man away, even if he had to gag and bind her. His eyes still on her face, he said slowly, "There is something you should know. The man in the cellar is black. He is a Southerner, but he belongs to the Union Army." He saw her eyes widen, and he thought he knew the reason. "Yes, that's right," he went on in a voice laced with mockery, "he is a Union soldier, Miss Desiree, and that makes him the enemy of all you stand for. He has taken a stand against slavery, he has actually dared to join in the fight for freedom. There, now you know. Are you sure you wish to soil your hands?"

Suppressing the sharp retort that sprang to her lips, Desiree sighed. "You are really very stubborn and difficult, and I don't know why I bother with you. As for what I stand for, you know nothing about it."

"I thought I did, Miss Desiree, but I am no longer certain."

"Good. Perhaps I make progress. By the way, that is the second time you have called me 'Miss Desiree.' It is done to goad me, I know, but I do wish you would call me 'Dessi.' " She smiled at him brilliantly. " 'Dessi,' please, it's so much friendlier." Her smile disappearing, she stared into his eyes. "There is something puzzling me, Christopher Fairfield. You are—"

"I go under the name of Wakely," Christopher interrupted. "You might remember that."

"Wakely, then. As I was saying, you are a white man, and you are also a Southerner. May I ask why you bothered with this Union soldier? Is he not your enemy, too?"

"I don't take sides," Christopher said shortly. "I told you my reasons for joining the army."

"I know," Desiree said hastily, "it was not out of patriotism."

"Exactly."

"Even so, you are not a traitor either, and your duties did not call upon you to rescue this soldier. Why did you do it?"

He regarded her from beneath frowning brows. "Isn't it obvious? I don't consider it a traitorous act to rescue a fellow human being. Does that answer your question?"

"It does indeed, and we are in perfect accord, Christopher Wakely," Desiree said, placing a slight stress on the last name. "Well," she went on, "don't just stand there. Let's go."

Would he ever understand her, Christopher wondered, or even understand himself? He feared for her safety, and yet, mingled with his fear was excitement. The excitement of seeing her constantly, working with her on some cases, of just knowing that she was near. Surrendering to an impulse, he took her arm and drew it through his own. "As you say, Dessi," he said, smiling, "let's go."

Josh stirred as hands touched him. Trying to collect his feverish, wandering thoughts, he stared into the face of the white woman who was bent above him. She had hair that had the brilliance of fire, and her smiling eyes were the color of violets. Josh sighed happily. The war had been only a bad dream after all, for here he was at Twin Oaks, safe at last, and the legendary Flame was here with him. The Flame was a woman, and she was no legend. Tildy had told him so. Awed, Josh reached up a weak hand and touched a lock of the bright hair; it clung reassuringly to his fingers, soft, vital, living. She was really there. She was not just a figment of his imagination. "Tildy say that you the Flame," he said in a labored voice. "Still cain't hardly b'lieve that the Flame a female."

Behind her, Desiree heard the sharp intake of Christopher's

breath, but she did not look at him. "Yes, Josh," she said gently, "Tildy told you the truth. I am the Flame."

"Knows it now, ma'am. Recollect you tellin' me 'bout your organization." The expression in Josh's eyes changed. "You ain't gonner let Miss Youtha fin' me, is you?"

"She won't find you. I promise. Don't you worry, Josh, everything will be just fine."

Josh's hand dropped heavily. "Martie," he muttered. "Ain't gonna make it without Martie. I need her and love her."

"Martie's safe, Josh. Amos got her away. Don't you remember?"

"Amos got her away," Josh repeated. "Remember now. I . . ." His words were cut off as his head dropped heavily to one side.

"Christopher!" Desiree said sharply.

"I'll see to him." Kneeling, Christopher took Josh's wrist between his fingers. "Passed out," he said briefly. He gave her a sidelong look. "I guess the excitement of seeing the Flame again was a little too much for him."

"Christopher, I—"

"It's true, Dessi, isn't it?" Christopher interrupted. "You are the Flame. You helped this man to escape, and the woman he spoke of."

"Not single-handedly." Desiree smiled at him. "Yes, Christopher, I am called the Flame."

Christopher laughed softly. "Your name is revered among the black people, revered by me too, and you turn out to be a woman! I'm sure the planters must breathe fire and fury whenever the name of the Flame is mentioned. What a rare joke on them."

Desiree looked at him curiously. "How is it that you accept my word without question? I could be lying, you know."

"Your word alone might have been difficult for me to swallow. It was he who convinced me," Christopher said, indicating Josh. "I heard him, I saw the look in his eyes. It was as though he had seen a vision."

Desiree flushed. "A lot of nonsense has grown up around the name of the Flame. I happen to be the head of a freedom-fighting group which has been successful. There is no more to it than that."

"Isn't there?"

"No. I am no romantic adventuress. I happen to be a very

sensible and practical person, and I know how to get what I want."

"You are too modest."

"Nothing of the sort," Desiree said angrily. "I am just stating facts, so there is no need to mock me."

"Would I do that?"

"Yes, you would. You have done nothing else but mock me."

"You wrong me, Dessi." Rising to his feet, Christopher took her hand and pulled her up. "My head may be spinning with the things I have learned, but I have no time to dwell on it now. You stay here with Josh. I'm going to scout around for a gray uniform. We can't very well take him with us dressed like that. You agree?"

"I agree." Desiree felt almost lightheaded with happiness. Christopher seemed to have changed completely. He was smiling at her, and that smile was very warm; his eyes were no longer shuttered against her, but almost tender in their expression. From now on, she felt sure, there would be a new understanding between them. "Christopher," she called as he reached the door, "I said that I know how to get what I want. Remember?"

Christopher turned. "I remember. And is there something you want, Madam Flame?"

"Yes."

"What is it?"

Desiree laughed. "You'll find out in good time, Christopher Wakely Fairfield."

14

Cemetery Ridge, Gettysburg. It had turned into a massacre! But the Confederates, under the command of General Longstreet, continued to assault the stone walls behind which the Union infantry lay. Knowing that they could not hope to win against the superior Union forces, they fought with reckless courage, with an untiring ferocity that was born out of desperation. Union guns, pushed so close together that their giant wheels were all but interlocked, presented an almost solid wall of blazing death as the infantry fired charge after charge into the ranks of the weary Confederate soldiers. Almost cut in half by the merciless rain of fire, gray-clad forms went down, piling on top of each other. Still the Confederates attacked. Using the bodies of their fallen comrades as stepping-stones, screaming their wild rebel yell, some of them managed to gain the tops of the walls. In hand-to-hand combat they thrust fiercely with bayonets, they reversed their useless muskets, using them as clubs, wielding them with such savagery that many of the Yankess fell before the onslaught. But this battle, like the battles for Round Top and Little Round Top, was already lost to them, and even as they fought, they knew it. Nothing could save the Confederate force from certain annihilation unless they drew back now.

Fighting side by side with his men, General Longstreet had long since abandoned the hope of turning defeat into victory. In these unfortunate encounters at Gettysburg the Confederate losses had been great, and he had been reluctant to expose his men to the withering fire coming from Cemetery Ridge, where the Yankees, determined to hold their strong position, had gathered in great force. But the attack had been ordered by Robert E. Lee, and one did not lightly disobey a command from the great general. Names of other battles whirled through Longstreet's tired mind. Bull Run, Wilson's Creek, Shiloh, Second Bull Run, Fredericksburg, Vicksburg, Chancellorsville, where Stonewall Jackson had been mortally wounded in a tragic accident. All of them had been Confederate victories. Fair Oaks, where the Yankees had won the struggle. Blue Ridge, another Yankee triumph. Antietam Creek, where they had managed to stop General Lee's advance. And now Gettysburg, with the Yankees victorious again.

Longstreet started as a soldier fell against him. Blood poured from the man's mouth as he fell, spraying the front of the general's uniform. The massacre must stop, Longstreet thought wildly. He would no longer be responsible for the loss of so many valuable lives. In a sudden lull between the fighting, he roared out his order. "Retreat! Get back to Cemetery Ridge. Save yourselves, lads!"

The guns spoke again, firing at the retreating Confederates. Half-deafened by the thunderous sound, choking on the billowing black smoke, Desiree stumbled after Christopher, trying to emulate his zigzag course across the open field to where the main body of the Confederate dead and wounded lay. Desiree pressed her lips tightly together, trying to subdue her rising hysteria. The dead! There were so many of them. They dotted the field, limbs already taking on the stiffness of death, gray uniforms torn by bullets and soaked with blood. Another scene out of the never-ending nightmare of war. There were other bodies, piled on top of each other like cordwood. Were there any among that pile who still lived? Desiree wondered wildly. Were they even now struggling to extricate themselves from their dead comrades? It was a thought not to be borne.

Coughing, trying to ease the stabbing pain in her side, Desiree paused for a moment. Her red-rimmed eyes, smarting with smoke, strained to see Christopher. He and other members of the medical team, crouched low against the firing, were dragging bodies toward the shelter of some nearby trees. For the first time Desiree noticed that the Confederate soldiers, with General Longstreet at the head of the straggling column, were in retreat. Soldiers only slightly wounded were doing their best to support the more serious cases. Her heart leaped with terror. With the withdrawal of Confederate covering fire, Christopher and the others were completely vulnerable to the Yankees. They would be cut down or taken prisoner. "Christopher!" she screamed. "Pull out, pull out!"

Almost as though he had heard her, Christopher looked toward the place where she was standing, then looked quickly away. He had not heard her. Her cry could not make itself heard above the still-booming guns and the moans and the screams of the wounded. Desiree rushed forward, waving her arms frantically. She fell heavily, sprawling over a body that lay in her path. Stunned, rigid with shock, she stared at the dead Confederate soldier. He was a black man, though the only way she could tell was from his outflung hands. The top of his head had been shot away, and the blood pouring from the ghastly wound had coated his face and neck with sticky scarlet. Sobbing, fighting back nausea, she gently touched the soldier's cold hand, her thoughts turning to Josh. Confined to the camp hospital, he had not been noticed at all. Everything had been in confusion, and to those in authority he was just one more wounded soldier. Josh had had little to say to those about him, and even with Christopher and her, he had been reticent. His wound healed, and one night he was no longer to be found. He had slipped away under cover of darkness, presumably to find a Yankee squadron. Where was he now? It might even be, if he still lived, that he was one of the Yankee defenders hidden behind the barrier of the stone wall.

Desiree tried to raise herself, but her body, still held in the grip of shock, would not function. Two years of war, she thought bitterly, and still no end in sight. Slaughter, suffering—it had almost become a way of life. The war had changed many things, and Christopher most of all. Thin, haggard, his eyes sunk into dark hollows of fatigue, his desire for vengeance apparently completely forgotten, he toiled indefatigably to save the broken and maimed men who were brought to the camp hospital. Christopher, with the stench of death forever in his nostrils, his gray shirt stiff with the blood of the victims of this terrible war. Christopher, who had turned into a patriot after all.

Desiree heard the shouting, and she looked up sharply. The guns had stopped. The Union soldiers were pouring over the wall in a dark blue wave, heading straight for the small group of laboring men. She saw Christopher sprawl forward on his face, felled by a rifle butt, saw the others struggling in the grip of the soldiers. "Christopher!" The paralysis leaving her limbs, Desiree jumped to her feet and rushed forward. Reaching the spot, she took one despairing look at Christopher, and then launched herself at a blue-coated officer. "Leave them alone!" she shrieked, battering at his chest with clenched fists. Swept away by long-withheld hysteria, she reached up a hand and lashed him savagely across the face. "God curse you, you filthy Yankee swine!"

"Well, now, it seems we've caught us a female Johnny Reb." His eyes glittering with fury, Captain Morrison gripped the frantic girl by her shoulders and held her away from him. "Thin as a pipestem," he pronounced, "and none too clean. But a camp follower is a camp follower. I haven't had a woman in a long time, and I might as well avail myself of you." He turned to a soldier standing near him. "Forbes," he barked, "take our Southern belle away and get her cleaned up. I don't fancy making love to a woman who is stinking with the blood of Johnny Rebs. After I've finished with her, you can throw her in with the rest of the prisoners."

The grin wiped from his face, Forbes jumped to attention. "Yes, sir." He grasped Desiree's arm, pulling on it savagely as she tried to resist. "Come on, whore, you heard the captain."

The members of the medical team, menaced by the drawn weapons of the Union soldiers, stood quietly now, their eyes averted. "Jamie," Desiree called frantically, "is Christopher dead?"

Jamie Peters looked down at the sprawled body. "I don't know, Dessi. But if he's alive, I'll do my best to help him." His eyes turned to Captain Morrison. "Sir," he said stiffly, "Miss Desiree Grayson is no camp follower. She is a nurse attached to this branch of the Confederate Army. I ask that you treat her with honor."

"You may ask nothing of me," Captain Morrison snapped. "You damned rebs need to be taught a lesson, and if you can't keep your women away from the war fronts, you must expect it to include them too."

Jamie Peters looked at the erect figure of the captain, a burning hostility in his eyes. "Sir," he began, "I would—"

Captain Morrison cut him off. "Silence! Since you are so concerned with this particular woman, you will be able to see for yourself how she has fared when she joins you at Camp Wetherby."

"Camp Wetherby!"

Captain Morrison smiled. "Ah, I gather from your tone that you have heard of it."

Jamie moistened his dry lips. "My God!" he exclaimed hoarsely. "Sir, I appeal to you! You cannot possibly place a woman in that hellhole."

"Can I not?" The captain's smile widened. "A woman is no novelty at Camp Wetherby, I assure you." The smile turned into a sneer. "You will find many other choice specimens of femininity residing there. You will enjoy yourself, reb, for although Wetherby is large enough to be partitioned off, we allow spies of both sexes to mingle freely."

"Miss Grayson is a patriot," Jamie said desperately, "but she is no spy."

Captain Morrison nodded. "Spy, patriot, what's the difference? I'll tell you something, if every one of you flaming patriots were locked away, the world would be a peaceful place and we would not be fighting this damnable war." The faint sneer leaving his lips, he turned once more to the gaping Forbes. "Well, soldier, what are you waiting for? I told you to take the woman away. After she's been cleaned up, put her in my tent."

"Yes, sir. At once, sir." Forbes's fingers bit into Desiree's arm. "Come along peaceable now," he whispered urgently. "You don't, and I'll land you a bash on the jaw."

Desiree did not hear him. Pictures of blood and death and horror swirled in her darkening mind, the grim toll of the many hard-won Confederate victories. She thought of the ghastly wounds she had dressed, the shattered limbs. Even when she had managed to snatch a few moments of much-needed sleep, the screams of the tormented men had pursued her into her dreams. She had listened to last confessions from youths who were hardly old enough to know the meaning of sin, and had closed the lids over countless dead and staring eyes. At the request of dying soldiers, she had written pathetic last good-byes to mothers, wives, sweethearts, while she herself was so torn apart by grief that she could hardly pen the words. She had watched Christopher grow gaunt, his dark eyes tormented in his drawn face, his hands compassionate as he worked over each fresh case. And every day she had faced the dread possibility that her father might be one of the broken men who were daily carried into the makeshift field hospital. With Christopher and others of the small team, she had assisted at operations. Vomit rising high in her throat, she helped to hold down the helpless victims of war as the harassed and overworked surgeon swabbed out gaping wounds and drew them together as best he could, or hacked off a gangrenous limb. They had all endured so much these last two years. Was this to be the end of it, confinement in a Union prison? Camp Wetherby! Who in the South did not know of that dread place? One would be better off dead than a prisoner in that particular camp. Dead! The word prodded at her agonizingly. Christopher was lying so still, his face buried in the trampled bloodied earth of the battlefield. He was dead; she was suddenly convinced of it, and without him she had no reason or wish to go on. In a last token resistance she clawed feebly at Forbes. The last thing she heard, just before the blessed darkness enveloped her, was his outraged gasp.

Unable to hold her deadweight, Forbes's fingers automatically relaxed their tight hold. Meeting his captain's furious eyes, he spluttered, "The bitch clawed my face, sir."

"You think that's bad, Forbes?" Captain Morrison's voice was quietly menacing. "It is nothing to what I'll do to you if you don't carry out my command at once."

"Yes, sir." Forbes touched a nervous hand to his smarting cheek. "I'll put her in your tent, sir."

"Not until she's been cleaned up, idiot. Take her to the bathing tent first, and then transfer her to mine. Do you understand now, or must I walk behind you repeating my order?"

Suppressing his resentment of this overbearing and arrogant officer, a resentment that was shared by all his comrades, Forbes said quietly, "I understand, sir."

"Good, Forbes. I was beginning to think you were not only an idiot, but deaf into the bargain."

Damned swine! Forbes silently retorted. I hope we live through this war. I'd like to meet up with you when it's over, by God, I would! Acutely aware of the bitter hostility emanating from the captured soldiers, Forbes stooped down and gathered Desiree into his arms. Rising with some difficulty, he shot a swift sidelong glance at Captain Morrison's ominous face, and then walked stiffly away. Bloody goddamned war, he thought, staring down at the unconscious face. Stupid, bull-headed, goddamned rebs! A strand of Desiree's hair blew across his mouth. Puffing the strand impatiently away, Forbes was suddenly outraged. Disgraceful when a bit of a lass like this one followed after the soldiers. It was true that the soldiers had to have some release, and the camp followers provided a welcome respite from war, but they were usually worldly-wise females of a more mature age. Forbes's mouth tightened into a hard line of disapproval. Why, this girl must be every bit as young as his daughter. If his Flora should ever take it into her head to behave so boldly, he would beat her senseless. But then, Flora could not possibly behave like this slut, it just wasn't in her. Flora was perhaps a little dull, Forbes admitted reluctantly, but she was a good girl, well-brought-up and gentle and demure in her manners. Her mother, who had the say in most domestic matters, had seen to that. At the thought of his wife, Forbes's mouth tightened still more. Miriam was a cold woman, and Flora was very like her. A great pity, that.

Arriving at the tent allotted to the soldiers for bathing, Forbes was not surprised to find it empty. With the battle over and the Confederate Army routed, temporarily at least, the last thought in the minds of his comrades was bathing. The supervision, the strict military authority that bound their lives, would, as it had after other victories, be relaxed. Only the sentries would be patrolling, alert for any movement from the enemy. The others would be lounging about, drinking, eating, and, he thought sourly, no doubt guzzling his share of the drink.

Setting his slight burden down on the hard camp bed, Forbes breathed a sigh of relief. If this specimen was an example of the much-vaunted Southern belle, he thought, his eyes running over her, he didn't think much of them. For once Captain Morrison was right; this Desiree Grayson certainly was as thin as a pipestem, and with no claim to beauty, unless it be the thick, dark, extraordinary long eyelashes that shadowed her cheeks. Lank hair, which seemed to be some kind of a reddish color, wisped about a wasted face, from which the cheekbones jutted so sharply that they gave the impression that they were about to burst through the skin; her lips were colorless, and the stains of fatigue beneath her closed eyes stood out like bruises.

Continuing to study her, his head on one side, Forbes chuckled. Captain Morrison had spoken the truth when he'd said that he hadn't had a woman in a long time. He could have had any one of the brazen women who visited the campsites, but he had held himself aloof. So what made him want this one, who looked as though a rough touch would break her in half? A nurse, the reb had called her. A likely story! What respectable female would choose to nurse on the battlefield itself? Girls who had a wish to nurse the soldiers could do so just as well at home. Take his Flora, for instance. Every day, so her mother had written, she went to Kempton Hospital, which was beginning to fill up with the wounded. Sometimes, when the hospital staff was rushed, Flora helped tend the less serious cases, and then at other times she was set to rolling bandages. His thoughts breaking off, Forbes turned away. With a last look at the girl on the bed, he went off in quest of hot water.

Desiree lay on the narrow bed, sunk fathoms deep in exhausted sleep. Outside, the laughter and the drunken singing of the victorious soldiers swelled, but she did not stir. A soldier, pushing aside the tent flap, stared hard at the sleeping girl. "Will you look at that!" he exclaimed. He grinned as his comrades crowded closer, all eager to view the captured female reb. "You can say what you like about that old bastard Morrison," he went on, "but he sure knows how to pick 'em." His eyes were faintly wistful as he looked at the wealth of bright hair spread out upon the hard pillow. Her face was too thin, but her features were perfectly formed, and the arched eyebrows and sweeping dark lashes gave her a mysterious look, he considered. He sighed. "Give her some rest and fatten her up a bit, and Morrison's got himself a raving beauty."

"There won't be time to fatten her up, Drew." Slouching

forward, his hands stuck into his pockets, Forbes peered into the tent. "You know the captain, he's strictly a one-timer, and then it's on to the next woman."

"Maybe it'll be different this time, Forbes. Morrison ain't had himself much lately. He don't even look at Betty, and she's the best of that bunch of whores we picked up."

Forbes shook his head. "It won't be different, I know that swine only too well. After he's finished with this one, she goes straight to Camp Wetherby."

Drew sucked in his breath sharply. "Wetherby, eh? It's a dirty shame. I wouldn't like a sister of mine to go to that place. It's enough to kill any delicately bred female."

Forbes gave him a jeering look. "I doubt this one's delicately bred, for all her fancy looks, and we ain't talking about your sister, Drew. Besides, Captain says that Grayson's a spy."

Drew, who was inclined to be pugnacious, grinned suddenly. "If Grayson's a spy, I'm Abraham Lincoln. And even if she is, she can spy on me anytime she's a mind to. Wish I'd had your job, Forbes, you cleaned her up real pretty. I sure as hell envy Morrison."

"I was there," Forbes answered him sullenly, "but Sue Ellen cleaned her up for me."

"So that's where the bitch went. You might have tipped me off. I was hunting for her." Drew's blue eyes twinkled. "Sue Ellen's too full of herself to relish fussing over another female. How'd it go?"

Forbes's lips compressed. "Having Sue Ellen there didn't do me much good. I had to stay and hold Grayson down."

"Hold her down, a little bit of a thing like that! Go on with you, Forbes, she don't look like she's got the strength of a kitten."

"That's all you know. Bloody spitfire, is that girl. Maybe you wouldn't think it to look at her, but she pretty near tore up the tent." Forbes heard the stifled laughter of the other men, and he turned on them indignantly. "Snigger all you please, but it's true. She fought Sue Ellen like a tigress. Landed her a punch in the eye that would have done credit to a man."

"Stretching it a bit far, ain't you, Forbes?" Drew drawled mockingly.

"Was you there, then?" Forbes demanded truculently.

"No, but I'd like to have been. If she gave you so much trouble, how'd you get her quieted down?"

"Gave her a clip that put her out. Had to. Sue Ellen got on with the job. Washed her hair and everything. She came to while it was going on, but she didn't fight no more. Kept on asking about Christopher Wakely. And you'd not believe this, but after all that trouble she gave us, she had the nerve to beg us to bring her news of him."

"And who's this Christopher Wakely?"

"One of the rebs we captured. Grayson's real worked-up about him. She seems to think he's dead."

"Is he?"

Forbes shrugged. "How the hell would I know? Him and the others were shoved into a wagon and taken straight off to Wetherby."

Drew looked at the girl, his eyes softening. "It's a long way to Wetherby. Could be they'll be rescued by a reb patrol."

"You sound like you want it to happen," Forbes growled, darting him a suspicious look.

"Me? I don't care one way or the other."

"Well, they ain't likely to be rescued. With all the raiding them rebs done on our wagons, the boys'll be keeping a special lookout. I heard Morrison give the order for the inside guards to be as fully armed as the outriders. If the rebs try anything, they'll be in for a painful surprise."

"This Wakely she's asking about," Drew persisted, "was he injured?"

Forbes nodded. "Got himself knocked on the head. Don't know how bad it was. He was still out when I went off with the girl."

Drew hesitated, then said impulsively, "Look, why don't you find out about him? It wouldn't hurt you none."

"Not me," Forbes said firmly. "I ain't making inquiries about no reb. Grayson'll have to wait until she gets to Wetherby to find out about him."

"Ain't you the softhearted one, Forbes?" Drew mocked. "What's the matter? You upset because you didn't guess what was waiting under all Grayson's dirt? If you had, I bet you'd have had first go at her, eh?"

"And how'd you know I didn't? I was with her a long time before she calmed down. I thought I'd maybe have to stay longer, but seemed like she just couldn't keep her eyes open no more."

"You didn't touch her, Forbes," Drew stated with calm conviction. "You're too scared of Morrison."

Incensed, his eyes flashing with anger, Forbes scowled blackly. "I ain't scared of no one, Drew, so you can shut that stupid big mouth of yours."

"Ah, now I've gone and made you mad!" Looking around, Drew winked at the other men. "Ain't it a shame about poor old Forbes? I bet he'd have really enjoying soaping her down." He paused significantly. "Once he'd knocked her out, that is."

Uncomfortably aware of the silent censure of the other men, Forbes defended himself hastily. "If you'd been in my place, you'd have done the same thing. She was like a goddamned wild thing, I tell you, biting and kicking and scratching, and punching out with her fists. And curse! She can curse as good as any man, so don't let them angel looks of hers deceive you." He glanced across at Desiree, and then, in a desire to reestablish himself, he added placatingly, "Still, like you say, Drew, she's cleaned up real good. Maybe a bit too thin for my liking, but pretty enough."

"Pretty? Beautiful's more the word, I'd say." As he studied Forbes's flushed face, Drew's eyes grew faintly malicious. "Look at that hair, man," he prodded. "You ain't gonner tell me you wouldn't like to burn your hands on that?"

"Forbes ain't interested in the hair on her head, Drew," another man put in. "Down lower's where all the honey is, ain't that right, Forbes?"

"Sure is." Forbes's sullen expression lightened into a knowing smile. "Conners has got the right idea, Drew. There's honey down there, all right, and a hell of a sight more burn." Noting Drew's too-obvious discomfort, he added jeeringly, "You agree, don't you?"

Drew reddened. He was old-fashioned at heart, a fact which he had tried hard to hide from the other men, and he had been taught by his stern father to revere women. "Sure," he answered, trying to speak offhandedly. "I guess so."

"You guess so?" Forbes opened his eyes wide in pretended astonishment. "Where have you been all your life?"

Cursing his betraying flush, Drew said angrily, "Why don't you just shut up, Forbes!"

Forbes grinned. "Got you going, have I, Drew?" He stabbed a finger toward Desiree. "That ain't your sister in there, you know, nor yet one of them prissy church ladies you're used to. That's a real hellion, that is." Frowning, he touched his face. "See this little decoration she gave me? Them scratches would have been a hell of a sight deeper if the bitch hadn't passed out. And look here." He pushed up his sleeve, exposing deep, angry-looking gouges. "See what she did to my arm. She done that when I was holding her down for Sue Ellen."

Drew, who fully returned Forbes's dislike, felt a sneaking admiration for the girl's spirit. "And what did you expect?" he said coldly. "If one of our women got herself captured, she'd fight too. I'm sorry she was a little too much for you, Forbes."

"Don't give me any of your smart-ass talk, Drew. I suppose you think you could have handled her better?"

"Some," Drew answered.

"Oh, sure." Forbes sneered. "I reckon you didn't know where to put it when you first got a woman in your tent. Flo told me you were kind of innocent-like. Spouting a lot of fancy talk and handling her like she was something precious." He backed as Drew took a menacing step forward. "All right, all right, I take it back." Turning to the others, he said truculently, "Sorry to disappoint you, but there ain't going to be no fight between me and Drew. I've had enough for one day. Oh, I'll fight him, but it's a pleasure I'm saving up for later. I've got a better idea for you. The girl's naked under that blanket. You can all go in and take a look at her, if you like. But you'll have to make it quick."

Offended anew by something in the man's expression, Drew said coldly, "Why would we want to do that? We've seen women before." Frowning, he scanned the circle of faces. A few, like himself, appeared to be uncomfortable with the idea, but the majority seemed willing to take Forbes up on his offer. "We've got women waiting," he went on, "so why waste time taking sly peeks at this one? Besides, we'd best get away from here. Morrison'll likely be along soon."

"I thought you said it was me who was afraid of Morrison?" Forbes interjected sarcastically. "If you ask me, Drew, you ain't too brave yourself."

"I'm not a fool, if that's what you mean," Drew replied

curtly. "Anyway, I'm thinking of the girl more than Morrison. If she should wake up and find us all gaping at her, she'd have every right to set up a squawk. We'd be in a mess then."

Secretly Forbes agreed with him, and he was already regretting his impetuosity, but he would not back down now. "What makes Drew think he can speak for all of you?" he said in a brisk voice. "Don't take any notice of him. If the girl was going to wake up, she'd have done so long since, what with all the noise you lot have been making."

"Ain't natural for her to sleep like that," Conners put in. "Maybe she's unconscious."

Forbes shook his head impatiently. "Nothing of the sort, she's just worn out. When she quieted down a bit, she told Sue Ellen that she hadn't slept in days." He looked at Drew. "Now we've got that settled, you coming?"

Drew shrugged. Conscious of a wish to stand well in the eyes of his comrades, he said casually, "Might as well, then."

"Drew's blushing," Forbes cried. "I always knew he was straightlaced under all that big talk." Avoiding Drew's kindling eyes, he went on quickly, "Detail a man to stay outside and watch for Morrison. The rest of you come on in."

As silently as possible, the men filed toward the bed. "And here she is," Forbes said in a low voice, throwing back the blanket, "our very own genuine captured Southern belle. She's maybe a mite scrawny, but you'll have to admit she goes in and out at all the right places."

Quietly, so as not to attract attention, Drew detached himself from the throng about the bed. He was not a prig, he defended himself, and certainly he was not straightlaced, it was simply that he believed in fair play. It didn't seem quite right to stand there staring at a defenseless girl.

"Touch her," Forbes said, his voice pitched slightly louder now. "That's right, Johnson, don't be afraid. It'd take a trumpet blast in her ear to rouse her. There, don't she feel good? Sort of like having a great big woman doll to play with, ain't it? If it wasn't for the fact that I'm bighearted, I'd charge you fellows for a feel."

"Will you listen to that bloody idiot," Benson said, joining Drew. He shook his head in disgust. "I never did like Forbes, and I like him even less now."

"Let him get on with it." Drew nodded to two other men

who had followed Benson. "They'll get tired soon enough of his foolery."

"I wouldn't bet on it," Benson answered gloomily. "Look at Sanderson. He's really enjoying himself."

Sanderson, after staring hard at the naked girl, had placed his hand on a soft breast. His face was flushed, and he appeared to be unconscious of the ribald comments this action aroused. "Very nice indeed," he muttered, stroking her. "That's a lovely pair of tits. Morrison ought to have himself a real good time."

The man standing next to Sanderson shook his head. "She's got good hair," he commented, "but I can't see nothing else in her. I like my women a bit fleshy, and this one's naught but skin and bones."

Sanderson gave the speaker an impatient glare. "Sure she's skinny," he said impatiently, "but she's class. Trouble with you, Joe, you don't know class when you see it."

"That so?" Joe answered pugnaciously. "Well, let me tell you something, Sanderson. That whore you was bumping a while ago wasn't fit for pigs to snuffle at."

The men ignored this by-play. Encouraged by Sanderson's example, they bent over the girl, trailing their fingers over her breasts, gently tweaking her nipples, and caressing her stomach. Forgetting caution, the eager, furtive touches became rougher, bolder. Desiree stirred as a hand was thrust between her legs; her eyes half-opened, stared uncomprehendingly; then, weighted by weariness, they closed again.

Forbes heard the little muttering, protesting sound she made beneath her breath, and he took instant alarm. Things were not going the way he had planned. Most of the men were more than a little drunk, and they were getting out of hand. "Don't touch her there, Davis," he said, pulling at the man's arm. "Stop it, you fool! If she wakes, she'll start hollering, and then we'll all be in trouble."

Davis gave him a surly look. "I didn't come in here for a feel," he said, pulling his arm free. "I got other ideas in mind."

Forbes's eyes searched for Drew. His back turned, he was standing near the entrance, talking to the other three men. "Drew?" Forbes went quickly toward him.

Drew turned and looked at him. "Something gone wrong, Forbes?"

"You can see that for yourself, can't you? I . . . I reckon this wasn't such a good idea."

"So what do you want from me?" Drew said coldly. "I tried to stop you. Remember?"

Forbes flushed beneath his critical gaze. "All right, so you've had the last laugh. Listen, you men have got to help me get 'em out of here, otherwise that bunch of bloody animals'll be having her off the bed and pounding into her." He looked appealingly at Drew. "If you don't help me, I don't know what in the hell I'm to do."

"Walk away from it," Drew suggested.

Forbes wrung his hands together in agitation. "I can't. While me and Sue Ellen was bathing the girl, I got a message from Morrison saying that I was to stand guard."

"That so? In a bit of a mess, ain't you?" Straightening from his lounging position, Drew nodded to his companions. "All right, Forbes, we'll help you herd them out, but it's for the girl's sake, not yours."

"I know." Forbes attempted a placating smile. "Let's get to it, then."

"Morrison's coming." The soft call came from the man who had been left outside to guard. He poked his head through the tent flap. "I seen Morrison in the distance," he added, "and it looks to me like he's heading this way. You'll be all right if you hurry."

"Oh, Christ! Thanks, Baker. Get on in here and help us."

Baker entered the tent reluctantly. Most of the men, contrary to Forbes's dire expectations, were amenable. Frowning, grumbling beneath their breath, they surged outside, where they promptly scattered. Only Davis proved difficult, until Drew and Benson, losing patience, obtained a tight grip on his arms and hustled him out. The sight of Captain Morrison's tall, portly form advancing rapidly sobered even the recalcitrant Davis. With a muffled exclamation he darted away, closely followed by Drew, Benson, and the other two men.

By the time Morrison gained his tent, Forbes was in place outside, standing stiffly erect. "What's been going on?" Morrision turned his hard eyes to Forbes.

Forbes gazed steadily into the middle distance. "All's quiet here, sir. Nothing to report."

Morrison stared at him. Suddenly remembering the girl, he

felt suspicion stirring. "Nothing to report, eh?" he snapped. "Then why are those men rushing about the camp like hooligans?"

Ignoring the sinking feeling inside him, Forbes answered hoarsely, "I couldn't say, sir." He shot a swift look at Morrison, and the sight of the captain's scowling face told him that his answer was not acceptable. "Likely they're drunk, sir," he said reluctantly.

Morrision stiffened. "Drunk! Did you say drunk?"

Forbes coughed uneasily. "Sergeant Freemont issued the liquor ration as usual, sir. The . . . the boys like to let down a little after a battle, sir, but there ain't no harm in them."

"Did I ask for your opinion, Forbes?"

"No, sir."

"Then until I do, oblige me by keeping your mouth shut."

"Yes, sir. I'm sorry, sir."

"All right, Forbes, you may go."

Forbes saluted smartly and walked swiftly away. "Damned drunken rabble, the lot of them!" Morrison muttered, glaring after Forbes. He made a mental note to see the generous-handed Sergeant Freemont in the morning. He would advise him that the liquor ration was to be cut in half, and that strict discipline must be maintained at all times. After a battle, especially one that had turned into a victory, a certain amount of laxity was permissible, even desirable, for one must always keep in mind the morale of the men, but Freemont and his fellow noncommissioned officers were allowing their squadrons to get entirely out of hand.

Frowning, rubbing thoughtfully at his nose, Morrison reflected on the hard-won battle for Gettysburg. For the first time he found himself questioning whether or not the enemy was capable of being crushed. As a fighting force, the Confederacy had proved that it was not to be despised. They were smart, wily, intrepid fighters, and they were filled with a burning determination to preserve their threatened way of life. Against such determination, even the superior might of the Union forces might very well falter and break. Dismissing his disturbing thoughts, his fleshy lips tightening to a thin line, Morrison turned on his heel and strode into his tent.

Desiree lay on her side, her long red hair spilling over the bed and all but touching the floor. Morrison stared, dazzled by its rich color and shimmer. He thought of the thin, shrieking, half-demented girl who had launched herself at him, striking with clenched fists, screaming curses. She had seemed drab enough to him then, and he found himself wondering if the rest of her could possibly match that glorious hair. Even as the thought entered his mind, Desiree gave a long, wrenching sigh and turned over on her back. Morrison held his breath, waiting for her eyes to open, but the heavy lashes did not flicker. No matter, he'd wake her soon enough. He examined her closely, a smile of pleasure curving his lips. Her face was thin, the hollows beneath the high cheekbones too deep, and there were lines of fatigue etched into the shadows beneath her eyes and about the full, soft mouth, but nothing could detract from or disguise the fact that she was a beauty. His smile lingering, he fingered a lock of her hair. Amazing to think that, in the prosecution of his duties, he had actually forgotten about her. Would she fight him? he wondered. Would she strike out at him, as she had done on the battlefield, would she call him "filthy Yankee swine"? He hoped that she would. The thought of being forced to subdue her gave him a curious pleasure that added greatly to his anticipation.

Desiree stirred again, a faint frown drawing her arching brows together. Stooping over her, Morrison caught his foot in the carelessly replaced blanket, dislodging it. Staring at her, he drew in his breath sharply. He had never liked full-fleshed women, and in his eyes she was perfect. Her limbs were long and slender, her breasts perfectly shaped, the unaroused nipples a dusky pink. Her waist was tiny, her hips a gentle curve. His eyes lingering on the fiery triangle that guarded her womanhood, he put one hand over his hardening organ, feeling the throbbing bulge of it stretching the tightly fitting material of his breeches. Rubbing at it, he touched her breast with his other hand, his fingers teasing at the nipple. Watching the nipple swell, he began to shake. Straightening up, he rapidly divested himself of his clothing. "Wake up, you," he said hoarsely. "You hear me, you rebel slut? Wake up, curse you!"

Desiree flung her arms above her head. "Christopher!" The name burst from her lips like a sob. "No, no, it's not true. Come back to me, Christopher, come back!"

Glaring at her in frustration, Morrison climbed onto the bed. Parting her legs roughly, he fitted his corpulent body to hers. He felt the outrushing of her breath as his weight settled fully, the leap and quiver of her muscles. "That's right," he said loudly, "I know you're awake." He smiled grimly. "Don't try playing games with me, or you'll regret it."

15

Desiree gave a choked scream as she awoke to a burning pain. Hard, bruising hands were tugging at her, a loud voice with a faintly nasal twang was commanding her to awaken. She felt the burning pain at her breasts again. "Don't!" Raising her hands, she pushed the source of the hurt violently away.

"Hurts, does it?" the loud voice said. "It'll hurt still more if you don't do as I say. Wake up, bitch!"

"A moment. Give me a moment." Her voice sounded unlike her own; it was slurred, strange to her ears.

"I'll give you a moment, but no more than that. Open your eyes. Look at me."

Stubbornly, her body tense, Desiree kept her eyes closed. The only thing that emerged clearly from her fogged brain was the memory of the dream she had had, a pleasant dream that had turned into a nightmare of terror. In her dream she had been walking with Christopher along the winding avenue that led to Twin Oaks plantation house. Trees reared above them, their leafy branches interlocking to form a pleasant shaded walk that effectively shut out the fierce sunlight. A cool breeze, oddly at variance with the weather, came whispering through the branches to cool their flushed faces. Desiree was suddenly so happy that she wanted to dance, to sing. Christopher was by her side, his hand holding hers, his dark eyes looking at her with love. The war was over, the guns silenced forever, and they had come through their baptism of fire without tragic incident. What more could anyone ask?

Christopher hung back a little as they reached the end of the avenue, but she tugged at his hand, leading him forward. There was the plantation house, the sun reflecting from its white walls in a shimmering haze. Flowers clustered thickly along the sun-warmed walls, their colors brilliant, the mingled perfumes heady. A magnolia tree sprawled shade over the upper part of the house, and a mockingbird called from behind a barrier of glossy dark green leaves.

The smile left Desiree's lips. Everything was the same, she thought uneasily. Too much the same. In the distance she could see Negroes at work in the fields; their voices and their occasional laughter drifted to her faintly. Twin Oaks was as it had always been, the house, the lands, the Negroes, all miraculously untouched by the ravages of war. "I don't understand." Desiree's hand tensed in Christopher's. "Everything is so serene, so perfect. And yet how can that be? How can Twin Oaks have survived in a land laid waste by war?"

Christopher did not answer; his eyes were on the opening door of the house. It opened to its widest extent, and Tildy stepped from the shadows into the bright sunlight. She stood still for a moment, her eyes widening in the broad black face. "Miss Dessi!" She ran forward as fast as her bulk would allow. "Where you been?" she scolded. "I done search for you everywhere." Her earrings swung against her cheeks as she nodded her head to emphasize her words. "I declare, chil', if you ain't enough to worry a body to death!"

Hypnotized by the flash and glitter of the earrings, Desiree said slowly, "But you know where I've been, Tildy. Juniper must have told you."

"Don't know, Miss Dessi."

"I've been helping to nurse the wounded soldiers." Desiree gave a long, relaxed sigh. "It's so good to be home. This war has been a long time ending."

Tildy frowned fiercely. "Now, then, Miss Dessi, you knows I ain't likin' games. Ain't been no war that I knows of. You listen to me, missy, your daddy so mad that he fit to be tied. Why you always got to go off on your own an' fret us so?"

"Christopher!" Suddenly frightened, Desiree looked at him pleadingly. "I don't understand what she means. Tell her about the war."

Tildy puffed out her lips angrily. "This another game, Miss Dessi? What for you talkin' to the air?"

"Tildy, don't!" Desiree's hand felt cold as Christopher drew his away. "Don't do this to me, Tildy! You remember Christopher Fairfield, don't you?" She smiled, trying to ignore her growing fear. "I want you to congratulate us. We are going to be married."

"Married?" Tildy stared at her, and there was fear in her eyes. "Miss Dessi," she whispered, "don't say such things. How come you tellin' me that you is goin' to wed with a dead man?"

"Dead!" Desiree's heart jerked in a spasm of terror. "Are you blind?" she cried. "Can't you see that he's standing here beside me?" She gripped Christopher's arm with numbed fingers, silently pleading with him to say something. He shook his head as though reproving her, but the dark eyes looking into hers were incredibly sad. "Tildy"—Desiree's voice broke—"tell me that you see him!"

The firm shake of Tildy's head set her earrings swinging again. "Cain't tell you that, Miss Dessi. Ain't no one there." She took Desiree's hand in hers and held it comfortingly. "Poor chil', you look so tired."

Desiree stared at her, feeling a trembling urge to give in, to relax in the comfort of those huge arms, to let Tildy, as she had always done, make everything right in her world. "I . . . I am tired," she stammered. "I can't remember when I last slept."

"I knows it, honey." Tildy smiled at her. "Come with me. Everythin' be fine by mornin'."

The urge left Desiree. It was all wrong. Tildy must be made to acknowledge Christopher. "No, Tildy, no!" She pulled her hand free. "Christopher is here, you know he is. Why do you persist in saying that he is dead?"

Tildy sighed. " 'Cause he is, Miss Dessi. Done hear he got himself killed in a riot at Buxton Prison."

"It's not true! Use your eyes, Tildy. Look at him!"

Tildy's lips tightened into a familiar grim line. "This game gitting purely tiresome, Miss Dessi, an' I ain't wantin' you to play it no more."

"Please, Tildy!"

"I likin' to oblige you, Miss Dessi," Tildy answered gruffly, "but cain't look at somebody who ain't there. Christopher Fairfield dead, I tell you."

"Oh, God, Tildy, don't torment me, don't!" Desiree stared at her with wild eyes. "Please! I can't bear any more."

Giving her a pitying look, Tildy turned from her and walked slowly away. "I be in the house if you needin' me," she called over her shoulder. "Come 'long with me, it the bes' thing. Ain't no use to be grievin' for what's gone."

Frozen, unmoving, Desiree stared after her. With Tildy's going, the sense of dreaming peace had vanished. The tranquil blue of the sky had darkened to a heavy, brooding gray, and she could no longer smell the sharp, sweet tang of the grass or the mingled perfumes of the flowers. She turned her head, and somehow she was not surprised to find that Christopher no longer stood at her side. She flinched as her ears were filled with the rattle of musketry fire, and following on like a deadly echo, the deep-throated booming of cannon. "Charge!" Above the tumult, someone roared a desperate command. "Onward, lads, onward. Show the Yankess what we're made of!"

Desiree tugged at the high neckline of her plain gown. She was choking on smoke, and all about her men were falling. She could hear the frantic whinnying of terrified horses, the screams of badly injured men, and the choked, agonized sounds made by the dying. "Retreat!" The desperate voice issued a new command. "Save yourselves, lads!"

Desiree put her hands over her ears. She was going mad. She was hearing things, seeing things that could not possibly be. There was no war, there never had been a war, Tildy had said so. "Tildy, wait for me, I'm coming!" Tears streaking her face, she took a lurching step toward the house, and saw it dissolve before her eyes. "Oh, dear God!" she screamed. "Where are you, Tildy? Help me, please help me!"

There was no answer. Desiree backed away, her horrified eyes on the place where the house had once stood. Twin Oaks was no more. Her world was no more! The musketry fire began again. Beneath her feet the ground trembled and shifted, and suddenly she was kneeling on a trampled battlefield, crouched over a black soldier with the top of his head blown away. His outflung hands with their pale pink palms seemed to be entreating her to aid him. Her tears began again, gushing from her eyes, blurring those vulnerable hands. "Poor boy, there is nothing I can do for you, nothing!" Sobbing, she touched a finger to the sticky scarlet that coated what was left of the soldier's face. Christopher! Her mind went back to him. If Christopher was dead, then nothing was of any use. Not her ideals, for which she had fought so stubbornly, not life, for she would have no use for it. She buried her face in her hands, rocking to and fro in her anguish. "Christopher!" she choked. "It can't be true. Come back to me, please come back!"

"Ain't I tol' you he dead, Miss Dessi?" Tildy's inexorable voice was borne to her on the smoke-polluted wind. "Done hear he got himself killed in a riot at Buxton Prison."

Desiree's hands dropped. It must be true, then. She had never known Tildy to lie. As she faced the truth, a coldness that was akin to death settled over her. Christopher was dead. She would never see him again. But Tildy had been misinformed. No prison could cage Christopher Fairfield for too long, and he had died as he would have wished, a free man. She touched a hand to the blasted earth. It was this battlefield that had seen the end of his stormy, troubled life, this earth that had soaked up his blood. July 1863. For as long as she lived, that date would be engraved on her memory. "I love you, Christopher, I will always love you. God bless you, my darling."

"What are you whispering about?" A brusque voice spoke in Desiree's ear. "Come on, whore, I've had enough of this. You asked me to give you a moment, and it's over now." Hands shook her roughly, chasing the last lingering mists of the nightmare away, bringing her abruptly awake. The man! How could she have fallen asleep again, how could she have forgotten him?

"Fell asleep, didn't you?" the brusque voice said. "Either that or you were playing possum." The hands shook her again. "Come on, I've been very patient with you." A finger touched her face. "Crying, eh? What the hell for? I won't be the first man you've bedded down with, and if you survive Wetherby, I won't be the last."

Desiree's mind was open now, receptive. Camp Wetherby,

the infamous Yankee prison! Cemetery Ridge. The battle lost, as she was lost. The rifle butt rising, crashing against the back of Christopher's head. The fight with the soldier and with the woman he had addressed as Sue Ellen, and then the soldier's fist exploding against her jaw. When she had come to her senses again, the woman with the brightly painted mouth was gone, but the soldier was still there. She had spoken to him, but she could not recall her words. Back now in the painful present, she felt crushed beneath the heavy weight of the body that covered hers. Her eyes flew open, fixing on the ruddy face bent above hers. Rage mingled with her fear for Christopher, giving her a surge of false strength. "Get away from me!" Her violent push, catching Morrison by surprise, sent him tumbling to the floor. Laughing hysterically, Desiree raised herself on her elbows and looked down at him. Words emerged from the hysteria, shaky but clear. "How dare you attempt to force yourself upon me. I remind you, sir, that I am your prisoner, not your plaything."

Glaring at her, Morrison felt sick with fury. The arrogance of her! She had humiliated him, laughed at him, and, by God, she had to pay for that. He'd teach her a lesson she would never forget. "Shut your mouth, you slaver bitch!" he shouted.

Desiree's eyes roved over his naked, awkwardly sprawled body, a vivid scorn in their violet depths. "For your information, sir, I don't happen to believe in slavery. Though if pigs like you were to preach to me of the evils of the system, I might very well begin to see some merit in it." She laughed again. "But at the moment, the point at issue is not slavery, but rather your reprehensible conduct." Trying not to let him see her fear, she pushed back her hair from her eyes and looked at him challengingly. "You will either treat me as a prisoner, or you will allow me to go free."

"I'll treat you any way I please, reb!" Getting to his feet, Morrison lunged for her. "Like this, for instance." His hand lashed against her cheek, snapping her head back. "And like this." He hit her again. "Hurts, doesn't it?" he growled, thrusting his hot face close to hers. "And there's plenty more where that came from."

Stunned by his savage attack, her face fiery with pain, Desiree swallowed hard as she conquered an inclination to burst into tears. He would like tears, it would delight him to see her humbled, but she would die first. Her pain-muddled brain dredged up words. "Scum!" she panted. She spat in his face. "Yankee scum!"

Seething, Morrison wiped the spittle from his face. Everything that was cruel in his nature surfaced, sending a rush of blood to his head. He had enjoyed hurting her, he thought, looking with satisfaction at the flaming brand of his fingers against her pale cheeks. And before he was through with her, he would hurt her still more. "For Dixie Land you'll take your stand," he jeered, slightly misquoting the words of the song composed by Dan Emmett. "Well, let's see how brave you really are. Let's see if you'll live and die for Dixie." Seizing her by the hair, he twisted it savagely, laughing as she gave a moan of pain. "By the way, in case you are interested, my name is Brian Morrison, Captain Brian Morrison. Do you think you can remember that?"

Desiree forced her pain-bitten lips into a mocking smile. "Since I . . . I am not interested"—she jerked out the defiant words—"I will be unable to remember."

"Is that a fact?" Morrison gave another twist. "In that case, perhaps you'd care to repeat your insult—if you dare, of course. Go on, let me hear it again."

Half-fainting, Desiree screamed the words at him in desperation and pain. "Scum, scum, scum! Yankee bastard!"

As Morrison held her down with a heavy hand to quell her struggles, a surge of bitterness mingled with his rage. Who did she think she was? he raged inwardly. Didn't she know when she was beaten? And where was the fear he craved to see? Goddamn Southern aristocrats with their tobacco fields, their cotton fields, their majestic white-columned houses, and their black slaves who ran to do their every bidding. This girl was one of them, he had no doubt of that, there was breeding in her voice, in the very look of her. Southern aristocrats, so called, why, if he had his way, they would all be wiped from the face of the earth, or failing that, be humiliated beyond all hope of recovery, which was something that he hoped this war might accomplish. Morrison, the son of a printer, was self-educated, and it was from the inflammatory pamphlets produced by his father from time to time that he had imbibed his present ideas. At eighteen, he had taken a situation with a prosperous tobacco importer; it was then that he had obtained his first view of the South and the gracious living that went with it. In the pursuit of business, he was sent to Georgia, where he was received cordially at Bell Alley, the flourishing plantation of Beauford Tanner. Business concluded, he had been invited to stay to dinner. Beauford Tanner had been charm itself, but nonetheless Morrison had believed that he detected condescension beneath the civil words. Just before dinner was about to be served, he had caught his first glimpse of the wife of his host. Arabella Tanner was a thin, nervous woman without any great looks to recommend her, but in her colorful silk gown, the great hoop skirts swaying and rustling, her hair in a gleaming coil from which honey-colored ringlets descended to touch her half-exposed powdered shoulders, she had seemed to Morrison like some dainty creature out of a fairy tale.

Like her husband, Arabella had exerted herself to charm their guest from New York, but Morrison, his first bemusement over, had found himself irritated by many things about her, her simpering smile, the coy flirtatious looks she directed at him every so often, her ceaselessly fluttering fan and the flash of her jewel-laden fingers. Comparing her situation in life with his mother's hard lot, he had condemned her as a vapid and useless member of a society he despised. These rich Southern women, he had told himself with growing indignation, were undoubtedly all cut from the same cloth as Arabella Tanner. Watching her covertly as he consumed the four courses of an excellent meal, listening to her gay, inconsequential chatter, he had longed to bring her low. How would this perfumed and silk-clad woman react, he had wondered, if she should be brought face to face with the more sordid facts of life? Many years had passed since that visit to Bell Alley, but the question had continued to haunt him.

Wondering at his silence and his vacant stare, Desiree stealthily endeavored to detach her hair from his loosened grasp. Instantly, his attention brought back to her, Morrison's fingers tightened. He glared down at her, smarting anew with the memory of his humiliation at her hands, the insults she had flung at him, her outright defiance of his will. Arabella Tanner, this girl, Desiree Grayson—they were all the same. Grayson, if he was to believe the Johnny Reb who had spoken out in her defense, was a nurse, not a whore, as he had first believed. A nurse! He sneered inwardly. Playing at it, more like. Like Arabella Tanner, she would swoon away should she be asked to tend real injuries. If the Johnny Reb had spoken truth, so much the better. He would break her, he would expose the soft rotten core beneath her posturing and her playacting. An idea flickered in his mind, and he wondered why he had not thought of it before. With Grayson, he would have the answer to that long-ago question. He turned his head, watching the passing shadows of soldiers thrown onto the tautly drawn canvas wall. "Don't move," he said curtly to Desiree. "I wouldn't like you to miss the little surprise I have in store for you." Releasing her, he snatched up the fallen blanket and draped it about himself. "Lie still, my dear," he said, striding toward the entrance. "Gather your strength, for you'll have need of it."

Trying to control the fresh panic inspired by his words, Desiree attempted to sit up. She must do something, anything. She could not just lie here and submit. With a stifled gasp she clutched at the sides of the narrow bed as her head began to whirl and the lamplit walls to close in upon her. Hastily she lay down again. It was bad enough to be conscious and at Morrison's mercy, she told herself, but unconscious, she shuddered to think of what he might do. Besides, she was not thinking clearly. With Morrison just outside the tent, she would be foolish to break and run. Such a futile attempt would provide laughter for him, and it would bring him and his cohorts down upon her like a pack of hungry dogs. She listened to the deep burr of Morrison's voice, to the other voices answering him, but she could not make out the words. Later, perhaps, when Morrison slept and the camp was quiet, she would make the attempt.

She lay there rigidly, her hands covering her maltreated face, and something that Morrison had said came back to her like a mocking refrain: "For Dixie Land you'll take your stand . . ." Well, she had taken a stand for Dixie Land, but not in the sense that Morrison meant. Her efforts in this war were for the sake of the suffering men who were in such desperate need of care, not an attempt on her part to keep slavery alive. Her ideals were the same as they had always been—the same ideals, she had later found, that Christopher cherished.

Flinching, Desiree moved restlessly. Christopher. It always came back to him. For as long as she lived, it always would. Impossible to try to forget him, impossible to block the pain of memory from her mind indefinitely. Oh, God, she mourned silently. Is he alive, is he dead? I must know! Don't you see that? I must know!

Dropping her hands, Desiree glanced toward the tent entrance, and formed her decision. She was destined for Camp Wetherby, Morrison had said so, and if Christopher still lived, she would find him there. Her soft mouth tightened to a determined line. Wherever Christopher was, she must be. She would make no attempt to escape from this place. Whatever Morrison did to her, she would not run like a frightened rabbit. Let him do his worst, she would come through it, she would survive, as she had done through these past harrowing years. She thought of something Christopher had said to her, and her lips curled into a faint smile. "You look fragile, but it is only an illusion. You are unbendable, unbreakable, you stare into the face of horror and death every day, and you do not flinch from your duty." He had taken her hand in his and held it briefly. "In view of what I have learned about your past activities, you should not amaze me, and yet you do. I admire you, Firetop, much more than I can say."

His words had been the beginning of a new understanding between them, and if they were not the declaration of love that she craved to hear, she cherished them just the same. From that moment on, he had changed, his hostility vanishing without trace. Without his defensive mask, she was enabled to see the true man beneath, warm, compassionate, tender. Only in one way did he still elude her; he was friendly and considerate, but he continued to hold her at a distance, reserving his compassion and tenderness for the wounded men. Would he ever love her? Sometimes hope was encouraged by a certain look in his eyes whenever they chanced to rest upon her. And yet even if he did love her, the barrier of social difference he had erected between them was strong, and she despaired of making him say the words that would topple it. Christopher, who had entered the war as a means of escape, a hiding place from possible pursuit, and had found himself irretrievably enmeshed by emotions he had not known he possessed. Christopher, the patriot, whose belief was not in the Cause for which most fought, but in a newly discovered love for his homeland. He had said to her once, "Let all the slaves go free, it is the way it should be, and I am as opposed to slavery as I ever was. But let the Yankee try to claim one inch of our land, and I am his enemy."

Startled by this vehemence from the usually silent Christopher, Desiree had said uncertainly, "But even without the question of the slaves, for which, presumably, this war is being fought, do you honestly think that the South can remain separate and apart?"

Christopher had shaken his head. "I don't know, Firetop, I honestly don't. But while we do remain apart, I shall fight for our right to do so." He smiled at her. "Without slavery, the South would be a beautiful place in which to live."

"You have changed, Christopher."

His smile had vanished, and she knew that she had touched on a place that he was not prepared to share. "Not so much as you might think," he had answered. He was silent for so long that Desiree thought he would not continue; then he said slowly, "If there is change in me, it is because I have learned to differentiate. I know the face of my enemy now." His rare smile returned. "It is not your face, Firetop."

"Phillips?"

"Yes, Phillips. I have not forgotten about him, but for the moment he is unimportant. I will find him eventually."

The bleak look had come back into his eyes when he spoke of Phillips, the soft-toned note of frightening menace to his voice giving her a glimpse of the Christopher she had not seen for some months now. Anxious to divert him, she had touched his arm gently. "Don't think about him," she urged.

"There was a time when I could think of little else." The twig Christopher had been idly turning in his hands broke with a sharp snap. "But circumstances alter cases, and these days I rarely think of the miserable little maggot." Throwing the pieces of twig away, he had turned to her and looked at her searchingly. "Why so concerned, Dessi? Does it really matter to you what I think or feel?"

"You know that it does."

"I really believe you mean that." Touching her face gently, Christopher had turned from her and walked away.

That gentle touch upon the cheek was the nearest thing to a caress she had ever received from him, and it vividly marked the difference between the bearded savage who had raped her and the man he was today. Desiree's heart twisted with pain. That fleeting touch might be all that she would ever have from him. Even if he should be alive, what chance would he have of surviving in a place like Wetherby? Like the rest of their team, he had worked day and night to keep abreast of the tide of wounded. Gaunt, haggard of face, carrying on on nerves alone, his strength badly depleted. Jamie Peters and Ralph Pargeter, the two other men in their team, had discussed Christopher with her once. "That man is a demon for work," Peters had said wryly. "It is almost as though something drives him on." Pargeter had nodded thoughtfully. "I think 'driven' is the right word, Jamie," he said slowly. "We all hate to see suffering, but it is as though Chris has his own personal vendetta against suffering and death." Pargeter's mild blue eyes turned inquiringly to Desiree. "You knew him before the war, didn't you, Dessi?"

Desiree nodded. "Yes." She was silent for a moment. "But not nearly as well as I know him now," she added.

Pargeter had exchanged a look with Peters, and Desiree, flushing, had wished that her tone had not been quite so fervent. "Then perhaps you know what drives Chris on?" Jamie Peters said quietly.

Desiree averted her eyes. "I can only tell you that he has undergone a great deal of suffering himself. Therefore he is extra sympathetic to the needs of others."

Jamie Peters had looked at her searchingly. "Suffering, Dessi? How and why?"

She knew that their feelings toward Christopher were friendly, especially Pargeter's, who had more than once said how greatly he admired him, but she had no intention of gratifying their curiosity. If Christopher wanted them to know about his past life, he would have told them. Unable to help the note of stiffness in her voice, she had answered almost coldly, "If you don't mind, I prefer not to discuss him further."

"All right, Dessi," Jamie said, "we didn't mean to pry."

"I know, Jamie." Desiree had been immediately apologetic. "I'm sorry."

"It's all right." Jamie rumpled her hair with a friendly hand. "We're all tired and inclined to be snappy. But seriously, Dessie, if you get the chance, you might try talking to Chris. We all do our best, of course, but Chris goes beyond the call of duty. If he's not careful, he'll burn himself out."

"That's true," Pargeter put in. "If you try taking everybody's pain on your shoulders, you're bound to crumble under the strain."

Frightened by the earnestness of them, Desiree had tried relieving the tension. "You make him sound like a saint," she said, smiling, "and I must confess that I have never thought of Christopher in quite that light."

Pargeter had looked at her blankly for a moment; then he had broken into a rumble of laughter. "A saint? Chris! Hell, no. For one thing, he's got the devil's own temper, and I've seen it displayed often enough when someone has been careless with a patient or jolted them and caused unnecessary pain." Pargeter winked at Desiree. "And for another thing, he can be damned formidable. "No, Dessi, he's far from being a saint, but he is a good man, and you can always rely upon him in a crisis."

Peters nodded in agreement. "You can indeed. I always find it reassuring to have Chris working by my side. Sometimes I think he knows more about healing than the doctor." He hesitated. "I'll tell you one thing, though, I'm glad Chris counts me as a friend, for I sure as hell wouldn't like to be his enemy."

The fear Desiree had tried to smother leaped to immediate life. "Why do you say that?" she questioned sharply.

Peters looked at her in faint surprise. "Nothing to get upset about, Dessi. It's just a feeling I have about him, that's all." He shrugged. "I daresay I'm wrong, my feelings usually are."

Not so wrong, Desiree thought, not where Christopher's hatred of Frazer Phillips was concerned. "What kind of a feeling?" she had persisted.

Looking uncomfortable, Peters had avoided her eyes. "Why not forget I said it? It's just my imagination working overtime."

But Desiree could not leave it alone. Had Christopher done something, said something to make Jamie feel the way he did? "I don't want to forget it, Jamie. Tell me."

Peters hesitated. "Well, if you insist on researching my feelings," he said reluctantly, "I believe Chris would make a dangerous enemy. I don't think I'd like to be someone who had done him an injury. I have this sense that he would be quite ruthless."

An injury, Desiree thought. An injury like the murder of his sister. Oh, yes, Christopher would be quite ruthless. Looking at Jamie, she had said uncertainly, "I suppose you know that we're all talking a great deal of nonsense."

Relieved, Jamie laughed. "Sure we are, that's what I tried to tell you. Me and my imagination, it will be my downfall one day. Anyway, Dessi, we've got nothing to worry about. We're all friends here."

But of course she had worried, only not in the way Jamie Peters thought. How could she help worrying, when every fresh day brought the dread that Frazer Phillips might appear among the wounded? And if that should happen, how would Christopher react, what would he do?

After that conversation, Desiree had observed Christopher as closely as she was able, and she thought she knew what Jamie Peters had meant. Christopher was friendly enough to his co-workers, and with the wounded he was gentleness itself, but in the rare times away from the field hospital, a change came over him. There was an aloofness about him then that held others at a distance, a wary quality, a faintly hard note to his voice, and an expression in his dark eyes that could be intimidating if one did not know him well. Sometimes, from the way he sat, hands tensely gripping the armrests of the chair, it was as though he was waiting for something disastrous to happen. Desiree knew, as the others did not, that these puzzling things about him were an inheritance from his imprisonment. Watching him, she yearned to say something that would take the tension away, but she knew that he had not yet reached that stage where mere words could comfort. Christopher alone could free himself from the hell his mind created. Would that time ever come? she would ask herself despairingly. Would he ever learn to trust?

Desiree's thoughts scattered as the tent flap was thrust to one side and Captain Morrison, still draped in the blanket, entered, closely followed by two other men. Her heart beating unpleasantly fast, Desiree sat up in the bed, shaking her hair forward in an attempt to cover herself. The two men with Morrison were drunk, she noted. One was staring at her, a foolish grin on his mouth, while the other hummed beneath his breath and held onto his comrade for support. Her eyes flashed to Morrison.

Reading her thoughts, Morrison said smoothly, "Yes, my dear, they are drunk. They'll be disciplined for that in the morning, but at the moment their sodden condition suits my purpose."

"And what purpose would that be?" Even as Desiree said the words, she knew what he meant to do. Her mind scurried in frantic circles, seeking a way out, finding none.

Morrison smiled, an unpleasant smile that did not reach his eyes. "It pains me to admit it, but I would assume that you are reasonably intelligent, therefore I have no need to answer that question." Throwing the blanket from him, he moved over to the bed and looked down at her. "It is true that the men are drunk, but not sufficiently so to impede them. Their alcoholic haze will not only cause them to work with a will, but it will add considerable gusto. Wouldn't you agree?"

Desiree moistened her dry lips. "If you have the faintest instinct of a gentleman, you will get out of here and take those two with you."

"Ah, the haughty Southern lady speaks." Morrison's eyes glittered with a cold light. "Don't try it on me, my dear, it won't work."

"You bastard!" Desiree's eyes blazed with an anger that was momentarily stronger than her fear. Naked, his hands on his hips, he stood posed before her, somehow obscene in his fleshiness. She looked briefly at his jutting penis, upward again into gray eyes that had lost their cold glitter and now burned with an avid light. Choking down the bile that rose in her throat, she turned her head away. "You are disgusting. You make my skin crawl!"

"Still defiant, eh?" Morrison's fingers pinched at either side of her jaw, forcing her head around. " 'Bastard,' I think you called me. Your language is not exactly that of a lady, and I must confess that it surprises me."

"Go to hell!"

Morrison's fingers tightened as she tried to jerk her head away. "My dear, you are ungrateful, and ingratitude has always made me quite angry." He looked into her eyes, enjoying the fear that had replaced the anger. "You know, you really must learn to count your blessings." His taunting voice dropped to a sibilant whisper. "Look at those two strapping young men who are so eager to provide you with enjoyment. It does your heart good just to gaze into their bright, unselfish faces, doesn't it? Think of it, three of us to service you. One at the well, my love, and two to look on. But in order that you should have no cause for complaint, we will change around frequently. You will enjoy Bates especially, for he is built like a giant. Renwick is a little smaller, but not much. As for myself, you can see that I am not lacking in that particular department. I think we will all fit inside you admirably." His hand fell away from her jaw. "You may speak now. Will you not tell me how grateful you are?"

Desiree's heart was beating so hard that she felt choked. "You are mad!" She brought out the words with an effort.

Morrison shook his head. "By no means, my dear, just determined to pursue an experiment that I have long had in mind."

"An experiment that will end in my death." Desiree raised her eyes to his. "The war will not last forever. Whichever side should win, there will be inquiries made as to the fate of prisoners."

"I have considered that. Never fear, we will stop short of killing you. After all, I want you to enjoy the luxurious accommodations at Camp Wetherby. It would be selfish of me to deprive you of that particular pleasure, and I have never been a selfish man."

Desiree wanted to weep, to beg, but she could not bring herself to do it. Why humiliate herself to no avail, when there was clearly nothing she could say or do that would sway him from his purpose? Trying to hide her terror, she managed to force a scornful smile to her lips. "Very well," she said hoarsely, "since I cannot prevent you, do your worst, and be damned to you!"

"Oh, I will, you can be sure of that."

"Of course. It is the kind of behavior I would expect from Yankee scum such as yourself."

"Unkind to condemn us all."

"You are mistaken. You are not representative of the Yankees, for which God be thanked. I admire the purpose for which this war is being fought, and the men who fight in it to help free their more unfortunate brothers. We have scum in our own ranks, I am aware of that, but you, I would imagine, are the worst example of both sides."

Morrison looked at her—pale, proud, seemingly unafraid now, words coming calmly and contemptuously from her lips—and his anger was fired to a new height. "Talking will not help you. I'll break you yet, you bitch!" He looked over his shoulder. "Bates, Renwick," he shouted, "get your lead asses over here!"

The two men glanced at each other uneasily, somewhat sobered by his furious tone. Running to his side, they both attempted a wavering salute. "What can we do for you, sir?" the taller of the two men said in a slurred voice.

"You grab her arms, Bates," Morrison snapped. "Renwick, take her legs. Hold the hellcat still, there is something I want her to do for me."

Shuddering, Desiree closed her eyes as their hands gripped her tightly. There was nothing else she could do but endure.

"None of that, whore, open your eyes." Morrison's open hand stung her bruised cheek in a light blow. "No more sleeping. Have you forgotten that it's playtime? Open your eyes, I say, or I'll force them open with my thumbs." He smiled grimly as Desiree's lids lifted. "Ah, I thought that would do the trick." Climbing on the bed, he straddled her, edging upward until his swollen penis was against her lips.

"No!" she shouted, turning her head away. "You will never make me do that!" The violence of Desiree's reaction satisfied Morrison.

"I won't? We'll see about that!" Morrison looked up at Bates. "Do you hear her, Bates? That's funny, isn't it? What about you, Renwick, don't you think it's funny?"

"Sir?" Renwick coughed, avoiding Bates's eyes. "Yes, sir, I guess it's funny."

"You guess? Don't you know, you fool?"

"Yes, sir, it's funny."

Bates frowned. "She looks kind of delicate, sir," he began hesitantly. "Maybe it would be better if we . . . if we sort of left things alone."

Morrison glared at him in outrage. "How dare you, Bates! I have told you what I expect from you and Renwick. You will take your turn with the girl, and you will give me a fine performance. That's an order."

Bates sighed. "Yes, sir, whatever you say."

"That's better." Morrison turned his glare on Desiree. Taking her head between his hands, he held it in a viselike grip, forcing her to look at him. Encountering the blaze of hatred in her eyes, he laughed softly. "In one way you are right, Bates," he said, still looking at the girl. "She does present an appearance of extreme delicacy, but by God, she's still got plenty of spirit." He winked at Desiree, as though they shared a joke between them. "No, you're not lacking in fighting spirit, are you, my love? Though this time I truly believe that the odds are against you. Don't you agree?"

He waited for Desiree to say something. When she said nothing, he went on in a light voice. "Bates, as you heard, is a little squeamish about this, but don't allow yourself to hope. He will do exactly as I say."

Desiree's eyes flashed upward to Bates. His hands holding tightly to her wrists, he was leaning over her, giving her an upside-down view of his face. He drew his head back quickly, as if ashamed to look at her. Desiree looked at Morrison again. "I hope for nothing from you, pig," she said quietly.

"You are upset," Morrison went on in the same light voice. "But you must not blame Bates for not rushing to your aid. He is shy with the ladies, but he believes in doing his duty by them, when ordered to do so."

"I'm sure he does," Desiree said bitterly, "especially when he realizes that he will be punished if he does not obey. But punishment or not, it is not the way a true man would behave."

"Ah, you are trying to stir up strife between officer and men, and it simply will not do, darling. You wrong Bates, you know. He is all man, so I have been given to understand. I grant you that his size is enough to put a delicately bred female off, but, undressed, you will find that he is truly magnificent, built like a stallion. Once he impales you on his spike, he will transport you to heaven, and what more could you ask for than that? Renwick, now, is a different matter. He is man enough to take his dip in the well, but he is in and out like a rabbit, which is rather daunting for a full-blooded woman."

The taunting voice went on and on, driving Desiree to the point of madness.

Morrison laughed and repositioned himself. Desiree gagged as his penis touched her lips once more.

A resolve grew in her mind. Her mouth opened, and a sound that was almost a snarl escaped her lips. Morrison, divining her intention, jerked back quickly, and her teeth grazed harmlessly over the taut, throbbing rod of flesh. Beside himself, he struck her again. For a moment longer he crouched there, glaring balefully into her pain-twisted face;

then he got off the bed. "The whore has made it clear that she has no time for details. She wants the loveplay to commence, and that being the case, we must do our poor best to oblige her." He nodded to the two men. "Throw her down on the floor, and we'll get on with it. I said *throw*," he shouted, as he noted the hesitant way the men were handling her. Dammit to hell, there's no need to be gentle, lads, she's not made out of china. Get on with it, let her know that we mean business."

Desiree gave a strangled cry as she hit the floor with a jarring thump that knocked the breath from her body. Through a mist she made out Morrison's red face looming above hers. "Hurry it up, Bates"—his voice was a harsh explosion of sound in her ears—"or I might change my mind about giving you first dip. You, Renwick, get your duds off. You'll take her after me. Jump, man, you know the lady doesn't like to be kept waiting."

Desiree heard the rustle of clothing, the sound of labored breathing. Someone approached her with a heavy walk that set the overhead lamp jangling and swinging. Hands thrust her legs brutally apart, and then Morrison was gone. Another man, huge, heavily muscled, was kneeling between her thighs. "Go on, man, thrust that goddamned spike inside her," Morrison's voice boomed from behind her. His hands kneaded her breasts, pinched savagely at her nipples. "We're waiting, Bates."

"Yes, sir." The words came in a groan from Bates. For a moment longer he hesitated, his eyes going to Renwick, who was standing awkwardly on bare feet, his clothes in a heap beside him; then he bent to his task.

Desiree's will to endure in silence broke and shattered as he entered her with a violent thrust that seemed to tear her apart. "No!" she screamed. Her hands flew out to twine in his hair, pulling at it desperately. "No, oh, God, no!"

In an instinctive movement, Bates struck her hands away. Deaf to her cries of agony, his conscience deadened, he jerked and shuddered inside her, his faint groans becoming louder as his passion mounted. His hands gripped her legs, lifting her, slid upward to her buttocks, fingers digging into her tortured flesh as he slammed against her in the madness of his approaching climax.

Barely conscious, Desiree felt the jetting of his hot seed inside her. Her lips moved silently, crying out a name. "Christopher . . . Christopher, help me!" It was as if she had willed him back from wherever he wandered, for suddenly he was there, vividly printed against the screen of her inner vision. His dark eyes were warm with compassion, and he was holding out his arms to her. She tried to lift her own in response, but they were too heavy. She gasped. Christopher had vanished, and she was falling from a great height, her tormented body twisting and whirling in space. Faces leaped out at her in that downward spiral—Morrison's, red and triumphant, Renwick's, his mouth agape, Bates's, white and sweating. Where had Christopher gone? She must find him, he was her only hope. The faces closed in on her, merged and became one, and then the merciful darkness claimed her.

Morrison got shakily to his feet and looked down at Desiree's crumpled figure. He felt a stir of uneasiness as he saw the bright blood on her thighs. Good God, Bates must have ripped her apart! His uneasiness increased as he saw her face. Even in unconsciousness the muscles of her face were not relaxed; her features looked pinched and somehow dwindled. Her mouth, too, was tightly held, the bitten lips blue-tinged. His heart leaped in a burst of panic. She looked as though she had died in torment.

"Is she dead, sir?" Frightened, cold sober now, Renwick began to scramble into his clothes. "God damn you, Bates, you're enough to kill any female!"

Bates turned a stricken face to him. "She's not dead, Renwick, but that's not my fault." Rising, he picked up his own clothes. "I shouldn't have done it, she was too little, and I was too much for her." His mouth twitched in a spasm of nerves. "M-maybe she will die."

Badly shaken, Morrison glared at him. "Be quiet, Bates!"

Bates sucked in a deep breath. Then, as though he had won an inner struggle, he said quietly, "I'll be quiet, sir, after I've said what I've got to say."

"And what's that?"

Bates flushed, momentarily confounded by his own daring, but he went doggedly on. "Just this, sir. If the little lady dies, I'm putting you on report, and myself along with you."

Morrison took a menacing step toward him, stopping short when Bates held his ground. "You dare to say that to me, you drunken fool! Since when has an enlisted man been able to put an officer on report?"

Bated looked at him steadily. "You know the rules, sir, as well as I. As an enlisted man, I can take no action against you myself, but I can report your conduct."

Defeated, Morrison turned away. "There will be no need for your damned report. I'll see she's taken care of."

"You won't touch her again, sir?"

"Of course not, idiot. Get out, both of you. Oh, Renwick, find one of the women and send her to me."

"Which woman, sir?"

Fuming, Morrison whirled on him, his gray eyes blazing. "Any one of them," he shouted. "I assume a whore will know how to take care of one of her own sisterhood."

"Yes, sir." With a swift look at Bates, Renwick departed hurriedly.

Bates looked as though he was about to say something; then, meeting Morrison's eyes, he desisted. Shrugging quickly into his clothes, he looked miserably at Desiree and then followed after Renwick.

Harry Drew entered the small tent hesitantly. Approaching Desiree, he assisted her to her feet. "Been sent to get you, ma'am," he explained. "Prison wagon's waiting."

"I know." Desiree leaned heavily on his arm. "I'm ready."

Drew looked down at her. "I can't bear to think of you going to that place, ma'am."

Desiree smiled faintly. "It doesn't matter. . . . I want to thank you for your kindness."

Drew flushed bright red with embarrassment. "I did no more than pop in and out. I . . . I wanted to know how you were."

"I consider that a great kindness." Desiree's weary face lit with a warmer smile. "Especially since your interest in my welfare might have got you into trouble with your superior."

"Stuck away in this tent as you were, away from the others, no one was to know except the guard." Drew's blue eyes kindled to a hot rage. "We all know what Morrison did to you, ma'am, the word has got around. We'll get him for it one of these days."

"No, please! Not on my account."

"Southerner or not," Drew retorted hotly, "you're a lady. He had no right to lay his dirty paws on you!"

"I'm much better now." Desiree's fingers gently pinched his arm, trying to urge him forward.

"That may be," Drew answered, "but you still look sort of frail to me." His gloom lifted, and he smiled at her. "But I was forgetting something, ma'am. I've got a present for you, something that'll make you feel a whole heap better."

Desiree looked at him with bewildered eyes. "Have you forgotten that I am a prisoner? You are not allowed to give me gifts."

Drew laughed triumphantly. "I can give you this one. Forbes was telling me that you were asking about Christopher Wakely, so I inquired around." He paused, aware of her sudden stillness. "I found out that he's still alive. He was hurt some, but he made it."

"Drew!" Desiree sighed. Releasing his arm, she looked up at him, and he was dazzled by her sudden vivid beauty. "Oh, thank you, Drew, thank you!" Impulsively she flung her arms about him and hugged him close. "God bless you. I shall never forget you!"

16

Desiree held up her hand to the candle flame, letting the light shine through it. Momentarily she was fascinated by its transparency and its almost skeletal appearance, and then her dulled eyes took on an expression of horror. How long would it be, she wondered, before she collapsed and died, as so many of the prisoners had done? And Christopher, how could she go on if anything should happen to him?

Shuddering, Desiree let her hand drop. Thinking back to that time when she had first set foot inside Camp Wetherby, she felt a trembling inside her. In the beginning, only Christopher had been real to her, his beloved face standing out from the other prisoners like a beacon of light, and then she had become aware of the prison camp itself. Camp Wetherby, consisting of a series of small wood and brick huts, with here and there a group of battered, weather-stained tents, housed murderers, thieves, prostitutes, bounty skippers, and felons of all descriptions, all of whom, regardless of sex, mingled freely with the prisoners of war. They existed under conditions of privation that were so frightful as to be well nigh unbelievable. The privies were so broken down that they were useless, and, as a scanty concession to the health of the prisoners, the guards had ordered that long trenches should be dug at various points. There was little water to spare to flush out these trenches, with the result that in the summer months an overpowering odor of human excrement hung over the camp, mingling sickeningly with the stench of unwashed bodies. Daily, men lost to hope coupled with the prostitutes, who sold their favors for an extra scrap of bread or a few sips of the insect-swarmed water.

Remembering, Desiree's hands clenched at her sides. It had been a long time before she could look unmoved upon such degrading sights, for the couples, oblivious of their audience, would fornicate freely. It had been longer still before she could choke down the hard, weevil-infested biscuits, the minute piece of rancid meat, without vomiting. But gradually, with the passing of the long, dragging months, she ate the starvation rations and drank the contaminated water almost with enjoyment. In common with the others, she would devise elaborate schemes whereby she might obtain more food, but she could not follow the women who, taking a lead from the prostitutes, would sell their bodies to the men for extra food. Even in her extremity, this one thing she forbade herself, for her feelings for Christopher ran too deeply to be ignored. Desiree thought drearily that except for her never-ending unspoken love for Christopher, it had been a long time since she had felt anything at all. Sometimes, when she was deep in the slough of her private despair, she would believe that an essential part of herself had been lost, that she was incapable of feeling, of being the woman she had once been, but then she would look at Christopher, and the warmth of her reaction would reassure her that her emotions were only temporarily stunted.

Pushing thought from her, Desiree turned, stepping carefully over the outstretched legs of the people propped against the wall. She made her way to the small, grimy window. Outside, a brisk March wind howled, raising a whirlwind of dust and bending the trees that stood just beyond the high wire fence that imprisoned them. In the failing daylight, guards tramped up and down, their boredom with their task clearly expressed in their carelessly slung weapons. Almost as though she could see into their minds, Desiree knew what they were thinking: Why bother to be vigilant? What can these living scarecrows do? They haven't the strength to lift their hands, let alone make a break for freedom. So the guards, ignoring the prisoners, rubbed their chilblained hands together and stamped their stoutly booted feet against the penetrating chill.

Desiree's attention was drawn to the prisoners. Those who were hardy enough to brave the frigid air had congregated in little groups, well away from the hostile guards, their heads bent together in conversation, arms hugged about them in an effort to keep warm. Many of the prisoners of war were barefooted, with only the tatters of their gray uniforms to protect them from the elements. Others had the soles of shoes tied to their feet with string, and some had their feet wrapped in rags.

Unaccustomed tears stung Desiree's eyes. It was a pitiful thing to see the soldiers of the proud Confederate armies so reduced. Turning her head, she looked at the rough calendar scratched on the wall beside the window. Counting the scratches swiftly, she calculated the date to be the twenty-eighth of March 1865. Her heart plunged as she stared at the markings. 1865! And the war had been raging since 1861. Dear God! Would it never end, must the killing go on and on? Why didn't God stop it, why didn't He put out His hand and say, "Enough!" Thinking of the captured soldiers recently brought to Camp Wetherby, Desiree bit down hard on her quivering lower lip. From these battered and shocked men, she had learned that the war was as good as lost to the Confederacy. Southern homes were in ruins, the price of food was sky-high, and General Sherman had reduced that strategic point, Atlanta, almost to rubble. One soldier, weeping from mingled pain and grief, had told Desiree that General Lee was in despair. "A series of miracles must happen," General Lee had been heard to say, "or else I greatly fear that the Southern Cause is doomed." These words from the intrepid, fire-eating, never-say-die General Lee! It showed how far along the road to failure the South had progressed.

Although she had never espoused the Cause, Desiree shivered as if from an anticipated blow. What would the loss of the war mean to her father, if he still lived? What would it mean to the other planters, to all of the people? Trying to stem her surging thoughts, Desiree looked away from the calendar, her eyes seeking out Christopher. He was standing at the edge of the group nearest to the window. He seemed to be listening intently, but, as usual, he was contributing nothing to the conversation. "Doc, the man of mystery," the soldiers called him. In every way, except for the actual degree, he was a doctor, and the men thought of him as such. In their rough way, they might be said to love him, and certainly they respected him highly, not only for his skill, but for the compassion he brought to his work. He was waiting now, Desiree knew, for the imminent arrival of a fresh batch of prisoners.

Desiree pressed her fingers to the cold glass, her eyes growing tender as she surveyed him. His dark hair, blown by the wind, was wildly disarrayed, and his face, from which the deep tan had long since faded, looked almost purple with the cold. Her heart twinged painfully. He was so gaunt that he looked taller than ever, and his dark eyes were sunk deeply into hollows. He was only the ghost of the man he had been, but he had a fiery spirit that would not die. Dearest Christopher! Very soon he would become "doc" to the new arrivals. They would rely upon him as the others did. They would gaze hopefully toward the door for his arrival, and when he came toward them there would be that look in their eyes that she had seen so many times before, a look of unquestioning trust.

Breathing on the glass, Desiree rubbed a small patch clear with the end of her ragged sleeve. Christopher, as usual, would do all in his power to alleviate the suffering, but there were times when he failed. She thought of the stunned expression on his face when Jamie Peters and Ralph Pargeter, both suffering from the same type of fever, had died within hours of each other. There had been actual torment in Christopher's eyes when he had looked up at her, but at the same time it seemed to her that the line of his jaw had become harder, even more determined. "They're dead, Dessi," he had said in a carefully controlled voice.

She had gone to him and placed her hand on his shoulder. "You did your best."

"No!" His control breaking, he had risen abruptly to his feet. "Don't you see, Dessi. I should have been able to save them. I let them down."

"Don't say that!" she had cried out in protest. "No man could have done more."

He had not seemed to hear her. "Jamie and Ralph, both

dead. I failed them. But, by Christ, I'll try not to fail the other men!"

Desiree smiled wryly. It was not Christopher who had failed, it was she. Once he had called her "unbendable, unbreakable," but she had shown little of that spirit lately. Christopher, on the other hand, with few medical supplies to aid him, worked day and night. If he ever slept, Desiree was not aware of it. His sleeping position was beside her, and sometimes, waking in the night, she would put out a groping hand to touch him, only to find that he was not there. Often she would slip out into the night and follow him to the small, wretched hospital that served the prisoners. She would always find him there, tireless, his eyes burning with intensity, taking the place of the prison doctor, who had died six months ago from pneumonia. The prison authorities did not interfere, for they, unable to obtain another doctor, were only too glad to delegate authority.

Desiree's mouth tightened in self-disgust. It was true that in the past few weeks she had almost given up. Almost, but not quite, as Christopher would find out when the new prisoners arrived. She would be there at his side, as she had been in the past, doing what little she could. Turning away from the window, she walked over to her allotted space against the damp brick wall. Sitting down heavily, she drew her cold legs under her and settled the folds of her threadbare skirt over them. Her thoughts drifted on. She and Christopher, reunited, had teamed up once more, becoming the unofficial doctor and nurse. They bound up wounds, comforted the dying, and tried to instill courage and a fighting spirit in those in whom the flame of life burned low. But the wish to die, so prevalent in Camp Wetherby, they had been unable to combat. So many had died, succumbing to disease, starvation, or just plain giving up. Desiree pressed her trembling hands together. For a long time she had fought her growing weakness and her mounting despair, but in the end she had turned away from her duty, leaving the whole burden on Christopher's shoulders. But no more! Somehow she would make up for it. She wanted to be warmed by Christopher's rare smile, by the approval in his eyes. If she could not have his love, she could at least have something of him to cherish. "Christopher," she murmured, "why can't you love me?"

"Love!" a harsh voice exclaimed. "Who the hell needs it? I don't want love, I want food in my belly."

Startled, Desiree turned her head and looked at the girl who was seated a little distance from her. Melissa Travers had not spoken in months, and the eleven other people who occupied the small hut had grown used to her silence. "Melissa!" Desiree gave her a tentative smile. "You've said something."

Melissa Travers shrugged. "Didn't have anything to say before." Running her hands through her shock of untidy blonde hair, she turned her wild blue eyes to Desiree. "Just had to speak, nursie dear, when I heard you babbling on about love." Her lips curled into a sneer. "You should speak of death, for we're all going to die before this war is over."

A fierce resentment stirred in Desiree. How dare this girl make mention of death, when she had just made up her mind to return to the fight? "No, Melissa"—Desiree's voice shook with suppressed emotion—"you mustn't give in. You must hang on, it is the only way to survive."

"Survival is for the strong ones, like you."

A flush stung Desiree's cheeks. "I thought I was strong, but I'm not. I gave up."

Melissa nodded. "Yes, you did. But you've brought yourself out of it again."

Desiree looked at her curiously. "How do you know so much?"

"I've been watching you, nursie. It's surprising what you can see when you retire yourself from life."

Desiree felt a faint flutter of alarm. Before Melissa had relapsed into silence, she had been prone to fits of screaming hysteria. She seemed calm enough now, but it might be wise to choose one's words with care. "If I can come out of it, Melissa," she said cautiously, "so can you. Don't give up. You mustn't."

Melissa's hard defiance crumbled. Tears welled into her eyes and ran down her wasted cheeks. "I'm tired of feeling weak all the time. I just want to die!"

"Don't say that," Desiree said sharply. "You want to live. You must keep telling yourself that."

Melissa brushed a trembling hand across her wet eyes. "I don't want to discuss it. I'm sick of living. I was even before I came to this place. There, now you know, so leave me be!"

"I'm sorry," Desiree said gently. "Would you like to tell me about it? Perhaps I can help in some way."

"You help me. Huh! That's a good one. The truth is, I was a failure from the day I was born, and I'll likely die a failure."

"How do you come to be in Wetherby, Melissa?"

"I was caught stealing, that's how come." Melissa gave a mirthless laugh. "I was going to kill myself, you see, and I wanted material to make a new gown for my burial. I had only one gown to my name, and that had seen its day, so I figured if I couldn't look good in life, why not go out like a queen. Anyway, I had the material in my hands, peacock-blue velvet it was. I was just about to shove it under my coat when this man, the owner of the store, caught up with me."

Speechless, Desiree stared at her, her eyes soft with pity.

"You're wondering why I used to make such a fuss about being hungry, I suppose?" Melissa went on rapidly. "Well, that's easily explained. I want to die fast, not slow."

"No, Melissa," Desiree answered in a low voice, "I wasn't wondering about that. Tell me why you feel this way. Were you in love?"

"It's always a man, isn't it?" Melissa dried her eyes on the hem of her skirt. "But I don't want to talk about me anymore. Let's talk about you instead."

Desiree shrugged. "There's nothing much to say, I'm afraid."

Melissa studied her. "You've got secrets in your eyes, nursie. I'd say there would be a great deal to tell if you once let down your guard." She smiled faintly as Desiree averted her face. "It's all right, I won't press you. I don't like people prying into my life, and I won't pry into yours. But this much I will say, you'll never really give in, not all the way. The strong ones never do."

Desiree turned her head and looked at her. "What makes you so certain that I'm strong?"

"I know, that's all. You're like doc."

Desiree smiled at this reference to Christopher. "I haven't shown much strength lately."

"That's true," Melissa agreed bluntly, "but you'll make up for it. You were down for a while, but you're not the type to stay down, it's not in your nature. You and doc will make it, take my word for it."

"Will we? I wonder."

"Sure you will." Melissa hesitated, and then went on almost shyly, "Before I met up with doc, I thought of all men as heartless swine. But he's so different that he convinced me that there must be a good one here and there, if you look hard enough. A woman would be a fool to pass him up. He's worth everything."

Desiree thought of Christopher's past undeserved reputation. The scandal that had been attached to his name, the venomous gossip that had followed his every action. The wild Fairfield boy. The callous murderer. But he was innocent of murder, and he was no longer that wild, unruly boy. If the people who had condemned him could only know the true Christopher Fairfield, his strength, his compassion, his sensitivity, how quickly they would revise their opinions. "Yes, Melissa," Desiree said softly, "doc is different. He always has been. Only people didn't understand him, he wouldn't let them get close enough, and so they hated him for that difference."

Melissa's blue eyes opened wide. "Go on, you're joshing me. No one could hate doc."

Desiree shrugged. "They did. But it's a long story, and I don't want to go into it now."

"All right." Unoffended, Melissa nodded in agreement. "Am I right in thinking you've known doc for a long time?"

"You are. I've known him all my life."

"And you're in love with him?"

Bright color flooded Desiree's pale face, but she made no attempt at evasion. "Yes," she answered simply, "I love him very much."

Melissa smiled. "Sure you do. Even if I hadn't heard you just now, I'd have known. It sticks out all over you."

Desiree's flush deepened. "Am I really so obvious?"

"Maybe only to me. I told you, when you don't talk you observe a lot. What about doc, does he know?"

Desiree shook her head. "Of course not."

"Then why don't you tell him?"

"Tell him?" Shocked, Desiree started at her. "Oh no, I couldn't do that."

"Why the hell not? What have you got to lose?"

"You don't understand," Desiree said desperately. "He wouldn't be interested."

"I think you're wrong." Melissa folded her arms about her knees, half closing her eyes in thought. "I remember when you first came to Wetherby, the look on your face when you saw doc, the look on his. He loves you, all right."

Desiree's heart began to beat very fast. Could Melissa possibly be right? Did Christopher love her? Feeling almost light-headed with the hope that Melissa's words had brought to life, she said breathlessly, "He—he was relieved to see me, that's all. Nothing more than that."

Melissa grinned, an urchin's grin that lit her worn face to a fragile beauty. "Not going to let me down, are you, nursie?" she scoffed. "After all I've said about your strength, don't tell me you haven't the courage to go to him."

Desiree put her hands to her hot cheeks. "Why should it matter to you?"

Her grin fading, Melissa shrugged. "I guess it's because doc's been good to me. You, too, in your own way. Well, are you going to tell him?"

"I can't!"

"I see." Melissa looked at Desiree scornfully. "Then it's pride, you're afraid he'll turn you down?"

"P-perhaps."

"You're a fool, nursie. Forget about your goddamned pride. I know I'm right about doc, and you can't afford to throw away what little happiness you can get."

"And if you're wrong, Melissa?"

"I know I'm not. You want it all nice and tidy and wrapped up in blue ribbons, don't you? What's the matter with you, girl, you're in Wetherby, and you may be dead tomorrow. Take a chance, or forget about it altogether." Abruptly, Melissa turned her back. "I don't want to talk anymore," she said, lying down.

Her face still hot, Desiree's gaze scanned the few people who were sitting against the wall. Melissa had not troubled to lower her voice, and she wondered what they were thinking. Tom Melrose, as usual, was staring at the floor, his lips moving as he conducted a silent conversation with people only he could see. Poor Tom! Six feet four, and worn down to a shadow of himself. Sometimes he was normal, but more often he was not. His brain had been damaged from a head wound he had received at the Battle of Peachtree Creek, and the hardships he was forced to undergo at Camp Wetherby had not helped his condition. Hannah Forrester, who had been among the boldest and the hardest of the prostitutes when Desiree had first arrived at the camp, was sitting near the cold stove, her clawlike hands held out to a nonexistent flame. Now, too weak from semistarvation and the constant abuse of her body to walk very far, Hannah had simply given up. She spent most of her time in the hut, either sitting by the stove or with her back against the wall, staring vacantly into space. Of the other three people in the hut, two were looking Desiree's way, the other was sprawled on his back, sleeping.

Desiree lowered her eyes, shutting out their blank, incurious stares. Of course they had not heard, she told herself, they were not concerned with her or her problems. Their bodies might be in Wetherby, but their minds had taken them far away, to a safe, comfortable, happy world of their own. Desiree's lips firmed and her violet eyes took on a bright glow of resolution. She, too, would remove her mind from Wetherby. She would forget pride, doubts, the stupid conventions that had been bred into her, and which had taken a firmer hold on her than she had realized. With the remaining strength left in her enfeebled body, she would try to make her own world with Christopher. It might be that he did not love her, as Melissa so confidently claimed, but he was a man with normal desires, and she knew that she could make him want her. Melissa was certainly right about one thing, though—she could very well be dead by tomorrow. That being so, it was up to her to take what happiness she could get and, hopefully, give.

There was a hint of the old authoritative Desiree in the squaring of her shoulders, in the set of her jaw as she glanced at the prone Melissa. Even her voice had taken on a new and firmer note when she spoke. "Melissa, you were right."

"About what?" Melissa's shoulders shrugged in irritable rejection. "What do you want, anyway? I told you I didn't want to talk anymore."

"I know. But I thought you might be interested to hear that I've made up my mind. I'm going to find doc."

"What for, you going to roll bandages, or something?"

"I'm going to tell him that I love him, and that even if he doesn't love me, I want him."

"Good for you." Melissa turned over on her back. Without

opening her eyes, she added, "Why are you still here, then? Get going!"

Desiree rose to her feet and went steadily toward the door. Opening it, she was stayed by Melissa's faintly jeering voice. "You sure you'll be able to take him on, nursie? You look pretty feeble to me."

Desiree smiled. "I'm sure. The body may be feeble, but the spirit is just fine." Closing the door, she heard Melissa's soft, approving laughter.

17

Howling like a chorus of demons, the wind came swooping down upon Desiree as she left the doubtful shelter of the hut. It swirled out her hair in dulled streamers of red-gold, threw fine dust into her eyes, and pierced through her thin, shabby clothing with the stabbing ferocity of knives. Shuddering, blinking her smarting eyes in an effort to clear them, Desiree glanced about her. The little groups of men were dispersing, some entering their huts, others, the less fortunate, moving toward the tents, barren abodes with bare earthen floors, serving to keep off the worst edge of the wind, but contributing nothing at all in warmth and comfort. Doubtless they would attempt to while away the leaden hours in sleep, or else they would shoot homemade dice in a game of their own invention. They did not play for money, for they had none, nor yet for food, which was increasingly scarce. The whole purpose of the game was to take their minds off their troubles, and ease the ever-present burden of dread for their loved ones in the beleaguered South.

Sighing, her anxious eyes noting that Christopher was not among the listlessly shambling men, Desiree began to make her way toward the low, dingy-white building that served as a hospital. Her step quickened with her heartbeats as she drew near. Christopher would either be in the ward or in the little room adjoining it, which was used for the dispensing of medicines and dressings, when available, to the ambulatory patients. What would Christopher say when she told him that she loved him, when she offered herself to him? Surely he would not reject her? Oh please, God, don't let him reject me!

The guard, who was stationed a little distance from the hospital entrance, eyed the thin, redheaded girl with truculent blue eyes. Another whore, he thought sourly. The place was crawling with them. Damn it to hell! He did not like this new assignment to Camp Wetherby. He had joined the army to fight the rebs, not to play nursemaid to a lot of criminals, whores and prisoners of war. His simmering temper boiled over as the girl walked straight past him. "Hey, you!" Catching at her blowing hair, he dragged her back. "Where the hell do you think you're going?" He gripped her hair tighter. "You a patient? If so, show me your goddamned pass."

Wincing with pain, Desiree spoke through gritted teeth. "Let go of me. You're hurting me."

"I meant to." The man released her hair. "I'll hurt you a heap more," he said, his eyes boring into hers, "if you don't show me your pass."

Desiree rubbed at her smarting forehead. "I don't need a pass. If you don't know that, then you must be new to Wetherby."

The guard took a threatening step forward. "Don't you take that tone with me, missy. Sure I'm new," he added bitterly, "but that don't mean I'm going to take lip from you, or from any of the other choice specimens floating around here. You got that, Red?"

Desiree started at the barked question. "Yes." Nervous color flooded her face as she met his eyes. "I understand perfectly."

The guard, noting her reaction, smiled maliciously. No doubt she'd been full of fire and ginger at one time, she had that look about her, but Wetherby, from all he had heard about it, ground them all down to the same level. "Well now"—his smile widened—"don't you speak pretty, all honey and cream and magnolias. Must make you feel real bad that the South is getting whupped." He advanced his face close to hers. "It does make you feel bad that the rebs are losing the war, don't it? Come on, let me hear you say it."

Desiree drew back hastily, slightly nauseated by the strong gust of his liquor-laden breath. "Nothing can be said to be lost until the last battle has been waged."

"Ah, but it's about to be, little gal. Any day now. Grant and Sherman have really got the upper hand. Our troops are harrying them yellow, backbiting dogs, make no mistake about that. The rebs ain't got a chance with Grant and Sherman on their tails. Great men. You've heard of them, ain't you?"

"Naturally. Even in this place, we get news from time to time." Desiree, trying to compose herself, hid her trembling hands behind her back. "If you don't mind, I prefer not to discuss the war."

"Uppity bitch! You figure I'm some little black boy you can kick around?" His face hard and cold, the guard held out a gloved hand. "Perhaps you'd prefer to discuss your pass instead. Give it here."

"I—I don't have one." Despising herself for her nervous stammer, Desiree hastened to cover the small lapse with other words. "What I meant to say was, I don't need one."

"You don't, eh? We'll just see about that."

She hated him, his hard eyes, his heavy red face, his burly, well-fed appearance! He reminded her of Captain Morrison. Something moved strongly inside her—defiance, rebellion against this particular form of petty tyranny. In unconscious hauteur, her head rose. "You may ask any of the guards," she said coldly. "They all know me, and they will tell you anything you wish to know."

"That so, missy. Suppose *you* tell me all about yourself."

Desiree bit her lip. He was determined to bait her, it seemed. "There's very little to tell," she said in a low voice. "I am a prisoner, like the rest, but because I help doc, I am allowed to enter the hospital without a pass."

"You're lying, girl, and it won't do you no good to lie to me. Let's have the truth."

The tight control Desiree had exerted over herself vanished. Trembling visibly, her hatred showing, she cried out almost hysterically, "I'm not lying! The truth is easy enough to prove. Why don't you ask one of the guards, for God's sake!"

"In due time. In the meantime, I happen to know that there ain't no doc. I was told he'd died." He leered at her triumphantly. "What you got to say to that?"

He was doing it deliberately, trying to goad her into indiscretion. Taking a deep breath, Desiree said with forced calm, "The doctor did die. After Dr. Brinkley's death, there was no one to help with the sick and the wounded, so Christopher Wakely, who has a great deal of medical knowledge, took over. The prisoners christened him 'doc.'" Desiree looked at the guard defiantly. "I am quite sure you have already been told about Christopher Wakely."

The guard's eyes narrowed. "You saying I'm lying, girl?"

Loathing the need to appease him, Desiree shook her head. "Not lying. Perhaps you had just forgotten."

The guard shifted his long rifle to his right hand. "That's better," he grunted. "This Wakely, he that tall, dark reb the other guard let through?"

"That sounds like Christopher."

"I can't think why the hell he should have the freedom of the hospital. It don't seem right to me."

"But I've already told you why." Desiree's voice rose slightly. "With Dr. Brinkley gone, there had to be somebody to tend the sick."

The guard glowered at her. "That don't make me no never-mind. Reb, ain't he?"

"What difference does that make? Christopher is the unofficial doctor of Camp Wetherby. He is given no more privileges than the rest of us, but he is allowed to use his skill. The prisoners rely upon him. The officers and the guards both trust and respect him." Desiree laid stress upon the last words, and had the satisfaction of seeing the guard flush. "I have answered all your questions, I think," she added, looking at him scornfully. "May I go now?"

"You'll go when I say, not before. Who the hell do you think you are, anyway!" Propping his rifle against the low stone wall, the guard advanced upon her. "I don't like your tone, your insolent looks; in fact, I don't like nothing about you, whore, and I'm thinking you need a little lesson." Spinning her around, he kicked at her viciously, sending her sprawling. "That's much better," he said, placing his booted foot on her prostrate body. "Now you're in your proper place. Down where sluts should be."

Tears of pain and rage and humiliation stung Desiree's eyes. The pain was nothing, she told herself; she had no doubt that she could endure far worse in stoic silence. It was the humiliation she minded, the terrible humiliation! That she should come to this final degradation, dirty, half starved, clad in rags, writhing at the feet of this Yankee soldier, was too much to bear. If only she had a knife, the opportunity and the strength to wield it, she would plunge it deeply into his fat gut, and glory in his death agony. "Oh, God!" Doubling her fists, she beat frantically at the cold earth. "Dear God!"

The guard removed his foot. Kneeling down beside her, he grasped her hair and strained her head back. "God ain't about to listen to no rebel slut. You're just wasting your time calling on Him."

Laughing, he released his grip on her hair. "Eat worms," he said, pushing her face into the earth. "I'm told you prisoners don't get enough to eat, so I'm doing you a favor, darling. Them worms taste good, do they?"

"Take your hands off her," a cold, cutting voice said.

The guard looked up quickly. "Well, if it ain't Wakely," he jeered, eying the tall, gaunt figure coming toward him. "How's all them rebs you've been doctoring? I hope you've managed to kill off some of the swine."

"Get up!" His hands clenched into fists, Christopher stood over him. "On your feet, scum, or would you prefer that I drag you up?"

With an effort, Desiree managed to shake off the guard's heavy hand. "No, Christopher," she shouted, "for God's sake don't touch him! He'd like that, but you know what will happen to you if you do. Please! I'm not hurt."

"Ain't that touching, doc? The lady's pleading with you not to hurt me. That goes straight to my heart, it really does." The guard's eyes, as hard as blue pebbles, reflected the sneer in his voice. "But there, you ain't got the strength to do a damn thing, have you? Yeah, doc, it's pitiful to look at you, seems to me like a puff of wind would blow you over."

The dangerous light in Christopher's eyes intensified. "You are mistaken. Never allow yourself to be deceived by looks. I've a special reserve of strength for fat pigs like you. Will you get up now?"

The guard's smile was one of pure, fiendish joy. "Right, reb," he growled, surging to his feet, "you've asked for it, and you're sure going to get it. Where do you want it? Shall I smash your face in first, or would you maybe fancy a bit of fast body work?" He glanced down at Desiree. "You'd better stuff your ears, whore. Them bones of his are really going to be popping."

Desiree rolled over on her back. Christopher could not win in a fight with the hulking guard. For months now, he had driven himself to perform his duties at the hospital on nerve alone, but his physical strength had long since been depleted. Terrified for him, she shrieked out a frantic plea. "Christopher, don't! For my sake, please don't!"

Christopher looked down at her. For her sake, she had said. Every thought he had was of her, every feeling responded to her, and the love that had started on that long-ago day in the forest had grown steadily, turning into a torment of longing. But not even for her could he let this pass. Pain twisted inside him. She was so small, so pathetic now. "I'll be all right, Dessi," he said, avoiding the wild appeal in her eyes. "I can take care of myself." He turned back to the guard. "All right, pig, let's get on with it."

Desiree pressed her hands over her mouth to stifle her scream as Christopher ducked the first blow from the hamlike fist. She must get up, she must help Christopher. She looked down at her long, ragged nails. She would use them on the guard if she had to. Struggling to her knees, she caught a flicker of movement from the corner of her eyes. Turning her head, she saw an officer approaching. Her heart plunged and began to beat at a suffocating pace as she recognized the trim, erect figure. Captain Sinclair! He was reported to be hard and unyielding. Fighting with a guard was a serious offense. What would he do to Christopher? Captain Stacey, who had had the command of Wetherby before Sinclair, had ordered a man hanged for just such an offense.

Desiree's head snapped round again as she heard the thud of a blow. Christopher! He was down, there was blood trickling from his lips. Hanging offense, hanging offense, fighting with a guard is a hanging offense! The words thundered in Desiree's head. She wanted to hold on to Christopher, beg him not to get up, but already he was on his feet, his face grimly determined, rushing at the guard. All hope fled as

Captain Sinclair stopped before her. Moaning, she covered her face with her hands.

"Enough!" Captain Sinclair's voice cut through the tension-filled air like a whiplash. "Price, get away from that prisoner!"

Dropping his fist, the guard swung round. "C-Captain Sinclair, sir," he stammered.

Sinclair eyed him coldly. "How long have you been at Wetherby, Price?"

"Three days, sir."

"Perhaps you are not aware of the rules that govern this prison camp. Is that so, Price?"

Price's face turned sullen. "I know the rules, sir."

"Indeed." The captain swayed lightly backward and forward on his heels. "In that case," he snapped, "how dare you provoke a fight with a prisoner?"

Price started. "Me, sir! I didn't start it. The prisoner threatened me, and I wasn't about to take that from no reb."

Her hands dropping, Desiree saw Sinclair's cold eyes turn to Christopher. "Is that true, Wakely?" he said. "Did you threaten Price?"

Wiping the blood from his mouth with the back of his hand, Christopher looked at him unflinchingly. "Yes, sir, I threatened him."

"May I ask why?"

Christopher gestured toward Desiree. "He struck the lady."

Red-faced, spluttering, the guard glared at Christopher. "That ain't true, sir. I never touched her. She slipped and fell."

"You will be silent, Price." Sinclair extended his hand toward Desiree. "Are you able to rise?"

"Yes, sir." Desiree put her trembling hand in his and scrambled to her feet. Vaguely reassured by the expression in his brown eyes, she drew in a quivering breath. "The guard is lying, sir," she said quietly. "He—he kicked me."

Sinclair dropped her hand. "Yes. The incident was reported to me by another guard, and now you have confirmed it. I am satisfied that it is as the guard reported." He turned to Christopher. "If any more such incidents should occur, you will come to me and report them. What you will not do, under any provocation, is to threaten a guard, or attempt to strike him. Do I make myself quite clear, Wakely?"

"You do indeed, sir."

"Good." A faint hint of a smile hovered for a second about the captain's stern mouth. "It is fortunate indeed for you, Wakely, that you did not manage to get in a blow. Had you done so, it would have been my bounden duty to take stern measures with you." Sinclair turned to the sullen guard. "As for you, Price, you will go straight to the adjutant's office and place yourself upon report. I will follow you shortly."

Outraged, Price glared at him, rebellion flickering in his eyes. "But it ain't fair, sir."

"I will say what is fair, Price."

Forgetting to stand at attention, Price gestured wildly with his hands. "But, sir, he's only a stinking reb."

Sinclair's lips thinned to a straight, formidable line. "Arguing with your commanding officer is a further offense, Price. You may tell Adjutant Marlow that I will be adding to the charges against you." Turning his back on the infuriated guard, Sinclair addressed Christopher. "The lady looks weary, Wakely. I suggest you take her inside and let her rest for a while." He sketched a slight salute with the small cane he was carrying, and then turned to follow after Price.

"Christopher!" Desiree stumbled toward him. "Oh, Christopher, I was so afraid. I thought that he—that Captain Sinclair would—" She broke off, unable to say the words.

"You thought that he would order me to be hanged, as Captain Stacey did with Beau Newcombe?" Christopher finished for her. He made a wry face. "To tell the truth, Dessi, so did I."

"Yes, yes, that's exactly what I thought."

Christopher nodded thoughtfully. "Like yourself, I have heard of Sinclair's reputation for harsh brutality, but it seems to me now that it might be undeserved. I would say that he is a very different man to our late and unlamented Captain Stacey."

"I agree. And I thank God!"

"Don't dwell on it. It's over." Christopher looked at her curiously. "I had thought you had given up your duties at the hospital," he said slowly. "What are you doing here now, Dessi?"

She flushed. "Christopher, I'm so ashamed. Can you forgive me for letting you down?"

"Ah, Dessi, always so unexpected. Just when I think I

know you, I find that I don't know you at all. Will I ever, do you think?"

"You will, Christopher. If we live to get out of this place, I intend that you should know me very well."

"And what do you mean by that?" Elated by the hope that had sprung into such sudden and unexpected being, Christopher's eyes searched her face intently.

"I—never mind that for now. You haven't yet told me if you forgive me."

Relinquishing the hope, Christopher sighed. "There's nothing to forgive," he said, touching her face gently. "Nothing at all, Dessi." His hand lingered on her face. "You're very tired, I know. Very near the end of your strength."

The touch of his hand sent a racing warmth through her cold body. "I'm indestructible," she said in a shaken voice. "Don't you know that by now?" To cover her emotion, she added almost abruptly, "When do the prisoners arrive?"

Christopher shrugged. "Tonight, tomorrow, who can tell." He looked up at the sky. "It will be full dark soon. Go back to the hut and rest for a while."

"Will you come with me?"

"No, I'd better stay. Mayfield and Craig are on duty in the ward, but I might be needed for something."

"In that case I'll stay with you," Desiree said firmly.

"It's not necessary. The patients are quiet, none of them critical, and unless something untoward should occur, Mayfield or Craig can attend them."

"Possibly." Desiree's head lifted with the old arrogance that Christopher remembered so well. "But I have another reason why I must stay."

"And what is that?"

"I—I will tell you when I have gathered together my courage."

Christopher frowned impatiently. "To my knowledge, you have never lacked courage, so don't play games with me. There is no other reason. You are simply being your old obstinate self."

Desiree put her hand on his arm. "I am still obstinate, I know. I am still all of those things you once charged me with. But in many ways I have changed. Haven't you noticed?"

Christopher looked down at her hand. It was purple with

the cold, the long, slim fingers distorted with chilblains. His eyes lifted, studying her intently. Her glorious hair was dulled, her radiant beauty diminished by suffering and hardship, and yet to him she had never seemed more lovely. "Yes," he said huskily, "you have changed. You have become a wonderful woman. Someone I am proud to know. You have grit, endurance, many fine qualities. But some things can be pushed too far, Dessi, and I would not have you exhaust your strength."

"And what of your strength, Christopher? Do you have an unlimited supply?"

"It is different with me," Christopher said abruptly. Her eyes! he thought. They were such a clear, shining violet in her pinched white face. "But—but you," he continued with some difficulty. "You are such a little scrap of a thing."

"Size doesn't count." Desiree's air of composure belied her inner turmoil. "For a little while I lost sight of who and what I am. But no more. I can do anything I set my mind to."

"Ah, there speaks Madam Flame." In an unusually demonstrative gesture, Christopher took her hand and squeezed it gently. "But Dessi, although Wetherby, being somewhat isolated from the regular route, has not suffered an overwhelming influx of wounded, yet we have our share, and it does seem to me that you are too frail for such a burden."

"I am not." The soft look in Desiree's eyes was replaced by an expression of determination. "I have decided, so it is not the least use to argue with me. What you can do, Christopher Fairfield Wakely, I can do."

His dark brows rose at this use of his other and hidden name. "Well, it would seem that you are really on your mettle."

"I am indeed. I have returned to my duties, so you might as well get used to the idea."

"That is all very well to say, Dessi, but are you quite sure you have the strength to carry on?"

He had never spoken to her in quite this way before. Was it friendship, she wondered, or was it love that put that look in his eyes, that low, almost tender note in his voice? Love? She examined the thought. Yes, perhaps. How wonderful it would be to be loved by him. What a glorious adventure they would make of life. After the war, the hunt for him might be resumed, but nothing mattered if he loved her. They would leave the South behind them, perhaps go to another country. Maybe England. Somehow, some way, they would make a life for themselves.

"Dessi, what are you thinking about so deeply?" Christopher's voice sundered her thoughts. "I asked you if you were sure that you could carry on."

Desiree nodded. "I am very sure. Don't worry about me, please."

"I will find that last a little hard, but I'll do my best." Christopher's smile eased the lines of strain in his tired face, returning to Desiree an aching glimpse of the young boy who had stared at her with intense dark eyes, his mocking attitude both exciting and maddening her, his drawling voice calling her "Firetop." He had invaded her waking and sleeping dreams, and even then, although she had never been able to bring herself to admit it, she had known that her life would, in some way as yet unknown to her, be bound up with his. She started out of her thoughts as Christopher, dropping her hand, remarked in his customary cool tone, "Well then, Dessi, come along if you insist. You can help me check the medical supplies." He paused, shrugging, and then added on a note of bitterness, "The term 'medical supplies' is farcical, for very little remains to us."

Following him into the hospital, breathing in the odors of sick humanity, unwashed bodies, and putrefying flesh, Desiree felt a familiar despair. So much to fight, so little comfort for the sufferers, she thought, looking about her. The curtainless windows, minus many panes, had been boarded up here and there to cover the deficiency. The remaining panes, smeared, and starred with cracks, let in the whistling wind, fluttering the flames of the numerous candles that were, of necessity, kept continually burning in an effort to lighten the gloom. Balls of gray dust skittered over the bare, unvarnished, plank-wood floor, and, borne upward by the wind, disintegrated, sending swirls of dust motes into the air. Desiree tightened her lips. Dust, an old enemy, sweeping in from the open spaces that surrounded the prison camp, settling in a thick bloom over everything. Blood, disease, death, the screams of the badly wounded, the babbling of delirium, the smell of gangrene, of vomit, of suppurating wounds. Insufficient food to nourish and sustain, not enough hot water to cleanse the patients, or cool water to soothe fevered limbs.

Hands reaching out, eyes beseeching. Men lying on the cold floor, huddled in the spaces between the filled beds, covered with coats, army jackets, rags, anything that would keep them warm. She thought of herself, trying to talk brightly, to smile, to comfort, when the burden of her grief for the maimed and hopeless men seemed almost too great to bear. Leaning over the narrow, iron-framed beds, breath coming short, arms straining as she sought to heave slack bodies, tortured bodies, into more comfortable positions, bathing bedsores, bandaging gaping wounds, the indescribable stench forever in her nostrils. Carrying out buckets of night soil, coaxing, rallying, biting her lips to hold back her hysterical tears. Weary! Weary unto death, wanting nothing more than to drop down on the floor, close her ears to the pitiful sounds of suffering, close her eyes against all the tragedy and the ugliness, and never open them again in this life. She thought of the new prisoners who would be arriving, a great percentage of them wounded, sick, and her heart quailed. Could she do it again, did she have the strength, the endurance?

"Dessi?"

Desiree looked toward Christopher, and found that he was watching her intently. Color scalded her face. She hadn't realized that she had stopped short in the middle of the ward. What must he be thinking? Christopher would never make weariness an excuse for shirking his duty, she thought, starting toward him. He would go on and on until he dropped. Her quivering lips firmed and a flood of new courage poured through her. And so would she, she vowed.

"Dessi," Christopher said again, as she stopped before him, "what is it?"

Desiree looked at him, her eyes over-bright. "Nothing is wrong."

Christopher put his hands on her shoulders. "You look so haunted, Dessi. You are too hard on yourself. It is time for you to stop, more than time. For months you have done the work of six women. Do you think I haven't noticed or cared?"

"Do you really care, Christopher? I can remember a time when you did not."

That break in her voice, the look in her eyes! He wanted to sweep her into his arms and hold her close. "That was long ago, Dessi. I care now, believe me. Change your mind about returning here, please. I will understand, even applaud your decision."

"But I won't understand, Christopher. Don't you see, I have to prove myself."

"Nonsense! You have done so over and over again."

"It is not enough for me." Desiree forced her stiff lips to smile. "Here is where I belong."

Christopher's hands dropped from her shoulders. "No, Dessi, this is the last place where you belong." He hesitated, fighting an overpowering urge to give in. And yet how could he bear it if she should collapse and die? She would never belong to him, he knew, but when the war was over, he must know that somewhere she lived, as beautiful, as bright and shining, as she had once been. "I don't want you here," he said harshly. "Go on, you stubborn little fool, get out of here."

Her mouth quivered. "And where shall I go? I will simply exchange one hell for another."

Trying to hide his emotion, Christopher frowned at her fiercely. "At least, away from the hospital, it will be the lesser hell."

"No, Christopher, I belong wherever you are." Her eyes dropped before his startled gaze. What was the matter with her? She hadn't meant to blurt it out here. "Christopher"—unable to stop the words, she swayed toward him—"I love you so very much! Couldn't you bring yourself to love me just a l-little?"

"Dessi!" He couldn't believe what he was hearing. "My God! Do you know what you are saying?"

"Yes, yes, I am saying that I love you." Hot tears started to Desiree's eyes, making the stained floor shimmer in a mist. "I am saying that even if you can't love me in return, let me belong to you." She raised her tear-streaked face and looked at him pleadingly. "Please, Christopher, I have no pride left now. Let me have something of you to remember."

"Dessi." Christopher put his arm about her shoulders. "Dearest Dessi!"

A hand touched Desiree's ankle. "Miss Dessi," a hoarse voice begged, "will you tend my leg? It hurts real bad."

Desiree looked down at the man huddled on the floor. His face was contorted with pain, and his long, lean body was shivering under the coat that covered him. "Of course I will."

She smiled at him through her tears. "Don't worry. I'll have you comfortable in just a moment."

Christopher's arm tightened about her shoulders. "Not now, Dessi. Mayfield will see to him." He beckoned to the two men standing in the center of the ward. "Mayfield, change this man's dressing. And you, Craig, it's time for medication."

"Right, doc." Mayfield bustled forward. "I'll have him all right and tight in no time at all."

Christopher nodded. "If you need me for anything, I'll be in the dispensing room. Other than that, do you think you can manage?"

Looking at Christopher's dark, abstracted face, noting the unsteadiness of the usually firm mouth, the nervous twitching of the long, sensitive fingers, Mayfield smiled sympathetically. "Sure can," he said briskly. "Trust me, doc. I ain't about to let no one disturb you, and that includes Craig and his usual bunch of damn-fool questions."

Although he longed to be away, Christopher's conscience prodded uncomfortably. "There's Forbes. Perhaps I should be here, just in case he takes a turn for the worse."

"If he does, doc, I'll let you know. I know what to do for him, in any case. You trained me and Craig well, and that means you ain't got a thing to worry about."

Christopher shot a look at Desiree. Meeting her eyes, he found that he could not look away. It was Desiree who broke the spell. Her face scarlet, she looked down at the floor again. "Mayfield," Christopher said abruptly, "if the prisoners arrive, you be sure to call me."

Desiree looked up in response to Mayfield's exaggerated sigh. "You know I will, doc. I promise. Anyway, it's about time you had a rest."

"I—yes, I suppose so." Christopher ran his fingers through his disordered hair. "See you in ten minutes, then."

"No, you won't," Mayfield said firmly. "You take longer. You've been pounding this ward all day." Mayfield turned to Desiree. "You see that doc rests, little missy, God knows he's earned it."

The sympathy in his twinkling dark blue eyes shattered what remained of Desiree's composure. Cursing herself for her foolish tears, she let Christopher lead her past the row of narrow beds, the staring eyes, past Craig, who was watching them with equal sympathy, and into the little dispensing room. She gazed about the room as though she had never seen it before, her eyes lingering on the one chair, the rickety table that served as a desk, the almost-empty shelves, looking everywhere but at Christopher. Oh, God, what a fool she had made of herself! To imagine herself confronting Christopher and telling him of her love was one thing, the reality quite another. He wasn't interested. How could he be? Her beauty was gone, she was tired all the time, why should he be interested? In a few seconds he would devastate her with his scorn. He would tear down her dreams, trample them with his cold, repudiating words. Unable to bear the throbbing silence, she cried out wildly, "Christopher, I'm—I'm sorry!"

The closing of the door made her jump. "Look at me, Dessi." Christopher's voice sounded strained. "Come now, don't hang your head."

"I—I can't. I'm so ashamed."

"Ashamed of loving me?"

"No, never!" Her head shot up. "How can you say a thing like that?" Meeting the blaze in his dark eyes, her heart accelerated to a painful beating. He was angry. She had known that he would be. "I—I meant that I was ashamed of m-myself for embarrassing you," she stammered. "Christopher, I know you don't love me. Don't say anything, please. Just let me go!"

"You think I don't love you?" Christopher's voice sounded incredulous. "Oh, girl, you don't know, you just can't imagine how very much I care!" He moved away from the door. "Those things you said, did you mean them?"

Desiree stared at him with dazed eyes. He loved her! Suddenly she was laughing and crying at once, gasping out words. "Oh, I did, Christopher. I meant every word!"

"Dessi, my Dessi!" For a moment longer his eyes traveled over her, and it was as though he beheld a miracle. Then his shaking arms went around her, crushing her close, his voice murmuring her name as though he could never get enough of saying it. "There must have been a time when I didn't love you, Dessi, but I can't remember it. I think I must have been born to love you."

She had said the same, thought the same, but she had never expected to hear these words from the reserved and often grimly unapproachable Christopher. Consumed with wonder, held close in his arms, feeling the pounding of his heart against her, Desiree was transported back to another time, another place, a place of sunshine and dreaming peace, where the ugly shadows of war could not intrude. "Christopher, I love you, I want you!" She wound her arms about his neck, her fingers stroking his thick, curling hair, her body pressing close to his. "Say that you want me. Show me!"

His soft kisses took on urgency, burning on her face, her closed eyes, her quivering mouth, feeding the hunger inside her. "Oh, Dessi, you know I want you! But we must wait. You haven't the strength to endure."

"I won't wait, I can't!" She caressed his face with her fingertips. "These moments may be all that we have left to us."

It was wrong, he knew it, and yet her body was so warm and alive in his arms. He touched her breasts lightly, and felt the swelling of her nipples through the thin material of her bodice, and he was lost to reason. He kissed her mouth again, a long, lingering, hungry kiss of surrender. "I want to see all of you, Dessi," he said jerkily, putting her from him. "I'll light the other candles."

Desiree was swept with panic. She had grown so thin, her once-full breasts were meager, her ribs visible through her flesh. If a strong light should shine on her, revealing all of her pitiful secrets, she would revolt him. "No!" she cried out sharply. "The one candle is enough, and there is still light coming through the window."

"But there is not enough light. I don't want to see you in shadow, I want to see you clearly."

"No!"

Suddenly he understood, and he, who could scarcely remember when he had last cried, felt his eyes fill with stinging tears. To see her so humbled by doubt, his proud and beautiful girl, was more than he could bear. Coming close to her again, he stroked her face tenderly. "It shall be as you wish," he said softly, "no extra light. But Dessi, I want you to listen to me, and to remember it always. In my eyes you are beautiful, you will always be beautiful. When we have grown old, you will still be to me my darling of the radiant face and the flower eyes."

Her hands fluttered out, her fingers touching him lingeringly, tracing his features. "And for me you are the same.

You will never change. Ah, love, will we be given the chance to live out our lives, will we grow old together?"

Christopher winced. For the moment she had forgotten, but he was still Christopher Fairfield, convict, a man who must be perpetually on the run. He could not take Dessi with him, could not allow her to throw her life away. Inwardly mourning, he managed to smile at her. "We will be together, my darling," he said softly.

The glow in her eyes was suddenly quenched, and he knew that she was remembering. "Christopher—"

"No, Dessi," he interrupted, "don't think beyond these moments. Promise me!"

"I promise," she whispered.

Christopher's hands quivered as he helped her out of her one garment. He saw her eyes flinch away from his as the gown slid down and pooled about her feet, and he felt a rush of tenderness, a need to reassure her again. She was so pitifully thin in her nakedness, and yet so eternally beautiful to him. "Lovely!" he said huskily. "My lovely girl!" Bending his head, he kissed her breasts lingeringly.

At last, moving away from her reluctantly, stripping off his ragged clothes, spreading them out so that she need not lie upon bare boards, and wadding her gown to make a pillow for her head, Christopher could not help remembering that day in the forest some four years ago. The rape of Miss Desiree Grayson of Twin Oaks, for so he had labeled the episode in his mind, had begun in raging anger, in bitterness, in hatred for Elton Grayson, her father, but for him it had ended in love. When he had walked away from her, he had never thought to see her again. So much against them, so wide the barrier between them, and yet here she was, worn out, half starved, saying words to him that he had only dreamed of her saying. The barrier between them? Christopher felt a touch of the old bitterness as Frazer Phillips' face flashed into his mind. Little Charlotte Elliot. Chrissie, so small and drained in death. The crumpled handkerchief, stained with Chrissie's blood. Phillips, the murderer! He had no proof to use against the man, but he knew, dear Christ, he knew!

"Christopher!" Desiree's voice, sharp with fear, came to him. "What is it? You look so—so fierce."

Damnation to Frazer Phillips! He had not thought of the

man in months, and he would not think of him now. Smiling, he turned to Desiree. "It's nothing, sweetheart."

"But you were doing what you told me not to do," she accused, "you were thinking back to the past."

"A little," he admitted. "But deep thought is over. Only you and I are important." He moved toward her. "Dessi, my darling, are you sure?"

"I have never been surer."

Christopher hesitated, then he swept her up in his arms and carried her to the improvised bed on the dusty floor. He laid her down gently, and the solitary candle flame touched her hair with flickering yellow light, leaving her face and her body in shadow. Kneeling beside her, hearing her soft sigh, anxiety touched him again. She had felt so light in his arms. It had been like carrying a small child. Would he be too much for her? Did he have the right to further deplete her scanty store of strength?

Reading his mind, Desiree smiled at him. "Please don't worry about me," she said softly.

"But I do worry, Dessi. How can I help it?"

"Hush, love, hush! Where you are concerned, I have all the strength in the world."

Don't think, Christopher told himself sternly. Don't remember the misery of Wetherby, the cold, the hunger, the filth and the stench. Don't remember the gaunt, starved faces, the sick eyes, the suffering, the deaths. Live only for this moment. Think only of this one beloved woman. Think of Dessi as she was, radiant with health, glowing with that amazing beauty. Dessi, as she will be again, once this war is over. He felt a sharp stab of loss. The end of the war, and Dessi would be gone from his life. It could be no other way.

"Christopher?" Desiree's hand touched his stiff arm pleadingly.

Her arms enfolded him as he lowered himself upon her. He felt the touch of her naked body beneath his, the crushed softness of her breasts, her quivering legs, and his doubts were swept away on a tide of passion. Hungrily he began to explore her. "Dessi, my Dessi!"

Desiree moaned as his hands began tracing fiery paths. His lips touched her mouth, clinging with searing passion, moved downward to her throat, her breasts, his tongue teased her nipples, his lips drew them in, suckled them. She could feel the hard, throbbing bulge of him against her, and the ecstasy of the moment was almost more than she could bear. Her breathing shallow, she arched upward in a response that would brook no denial.

For a moment he was still, and Desiree trembled, waiting. Surprisingly, the first thrust brought a sharp pain, as if she had retreated back into virginity, and then just as quickly as it had come, it vanished. She began to move with him, pushing herself hard against him, wanting to absorb him entirely, glorying in the feeling of him deep inside her. He began to move faster, savage, urgent movements that shook her body. Her legs crept up to clasp his waist, and then, not satisfied, moved higher still. She felt him shuddering, the frenzy of his passion matching her own, and then the sudden hot spill of his release. "Dessi?" his whispering, tender voice in her ear. "Are you all right?"

She was sliding downward from the heights. She felt a glorious calm, a peace of mind such as she had not known in a long time. Christopher's arms were cradling her tenderly, so tenderly, telling her without words of his love. There was no war, no Camp Wetherby, no yesterdays, no tomorrows, no cares. Tears stung her eyes as she suddenly realized the foolishness of her little game. No use! She could not retreat into this world that her longing heart had created. Tomorrow must come, and with it the awakening to grim reality.

Christopher peered at her in the gloom, sensing rather than seeing that she was crying. He touched her face, felt her tears, and he was pierced with agony. "Dessi," he said in a choked voice, "don't cry, my darling! Did I hurt you?"

"No, love." She drew his head down and kissed his lips softly. Her voice was low, still trembling with the aftermath of passion. "I feel as though I have been born again."

Long after she had fallen into a light, shallow sleep, her words continued to resound in Christopher's mind. 'Born again.' If only one could wipe out past mistakes and start all over again. But it was not possible. Life rarely gave one another chance. Even if it did, and he was proved innocent, how could there be a union between an ex-convict and Desiree Grayson, the lady of Twin Oaks? The best thing he could do for Dessi was to get out of her life as soon as possible. If life at Camp Wetherby did not kill them both, it was what he would do.

Desiree started out of sleep as a knock sounded on the door. "Christopher!" She clutched his arm.

"It's all right, Dessi," he soothed. "Don't be afraid. That will be Mayfield, I expect."

Desiree smiled as she reached behind her for her gown. "I'm not afraid, not when I'm with you." Rising, she put it on quickly, smoothing the shabby folds over her hips. Watching Christopher as he dressed, she combed back her tumbled hair with nervous fingers.

The knock sounded again. "Doc," a voice called, "it's me, Mayfield."

With a last glance at Desiree, Christopher went to the door and opened it. "Something gone wrong, Mayfield?"

"Depends on how you look at it, doc." Mayfield's twinkling blue eyes looked subdued.

Christopher stepped out, closing the door behind him. His glance went to the occupants of the row of narrow beds, to the men lying on the floor between the beds. "Is Forbes all right?" he questioned sharply.

"He's all right, doc, so's the others. Captain Sinclair sent Sergeant Bannister over with a message not more'n a minute ago. He's heard from the runner who came on ahead that the wounded should be arriving in about a couple of hours. More'n a hundred of them."

Christopher stared at him, appalled. "My God! Where the devil will we put them all? The poor swine will die like flies."

Mayfield smiled, his somber eyes lighting up again. "I've saved the best for the last, doc. Wondering what to do with 'em ain't your worry no more. They've got a doctor coming with them. That ought to ease your load a bit, eh?"

Christopher's rigidly held shoulders slumped. "It eases my responsibility, but not my mind. The ward will still be overcrowded, the men will still die. All I can say is, God help them when they enter this pesthole."

Mayfield regarded him with affection. "Can't lay down the burden, can you, doc? It ain't in you. This doctor that's coming, he's lucky to have you working with him, and that's a fact."

"Thanks for your confidence, Mayfield." Christopher placed his hand on the man's thin, bowed shoulder. "But you and I and Craig, Miss Dessi, too, we're about at the end of our rope, eh?"

Mayfield looked at him, then said quietly, "Just about, doc."

Christopher nodded. "All right, Mayfield, let's get going. There's not much we can do, but we'd best make what little preparation we can."

Mayfield looked after the tall, thin figure as he strode away. "Christ help you, doc," he muttered. "Christ help us all!"

18

The March winds that had eddied so violently about Camp Wetherby, overturning tents, sending showers of stinging dust, leaves, and twigs swirling through the air, causing not a few deaths from congested lungs and fever, finally blew themselves out in a last furious display of Nature's power. April came, bringing with it pelting rains that churned up the iron-hard earth and spewed streams of mud everywhere. Relenting after a few days, the gray clouds parted and rolled away, revealing a light blue sky, with here and there a few innocent-looking fluffy white clouds.

Her sodden garments steaming in the warmth of the unexpectedly benevolent sun, her arms weighted down by the two large pails she carried, Desiree trudged wearily back to the hospital. This was the third trip she had made, departing from the hospital with the pails loaded with blood- and pus-soaked dressings that had gone beyond all hope of washing and restoring, burying the dressings in the oozing earth at the back of the prisoners' huts, and returning with her empty pails for more. Inside the hospital, with the arrival of more wounded, it was chaos, the air rent with the sounds of human suffering, thick with mingled odors of blood, vomit, sweat, urine, and feces. Many of the suffering men still lay in the small entrance next to the ward, crowded close together, untended. But Dr. Treherne, with his small staff consisting of Christopher, Craig, Mayfield, and Desiree, had given his assurance to Captain Sinclair that all the men would receive attention before nightfall. Dr. Treherne, up to his arms in blood, his eyes wild above his handkerchief mask, seemed to be on the point of collapse. Christopher was in like straits, and Mayfield and Craig, moving as directed, were all but asleep on their feet.

Desiree stopped, placing the buckets on the ground. And she? At this moment she would gladly give years of her life for just one hour of uninterrupted sleep. Her gaze fixed, she stood there rubbing at her aching arms. It was a nightmare, she thought, a nightmare from which there seemed to be no awakening. They were all working themselves to exhaustion, but the men were still dying, as much from disease and overcrowding as from the wounds themselves. Remembering an operation at which she had assisted this morning, she shuddered violently. The young soldier lying on the rough table, herself, swallowing vomit, helping Craig to hold on to his arms. Mayfield, at the other end of the table, holding on to the soldier's good leg, Dr. Treherne and Christopher stooping over the table. The soldier screaming and screaming as his gangrenous leg was sawed off. The overpowering stench penetrating the handkerchief mask she wore. The grating of bone, the spurting of blood. The soldier's eyes! Dear God, the expression in his eyes!

Shaking the memory away, Desiree picked up the buckets, forcing herself to go on. She must not collapse. The men needed her, Christopher needed her. So tired, so bone-weary, it was an effort to put one foot in front of the other. Everything seemed so far away now, as if the laughing, carefree girl, the dedicated woman she had become, who had thrilled to the element of danger in the work she had undertaken, had lived her life in another world somewhere beyond the mysterious stars. Twin Oaks, that stately, columned white building she had called home—it was hard to believe it had ever existed except in her imagination. The black people who had surrounded her, working with her in the cause of freedom, giving her their trust, loving her as she loved them. Tildy, smiling at her, sometimes scolding her, her hoop earrings swinging against her plump black cheeks in the vehemence of her discourse. Wilmers, grown old in bondage to Elton Grayson, tall, dignified, gray-haired, his eyes always so sad. Where were they now, all of her dear friends? Did they ever think of her, as she so often thought of them? Her father? Desiree's heart quailed. It was unbearable to picture him suffering, perhaps needing her. Was he alive, badly crippled by the ravages of war, in a Yankee prison camp, or was his body rotting on some battlefield?

War! Desiree stumbled, almost dropping the pails. It was inevitable that war must bring change, she thought painfully. We none of us can go back, we can never be as we were before. If this war had brought freedom for the Negroes, then some, herself and Christopher included, must term it to have been worthwhile. And yet so contrary is human nature that the heart and the mind will always yearn after what once was, will always cling to the dear and the familiar. Her mind flew to Christopher. Christopher, who loved her, but who was planning to leave her at war's end. She, who knew him as well as she knew herself, had read the signs in his eyes. For her sake, he would sever the ties between them, believing that he did the right thing for her. But his loss would kill her. He was her life, her only reason for being. Let him make his plans to free her from the undesirable Christopher Fairfield, but wherever he went, he would find her at his side.

Price, once more on duty outside the hospital, turned his head as Desiree stumbled past him, but his gaze skimmed over her without interest. Turning back to the two lounging Federal soldiers, he resumed his conversation. "Christ Almighty, Johnson!" he exclaimed. "You think it can be true?"

"I reckon so, Price. The way I got it, seems like General Grant received the formal surrender at Appomattox. At some courthouse, I believe it was."

Price gaped at him, excitement gleaming in his eyes. "You'd just better not be giving me the business, Johnson." His fingers tightened about his rifle. "If I find out that you are, I'll smash your head in."

The man who had been speaking shrugged. "That's your trouble, Price, you always got to get nasty. Look at the way you roughed up that redheaded girl."

Price's face went sullen. "Shut up!"

"Fine by me. Anyway, I'm not saying that what I heard is

God's truth. Could be a rumor, got to make allowances for that, but I'm inclined to believe it."

Price looked at the other man. "What about you, Farley, you believe it?"

Farley, who disliked Price, removed his pitying eyes from Desiree, who was still struggling to open the heavy door. He would have liked to run forward and help her, but if Price commented on his action, as the big-mouthed swine surely would, it would only lead to a fight. "Don't know," he answered coldly. Frowning thoughtfully, he rubbed at the bridge of his nose. "Maybe it could be," he conceded. "It's about time for the rebs to crumble, I reckon, seeing we've smashed them on all fronts."

Price nodded. "Damn right! High time, the obstinate swine! Dirty shame, ain't it, after them rebs doing so well in the beginning?" Abandoning his mockery, he turned to Johnson. "But if it's true, why ain't we heard nothing about this surrender? Bloody rebs! I want to hear hard facts about 'em, not a bunch of rumors."

Johnson, whose mother had originally hailed from Georgia, looked at him with hostility, vaguely resenting his remarks. "Can't wait to rub the rebs' noses in it, can you Price?"

"Hell to you!" Price retorted fiercely. "What do you want me to do, kiss 'em?"

Johnson shrugged the remark aside. "Well, anyway, it's just too goddamned bad about you, Price. You'll just have to make do with rumors, won't you? Takes time for the bigwigs to get around to telling us poor slobs the facts, you ought to know that. They don't mind us giving up our lives, but they ain't about to spoil us."

Price glowered at him. "Think you're funny, don't you?"

Recovering his humor, Johnson grinned at him. "Tolerably so, Price, which is more than I can say for you."

Appomattox? Formal surrender? Smashed them on all fronts? Getting the door open at last, Desiree eased through. Putting down the pails, she rubbed her aching back, her tired eyes seeking and finding Christopher. He was standing in the entrance hall, his back toward her, looking down at the miserable untended men lying on the cold floor. The words she had heard were driven from her head. There was something wrong. Something about his utter immobility that frightened her. Pulling up her handkerchief mask to block out some of the throat-catching stench, she went quickly toward him. "Christopher?" She put her hand on his arm. "Has something happened?"

"You might say that." Christopher's voice held a note that increased her fear. "Or on the other hand, you might say that prayers are sometimes answered."

"What do you mean?" Desiree's heart began an uneven beating. "Don't talk in riddles, please. Tell me what's wrong."

"Wrong? It depends on your point of view. There's someone I want you to see, Dessi." He pointed. "Look there."

Her eyes followed his pointing finger, the coldness of dread engulfing her. Lying between two men, his blue eyes staring vacantly ahead, was Frazer Phillips. He looked immeasurably older. His face was smoke-grimed and heavily bearded, streaked with the blood that still dribbled from the great gash on his forehead, but she could not fail to recognize him. Oh, God! Her nails drove into her palms. Frazer Phillips, here. But Christopher would surely kill him! Revenge for Charlotte Elliot, for Chrissie, his sister, for the undeserved years he had spent in Buxton Prison, it was here within his grasp. Murder! Yes, it would be this time, and it would spell the end of any chance they might have of a life together. She could not let him do it. Somehow she must stop him!

Christopher turned his head to look at her, and she suffered a further heart-jolting shock as she met his bleak eyes. "Well, Dessi, tell me who you see."

Her eyes wide and dark with terror, she dug her fingers into his rigid arm. "Please, Christopher!" She groped after other words, but they eluded her. There was so much she wanted to say, so much that she must say, but she could only stand there, trembling with her terrible fear, repeating senselessly over and over again, "Please, Christopher! Please, Christopher!"

She bit back a scream as Christopher, detaching her fingers from his arm, went to kneel beside Phillips. He said something to him in an undertone. For a moment he was still, crouched there over the man he so bitterly hated, and then he lifted his hand, waving it before the vacant blue eyes. Desiree's distracted mind suddenly released the words, they came tumbling from her mouth in a passionate plea. "Don't do it, Christopher, don't turn yourself into a murderer!" Almost falling in her agony of apprehension, she ran forward and knelt down beside him. "Oh, my darling, he's not worth it. If you will only listen to me now, I will never ask anything of you again. Please, I'm begging you!"

"Don't trouble yourself, Dessi." Christopher's voice sounded very weary. "Phillips has managed to elude me again. I would find no satisfaction in killing a blind man."

"Blind?" Desiree stared at him, unable to take it in. "You are saying that Frazer is blind?"

"Yes." In demonstration, Christopher's waving hand almost touched the staring, unblinking eyes. "I would not wish blindness on my worst enemy," he resumed, "and Phillips is certainly that. I think you can say that I have my revenge."

Desiree glanced from him to Phillips. "Can he—can he hear us?"

"I don't know." Christopher hesitated. "Judging from his lack of facial expression, I would say not."

"Christopher, what if his sight should return?"

Christopher shrugged. "You have nothing more to fear, Dessi, it's over. You were right, he's not worth it."

"Thank God!" Her control breaking, Desiree fell against him, sobbing helplessly. "Oh, Christopher, I was so afraid!"

"I know, love." Christopher put his arm about her, hugging her close. "Don't cry anymore. There'll be enough tears later for both of us."

"I don't know what you mean."

"You do. You understand me perfectly, so why pretend?"

"No, Christopher!"

"We have no future together, Dessi."

He sounded resigned, hopeless, as though, mentally, he had already relinquished her. "Don't you dare say that to me!" Desiree's voice rose in an anger that was born of fear. "I'll never let you go, never!"

"Hush!" Christopher said in a low voice. "I must go now. But we'll talk later. I promise."

"If we can find the time, you mean." Desiree's lips tightened as she saw him glance at the huddled forms, and she knew what he was about to say. "I know," she resumed bitterly, "you want me to stay here and reassure these men, those that are capable of understanding, that is."

"If you would, Dessi. After that, you will be needed on the ward. Dr. Treherne has been asking for you."

"Goddamn Dr. Treherne! Tell him I'll be along when I've

finished my task." Desiree waved her hands wildly. "Tell me, Christopher, what do I say to these men?"

"You know, Dessi, you've done it often enough before. Quiet their fears. Tell them that they have not been forgotten, and that we will get to them as soon as possible."

Staring up at him with burning eyes, Desiree laughed. "No, no, I'll tell them the truth this time. I'll say, 'Please don't take so long dying. We have no beds to spare, not even a square inch of floor. So do us a favor and die, there's earth aplenty waiting for you outside.' Will that reassure them, Christopher, will it?"

"Stop it, Dessi!" Christopher's harsh voice jerked her out of her incipient hysteria. "You're talking a lot of nonsense. You care as much as I do for these men, and you know it."

Desiree crumbled. "Oh, God, yes, Christopher, I do, and I'm sorry, so sorry! It's just that everything seems so hopeless, and I'm so t-tired."

"Of course you are. We all are." Christopher forced a smile to his lips. "But hang on, Dessi. It's so much worse for them. Remember that."

Desiree nodded. "As if you needed to tell me. But I never know what to say to them. They look at me so pleadingly, and it breaks my heart."

"There is nothing I can say to you, except that this tragedy must come to an end someday." Christopher stroked her arm, his touch as tender as the expression in his eyes above the mask. "I have faith in you, Dessi," he said, rising to his feet. "You will come through this."

Looking at him, Melissa's words echoed in Desiree's head: "You and doc will make it—" Poor Melissa, who had died three days ago, a victim of the prevailing dysentery and an urgent wish to die. She had not been buried in a gown of peacock-blue velvet, as had been her pathetic desire, but in a stained and torn shift. Fresh tears dampened the edge of Desiree's mask, and she rubbed impatiently at her brimming eyes. "Christopher, you must listen to me. We belong together, you and I. We will have a future. We will make one."

"Dessi, this is not the time or the place." Christopher hesitated, as if about to say more; then, raising his hand in a helpless gesture, he turned and walked away.

"Ma'am," a weak voice said. "I'm frightened, and I don't want to die. Please help me!"

Looking into the clouded brown eyes of the young man, Desiree felt hatred for herself. It was her hysterical, unthinking words that had created this fear in him. Taking a deep breath, she said warmly, "What's your name, soldier?"

"Tom, ma'am. Tom Foster."

"Well, Tom, we've no intention of letting you die." She spoke firmly, a smile touching her lips.

"But I heard you. You said—"

"I said a great many things, Tom"—Desiree hastened to interrupt the faltering voice—"and all of them foolish. You're going to be just fine."

Other voices began calling to her. Some, like Tom's, were weak and fearful. Others, expressing their fear in a different way, were belligerent, demanding attention. To each of them, as fitted their needs, she gave something of herself. Crawling on hands and knees, making her way among them with difficulty, she smoothed back tangled, lice-ridden hair from sweating foreheads, held twitching, fevered hands, and managed to restrain her tears at the sight of some of the terrible injuries. Keeping a forced smile on her dry, swollen lips, she coaxed, encouraged, gently bullied, and even attempted to make small jokes. Stooping over one soldier, whose blue-tinged lips and staring eyes testified to his terrible struggle to go on breathing, Desiree felt a violent revulsion of feeling. Jokes! Of what use were jokes to these ragged, dysentery-stricken, badly emaciated men? And yet what else had she got to offer them at this point? The men crowding the one ward were not only weakened by dystentery, but were the tragic victims of gunshot wounds, bayonet thrusts, and bursting shells. There was, too, the lack of medication that impeded efforts to aid the men. But even if the dedicated helpers had all the supplies they needed, even if they worked the clock around without pause, they still could not cope with the tide of wounded.

Desiree rose to her feet. Compassion directed that she remain where she was, however useless her presence might be, but duty said that it was time to return to the ward. Passing Frazer Phillips, she stopped abruptly. His slack face had come alive to suffering. "I can't see!" Frazer's voice emerged in a shocked whisper. "Is anybody here?" His hands made futile motions before his eyes. "Please! I can't see."

Kneeling down again, Desiree took his hands in hers. "Don't be afraid, Frazer. You're not alone."

"Dessi?" His head jerked to one side in a listening attitude. "Dessi, is that really you?"

"Yes, Frazer, it's Dessi."

Incredulity gave way to terror as the full horror of his affliction overcame him. "Why can't I see you? Oh, God, Dessi, I'm blind! I'm blind! Help me. Somebody must help me!"

His face contorted with fear, sweating heavily, Frazer tore his hands from Desiree's grasp, giving her a vicious push that sent her toppling backward. Rearing up, he shouted, "Sergeant Kingston, to me, to me! The Yankee swine are all around us. I'm blind, Kingston, you have to help me!"

Desiree threw herself at him, struggling to control him. With relief, she heard footsteps behind her, and then Captain Sinclair's sharp, clipped voice. "That man is out of his head, Wakely. He'll have to be restrained."

"He's blind, sir," Christopher said, "and he's very frightened. You, Craig, help Miss Dessi with him."

"Sure, doc. All right, Miss Dessi, you can let him go. I'll see to him."

Trembling with reaction, Desiree rose. "You're with your own men, sir," she heard Craig say. "Be still now, be still."

Captain Sinclair cleared his throat. "I came over here to tell you that I've rounded up some men to help you. You and the doctor can show them what to do."

"Yes, sir, thank you." Christopher's voice sounded distracted.

"That man, Wakely." Sinclair nodded toward Frazer. "He appears to have quieted down, but if he should start up again, perhaps I can find a spot to hold him for you. I'll have one of my men keep guard over him." He colored as he met Christopher's eyes. "Damn it, Wakely," he said testily, "I'm not an ogre. I'm just trying to help."

Christopher nodded. "I know, and I appreciate it. But he'll be all right. If we need help with him, we'll call on you." Christopher turned. "Phillips, I want you to listen to me. Your blindness may be only a temporary condition. Once we've examined you, we'll be able to tell you more. Do you understand?"

The madness faded from Frazer's face, to be replaced by

an expression of painful attention. "That voice," he mumbled. "I know that voice."

Christopher's hands clenched at his sides, but his voice was level as he repeated himself. "Did you hear me, Phillips? I said your condition may be only temporary. It could be the result of shock."

"Christopher Fairfield!" The breath rattled harshly in Frazer's throat as he brought out difficult words. "It is you, isn't it? Don't try to deceive me, Fairfield, I'd know your voice anywhere. I should know it, I've heard it in all of my nightmares."

Sinclair stared at the twitching face of the blind man. "You know this man, Wakely?" he said sharply.

"Yes, sir, I know him."

"Why does he call you Fairfield?"

"It's a long story." Christopher's eyes met Desiree's, their expression warning her to keep silent. "I haven't the time to go into it now, sir."

"I'm blind," Frazer said in a dead voice. "Does that make you happy, Fairfield?"

"No," Christopher said curtly. "I have told you that the condition may not be lasting."

"But I know different." For a moment frenzy threatened to overcome Frazer again; then, with an effort, he pulled himself together. "What are you doing here, Fairfield?" His hands groped in the air, as though trying to establish contact. "Fairfield, the voice of my conscience. Are you really here, or am I having one of my nightmares again?"

Desiree's heart contracted painfully as Christopher knelt and took one of the groping hands in his. It was not in him, she thought with a rush of pride and love, to refuse comfort to a suffering man, not even when that man was Frazer Phillips, his enemy. "I am real enough, Phillips," she heard him say in a quiet voice. "I'm helping the doctor take care of the wounded."

A curiously sly expression crossed Frazer's haggard, bearded face, and his hand turned in Christopher's, his fingers clutching desperately. "I know well that you hate me, Fairfield, but if you'll help me now, we can strike a bargain, you and I."

Christopher's face froze into an expressionless mask that hid his seething emotions. "I do hate you, Phillips, you're right about that." His voice was as expressionless as his face. "But you need have no worry on that score. It's my duty to help you, and you can be assured that I'll carry out that duty."

"I don't want you to carry out your goddamned duty!" Frazer almost screamed the words. Quieting again, he went on in a feverish voice, "I'm afraid, don't you understand that? Ghosts, Fairfield, ghosts, they're with me all the time. I can't control them anymore. And now that I'm blind, I won't be able to defend myself."

"You will quite possibly recover, Phillips."

Frazer shook his head wildly. "Even if I do recover, I don't want to live. The bargain, Fairfield, the bargain. You help me to die, and I'll clear your name." His clutch tightened as Christopher attempted to disengage his hand. "Listen to me, Fairfield, listen! You're the very one to help me, because you have everything to gain. Don't you understand?"

"Be quiet, Phillips. You're talking too much."

"No, no, I've got to make you understand. Once you hear what I have to say, I know you'll help me. I killed Charlotte Elliot. I stood by and let you take the blame. I always hated you, and I was glad you were convicted, do you hear me, Fairfield, I was glad. I wanted you to hang. That was my only regret, that you did not hang."

Christopher's voice was strained. "Why so much hatred? You had position, wealth, influence, everything that I did not have."

"I don't know. Does it matter?" Again the sly look crossed his face. "All you have to remember is that I killed Charlotte, and that I am the only one who can clear your name. I slit Charlotte's throat, Fairfield, and I left her there in that alley to bleed to death."

Christopher's hand jerked in Frazer's. "I guessed as much, Phillips, but I had no proof."

"You have it now," Frazer cried. "You can write down my confession, and I'll sign it. I'll do anything, if you'll only help me to die!"

"And Chrissie? Tell me about Chrissie, Phillips. Did you kill her too?"

"Chrissie, little Chrissie! Day and night she haunts me. I

hear her voice: 'Die, Frazer, die! I'm waiting for you—' I can't stand it anymore, Fairfield, I can't!"

"Why did you kill Chrissie?"

"I didn't." Frazer gave a despairing cry as Christopher pulled his hand free. "Don't leave me, Fairfield! Chrissie's death was an accident, I swear it to you. I was angry with her, I can't remember why. But I pushed her, she fell, hit her head. I tell you it was an accident. You have to believe me!"

Christopher waited for the violence to come, the raging anger that would enable him to kill this man who had first robbed him of valuable years of his life, had indirectly been responsible for his father's death, and who had then, by an act of anger, erased that bright and lovely being, his sister Chrissie, but, oddly, he felt nothing. Drained mentally and physically, he could only crouch there, staring into Phillips' distorted face. It was the touch of Desiree's hand on his shoulder that roused him. He looked up at her, and the tenderness of her expression brought the stinging tears to his eyes. "Dessi, I—" His voice broke.

Desiree smiled. "I know, love, I understand. No need to say anything now."

Christopher nodded. "I can't talk anymore now, Phillips," he said in a controlled voice. He stood up. "I must go. I'll get back to you later."

"You'd better!" Frazer cried. "Give me what I want, and I'll clear your name. I can do it, I'm the only one who can. Don't you forget that, Fairfield."

"I'm not likely to forget," Christopher answered curtly. He looked at the staring, open-mouthed Craig. "Settle him down, Craig, and then return to the ward."

Craig's mouth closed with a snap, and the look he gave Christopher was one of devotion. "Sure, doc."

"Thank you, Craig." Turning, Christopher walked away, followed by Sinclair and Desiree. "Wait a minute, Wakely." Sinclair's voice stopped him.

"Yes, sir?" Christopher turned and met Sinclair's eyes. "Is there something I can do for you?"

Sinclair shook his head. "No. But perhaps there is something I can do for you."

Christopher's dark brows rose in inquiry. "And what would that be, sir?" A faint, sardonic smile touched his lips. "If it is your intention to lock me away until such time as you can hand me over to the law, you will make things extremely difficult for Dr. Treherne."

Sinclair's eyes glinted frostily. "Curse you, Wakely, you're a hard man to communicate with." He hesitated, and then went on quickly, "You were charged with murder, I take it? A murder of which this man, Phillips, is guilty?"

"Yes."

"And that's all you intend to say, I suppose?"

"For the moment, yes."

Sinclair nodded. "Have it your own way. But I'd like to help you, if I can. Whether or not Phillips signs a confession, I am willing to testify that I heard him confess to this murder."

Desiree's hand groped for Christopher's. He felt the urgency in the pressure of her fingers, but he did not look at her. "Why would you do that for me, Captain Sinclair?"

Sinclair's smile was wry. "Don't be so suspicious, Wakely. I assure you there are no strings to my offer."

"I apologize, Captain. Let us say that the circumstances of my life thus far have bred suspicion."

Sinclair nodded. "After what I have heard, that is understandable. We have fought on different sides, you and I, Wakely, but I have a passion for justice. May I give you a piece of advice?"

Christopher hesitated. "Please do."

"I advise you to write out that confession as soon as possible, and have Phillips sign it." Sinclair paused, and then added dryly, "Even if you have to resort to trickery, do it."

For the first time Christopher relaxed. "The thought had crossed my mind," he answered. "That is exactly what I will do."

"Good. You know, Wakely, had we met under different circumstances, I could have liked you."

Christopher's eyes softened. "I was just thinking the same thing about you, sir."

"Yes, well—" The color high in his face, Sinclair turned away abruptly and beckoned to the men who crowded the doorway. As they came forward and stopped before him, he addressed them in his customary brisk, no-nonsense voice. "You are to help Dr. Treherne in any way you can. You will take your orders from him, and from this man." He gestured toward Christopher. A subdued muttering arose, and he quelled it sharply. "Silence! If I hear of any incidents, such as fighting, or flagrant disobedience to the orders given to you, you will be hearing from me, and in a way you will particularly dislike." His eyes went from one face to another. "It is not customary to give aid to the enemy, or to take orders from him, therefore I can appreciate your feelings. However, in an emergency of this nature, the differences created by war must be temporarily put aside. I hope I have made myself perfectly clear?"

"You have, sir." A tall, sandy-haired man spoke up. "What you mean is, we ain't to look upon these sick men as our enemies, but as human beings in need of help. Ain't that right, sir?"

"Exactly." Sinclair nodded approvingly. "Very astute of you, Carver."

Carver beamed proudly. "I don't know what the others think, sir, but speaking for myself, I reckon you're all right."

"Why, thank you, Carver. Perhaps we had better not inquire too closely into what the others think." A general laugh greeted this. When it had died, Sinclair resumed, "Thank you, gentlemen, for your cooperation. On your way now. Dr. Treherne will show you what to do." With a nod to Christopher, and a faint smile in Desiree's direction, Sinclair turned and strolled away.

Not quite able to believe what she was seeing, Desiree stood there like one in a dream. Yankee soldiers in the ward, clustering around the harassed Dr. Treherne, their smiling, friendly faces showing him that they were willing to help. Incredible! And it had been brought about through the goodwill of Captain Sinclair, that much maligned man, whose cold eyes were ill-matched to his warm and compassionate heart.

"Christopher"—she turned to him quickly—"isn't it wonderful?"

"Wonderful indeed, Dessi. Especially when you think that these same men will, later, make every attempt to kill each other."

"I know." A shadow crossed Desiree's face. "Christopher, do you really think you can get Frazer to sign a confession?"

Christopher put his arms about her. "Yes, Dessi, I do. Phillips wants to die very badly. He'll sign."

"But if he should recover his sight, he might change his mind."

"I don't believe he will. His conscience is eating him alive. If ever a man had a death wish, it is Phillips."

"Christopher?" Desiree looked up at him, her eyes troubled. "You—you won't help Frazer to die?"

"How can you ask me such a question? Phillips must either learn to live with himself, or else he must bring about his own death. I'll have no hand in it."

"I'm so glad!" Desiree clung to him. "If we get through this war, everything will come right for us. You'll see, my darling. Promise me you'll never leave me!"

"Dessi, are you sure of what you want? Really sure?" Christopher asked doubtfully. "I am still Christopher Fairfield, and you will still be the lady of Twin Oaks."

"I'm sure. This war will have changed everything, of that much I am certain. But even if there was no change, I would storm any barrier to get to you. I love you, Christopher, does that answer your question?"

Christopher's rare smile lit his face. "And I love you, Dessi, so much more than I will ever be able to tell you." He put her from him firmly. "Now go, Madam Flame, Dr. Treherne is looking our way."

19

The old man lay stretched out on the grassy bank that bordered the rutted, dusty road. With his hat over his eyes to block out the fierce summer sun, and his prominently veined black hands clasped lightly on his stomach, he appeared to be at his ease, but his muscles were stiff with tension, his ears almost painfully alert. Every day, since the shattering news that General Lee had surrendered to General Grant at a place called Appomattox, the old man had kept patient vigil. April turned into May, May into June before he was finally rewarded. At first there had been only a trickle of homecoming Confederate soldiers, many of whom did not belong to Hawleigh County, but were simply passing through on their way to other destinations. Then the trickle had developed into a steady flow of exhausted, starved-looking men. Haggard of face, the rags of their gray uniforms fluttering, they went limping past him on shoeless, lacerated feet. Suddenly, with the advent of the soldiers, the quiet road would come alive with running women, with children, and with the older men whom the war had passed by. They would stand by the side of the road, breath caught, eyes searching as the emaciated ghosts of a lighthearted, carefree past shuffled by. Sometimes there would be tears, bitter disappointment, other times when the searching eyes would light with an incredulous joy. Glory be to God, he was here! He had come home! Women, pulling their particular loved one from the line, laughing, crying, hands touching the gaunt body as if to reassure themselves that he was really there, patting, murmuring soft endearments, and then suddenly clinging to him, covering the worn, bearded face with kisses. The older men, over-hearty in their emotion, beaming, clasping hands, thumping shoulders, and trying to hide their own tears. Children laughing, shouting wild with excitement, kicking up the fine white dust of the road, shrill voices calling—*Look there! That's my brother. There's my daddy. He's home from the war!*

Sometimes others came to watch the reunions. The widowed, the sad-faced old people, the solemn children, all those for whom there would be no returning soldier. The heartbreaking queries for Jimmy, who had died at Shiloh, for Beau, who had given up his life at Gettysburg. Other battles, other names, but the pattern of the queries always the same. Trembling fingers clutching at the tired, staggering soldiers, haunted eyes in tear-stained faces, the pleading voices. *Did you see my boy die? Were you with my husband, my son, my brother, when he died? Did he suffer? Did he ask for me, speak my name, send a message? Please, please, is there anything at all you can tell me? I have to know, I must know!*

Wilmers, seated like a black statue upon his grassy bank, the silent witness to these harrowing scenes, was purged of all bitterness against the white folk who had so harshly enslaved his people. There was a kindship in grief, he had found, and so many had died that the grief far outweighed the joy. Watching, listening, he would feel very old, very tired, and their grief, mingled with his own, was a heavy burden on his heart. White folk! If they did not enslave you one way they enslaved you another. The irony of it was that, despite everything, he had loved Elton Grayson, and he was shattered by his death. Every day he searched the road, hoping for some sign of Elton Grayson's daughter, who had become to him as his own daughter. Sometimes, mentally counting the passing of time, it would all seem too much to bear, and he would be tempted to abandon his vigil. General Lee had surrendered in April, and now July was fast approaching August, only five more months left to this year of 1865, and still Miss Dessi had not returned. Was she dead? Horrified, he would push the thought from him. Death had no connection with his bright and beautiful mistress. It could not touch the Flame, she who had been the hope of his people. Firmly, refusing to give in to despair, he would tell himself, She will come today. Miss Dessi will surely come today. She was loved, she was needed, and she must not be dead!

Removing his battered straw hat from his eyes, Wilmers sat up straight. A sigh shuddered through him as he thought of Juniper, Miss Dessi's maid. Six months after Miss Dessi had left Twin Oaks, on the very day they had received the news of Elton Grayson's death, Juniper had come to him, her face streaked with tears. "Cain't bear it no more, Wilmers," she had sobbed. "Now that we hear master's dead, I got to tell you 'bout Miss Dessi."

"What you talkin' 'bout, you fool gal?" Fear had knocked at Wilmer's heart, and he had regarded Juniper with more than his customary sternness. "What's this 'bout Miss Dessi?"

"That day master went off to the war," Juniper had faltered, "he didn't come to say good-bye to Miss Dessi, and so he didn't know that she was already gone."

"Ain't tellin' me nothin' I don't know." Wilmers had forced himself to be patient. "I 'member how you let us go on searchin' for Miss Dessi, an' you all the time knowin' she'd run off to stay with a friend. Tildy was real provoked at you."

Juniper hung her head. "Ain't no friend," she said in a muffled voice. "I lied to Tildy, lied to you all. Miss Dessi made me promise not to say nothin', an' I was just tryin' to protect her."

"Protect her from what?" The fear very real now, Wilmers fought to control himself. "If Miss Dessi ain't with her friend, then where's she at? Speak up, gal! Where's she at?"

"She—she gone off to nurse the soldiers. Leastways, that what she told me she was goin' to do."

Thunderstruck, Wilmers had stared at her. "That time Master Grayson come home for a few days, why didn't you tell him?"

"I was afraid to say anythin'." Juniper wiped her eyes with the corner of her apron. "Master, he was upset enough 'cause Miss Dessi run off, an' he didn't know where she was." Juniper looked at Wilmers, her tear-filled eyes pleading for his understanding. "How could I tell him that Miss Dessi gone to nurse the soldiers, an' that she might—might be—" Her voice trailed away.

"Might be what? Speak up, gal!"

"Might be dead," Juniper whispered.

The coldness of Wilmers' dread made him want to strike the girl. "Don't you never say that again!" he shouted. "Ain't it bad enough that master's dead, without you flappin' your mouth 'bout Miss Dessi? She's alive, I tell you. I got to believe that!"

Yes, Juniper thought, he had to believe it, it was the only way he could survive, for his life was bound up with the Graysons. Frightened by his emotion, she averted her eyes from the old butler's contorted face. He had both hated and loved Elton Grayson, the love stronger than the hate, but Miss Dessi he had worshiped without reservation. If he should hear of her death, it would put him in his grave. Juniper had said quickly, soothingly, "I'm hoping she's alive, Wilmers, I surely am. We all love Miss Dessi, 'cept maybe that Clover."

Wilmers rubbed a shaking hand across his eyes. Strange how vividly that conversation stood out in his mind, and yet it had happened almost three and a half years ago, and Master Grayson had been dead that long. Juniper was gone, along with many others, and nothing was the same. Elton Grayson? He had fallen in battle, his life snuffed out in the first months of the war. They had received the news from Oliver Tindell, a cousin of Master Grayson's. Master Tindell, at sixty-five years of age, was too old to join in the fighting, and when most of the house and field slaves fled, he had undertaken the management of Twin Oaks. But the coming of the Yankees had changed all that.

Wilmers bit down hard on his lower lip. The coming of the Yankee soldiers! Would he ever be able to forget it? They had swarmed all over the plantation house like blue-uniformed insects, pillaging, destroying, and finally setting fire to the house. The sound of their laughter, as the flames leaped high, making a jagged, flickering pattern against the sky, was in his ears now. Treasures saved from the flames had been spread out on the ground before the burning house. Miss Dessi's gowns, looking like so many limp, colorful blossoms, her jewelry, her perfumes. Boxes of carefully hoarded food, silver, china, vases, and valuable paintings, jumbled together with bottles of wine and brandy. Even Miss Dessi's gowns, which he had thought they might leave behind, had been carried away.

Caught up in painful memory, Wilmers clasped his shaking hands tightly together. The few servants who had remained at Twin Oaks were hysterical with fear, even Tildy's militant spirit had been temporarily quenched by the devastation, and Master Tindell, who had been injured by a falling beam, was lying unconscious, and so, in the absence of white authority, he had deemed it his duty to intervene. Picking out a burly blond man, who seemed to be the leader, he had begged him at least to leave the food behind. "That food been stored to help us through the trouble, suh," he had said, his voice trembling despite all his efforts to exercise control. "Cain't hardly git food no more, an' if you take it, we'll maybe starve."

"Eat roots, nigger, I hear they're powerful good. They'll keep you going for months. Now get out of my way." The blond man had pushed him, so that he had landed beside the sprawled body of Master Tindell. It was then that Tildy had recovered her spirit. Waddling rapidly forward, she had stood solidly before the blond man, hands planted on her hips, her eyes flashing. "You'll be leavin' that food behind," she shouted, "and my missy's gowns. Them gowns ain't no use to you nohow."

The blond man had seemed to be amused at first. "Them gowns'll likely fit my wife, old woman. As for the food"—his eyes were malicious—"it'll do you good to go without. You're fat enough already."

Losing her head, Tildy had launched herself at him, her balled fists striking out wildly. "You ain't nothin' but scum!" she screamed at him. "You git off this place. Go on, git!"

"Nigger bitch!" His face scarlet with anger, his eyes blazing, the man hauled off and hit her hard. "Call me scum, will you! It's a white man you're talking to, and don't you forget it. Why the hell we had to fight to free bloody black bastards, I'll never know."

"There's more'n one slavery, white man." Tildy spoke thickly through split lips. "There's the slavery of your hatred for my people. Sure you're in a fight to free us, but we ain't never gonna be free in the eyes of folks like you. I only hope to the good God that they ain't all like you."

Like a goaded bull, the man turned to the excited soldiers.

"This nigger thinks I hate her!" he shouted. "Can't have her thinking that now, can we, men? Get on over here, if you want to watch me show her how much I love her."

The men crowded close, and the blond man turned his venomous eyes to Wilmers and the frightened servants. "Any of you niggers move a muscle while I'm showing this bitch my love, and I'll shoot you down."

What followed was another part of the nightmare which Wilmers would never be able to forget. Stripped of her clothing, Tildy lay on her back, two soldiers holding her arms. Another two, having jerked her legs wide apart, held them pinned to the ground. Grotesque in her enormity, her great breasts heaving, Tildy was nonetheless a gallant if pathetic figure as she continued to scream her defiance. "Scum! White trash! A Southern gentleman'd have the likes of you whipped off his place. You ain't fit to live!"

"We'll see about that." Laughing, excited by his audience, the blond man divested himself of his jacket and breeches. Clad only in his shirt, he knelt between Tildy's legs, his hand caressing his hard penis as he posed there for the benefit of the onlookers.

"Get on with it, Addison," a nervous voice shouted. "General Horner and Captain Fulton ain't too far behind us, so if you're going to stick it into the old girl, you'd better hurry."

"Sure thing," another joined in. "Old Horner ain't going to like us taking loot, let alone raping one of his precious niggers. Both Horner and Fulton is nigger lovers, you know that for yourself."

For a moment Addison looked disconcerted, then he shrugged. "What them two don't see, they won't grieve about," he said in a loud voice. "Some of you pack up all that stuff and get it out of sight. The rest of you stay here. I'm raring to go, and I'll soon have this nigger panting. Just watch me."

Oblivious to the sudden flurry of activity as the soldiers hastily crammed the loot into anything that would hold it, Addison swarmed over Tildy like a wild animal. His tongue licked at her flesh, his teeth bit at the great mound of her stomach, and his hands mauled at her breasts, his fingers pinching at the nipples so that they stood hard and erect. Lowering his head, he began sucking at the thrusting, tiny spears of flesh. "You like that, nigger babe?" he panted. "Tell old Addy that you like it. Hey, men, look at her squirm. She ain't so old that she can't feel nothing, are you, babe?"

Tildy's eyes were closed against him, her mouth a tight, suffering line, but Wilmers, watching the flicker of expression that crossed her face, knew that against her will she was becoming excited. Her mouth opened on a moan, and her breath came pantingly as she sought to push herself upward.

Grinning widely, Addison slapped her heaving stomach. "Ain't she something! Old as she is, she can't hardly wait to feel it inside her. All right, boys, you can let go her arms and legs. You ain't going nowhere, are you, babe?" Tiring of his mauling, Addison poised himself above her. "Here it comes," he shouted, "here's every nigger bitch's friend. This is gonna ease your itch, and then some."

The force of his entry wrung a scream from Tildy, and with that scream her mounting excitement died. There was agony in her wild cries as Addison forced her legs up and rode her like a maniac. "No, no!" Tildy whimpered. Her voice rose to a scream again as his thrusting increased in savagery. "Don't! Oh, sweet Christ, you're killing me. Oh, I hurt so bad, so bad!"

When Addison finally withdrew, he stared at her agonized face for a moment. Then, bending his head, he bit at her nipples. "There, old lady, that'll teach you not to call a white man names." Rising, he began to dress quickly. His eyes meeting Wilmers', he said abruptly, "Don't look so down, old uncle, we'll be gone soon." He pointed to Tildy and the unconscious Oliver Tindell. "Drag 'em both away. And listen to what I'm saying, because I ain't gonna repeat it. You say one word about this to anyone, and you ain't gonna live long. You got that, nigger?"

Angry, condemning words had crowded to Wilmers' lips, but fearing reprisals against the other women, he had choked them back. His eyes mirroring his scorn, he had nodded in answer. Juniper begun to wail as she helped him lift Tildy to her feet. "Look there, Wilmers! Tildy got blood running down her legs. That white man gone an' bust her up inside."

"Be quiet, gal," Wilmers said sharply.

"But Tildy old, Wilmers, she ain't able to stand it like a young 'un. That man, he rip into Tildy like he one of master's stallions."

"I said hush your fool mouth, gal, less you a-wantin' to be

next." Seeing the fright in Juniper's eyes, Wilmers had added, "He wouldn't think nothin' of throwin' you down, you 'member it, gal."

Wilmers put his hands over his ears, as though to block out those ugly voices from the past. The Yankee soldiers had departed, leaving Twin Oaks a ruin, and Tildy the ghost of her old bustling, domineering self. Master Tindell had never recovered consciousness. When he had drawn his last breath, Wilmers had gone to the white neighbors and told them what had happened. It turned out that Master Tindell had had no other close relative, and so he had been buried in the family graveyard, next to Master Grayson's wife.

Wilmers' ears caught a sound, and he turned his head sharply. More soldiers were coming down the road, several of them this time. He heard excited voices as women and children assembled to greet the men, but he did not look at them. Glory be to God, there was a girl among them! He waited, his heart pounding fast. Miss Dessi? Oh, dear good Lord, let it be Miss Dessi! His excitement died and he felt a sick disappointment as the girl, supported by a tall, dark man, drew near. She stopped her stumbling walk, breathing heavily as she clung to the man. The returning soldiers did not appear to see her, for they jostled her roughly as they passed. She made no move to go on, and Wilmers thought that she must be at the end of her endurance. Knowing that she had not seen him, Wilmers studied her intently, his eyes taking in the white, pinched face, the lank, dull hair that surrounded it, streaming past her shoulders to her waist. A heavy weight, that thick hair, for one so painfully thin, he thought pityingly. He looked at her bare, bleeding feet. Wherever the poor child was bound for, she would be lucky if she reached her destination. There was something vaguely familiar about her. Had he seen her before, did she come from these parts? Perhaps she was from Lonville, a few miles east of Hawleigh County.

Troubled as the sense of recognition grew, Wilmers' scanty brows drew together in a frown. He became conscious of fear, of a longing deep inside him, and he could not understand either emotion, or why the sight of the girl had begun to affect him so strongly. For some reason, he reluctantly admitted, she made him think of his mistress. That poor emaciated creature, with her nondescript hair, who looked as though she had seen hell, actually made him think of his Miss

Dessi! Shuddering, he tried to reject the feeling. It was the waiting, the endless waiting, that must be it. It had finally turned his brain.

Wilmer's eyes turned to the tall man supporting her, and again he had a flash of recognition. It must be that they both had a likeness to people he had known. There was no other explanation that he could think of. The girl turned her head, her dry lips moving as she said something to the man. Wilmers listened intently, hoping to gain some clue to her identity, but he could distinguish only a few words: "Soon home—not far—"

Wilmers drew in a sharp breath. "Soon home." He turned the words over in his mind. So she must be from these parts. The tall man's answering voice was stronger, and it came to him quite clearly. "I know, Dessi. I know, darling." There was a moving tenderness in his voice, a great love. "Do you think you can make it, Dessi?"

The girl's voice rose, losing the slurred notes of weariness. "Make it? Of course I will. I can do anything when you are with me, Christopher."

Wilmers sat there frozen. Dessi, Dessi, Dessi, the name tolled in his brain. And then he knew the reason for the strong emotion that the sight of her had aroused. There might well be other girls with the same name, but that was his Miss Dessi! His eyes filled with tears as he watched her resume her painful walk. What had the war done to her, the lovely child he had watched over and protected, who had grown into an equally lovely woman, and had become the bright hope of his people? He hadn't known her, except perhaps in his innermost being, God forgive him, but he had not! Despite everything, the suffering of others, the lack of everything that made life worthwhile, she had still been to him untouchable, lifted above the common mortal by his own love for her, and by her unquenchable spirit. And so he had continued to picture her as he had last seen her, graceful as a swaying flower in her brilliant gown, breathtakingly beautiful, her hair fiery in the light, her violet eyes glowing. Now her pitiful condition had brought home to him the fact that his beloved girl was, after all, only mortal. She was not a goddess to be worshiped, she was a flesh-and-blood human being who had suffered along with the rest of them through this terrible war that had wrought such drastic changes. He felt a rush of love for her that was so strong that he was momentarily giddy with the force of it.

"Miss Dessi!" Coming out of his shock, Wilmers slid down the bank and rushed after her. "Miss Dessi!" Grasping at her thin arm, he pulled her out of the line. "I knew you comin' home one day," he babbled. "I been keepin' watch."

"Wilmers?" Shadowed violet eyes looked into his. Trembling lips formed his name once more, and then the weary face lit with a smile of such radiance that Wilmers knew beyond any doubt that the beautiful girl he had remembered so well would one day reemerge. "Wilmers, it really is you!"

"It's me all right, Miss Dessi. Been waitin', been cravin' a sight of you." Wilmers' eyes went to the tall man, who was smiling slightly, and another piece of the puzzle clicked into place. Christopher Fairfield! But he was wanted for murder. What was he doing with Miss Dessi? Clearing his throat, Wilmers said huskily, "How do, Master Fairfield, suh."

"You remember me then, Wilmers."

Wilmers nodded. "You been away a good many years, even before the war, but I 'members you, suh." He attempted a smile. "Should do—didn't I watched you grow up?"

Desiree did not appear to be listening. "Wilmers!" she said again, as though she could not quite believe he was standing before her. With a sudden movement, she put her arms about him and kissed his wrinkled cheek. "It's so good to see you! But I thought—that is to say, I had not expected to be greeted by anyone from home."

Wilmers found that he could not speak for a moment, then he said in a choked voice, "Ain't many of us left, Miss Dessi, but I was determined that I ain't never goin' to leave you. Loves you, I do, an' ain't never lettin' you git out of my sight agin."

"I love you too, Wilmers." Desiree saw his eyes go to Christopher, and she said in a quiet voice, "You are wondering what Mr. Fairfield is doing here with me?"

Wilmers nodded, "Was wonderin', yes, Miss Dessi."

Desiree's smile lit her face again. "It's a long story, which you will know in time. But I will tell you this much now. When things have returned to normal, Mr. Fairfield and I are going to be married."

Wilmers' eyes registered his shock. It could not be, it must not be! Christopher Fairfield was a hunted man. When he ran again, that meant Miss Dessi would go with him! Taking pity on him, Christopher said gently, "Things have changed, Wilmers. You need not fear for Miss Dessi."

The blood surged to Wilmers' face as, for the first time, he spoke bluntly to a white man. "Cain't help fearin', suh. You still wanted for murder."

"I didn't kill Charlotte Elliot, Wilmers, and I have a signed confession from the murderer to prove it."

Wilmers blinked, trying to hide his surprise. He looked at the scarecrow-thin man, and saw the smile lurking in the dark eyes. "I'm glad, suh," he said simply. "You was a real rapscallion, but I always did like you."

Desiree looked at the crowd of people milling about the soldiers, and she became more than ever conscious of her own weariness. "We can't talk here," she said with something of her old firmness. "Let's go home." Linking one arm in Wilmers', the other in Christopher's, her voice dropped as she added shakily, "Home. How I have longed for it!"

Feeling the trembling grip of her bone-thin arm, Wilmers felt his joy fading. How was he to tell Miss Dessi about her father, about Twin Oaks? What would her feelings be when she saw the charred ruin? Taking a deep breath, Wilmers began to speak. He told of the death of Elton Grayson, of the harrowing events that had followed. When he came to the burning of Twin Oaks, the looting, the rape of Tildy, and the death of Oliver Tindell, he had to force himself to go on. "Me an' Tildy been livin' in the slave cabins," he concluded in a strained voice. "The others all run off."

Tears ran down Desiree's cheeks as she mourned the death of her father. In her heart she had felt that he must be dead, but to hear it put into words created an overpowering grief that she had not the strength to combat. Her father! Twin Oaks! All gone. How was she to bear it? "Christopher!" Her faint voice was a cry for help as she sagged between the supporting arms.

Without a word, Christopher gestured to Wilmers to stand back, and then he picked her up in his arms. "It's all right, darling," he whispered. "I'm here."

"Suh," Wilmers protested, "you ain't got the strength to carry her. Best let me do it."

Christopher did not look at him. "I'll find the strength,

Wilmers. You go on and tell Tildy that Miss Dessi has come home."

Wilmers stared after the staggering form. "I will find the strength," Christopher Fairfield had said. Yes, Wilmers thought proudly, he would always find the strength to do whatever was necessary, and so would Miss Dessi. Two strong people united together by the bond of love, together they would remake their world from the ruins of the old. "You've come home too, Master Fairfield," he muttered. "Always did like you, no matter what folks said 'bout you. You're right for my Miss Dessi. You're just exactly right." Smiling, he ran past Christopher. "I'm on my way, Master Fairfield," he called back. "Cain't hardly wait to see that ol' Tildy's face when I tell her you comin'."

The sun was dipping behind the distant hills as Christopher stood with Desiree before the burned-out shell that was all that remained of the plantation house. He put his arm about her and drew her close to him. "In time I will restore Twin Oaks, Dessi," he said softly. "It may never be as it once was, but I will restore it. Do you believe me?"

Desiree looked at him, her love shining from her eyes. "I believe you. But you must not leave me out. We will both have a part in the restoration."

"I love you, Dessi." Christopher kissed her upturned face. "I will spend my life trying to make you happy."

Smiling, Desiree gently released herself. "Come, let's go home." Together, their hands linked, they walked in the direction of the slave cabins.

About the Author

Constance Gluyas was born in London, where she served in the Women's Royal Air Force during World War II. She started her writing career in 1972 and since then has had published several novels of historical fiction including *Savage Eden*, *Rogue's Mistress*, and *Woman of Fury*, available in Signet. She presently lives in California, where she is at work on her new novel.